THE EMPIRE OF TIME

DAVID WINGROVE

DEL REY

1 3 5 7 9 10 8 6 4 2

First published in the UK in 2014 by Del Rey, an imprint of Ebury Publishing
A Random House Group Company

Copyright © 2014, David Wingrove

David Wingrove has asserted his right to be identified as the author of this Work in
accordance with the Copyright, Designs and Patents Act 1988

The Random House Group Limited Reg. No. 954009

Addresses for companies within the Random House Group can be found at:
www.randomhouse.co.uk

A CIP catalogue record for this book
is available from the British Library

The Random House Group Limited supports The Forest Stewardship Council®
(FSC®), the leading international forest-certification organisation. Our books
carrying the FSC label are printed on FSC® -certified paper. FSC is the only
forest-certification scheme supported by the leading environmental organisations,
including Greenpeace. Our paper procurement policy can be found at:
www.randomhouse.co.uk/environment

Printed and bound by Clays Ltd, St Ives PLC

ISBN 9780091956158

To buy books by your favourite authors and register for offers visit:
www.randomhouse.co.uk
www.delreyuk.com

Contents

For Susan,
Always for Susan

On Time's Progression

It might be noted at the outset that this work is told, not in a direct and chronological fashion, but by great leaps forward and back through time. This is, I'd argue, how it should be. It is, after all, a time travel novel. Oh, H G Wells might have done things differently in his day, leaving out those complications that seem to come with the territory, but I am quite certain that had he, like I, witnessed more than a century of development of this sub-genre, he might have told it in the same way, experiencing all that happens through Otto's eyes, through Otto's thoughts; sharing each moment *as* he experiences it, and, by that means, giving the reader the very feel of travelling in time.

Roads To Moscow was originally written, and was always intended to be, a singular work, though of considerable size. Throughout its six-year gestation, and through all the changes of mind and direction the work took, there was never any question in *my* mind that the story that began in Chapter 1, in the dark and distant depths of the ancient Prussian forest, should be the same story that culminates in Chapter 468, long years later and in the futuristic environment of Four-Oh.

And so it is presented. Only... not in one book but three; those three books intimately connected – *laced together*, if you like – to form a seamless whole. Three books which, part through design and part through chance, came to chart the various stages of Otto's 'education'; an education that in a very real sense, *is* the work. What Otto learns, scene by scene, chapter by chapter, reflects how we, as a species, must change. Or die.

Three books, then, each with its own distinctive feel, each charting a stage in the development of our hero, Otto, each taking us one stage further, and yet each embedded in the others, bound together event by event, until, at the end, we share some flicker of his understanding of the world.

And so my singular trilogy, my journey back and forth through Time, on roads familiar and yet strange. A brief flirtation with infinity. A worm, swallowing its tail. Or simply a lesson in how to become fully human. Here it is. Make of it what you will.

David Wingrove, January 2014

'Tok, Ick, jraule nicht vor Dir!'
['Death, fear thee not!']
  – German dialect, 18th c.

CHARACTER LIST

Adelbert — Grand Master of the Guild in Asgard, 2747 (part-human bio-mechanisms).

Alekhin — Russian time agent, acting as part of Nevsky's entourage. A bodyguard.

Alpers — 'student' on Four-Oh.

Axel — Chief of the Curonians.

Balk, Hermann — thirteenth-century *Hochmeister* of the Teutonic order of St Mary's Hospital in Jerusalem; in charge of the Northern Crusades in wildest Prussia.

Batu — the Great Khan himself, leader of the Mongols in the 13th century.

Behr, Otto — our narrator; a German '*Reisende*' or time traveller.

Bella — one of the women at the platform in Four-Oh.

Bobrov — Russian time agent and killer of at least a dozen German agents.

Brigitte — one of the women at the platform in Four-Oh.

Burckel, Albrecht — German time agent and 'sleeper' in 2747 AD.

Chkalov, Joseph Maksymovich — otherwise known as Yastryeb, 'the Hawk', and Grand Master of Time for the Russians.

Conrad — Brother of the Northern Order (13th century).

Dankevich, Fedor Ivanovich — Russian time agent. Otto has shot him at least twice, the last time 'fatally'.

Diederich — German ex-time agent and leading physicist from Four-Oh.

Dieter — eldest of the students at Four-Oh.

Dietrich — Master of the Northern Order, 13th century.

Ernst – see Kollwitz.

Frederick the Great — Prussian King, Frederick II, known more commonly as 'Old Fritz'. Fighting against overwhelming odds, he helped Prussia survive the Seven Years War, where he was faced with the alliance of France, Austria and Russia.

Freisler — German '*Reisende*', or time agent; Hecht's special henchman – his '*Jagdhund*' or bloodhound, responsible for doing all the dirty work.

Friedrich, Caspar David — assumed name of '*Reisende*' Seydlitz in 1836.

Funk, Walther — President of the Reichsbank and Minister of Economics for the Nazis, in the 20th century.

Gehlen, Hans — aka 'the *Genewart*'. Architect of Four-Oh, scientific genius and inventor of time travel. Has existed for 200 years as a gaseous presence in the midst of the artificial intelligence known as Four-Oh. Twenty-eight years old in 2747.

Goebbels, Paul Joseph — Minister of Propaganda in Nazi Germany, 20th century.

Gotz, Carl von — *Flugeladjutan*t to Frederick the Great (18th century).

Gruber — one of the eight '*Reisende*' carrying Seydlitz's DNA. In his early twenties and 'turned' by the Russians.

Gudrun — King Manfred's giant niece, twin to Fricka; also niece to Sygny and Tief. In 28th century.

Gunner — German '*Reisende*' or time agent.

Hagen — Manfred's arrogant giant sixth son; his third wife Gunnhilde's son.

Haller — student on Four-Oh.

Hecht — 'The Pike'; Meister of the Germans at Four-Oh.

Hecht, Albrecht — Hecht's older brother and keeper of the Archives back in time.

Heinrich — "Henny", Burckel's friend, a revolutionary (*Undrehungar*).

Helge — one of the women at the platform in Four-Oh.

Hermann of the Cherusci — known to Rome as Arminius, 1st century AD.

Heusinger, Klaus — '*Reisende*', loyal to Four-Oh. Acts as Otto's secretary in Asgard in 2747.

Hiedler, Johann Georg — itinerant miller and grandfather of Adolf Hitler.

Himmler, Heinrich — *Reichsführer* of the *Schutzstaffel*, or SS, and leading Nazi figure in 20th century Germany.

Hitler, Adolf — Führer ('leader') of National Socialist or Nazi party, in 20th century.

Horst — assistant to Diedrich on Four-Oh.

Iaroslavich, Alexander — see Nevsky.

Inge — one of the women at the platform in Four-Oh.

Jodl — armourer for Four-Oh. In his late sixties and an ex-'*Reisende*' or time agent.

Johannes — Brother of the Northern Order, in 13th century Prussia.

Kabanov — Russian time agent.

Kalugin, Grigori — Russian time agent and brother of Ivan.

Kalugin, Ivan — Russian time agent and elder brother of Grigori.

Karen — one of the women at the platform in Four-Oh.

Katerina — Otto's love. See also Razumovsky.

Kollwitz, Ernst — a '*Reisende*', or time agent. Otto's best friend and travelling companion; damaged in the Past.

Kondrashov, Alexi — Russian time agent, brother to Mikhail.

Kondrashov, Mikhail — Russian time agent and brother to Alexi.

Kramer, Hans — red-haired *'Reisende'*.

Krauss, Phillipe — double-agent, working for the Russians and responsible for 'turning' eight German time agents.

Kravchuk, Oleg Alekseevich — agent of the Mongols in 13th century Russia, and – in some time-lines – married to Katerina.

Kubhart, Klaus — Ernst's replacement in 13th century Russia.

Kurst, Herr — innkeeper in Dollersheim in Austria in 1836.

Lavrov — Russian time agent.

Leni — female courier in Four-Oh.

Lili — one of the women at the platform in Four-Oh.

Locke — one of the eight German time agents 'turned' by the Russians.

Lothar — German head of translations at Four-Oh; expert on *ge'not*.

Luder — Brother of the Northern Order (13th century).

Luwer, Hans — artefacts expert, based on Four-Oh. Uses his other selves to multi-task. Has a woman somewhere in Time.

Manfred — King of Greater Germany for 87 years. Three times the size of normal humans, he is a tenth-generation *'Adel'*.

Manfred — three-year-old son of Gehlen.

Manninger, Lucius — alias of Otto in Asgard in 2747 – acting as the envoy of the Confederation of American States.

Maria — grandmother of Adolf Hitler, but actually a female Russian time agent.

Matteus — young student at Four-Oh.

Mindaugas — Grand Prince of Lithuania.

Muller — innkeeper of the Black Eagle tavern in Potsdam in 1759.

Muller — student on Four-Oh.

Nemtsov, Alexandr Davydovitch — Russian time agent, working in the Mechanist Age (23rd – 25th centuries).

Nevsky — Alexander Iaroslavich, Russian orthodox Prince of Novgorod in the 13th century. Victor of the Battle on the Ice (on Lake Peipus) in April 1242; a battle which ends the expansive Northern Crusades.

Oleg — Razumovsky's steward.

Ooris — Neanderthal female back in the Haven.

Otto — see Behr.

Petsch — greatest artist for a thousand years; living in 28th century.

Postovsky — Russian time agent.

Razumovsky, Katerina — eternal love of Otto Behr. Daughter of Mikhail. Lives in Novgorod in the 13th century.

Razumovsky, Masha — wife to Mikhail and mother of Katerina.

Razumovsky, Mikhail — rich boyar, living in Novgorod in the 13th century. Father of Katerina.

Reichenau, Gudrun — 'daughter' of Michael (he claims).

Reichenau, Michael — *Dopplegehirn*, and Supervisor of *Werkstatt* 9. Also somehow involved in time travel.

Ribbentrop, Joachim von — Foreign Minister for Nazi Germany, 20th century.

Ritter — German time agent.

Rothaarige — 'the red-haired one', manager of the club of the same name in Neu Berlin in 2747.

Schmidt, Andreas — alias for Russian time agent Dankevich.

Schmidt — home owner in Berlin in 1759.

Schwarz — one of the eight 'turned' by the Russians, and carrying Seydlitz's DNA.

Seydlitz, Friedrich — advisor to Frederick the Great, and one of the greatest cavalry generals of the 18th century.

Seydlitz, Max — '*Reisende*', in charge of Project Barbarossa, an attempt to change history in Hitler's favour.

Streicher, Julius — Nazi Gauleiter of Nuremberg, in 20th century.

Subodei — Mongol chief in 13th century.

Sygny — King Manfred's aunt, assassinated in 2747.

Taysen — stable owner and ostler in Potsdam in 1759.

Tief — Chancellor to King Manfred in Asgard (2747). Uncle to Princess Gudrun. *'Adel'*.

Tomas — young student at Four-Oh.

Urte — one of the women at the platform in Four-Oh. In love with Otto. Also an expert physicist, technician and mathematician.

Vyshinski — trader in 13th century Novgorod.

Werner — Brother of the Northern Crusade, in 13th century Prussia.

Werner — gene surgeon in the Neu Berlin of 2747.

Yastryeb — see Chkalov. Grand Master of Time for the Russians.

Zarah — most senior of the women who run Four-Oh's operating systems. Sweet on Otto.

Zieten, Hans Joachim von — cavalry general in Prussian army, and advisor to Frederick the Great.

Part One

The Tree Of Worlds

'There was a Vala who sang of the end of all things, of the doom of the gods and men, of the last dread battle and Odin's death, and of the coming of Surtur, whose flames shall consume the world. In mid-air she sang, and at high noon. Odin, sitting in his throne of gold, was silent, and listening he understood, for from the beginning he had foreknowledge of the end. Yet was he not afraid. He awaited Ragnarok, 'the Dusk of the Gods', as in youth he had waited, and now he was grown old.'

– Donald A. Mackenzie, *Teutonic Myth and Legends*

1

Picture this. Forest. One hundred miles of dense, forbidding forest on every side, cut through by streams and rivers that flow between the dark, straight stands of pine, mirror bright beneath the moon. And here, on an island in a river, behind a stoutly built stockade, is a wooden fort and a tower and a crude stone chapel. This is Christburg, built three years past on ground cleared from the virgin forest and defended against the heathen.

Two guards man the tower, casting their weary eyes to the foreboding blackness of the surrounding forest. Deep snow carpets that bleak, unforgiving space between the fort and the river, while overhead a full moon shines down from a clear, blue-black sky.

It is cold. Bitterly cold. Breath plumes in the air as the guards rub their gloved hands together and stamp their feet to keep warm.

This is the edge of the Christian world. Beyond is only darkness: a hostile wilderness in which the heathen Prussians eke out their godless lives, praying to rocks and trees and the demons of the air.

In the chapel the knights and priests are gathered, beneath the bright silken banners of the Order. Hermann Balk, the *Hochmeister* himself, the *Magister Generalis*, is there, along with six of his knights.

Beside them are two dozen knights of the Teutonic Order of St Mary's Hospital in Jerusalem, along with nineteen priests aged between eight and seventy. Kneeling on the cold stone floor, they pray to the Virgin, goddess of this holy war, asking her blessing.

And, at the back, one other. Myself. Otto Behr, supplicant of the Order these past six months.

There is a moment's silence and then the *Hochmeister* stands, turning to look out across the bowed heads of the gathering. The candles on the altar waver, sending up their incense into the darkness of the rafters. As one, the congregation raise their eyes and look back at him. Meister Balk is a tall, gaunt figure, grey of hair and clear of eye. Like all the other knights, he wears full armour and long leather boots. About his shoulders is a white mantle, the emblems of cross and sword emblazoned in red upon the left shoulder.

This is a special moment. Tonight, I will become a member of the Order, a monk-warrior, obeying the strict rules and codes of the Brotherhood. Smiling grimly, Meister Balk looks to me, then gestures for me to rise.

I move carefully between the kneeling figures until I am directly in front of him. My scabbard is empty, my sword lain across the altar behind him. His grey eyes search mine, a stern pleasure in them; then, without preamble, he begins:

'Otto ... do you belong to any other Order?'

'No, Meister.'

'Are you married?'

'No, Meister.'

'Have you any hidden physical infirmity?'

'No, Meister.'

'Are you in debt?'

'No, Meister.'

'Are you a serf?'

'No, Meister.'

The Meister pauses, a glint of satisfaction in his eyes, looking about him at the watching knights, then, with a nod, begins again.

'Are you prepared to fight in the Palestine?'

'Yes, Meister.'

'Or elsewhere?'

'Yes, Meister?'

'Will you care for the sick?'

'Yes, Meister.'

'Will you practise any craft you know as ordered?'

'Yes, Meister.'

'Will you obey the Rule?'

My voice rings out, clear in that tiny stone chapel.

'Yes, Meister!'

Again, the Meister nods.

I have answered the five Noes and the five Yeses. All that remains is for me to swear my loyalty to the Order. I turn, facing the others, the practised words coming easily to my lips.

'I, Otto Behr, do profess and promise chastity, renunciation of property, and obedience, to God and to the Blessed Virgin Mary, and to you, Brother Hermann, Master of the Teutonic Order, and to your successors, according to the Rules and Institutions of the Order, and I will be obedient to you and to your successors, even unto death.'

There are smiles now on the faces of many of those watching me, smiles of pride and satisfaction. I have lived and worked with these men and they know my qualities. Now I am one of them. A *Brother*.

I turn back. Meister Balk takes my sword and, holding it flat across his palms, offers it to me. I take it and, lifting it in the air, kiss the embossed cross upon the pommel, then turn to face the others, repeating the gesture.

Slowly I draw it through the air, making the sign of the cross. Then – and only then – do I sheath it again.

I step back through them to my place, then kneel, facing the *Hochmeister* as we begin the final prayers. Yet we are not halfway through the first of them when there is a baleful shout from without, followed moments later by a hammering on the outer door.

Meister Balk strides across and throws it open. Framed in its whiteness is one of the guards. He falls to his knees, head bowed.

'Meister, you must come at once!'

'What is it, Brother William?'

The young man looks up. The horror in his eyes turns my stomach. All about me the knights are getting to their feet.

'It is Brother Werner, Meister. He ...' The young man swallows. 'The Prussians have *returned* him.'

If the *Hochmeister* feels anything, he conceals it well. Turning back, he looks to us.

'Johannes ... Otto ... come. Let us bring our brother back inside.'

2

His body lies there, not fifty paces from the fort. They have stripped him and lain him like a star upon the snow, his pale limbs smeared with blood. Kneeling beside him and seeing the rictus on his ash-white face, I feel my heart break. He is snarling, as if still in pain, even though his brief life here is ended. He was the youngest of us, perhaps the finest. Looking closer, I see the ice crystals in his blood. He has been dead some time.

They have disfigured him badly: cut off his fingers and his feet, and opened up his chest with an axe. His eyes have been gouged out and his ears cut off, his tongue cut from his mouth. Worse still, they have carved the sign of the cross into his crudely shaven skull. And all of it while he was yet alive. For that is their way, these Prussians.

Coming alongside me, Johannes groans, then kneels, crossing himself. I do the same, then look up, searching among the trees on the far bank for any movement. The enemy are watching us, looking to see how we react. I meet Johannes' eyes, and we both stand, drawing our swords. Stepping forward, I plant myself there, prepared to defend the body until help comes from the fort. There are shouts now from that direction. I hear the gate swing open once again, the sound of quick, crisp footfalls.

Meister Balk himself has come, along with two others – young knights, not Brothers yet, barely a season into the service of the Order. Seeing the body they stop, then turn away, to be sick in the snow.

I look back, my eyes on the frosted plank bridge, knowing that if they are to attack, they must attack from there, and soon. Touching my arm, the *Hochmeister* urges me forward.

'Otto, Johannes – to the bridge! You must delay them until we get him back inside.'

I see them now, moving among the trees, and feel a natural hatred towards them for what they've done. Werner was my brother-in-arms, my comrade. When I think of him, I think of his smile, of his laughing eyes, which even the strict, almost masochistic rigours of the Order could not repress.

It is not that we are better men than they. No, for I have witnessed atrocities enough. We have burned their villages and killed their wives and children. And for what? For the Virgin and her son? To bring God to the heathens of these accursed woods? I know this, and yet the urge for vengeance – to cleave these Prussian bastards limb from limb – overwhelms me as I stand there facing them across the river.

Meister Balk barks orders behind me. He and the young knights have begun to drag the body back to the fort. At that very moment there is sudden movement among the trees across the river as a dozen or more men charge towards us. There is the hiss of crossbow bolts flying through the air, launched by our men in the stockade. Choked cries come from our attackers.

Johannes looks to me and smiles grimly, then takes a fighting grip of his sword. I do likewise, bracing myself to meet their attack. But something's wrong. Out of the corner of my eye I see a movement, below me and to my right, and realise with a shock that the river has frozen over in the night and that our enemies have crossed upon the ice and are now not merely in front of us but to our sides also, on the near bank of the river. Even as I call a warning, they climb the banks and throw themselves across the space, outflanking us as they try to cut off the little party that is halfway across the snow.

And now our men see the danger from the walls. There are shouts. A moment later, a group of knights ventures out, hurrying towards the *Hochmeister* and his party.

But that's all I see, for in that instant the enemy are upon us. Johannes grunts and swings his heavy sword. I hear the wet sound of metal cleaving flesh, the heathen's chilling scream, and then I too am in the thick of it, parrying a spear-thrust, then hacking at an arm. A severed hand flies up and falls, steaming obscenely on the frosted planks. For a moment it is as if I am unconscious. I thrust and parry and swing and cleave, numbed to the horror. My instinct to survive outweighs all else. Slowly we fall back, giving ground, yet keeping the small force of Prussians at bay. Then, suddenly, Johannes stumbles on to one knee. I stand in front of him, to shield him while he gets back to his feet. Yet even as I do, an axe swishes past me and thuds into his back.

I turn, bringing my sword up viciously, taking the man's head clean from his shoulders. It's a feat that shocks me as much as it shocks the Prussians. But I am outnumbered now, eight to one, and the space between me and the fort is alive with barbarians. Slowly I move back, fending them off, my sword scything the air about me, but it is only a question of time.

I kill another of them, noting, as I look past his fallen body, that there's no sign of the *Hochmeister*, or of the group of knights who'd sallied out to help. All of our men are fallen. I am alone out here and the main struggle now is at the gate where, using ladders and logs, the Prussians are seeking to force an entry into the stockade. The fighting is fierce there, but I have no time to watch, for the ragged group about me now begin to press their attack with renewed vigour, thrusting at me with knife and spear and axe, forcing me back step by step. One mistake and they will be on me, like wolves on a fallen traveller.

For a moment I press back at them, wounding one, cutting the tendons of another. He falls with a timid cry. But more of them are coming – a dozen or more, freed from the struggle at the gate – and their cries urge my attackers to greater efforts. I lift my sword to fend off a swinging axe, then grunt as a spear thrust catches me on the upper chest. My armour deflects the blow, but it's enough to send me tottering back, my sword falling out of reach.

There are shouts from my attackers. Shouts of delight. They're grinning now as they watch me trip and tumble down. As I sit up, they form a circle about me, their bearded faces pushed towards me, mocking me, calling to me in their barbaric tongue – Curonian, I note, not Prussian.

'Let's skin the whoreson!'

'No, let's drain him like a pig!'

'Burn him!'

'Let the women have him!'

There's laughter at that, but then the faces turn, watching as flames begin to rise up from the fort. And when they look back, the laughter's gone, and there is nothing but murderous intent in their cold, dark eyes. Even so, they wait, and eventually another of them comes, a chieftain by his look.

He stands over me, a bear of a man, the comparison emphasised by the thick black fur he wears. There's a wildness in his face that suggests a hint of madness, but maybe that's just bloodlust. He looks down at me, enjoying my helplessness; his yellowed teeth form a grin. Then he looks beyond me to one of his fellows, who throws him my sword.

Catching it cleanly, he raises it high, then looks about him. The others bare their teeth and howl their approval, like wolves. Lifting the sword up and back, he brings it down, grunting with the effort ...

The blade cuts the air. But I am no longer there.

3

With a pop of displaced matter, the great circle of Four-Oh shimmers into being, beneath me and about me. Surprised faces look up from screens at the surrounding desks, their surprise turning quickly to concern as they see the blood that laces my arms and chest.

Young Urte is there, and Karen, Helge – eight months pregnant by the look of her – and Brigitte, herself in the first stages of pregnancy. And Bella, and Lili and ...

I stagger and then, as the 'shield' evaporates, let Ilse and Helge reach up and help me down, realising only then just how much the fight has taken out of me. I am bruised and cut, but otherwise the only serious hurt is to my pride. I have failed, and the price of my failure has been the wholesale slaughter of my friends. My brothers—

As they lead me across and·sit me in a chair, I find myself overwhelmed with sudden grief at the loss.

'What is it, Otto? What happened?'

I look up. 'Where's Hecht?'

'I'm here,' Hecht answers, as the hatch hisses back and he strides into the room. He comes across and, leaning over me, stares into my face.

'You're like him,' I say.

Hecht's eyes ask the question.

'*Hochmeister* Balk. He was tall, like you, and his eyes ... are you sure?'

'No connection,' he says, and straightens up. 'So what happened?'

'Curonians. A raiding party from the north. I think they must have known Balk was there. If so ...'

It goes unsaid. Yet Hecht nods. Russian agents. It had to be.

'Are you okay?'

'Physically, a few cuts and bruises, but ...'

Hecht stops me with a look. 'De-briefing in an hour. Before then, go clean up. And see Ernst. I'm told he has some news for you.'

I nod, then look about me. The women are smiling now, pleased to see me safely home.

'It's good you're back,' Helge says, touching my cheek fondly. 'And now that we know ...'

We can put things right back there. But will we? Or does Hecht have other plans?

4

Ernst is mid-sentence as I enter the classroom. His six young students – the youngest eleven, the eldest fifteen, their close-shaven heads showing a stubble of ash-blond hair – stare up at him, their backs to me as I step in through the hatch.

The lecture theatre – one of eight – is a comfy, cosy space, the shelves on its walls filled with colorful artefacts from the ages we have visited – fragments of many different pasts. Teaching aids, for when words aren't enough. Oh, none of it is authentic, yet authenticity is something of a philosophical concept in this case, for these are *perfect* copies.

I smile, warmed by the familiarity of it all. On the wall behind Ernst, in large gothic lettering, is the slogan:

11

NEVER GO WHERE YOU KNOW YOU'VE BEEN BEFORE

Ernst looks up, glancing at me, and then his eyes fly wide open. A big beam of a smile lights up his face.

'*Otto!*'

The young students turn in their seats to stare as Ernst walks over and embraces me.

'Careful ...' I groan. 'My ribs.'

Ernst stands back, not sure whether to be concerned or to grin like an idiot. It's six months subjective since I last saw him. As for him ...

I frown. 'When is this?'

'August,' he answers. 'August eighteenth.'

I nod. *August the eighteenth, 2999.*

'Did you ...?' He nods at my attire. 'Did you become a Brother?'

I nod, and as I do, I see, behind him, how the eyes of the young men widen with awe at the thought. If there's a single model for us, it is the Order. The Brotherhood of Teuton Knights. And I have been there. I can see how much they envy me for that, see how their eyes drink in the sight of my battered armour, the bloodied mantle that covers my shoulders. I am a hero from the Past, and they admire me.

My blood, incidentally. For nothing that's not mine could pass through the screens on to the platform.

I sigh wearily, and Ernst's expression changes. He looks at me, concerned. 'Are you okay? You look—'

'As if I've been in a fight?' I smile, but the tiredness is beginning to gnaw at me. I need to bathe, to sleep. I need ...

'Look,' Ernst says, putting a hand out to touch my shoulder. 'I know this isn't the moment, but will you speak to the boys? Tell them about your experience? They've been learning about the situation back there, but ... well, it would be nice to have a first-hand account.'

I smile. 'Sure. Later. Hecht said you had something to tell me.'

Ernst glances back at the watching students. 'It can wait.'

'All right. Then I'll see you—'

'Tonight,' Ernst finishes for me. 'We've a session at eight.' He laughs, seeing how blank I look. 'It's just after eleven, Otto, in the morning.'

'Ah.' And I laugh. But it's hard sometimes, making these jumps through time. Harder than you could ever imagine.

5

Nothing stays the same for ever. Not even the Past.

Hecht's room is long and wide, the ceiling low, except in the central space where he seems to live, connected to his terminal. There, where the floor sinks down two feet, the ceiling also climbs to form a dome above his work space, the twelve black glass panels reflecting the faint fluorescence of the tree that hovers in the air above his desk.

Hecht's room is always dark. As you enter, you can see Hecht's face in the glow of his screen, austere, carved, the only bright thing in that shadowed environment. All else is glimpsed vaguely in the surrounding darkness: his pallet bed, his shelves of books, his clothes – in boxes, as if he's never quite moved in – and other things.

As I enter he looks up and across at me, his fingers still moving over the pad.

'Otto.'

He smiles faintly as he says it. Like the women, he is pleased to see me home, safe and in one piece.

I walk across, then sit cross-legged on the floor, facing him, the terminal to my right, the Tree above us both, its faint, yet ever-pulsing lights like the flow of life itself.

'So?' Hecht asks, not looking up from what he's doing. 'What went wrong?'

I have been thinking about this from the moment I recognised their dialect as Curonian, not Prussian: asking myself why they should be *there* at just *that* moment in time, and having argued the pros and cons in my head, I'm certain now.

'There must have been a Russian agent at Marienburg.'

Marienburg on the Baltic coast is one of the Order's fortresses, twenty miles west of Christburg. It was from there that Meister Balk set out to ordain me into the Order. As for the Curonians, we know they've been working with the Russians for some while.

Hecht glances up. 'It could just be coincidence.'

'It could, only with Meister Balk dead, and especially after the slaughter of the Sword Brothers at Saule earlier in the year, well, I can't think of two things more likely to destabilise the Order.'

Hecht smiles. 'Do you want to know what happened?'

I shrug, as if not bothered, and yet I do, for Balk's death, three years before his due time, was certain to have caused ripples, if not the collapse of the Order's Northern Crusade altogether, and without that ...

Without that, there would be no Prussia, no Frederick, and, ultimately, no Greater Germany. The implications were enormous. And yet it can't have happened that way, for if it had, things here would have changed.

Hecht glances at the screen one last time, then removes his hand from the pad, concentrating his attention on me.

Hecht has grey eyes. Some say they're cold – cold with the strange, dispassionate fervour of the intellectual – yet I've never seen that. I understand the icy fire that burns in him, for it burns in me too. And when he smiles, those same grey eyes are warm. Warm with a father's love for his children. Or perhaps that's just for me, his favourite, his *Einzelkind* as he calls me, as if any of us here could be an 'only child'. Yet I know what he means, for I am the wolf that hunts alone. Yet they are wrong. It is just that I do not properly fit into this regimented world of ours, although I try. Urd knows I try.

Hecht watches me a moment longer, and then he smiles. 'What happens is this. The Crusade does indeed falter. Support for it from the Papacy dries up. Moreover, the Swedes, dismayed by the failures of the campaign, do not invade the northern lands in 1240. They stay at home, and so Nevsky never becomes Nevsky, for there are no battles on the Neva or Lake Chud. Von Gruningen becomes Grand Master both of the Prussian and Livonian Orders, and under his leadership things go from strength to strength. In 1246 the Crusade is renewed with massive support from the Western princes. As a result, the heathen Prussians are suppressed, the Curonians defeated at Krucken.'

'Then ...'

'Time heals itself, Otto. As is its way. From 1250 onward you would scarcely know the difference.'

'And Nevsky?'

'He has his moment. But not as Nevsky. As ever, a few names change, the odd detail here and there, but Time ... Time flows on.'

I smile. 'Who did you send back to find out?'

'Kramer, and Seydlitz.'

'*Seydlitz?*'

My surprise amuses him. 'I thought he needed to get out in Time. He's been too wrapped up in his project.'

'Barbarossa?'

Hecht nods. 'Yes, but I wanted him away from here, while the Elders met.'

'They've *met?*'

Hecht sits back slightly. He is a tall, gaunt-looking man, yet the black one-piece that he's wearing makes him seem part of the

15

shadows. Only his face is distinct; that and his hands, which rest on the edge of the desk as he studies my face.

'Let's say I consulted them.'

'And?'

Hecht smiles, then changes the subject. 'You understand now how weak they are back there?'

For a moment I don't understand. Does he mean the Teuton Knights? Or is he talking about the Russians? The thing is, we're both spread thin. I mean, three thousand years, and only a couple of hundred agents to police them. No wonder we miss things. But then, so do they. It's a game of chess – the most complex game imaginable – only the moves can be anything, and the board . . .

The board is everywhere and any time.

I look up at the Tree.

It is not a tree like other trees. This is a Tree of Worlds, a tree of shining light, its trunk representing our reality, a thick thread of pearled whiteness, its various, multi-coloured branches the time-lines in which our agents operate.

Eight hundred and seventy souls inhabit the *Nichtraum* – the 'no-space' – of Four-Oh, at the last count. Of those, one hundred and seventeen are out there right now, in the Past, fighting the Russians, each one linked through Time and Space to Four-Oh. Their presence out there shapes the Tree, their living pulse forming *its* pulse. If any one of them should cease, then one shimmering, delicate branch ceases also, leaving only an after-image.

One whole alternate history snuffed out.

I look to Hecht. 'And you want me to find out just how weak?'

'In time. First you need to get some rest. I hear you're talking to Ernst's students later on.'

Is there anything Hecht doesn't know?

'He wants me to give them a first-hand account.'

Hecht laughs. 'Well, you can certainly give them that. Do you realise how strongly you smell, Otto?'

I grin. 'I can't say I've noticed.'

'No, but the women did. Oh, and Otto …'

'Yes, Meister?'

'Try to be kinder to the women, now you're back. They're only doing what they're supposed to do.'

6

You might wonder what Hecht means by that, and I ought, perhaps, to explain. Only, I *am* kind. Kinder than Hecht imagines. He's right, of course. I do have problems with that side of things, not with sex itself, but with the way we as a *Volk* handle sex. Oh, and I know the arguments. With so few of us, we need to take every opportunity we can to diversify the gene pool. Intellectually I can see the need.

Some argue that we could arrange this differently, mix up our genes in the laboratories and attain diversity by that means, but the counter-argument is strong. We are a *Volk*, not a group of families – Engel, Fischer and Muller, Schulz, Vogel and Ziegler, with all of the clannishness that involves – but a *people*. Change how we go about breeding and we would lose that. Our sense of oneness comes from knowing that we are one single family, that all mothers are *the* mother, all of our children *the* children of that one, singular mother, whomever's womb nature uses for the task. As for the physical, sexual side of things, that's there to bond us, man to woman, flesh to flesh. To do it otherwise is unthinkable. Or so I'd argue, if pushed. Because intellectually I *can* see the need. Emotionally, however …

But you don't need to know that. Not yet. Only that I find it hard, the way we do things here in Four-Oh.

Back in my quarters, I strip off and shower, then lie on my bed naked, my fingers laced together behind my head as I run things over in my mind.

It's hard at first to focus. Coming back, re-immersing myself in the hustle and bustle of Four-Oh after the cultural rawness of the Middle Ages, is never easy. My mind tends to be in two places at once for a while. But there are disciplines, and I use one now to clear away the mental clutter and attend.

It's very simple. If the Elders – the senior *Reisende* – have met, then a decision has almost certainly been made on Seydlitz's project – either to go ahead or, and the thought troubles me, to abandon it entirely.

I try to put myself in Seydlitz's position, try to imagine what it would be like to be turned down after putting in so much. After all, he's worked on his scheme for eighteen years now. And not just any eighteen years scattered through Time – but eighteen years *subjective*, as measured by his body's slow decay. He's still a young man, young enough, perhaps, to embrace another cause, another project, but I've seen men changed by the experience of rejection, seen them turn in upon themselves. If that were to happen to Seydlitz ...

They may, of course, have endorsed it. In which case ...

I smile, suddenly, strangely certain that that's what's happened, and the thought of it – of that great switch of manpower and man-hours to a new alternate time-line – gives me the kind of thrill that only an agent, operating out there in Time, can feel.

A new world order is about to be born. Something that didn't exist is about to be conjured into existence, with new choices, new branches, new diversifications.

A new move on the great board.

The thought reminds me of where I've just come from, and a wave of sadness envelops me, but I'm tired now, and, closing my eyes, I sleep ...

And am woken at seven by Ernst's soft *suden Deutsch* accent, reminding me of where I need to be at eight.

I dress, choosing a simple black one-piece not unlike Hecht's own, then, remembering the boys' faces, decide to summon Jodl, the armourer.

He's there instantly, as if he's been waiting for my summons – which is quite possibly true. He would have been informed the moment I got back. Now he steps into the room and stands there, head lowered, as the hatch hisses shut behind him.

He's a small compact man in his sixties, and he would dearly like to turn back the clock and be a *Reisende* again, only Hecht won't let him. These days his expertise is harnessed in other fields, which is what will happen to all of us when – and if – the time comes.

'I'm seeing Ernst's students,' I say, turning from the mirror to look directly at him. 'I thought it might be nice to look the part.'

He nods, then goes to speak, but I anticipate.

'I'm fine,' I say. 'A few cuts and bruises, that's all.'

Jodl almost smiles. 'You want me to clean the armour you were in, or bring your second suit?'

'The second suit will do.'

He hesitates a moment longer, and then he's gone, the hatch hissing shut behind him, returning an instant later, a hover-cart in tow, upon which is a brand-new suit of armour, my sword, a shield, and a second set of crusading Brothers' clothes.

'You didn't have to,' I say. 'There *was* time.'

He looks at me sternly but says nothing. Jodl prides himself on his efficiency. To be thought the least bit tardy ...

'Ernst isn't well,' he says, as he hands me the first item from the cart.

'Oh? In what way?'

'Look at his eyes. He hasn't been sleeping. And his hands ...'

I nod. It doesn't surprise me after all Ernst has been through. The only surprise is that he's sane at all.

I strip off the one-piece and begin to dress again. 'He'll be okay now that I'm back.'

Jodl looks me in the eye. 'Maybe.'

'No, he will. He's missed me, that's all.'

He looks away, then hands me another item, making no comment, but I know that behind that perfect mask of a face his thoughts are buzzing like a disturbed hive. Like all of them, he wants to know what I saw, what I did, who I met. And maybe I'll let him see a copy of my report when it's finished, only right now I don't want to discuss it. Not with him, anyway. Jodl has a way of asking all the awkward questions. And I'm not sure I'm up to answering those kind. Not yet, anyway.

As I pull on the rough woollen shirt, I look at him, reminding myself. If you look close – really close – you can see the odd grey hair among the black.

Time. How slow time must pass for the occupants of Four-Oh.

7

'What is Time *like*, Master Behr?'

'Time is like the surface of a pond. And also like ...' I pause, then laugh gently. 'Time has a thousand qualities, but mostly, mostly it's the thread that holds the universe together. In Gehlen's equations ...'

I stop, seeing how the boys are looking at me, glazed over suddenly. That's the trouble with Gehlen's Time equations, you can't *visualise* them – they function on a totally abstract level – and the mind needs to be able to picture things before it can understand them properly. It needs to create workable metaphors. But Time . . . how can you explain Time? It's pretzel logic.

'Time,' I begin again, 'is like a river. There are many tributaries, but only one river.'

Or a Tree, or . . .

They grin back at me, and I realise I'm being teased.

I know these boys well. I've taught most of them now for two, maybe three years, since they first came out of the Garden. When we're not in the field or researching, we teach, passing on what we know to the next generation. Ensuring that the fight is carried on in the best way possible.

Matteus, the youngest of them, raises his hand.

'Yes, Matteus?'

'Did you kill anyone, Master Behr? Where you've just been, I mean—'

It's a good question. Because if *that* past doesn't become *the* Past, then surely no one 'real' is killed at all? Only it isn't so. The Past is *always* real, even when we make changes to it. As real as this.

'Yes,' I say, remembering. *Even one as young as you.* But I don't say that aloud, because it disturbs me, this capacity in me to become a killer, back there in the Past. You see, at times we must be assassins. That is our job. There's little room for moral qualms. Or supposedly so. Some find it easy, you understand. Myself? I find it the hardest thing to hate. Not for ideological reasons, anyway.

'And were you ever in real danger, Master?'

The questioner is a thirteen-year-old named Tomas, a big lad for his age, all muscle and brawn like a peasant's son, only I know he is the brightest of them all.

'You are always in danger, in the Past.'

'*Always?*'

21

'Yes, Tomas. For where we are, they are.'

'The Russians?'

'Yes.'

And their allies. For they, like we, are not averse to using what-ever or whoever is at hand to further their cause.

Which is?

To annihilate us. To rid history of any taint of us, the German people. While we, in our turn, strive night and day to do the same to them.

A game. But one with the most deadly of intents: a game called *Rassenkampf* – 'race war'. And don't flinch at my words. Think. For *this* is the truth of humanity.

Tomas's eyes gleam as he watches me. 'Did you kill any ... *Russians?*'

Ernst, sensing that we're about to be led off into a cul-de-sac, interrupts. 'Let's stick to the subject, shall we?'

'But ...'

'*Tomas.*'

Tomas falls silent. Beside him, Matteus raises his hand.

'Yes, Matteus?'

'Does it *smell* back there?'

There is laughter. As it fades, I answer him.

'Very much. And you know what? Every Age has its own dis-tinct smell. Where I've been, well, things were very basic back then. Their idea of sanitation and personal hygiene left much to be desired.' I smile. 'It's no place for a sensitive nose.'

They like that. There's more laughter. But Ernst, I can see, wants something deeper than this from me. I can see in his eyes just how much he's missing it, how much he wants to talk about how it *feels* to be out there, in Time.

I look down. When I look up again my features are sterner.

'Smell is an important indicator of the state of social development of an Age, yet it's one of the more superficial aspects. Just as each age has its own smell, so it has its own mind-set, its own store of beliefs, of *givens* ...'

'Religion,' Dieter, the eldest of them, says, and I nod.

'When you go back, you must immerse yourself in the mind-set of that era. To do otherwise ... well, it's not an option. Not if you want to stay alive. One must learn to become a man of that time in every detail: in look, in speech and in basic mannerisms.'

'What do you mean, *Reisende?*'

Reisende, he calls me. *Traveller.*

I pause, remembering just how hard it actually is: lying to yourself day in day out, pretending to be what you're not, paying lip service to things you cannot, *should not* ever believe. Especially all of that Nazi stuff. Looking back at those reverent boyish faces, I find I cannot tell them. Not the whole truth, anyway. Being a time agent is like being the biggest liar that ever was.

I compromise. I tell them part of it.

'What I mean is that you must be a kind of actor. You must embrace the pretence. You cannot – *must not* – be who you really are. To let anyone suspect ...'

'So you live a lie?' Dieter asks.

I backtrack a little, noting how Ernst is watching me now, the faintest smile on his lips.

'When you're there, and it really is only when you're there, you find yourself searching within your own character for those elements that coincide with the Age, which ... *reflect* it, I suppose. You give rein to those elements.'

I see that some of them are not following me.

'It *changes* you,' I say, and I note how Tomas, at least, nods, some small glimmer of understanding in his eyes. I know there and then that he'll make a good agent when his time comes.

But the others? What do I want to say to them? That you are

not who you think you are? That to become a traveller – a *Reisende* – you must learn to shed one skin and wear another?

Yes. Only that's not all. The truth is, it is an exhilirating, liberating, *revelatory* experience. And troubling, too, for sometimes you learn too much about yourself when the restraints are cast off; when one must live by a new set of rules simply to survive.

'Otto?'

I look to Ernst. 'I'm sorry. I was remembering.'

'Remembering?'

'How it was, the first day I was there. On the boat, coming down the river to Marienburg.'

But I say no more, because I don't want to frighten them, and if I tell them how I really felt that day, it will. You see, the Past is an alien country. It is brutal and unforgiving, and you cannot make mistakes – not with the Russians out there.

'Otto?'

'I'm sorry. I'm tired. I haven't quite adjusted back yet.'

But it isn't tiredness, it's sudden understanding. I know now that it was me. Something I did back there. A mistake, perhaps, or some carelessness on my part. Because there's no other way the Russians could have known.

'I'm sorry, boys, but ...'

The boys show a paper-thin understanding, but I can see they're disappointed. They wanted tales of glory, of adventure and raw excitement, and I have not delivered. Only I can't free myself of the notion that my mistake – whatever it was – cost the lives of almost fifty men. *Real* lives.

I need to lie down and close my eyes. I need something to keep me from remembering.

8

Ernst comes to me later, in my room.

'What is it, Otto? What happened back there?'

'I don't know. But I must have done something. Something that left a trace.'

He nods, then sits, facing me on the end of my bed. I watch him for a while, noting how silent he is, then ask: 'And you?'

His smile is guarded. 'They say I'm doing well ...'

'It'll take time,' I say, resting my hand gently on his arm. But I am unable to imagine how he feels, for Ernst is a *Reisende* – a 'traveller' like me – and this confinement here in Four-Oh, however necessary, is chafing at him, like a frayed rope against raw flesh.

'Otto?'

'Yes?'

'Will you speak to Hecht for me?'

I hesitate, then nod. It will do no good, of course, but how can I refuse? Ernst is my best friend. To say no to him is almost unthinkable. Yet if I were in Hecht's place, I would make the same decision, for to even think of sending him back would be disastrous – for *all* concerned.

Ernst stares at me a moment, then looks away.

'What?'

He looks back at me, then shrugs. 'I was just thinking. About the Past. About us.'

'We were a good team.'

'We were. Only ...'

He doesn't have to say it. He only has to look at me and I can see the damage, there behind his eyes, there in every line of his face. And I sense – as maybe he senses – that it will never change; that he will *never* get better. And I don't know how *I* would deal with that. Because I know that the Past is like a drug for me: I have a craving to go there, to see it and be a part of it. Without that ...

I cannot imagine it. I just can't.

'I'll speak to Hecht,' I say. 'I'll try to convince him.'

But when he's gone, I slump down on my bed, my mood dark, because I know I can't help him. And if you can't help those closest to you, then what kind of man does that make you?

I sigh. Maybe it's the business at Christburg, but suddenly I wonder what the point is to it all, and whether I'm not simply lying to myself thinking I can make a single shred of difference to what's happening. But what's the alternative? To give up? To let the Russians win?

No. Because this is to the death. And whatever doubts I have, I need to keep them to myself.

As if on cue, I hear Hecht's voice from the speaker overhead. 'Otto, I need you. At the platform. Now.'

And I go. Because this is what I do, who I am. And to do otherwise is ...

Unthinkable.

9

Kramer is the first to come through. Looking across at us, he grins. He's wearing a simple brown garment of the roughest kind of cloth and his reddish hair is cut pudding-bowl fashion. He'd look the part, the archetypal medieval peasant, were it not for the way he bears himself now that he's back in Four-Oh, his 'disguise' thrown off.

As he steps down, the air behind him shimmers once more and Seydlitz forms like a ghost from the vacuum, his tall, well-proportioned figure taking on colour and substance in an instant.

He's dressed in full armour, the mantle of a Livonian Sword Brother about his shoulders, and his ash-blond hair is cut short, crusader-style. He looks exactly what he is, an aristocrat, his princely bearing only emphasised by his aquiline, almost Roman nose.

I look to Hecht for explanations, but Hecht ignores me. Stepping across, he greets the two.

'Hans, Max ...'

They bow their heads respectfully, then look to each other, excitement written all over their faces.

'Well? What did you find out?'

'Russians,' Kramer says, his eyes gleaming.

'Two of them,' Seydlitz adds. 'We killed them.'

Or think you did.

Hecht smiles. 'Do we know who they were?'

Kramer looks to Seydlitz. 'We're not sure.'

'Not sure?' Hecht's eyes narrow. 'Then how do you know?'

'We overheard them,' Kramer says.

'We'd tracked them down, to an inn.'

'They were discussing what to do next.'

'So we pre-empted things.'

Hecht doesn't even blink. 'In what way?'

'With a grenade.' And Seydlitz grins as he says it.

'Ah ...' But before Hecht can ask, Kramer intercedes.

'We buried what remained of them. Made sure the site was hidden.'

Hecht smiles. 'Good. Then maybe this once they'll stay dead and buried.'

Unlikely, I think, knowing how carefully the Russians track their agents, how they'll venture back and extract their agents moments before we've acted against them.

But both Kramer and Seydlitz are novices at this; they've barely half a dozen trips between them and it's clear they've let their enthusiasm cloud their judgement. But Hecht says nothing. He smiles at them, as if they've done well.

'Is that all?'

Kramer shakes his head and looks to Seydlitz, who produces a slip of paper.

'What's this?' Hecht asks, handing the paper to me. I look at it and frown. On it is drawn a figure of eight lying on its side. It is like the symbol for infinity, except that drawn inside each loop is an arrow, the two arrows facing each other.

'It was a pendant,' Seydlitz explains. 'A big silver thing. The fat one had it round his neck.'

'And the other? Did he wear one?'

Kramer shrugs. 'He may have done. There wasn't that much of him left.'

Hecht nods then looks to me. 'What do you make of it, Otto?'

'I don't know. Some kind of religious sect?'

'Maybe.' But I know that if Hecht doesn't know, then it's unlikely anyone else does. The question is: is it significant or just some piece of decorative jewellery?

Hecht watches them a moment longer, then nods to himself. 'Come,' he says. 'I want to hear it all.'

10

They shower, then join us in the smallest of the lecture rooms. There, with the doors locked and the cameras running, we go through it step by step.

I stand at the back, looking on, as Hecht faces the two across the table. Neither looks nervous, but why should they? I am the one who made the mistake. Or so I'm about to find out.

The story's pretty straightforward. While Kramer infiltrated the Curonians, Seydlitz went directly to the Brotherhood's head-quarters at Marienburg where, posing as an emissary of the Sword Brothers, the Brothers of the Knighthood of Christ in Livonia, he'd spent the best part of a month sniffing around, under the pretext of soliciting aid for his own Knight Brothers who, at the battle of Saule earlier in the year, had suffered an almost terminal mauling at the hands of the Lithuanians.

'So,' Hecht says, looking to Seydlitz first. 'What did you find out?'

Seydlitz sits up straighter. Even dressed simply, as he is, he looks every inch the knight. 'I didn't recognise them at first.'

'Was it these two?'

Two faces appear on a large screen to the side, larger than life. Seydlitz is surprised, but I just grin. Hecht sent in another agent and didn't tell them.

'Yes,' Kramer answers. His voice is a whisper.

'Ah. Go on.'

Seydlitz tears his gaze from the image on the screen and looks back at Hecht. 'They were posing as envoys from Rome, sent by Pope Gregory the Ninth. And they were good. Very convincing.'

Hecht nodded. 'They speak excellent Italian, so I'm told.'

'*Did*,' Kramer says.

Seydlitz glances at him, then continues. 'Anyway, I didn't suspect them at first. Not for a moment. Then, one night, I went down to the harbour. I had this notion that maybe the Russians were posing as traders, and there they were, the two of them, talking to a rather wild-looking fellow – a boatman – in fluent Curonian.'

'They saw you?'

Seydlitz smiles. 'No. It was very dark. The thinnest sliver of moon and heavy cloud. But I could see them by the light of one of the braziers that were burning along the harbour front. I hid behind a herring boat and listened. That's when I found out. After that I began to watch them. Noted who they spoke to, who they went to visit.'

'And then?'

Seydlitz pauses. 'It was about six days later. I turned up at the palace and they were gone. I asked about and no one had seen them since the previous evening. I thought I'd lost them, and then I remembered the fellow they'd met up with – the Curonian – and I went down to the harbour again.'

'He was there, then?'

'Yes, but another hour and I'd have missed him. He was waiting on the tide.' Seydlitz smiles. 'I put my knife to his throat and questioned him. It seems they'd paid him a visit the night before. Told him they were heading up the coast to rendezvous with his fellow Curonians. He'd offered to take them, but they'd not been interested. Said they had their own transport.'

Hecht nods thoughtfully. 'They jumped, then?'

Kramer answers him. 'Must have done. One moment they were in Marienburg, the next a hundred miles up the coast.'

'You saw them?'

'Yes. It was late. We were eating supper when they strode into the camp. The Chief of the Curonians, Axel he called himself, was surprised to see them. It was clear he wasn't expecting them back so soon. But it was also clear – and pretty quickly – that the news they'd brought was just what he'd wanted to hear. They had a bit of a party that night. Those Russians sure can drink!'

'*Could*,' Seydlitz says pointedly.

Hecht looks to him. 'So what was happening back at Marienburg?'

'I found that out later, when I tried to see the *Hochmeister*. I was told he had already left, with a small company of knights.'

'You didn't see him go, then?'

'No. He just slipped away. Pretty secretively, if you ask me. But then I asked around, and one of my contacts – one of the higher-placed clerics – told me he'd heard a rumour about Mindaugas wanting to meet up with the *Hochmeister*.'

'Mindaugas, the Grand Prince of Lithuania?'

Seydlitz nods. 'He wouldn't say why, but it was pretty obvious. After his victory at Saule, Mindaugas was in the ascendant, and the Knight Brothers knew it. *Hochmeister* Balk knew he needed to buy time. A temporary peace with the Lithuanians would give him that.'

'So you think that's the reason he went to Christburg? To meet with Mindaugas and arrange a peace?'

Seydlitz looks past Hecht at me. 'I can't be certain, but it seems likely, don't you think? More likely than that he'd make that perilous journey just to enrol a single knight – however worthy – into the Order.'

I feel some of the tension leave me at Seydlitz's words, and thank him inwardly for saying them. Maybe it wasn't my fault, after all. Maybe this was – as Seydlitz and Kramer are suggesting – a well-worked Russian plan to get to Meister Balk and kill him and so destabilise the situation. Yet it is some coincidence, if so. And why not just take him, there in Marienburg? It's unlike the Russians not to be direct.

Hecht looks to Kramer. 'What happened next?'

Kramer looks to Seydlitz. 'We met up. At the pre-arranged jump location. Traded information. Then decided to jump back to the Curonian encampment and follow the Russians. See where they went, what they did.'

'You didn't think they'd just jump home?'

The two of them look surprised at that. It's clearly not occurred to them before now.

Hecht pursues the point. 'You don't think they might have waited for you? Deliberately travelled by horseback down the coast so that you'd find them and make an attempt against their lives?'

'*Waited?*' Seydlitz looks aghast. 'But why should they do that? They didn't even know we were there!'

'Didn't they?' Hecht pauses, then says, 'As you might have guessed, I sent in another agent. Just to be safe. To *protect* you. And what he discovered was interesting.'

He turns in his seat, indicating the screen. 'Our friend on the left there is named Kabanov, and his fellow – the largish man – is named Postovsky. They're both new to this era, which is probably why you – and Otto, there – didn't recognise them. That said, they've clearly done their homework well. Well enough to fool you, Max, and many a better agent, too. But even so, they made mistakes. Once alerted to them, our man jumped back to when they first arrived in Marienburg and kept a close eye.'

Seydlitz looks up. 'Who was it?'

Hecht smiles. 'Our agent? You want to know?'

Freisler, I say to myself, a moment before Hecht confirms it.

Both men look thoughtful now. Neither meets Hecht's eyes.

'So what did he find out?' I ask, walking over to the table.

Hecht looks up at me. 'I believe they knew who you were, Otto. And that we were sending other agents in.'

'Not possible,' I say. 'I took such care.'

And it was true. I had spent time in Thuringia, establishing my credentials as a knight, then rode all the way to Marienburg, along with other knight-supplicants, so that when the time came they could speak for me and guarantee my authenticity. It simply wasn't possible that they had penetrated my disguise.

'Freisler thinks they got lucky. That one of their agents spotted you before you spotted him. If so, it would be easy to jump him out of there and replace him.'

'And is there any evidence that they did that?'

'Freisler thinks so. He traced them back, and discovered that there was just such a change of agent shortly after you arrived in Marienburg.'

'And who was there before?'

'Dankevich.'

'*Dankevich*? Is he certain?'

Hecht nods.

'Shit ...'

There's a moment's silence, and then Kramer asks. 'So are they dead?'

'The Russians?' Hecht smiles. 'What do *you* think?'

Both men look down, deflated now, but Hecht seems unaffected.

'It was rash, perhaps, to ambush the Russians, only you already had all the information you needed. You knew who they'd spoken to, and who the traitors were. That could be helpful in some future campaign. All in all, you did well. But for now, we do nothing.'

'*Nothing*?' Kramer looks horrified. But I understand. For any of our schemes to succeed we rely upon an element of surprise – we need to be able to spring the trap before they can get any of their agents into that time-line to combat us.

Hecht spells it out. 'I'm not going to waste good resources getting drawn into a tit-for-tat over a very minor time-line. As you know, the Russians have more agents than us – a hell of a lot more – and there's nothing they like better than to involve us in a fire-fight over nothing.'

Kramer makes to object again, but Hecht raises a hand, brooking no argument.

'We leave it. Understand me, Hans? We let it go.'

11

'Why Seydlitz?' I ask, when he and I are alone again.

'Because the Elders have agreed.'

'Barbarossa?'

Hecht nods.

'Then ...'

'Seydlitz didn't know. Only I wanted him to get a taste of it again. It's been a while.'

Almost three years, if I've heard right.

'You think he's ready?'

'Don't you?'

I nod, remembering how I felt when my first project was green-lit by the Elders. 'What backup are you giving him?'

'He'll lead a team of eight.'

'Eight!' It's a lot. Twice what we usually send in. But then, this is a major operation – a direct assault upon the very heartland of Russia – and if this works ... 'Am I ...?'

'No, Otto. I want you at a distance from this one.'

I don't quite understand what he means, but I bow my head anyway, obedient to his wishes.

'So when does he start?'

Hecht stands, then walks over to the bookshelves. He takes down a book and, turning back, hands it to me. 'He's begun already. I sent him in an hour back.'

'But ...' And then I laugh. Sometimes it's easy to forget how elastic Time is here in Four-Oh. For though Seydlitz was with us only moments before, it's an easy matter to wait a while, send him back a few hours, then send him back again, to a thousand years in the Past.

'The platform was busy the next few hours,' Hecht says, by way of illumination, which explains how he knew when to be at the platform to greet Kramer and Seydlitz.

And the book?

I look to Hecht, puzzled. It's a collection of Russian folk tales.

'Open it. To the title page.'

I open it and stare, because there, on the title page, is a hand-written dedication, and beneath it, the same symbol the Russian wore around his neck … the lazy-eight with the facing twin arrows.

I try to make out the signature, but it's almost unreadable. 'Who is it?' I ask, but Hecht only shrugs.

'Maybe we should find out.' And he smiles. 'Just in case.'

12

That night I dream.

I am back there, in the summer of 1236. Sunlight bathes the broad, flat rock on which we rest, laying a veil of gold upon the river below us and the trees beyond. There are five of us – Johannes, Conrad, Luder, Werner and I – brothers-in-arms, waiting there in the warmth of that July afternoon for Meister Dietrich to return from leading a scouting party into the forest on the far bank.

He has been gone since early morning, looking for pagan settlements amid that wilderness of trees. It has been some time – almost a year – since we last raided them, and they have grown incautious once more. Or so the Meister claims.

Johannes is the first to suggest it. He makes a comment on the smell of young Werner, and, laughing, roughly playful, Conrad helps Johannes strip the young man and throw him from the rock, naked, into the water. He surfaces, spluttering yet laughing, taking it in the spirit in which it was meant, then turns on to his back and floats there, treading water.

'Come in!' he yells, and splashes water up at us. 'It's wonderful!'

No sooner is the invitation made, than Conrad jumps from the rock, a high, flailing jump that ends only feet from where Werner is treading water. Johannes and Luder follow moments later, and, reluctant but grinning nonetheless, I slip out of my clothes and, throwing my arms out, dive straight as an arrow into that golden sheet of dazzling, shimmering light.

As I surface, there are cheers. Werner looks at me in awe. 'Where did you learn to do that, Otto?'

I gasp, gripped by the coldness of the water, but stay there, making no move to get out, determined to show no sign of weakness before my Brothers.

'My father taught me when I was a boy.'

'You were a boy, Otto?' Johannes says, mocking my earnestness, and the others laugh. But not at my expense. There's a kindness in their laughter. The mockery is gentle.

I duck down and swim towards the river's bed, thrusting myself down through the chill, clear water until I'm below them, their pale, strong legs kicking slowly in the pale greenness above me.

I surface right between Conrad and Luder, surprising them both, and, placing a hand on each of their heads, thrust them down, ducking them.

For a moment the three of us struggle in the water, laughing and gasping, and then Luder kicks back, away, shaking the water from his head as he does.

My strength surprises them. I know they think me soft. Comparatively, anyway. For these are the toughest, hardest, most resilient bunch of men I've ever known. Their austere self-reliance – their ability to survive in any conditions – astonishes me. They seem to need so little.

We climb back up on to the rock and sit there for a while, at ease in our nakedness, letting our bodies dry in the heat of the sun, enjoying the simplicity of the day. For a while all are silent, as if keeping to their vows, then Johannes stands and, after stretching, pulls on his clothes again. All but the armour.

We do the same, then sit there, staring out over the canopy of the forest. It seems to stretch to the very edge of the world. In the daylight there's a real beauty to the scene, but at night ...

I shudder and look to Werner, noting how he is watching me.

'I miss them,' he says. 'My family. My brothers especially.'

'Ah ...'

But Johannes has less time for sentiment. 'We do our Lady's business,' he says, and all bow their heads, as if in a moment's prayer, at the reminder.

But Werner is young. Only a minute passes before he looks to me again and asks. 'Do you miss your family, Otto?'

'I have no family.'

Werner's mouth opens the tiniest fraction, as if that explains a lot.

'They were killed,' I add, then look away.

'Is that why you came here?'

I nod. But I know they are all looking at me now. We have these moments. Quiet, reflective moments, when it is possible to say such things. When the vows we have taken are less important suddenly than understanding why we're here, and whether it's for the same sad reasons.

For as hard and self-reliant as these men are, they are also very much alone, even in such company as this. Lost souls, they are, seeking atonement. But theirs is also a steely, unshakable faith, and if they knew who I really was they would kill me without a moment's thought.

Silence falls again. I close my eyes, then hear a sharp intake of breath. My eyes flick open and I reach out for my sword. And then I see what it is, and relax.

In the shallows on the far side of the river, in the shade of the overhanging trees, a huge black bear has come to drink. She stands up straight for a moment, looking across at us, sensing us there, and then she turns and, with a strange, protective little gesture, beckons her cubs forward.

They scuttle past her, keeping close, and then rest there, their tiny, dark-haired bodies half-submerged in the water as they drink. And all the while the mother bear stares across at us defiantly.

None of us moves. At most we sit forward a little, as if to watch the scene more closely.

Finished, the cubs scuttle back into the trees, play-fighting as they go. The mother half turns to watch them, then looks back at us, her massive body swaying a little from side to side as she does, weighing up what to do. Then, as if satisfied, she bends down and, using her paws, scoops water to her mouth and drinks, glancing up at us from time to time.

Satisfied, she straightens and raises her head. Lifting it back, she growls, but whether it's in warning or in thanks it's hard to tell, and in a moment she's gone. The river flows on, like a broad band of molten sunlight running between the banks.

I turn and look to Johannes, who's looking down now, thoughtful.

'We should have killed it,' Conrad says, feeling the edge of his sword with his thumb. 'We could still go after it. It can't have gone far.'

'No,' Johannes says, with a finality that surprises us all. 'Leave it. It has a right to be here.'

'I agree,' Werner says. 'At least until we clear this godforsaken land.'

There's laughter. As it fades, Werner speaks again, gesturing towards the unending forest. 'Imagine it. All of this turned to pasture. A chapel there, where the river turns.

'And there' – he turns and points – 'a thriving Christian village.'

I can imagine it only too well, for though it may take several more centuries, it will be very much as Werner says. I know because I've seen it.

From our right a call breaks the stillness, and as we stand and turn towards it, so Meister Dietrich and the others emerge from the trees on the far bank a hundred yards downstream.

'They've found one,' Werner says quietly, unable to keep the excitement from his voice. 'Look at them, they've found one of their villages.'

I can see it's true. Though the Meister himself is sober, stern of face, the Knight Brothers just behind him are grinning excitedly.

'Thanks be to our Lady,' Johannes murmurs and crosses himself, the others – myself included – responding in an instant. Then he turns, looking to us in disgust, as if we were still naked. 'Now dress yourselves, quick, my brothers, unless you fancy a good flogging from the Meister!'

And then suddenly I am back there in the forest, at night, walking silently through the moonlit dark towards the village. All about me are the shadowy figures of my brother knights. They walk slowly, with a dream-like slowness, their long swords drawn, their cloaks fluttering ghostly pale between the dark, arrow-straight trunks of the trees.

We are close now. Ahead of us there's light and laughter. Sparks fly up into the darkness from a great bonfire in a clearing not a hundred yards away. About the fire are a dozen or so huts, crude things of daub and wattle. Families crouch before them, their faces lit, their eyes drawn to the leaping flames. Dark figures dance and whirl about the pyre, dancing to a crude yet haunting melody played on a single four-stringed instrument, its strangely exotic sound drifting out to us. The villagers sway from side to side, caught up in the song, clapping along to its rhythm, and then, suddenly, a voice picks up the melody and is quickly joined by others.

I feel the hairs on my neck bristle. The sound is beautiful, so pure and innocent. But I've no time now for such sentiments. My wrist is aching from carrying the sword, the muscles of my right arm stiff with tension. We are almost upon them, and as we come to within yards of the clearing's edge, so the Meister's voice cries out and we begin to run, our fierce yells of rage drowning out their song, which falters and stops.

They're screaming now, running this way and that, trying to flee into the forest as our men go among them, swinging their swords viciously. And those who do manage to slip away find themselves confronted by a second line of our men, standing out there among the trees, waiting to cut them down.

A young woman tears herself from the small group and runs towards me, yelling, her arms out to me. Her dark eyes implore me not to harm her, but even as I step back, a crossbow bolt knocks her down. I watch in horror as her hands scrabble at the welling patch of red in her side, a look of shocked surprise in her eyes. She struggles a moment longer, then convulses, dying with a whimper.

I look up. The huts are burning now, forming a great circle of brightness in the midst of that primordial dark. I turn, in time to see Brother Martin swing his blade and cleave a fleeing infant crown to navel, the child tumbling like a split fruit on to the carpet of bloodied leaves.

I howl and try to throw my sword away, but the muscles of my wrist are locked. And even as I do, the Meister himself strides across and, bellowing in my face, shoves me towards a group of cowering peasants, who crouch before a blazing hut.

There's fear in their eyes, and an overwhelming hopelessness, and I want to tell them that I'm sorry. I want to say, 'I have to do this, or my own people will die', but I can't. I am trapped in the moment, unable to deviate from it, and as I raise my sword again, I groan aloud and call to Urd herself to make this end.

But Urd is not watching, not protecting me from this, and as the dream goes on, I am forced once more to watch as, one by one, they die at my hand, screaming like frightened children, their souls flying up into the darkness like windswept embers. And when it's done, I turn to find the Meister watching me, a broad smile on his face.

'There,' he says, clapping me on the back. 'Not so hard, is it?'

The fires are raging now on every side, filling the dark night with their dazzling light, the blazing thatch roaring, the sound like a great torrent of falling water, glowing embers drifting on the gusting draughts like fireflies, carrying the blaze into the forest, setting parts of it alight, while at the centre of it all, the Knight Brothers, helms raised, lean on their bloodied swords and look about themselves, grinning and laughing, as if they've won some great victory.

Only I can't fool myself like them. I want to tell them just how wrong this is, only I'm not here to do that. I'm here to help them establish a bridgehead in this pagan land. I'm here because Hecht sent me here. Because ...

13

Light flickers, flashes, and I wake, pooled in my own sweat, gasping for breath.

'Otto?'

Zarah is there, sitting across the room from me, watching. I sit up, planting my bare feet firmly on the floor, then look at her.

'Bad dreams?'

I nod, but find I cannot talk. I don't trust myself to talk.

'Hecht told me,' she says. 'Some of it, anyway.'

I look about me for a drink. Zarah stands and comes across, holding a cup out to me.

'Drink this. It'll help.'

I meet her eyes, asking an unspoken query, and she smiles and nods. 'Enough to keep you out for several days. But it's your choice. You can keep suffering if you want to.'

I take the cup and down its contents in three large gulps, then slump back down, letting Zarah place the blanket over me. My eyes are already closed.

'If you need to talk ...'

But it's not talk that I need. What I need is to forget. And not to dream. Not those kind of dreams, anyway.

'So?' She says, after a while. 'Didn't Ernst tell you?'

This time I answer her. 'Tell me what?'

'No matter.'

But when I open my eyes she's gone, as if she too were a dream.

14

It happens that way sometimes. Things change, and we with them – our clothes, our memories, the things we've done in our lives. And we might not even know about it, only Hecht keeps track and lets us know.

It doesn't happen often. Not the big changes. But when they do we all feel strange for a time, not quite knowing why.

When I next see Hecht, he seems different, though in what manner I'm not sure. He looks and acts the same. Only ...

'What is it, Otto?' he asks, amused by the way I'm studying him.

'Nothing.'

'Good.' He pauses, finishes something on the keyboard, then. 'Feeling better?'

'Yes. Much refreshed.'

'Good. Then we'll find you something to do.'

'I thought ...'

He looks up patiently. 'Go on.'

'I thought maybe I could take Ernst back. To the Haven. I realise it's your space, but he's going mad, being cooped up here.'

Hecht studies me coolly. 'Cabin fever.'

'What?'

'It's what they used to call it. What happened when people were cooped up together for too long. Cabin fever.'

I nod, then wait, and after a moment Hecht shakes his head. 'I'm sorry, Otto, but I can't take that risk. We tried it once, remember?'

I look down, disappointed. Though I knew it would be his answer, I'd hoped he might perhaps relent. After all, what trouble could Ernst get up to so far back in time?

'You want me to speak to him, Otto?'

'No ... no. I'll go and see him now.'

Ernst is teaching when I find him, the boys hanging on to his every word as he tells them an anecdote from one of his journeys back. It's one I know well, and I stand there listening in the shadowed doorway until he's finished, and then – and only then – do I make my presence known.

'It's true,' I say, stepping past the boys and grinning at Ernst, who is surprised to see me there. 'I was there, and that's exactly what happened.'

'You blew them up?' Tomas asks, eyes wide.

'That's right. They just walked right in and ... *boom*! They never knew what hit them!'

The boys are delighted, but it's not them I've come to see, and once Ernst has dismissed them, I sit him down. Only I can't bring myself to tell him. He so wants to go back again.

'Well?' he asks. 'What did Hecht say?'

'I didn't get to see him. He's very busy right now.'

'Busy?'

I nod. 'He's got a lot on his plate. Seydlitz's project for a start.'

'Yes, but ...'

'You'll just have to be patient,' I say, and hate myself for lying to him. 'I'll see him later. I promise. I'll ask him then.'

Ernst looks down. 'They're still watching me.'

'Watching you?'

'Assessing me. To see if I'm stable. I look up sometimes and it's like I can see them there, in the control room, watching me on the screen, looking for some nervous tick perhaps, or some self-betraying phrase.'

'I guess they have to be careful.'

'Careful, yes. But sometimes ...' He hesitates, glancing past me at the camera high up on the wall behind me. 'Sometimes I think it's more than that.'

15

Another night passes without rest, and when finally I sleep, I dream once more, awful bloody dreams where I am back there with the Knight Brothers, and of all the bad things we did in the name of Our Lady, and I wake, gilded with sweat, gasping for breath, as if I've been drowning in blood.

Unable to settle, I go to the sanctuary, where, before the image of Ygdrasil, the Tree of Existence, I give offerings to Urd, Goddess of Fate, Queen of Life and Death.

This is *our* religion, and in this I believe, strangely enough. Rational as I am, this fulfils some need in me. Why? Perhaps because it is the only faith that reflects both the strengths *and* weaknesses of mankind, a religion that does not ask its followers to be any better than its gods. And yet ...

Yet there is still a small, argumentative part of me that *does not* believe. My 'mathematical soul' as I call it. And that part finds such emotional comfort little more than a superior theatre show. Yet, cold as I might appear, aloof as I am, my emotional self believes. I know the gods exist, and that when I die my soul – yes, and my bodily self – will go to Valhalla, there to feast with the gods.

I close my eyes and lower my head, saying the words of the ritual.

'Great Mother Urd protect me and guide me. All-Father Odin, grant me the strength of will to do my duty.' And it is true. Urd *does* protect me and watch over me. She, above all, safeguards my deeper self. She *is* my strength. If ever I lost my faith in her ...

I open my eyes and look up at the World Tree, nodding to myself. The great ash is the image of our cosmos: its roots stretch back into the Past, its great trunk forms the Present, its branches unfold into the Future. So life is, and we ... we are but leaves upon that Tree.

I have travelled the length and breadth of Time, and I have seen more than mortal man ought, yet only here do I find myself truly at peace, body and soul at one. Here, yes, and in one other place.

But I shall speak of that another time.

I stand, and as I do, I realise that Hecht is there, just behind me, his back to the door.

'Forgive me, Otto. I didn't mean to intrude.'

'It's okay. I was just—'

Hecht smiles. 'I know. I come here every day.'

I nod, understanding the feelings that we share about this place. Even so, I feel embarrassed, as if I have been caught doing something illicit, something very ... *personal*. Sensing this, Hecht steps back a little.

'If you'd rather I came back ...'

'No ... come and worship with me.'

And, turning back, I kneel once more, bowing my head before the holy ash, even as Hecht kneels beside me and, bowing his head, takes up the litany.

Part Two

In the Footsteps of Napoleon

"One repays a teacher badly if one remains only a pupil"

– Friedrich Nietzsche, *Ecce Homo* (1888)

16

'Otto ... we need to talk.'

Freisler stands before me, blocking my way. If I asked him to move, he would; he's not an impolite man, but there's something about his manner that gives me pause for thought.

'Sure.'

'Not here,' he says, and places his hand on my upper arm. I look at it pointedly, and he removes it without comment. He knows I don't really like him – that I *instinctively* don't like him – but it doesn't seem to worry him. Nothing does.

He turns and, tapping in the code, makes the door open on to his rooms. As it hisses apart, he looks round at me and gestures for me to enter.

I step inside. Books line the walls. In one corner is a chair. Otherwise there's nothing. No bed, no table, and no sign in the room I glimpse through the archway that he has any of these things. It makes me wonder where he sleeps, or even *if* he sleeps. Fanciful, I know, but Freisler attracts speculation like that.

'Well?' I ask. 'What did you want to say?'

Freisler is a strange fish. He's a good twenty years older than me, and people say he was Hecht's favourite, once upon a time. Until I came along. Not that he's ever made any comment on it – not in my earshot, anyway – only I guess it might irk him, that he might see me somehow as his usurper.

He looks at me now with that cold, supercilious stare of his, eyes half-closed under those heavy lids, his long face almost nodding. They call him Hecht's *Jagdhund* – his 'bloodhound' – and there is a certain dog-like quality to him, only he's far too intelligent to deserve that sobriquet. Freisler is very much his own man, however loyal he is to Hecht.

'I thought you should know what happened back there,' he says, his voice clipped, businesslike.

'I thought I did. Someone spotted me as I went in. They changed agents and—'

I stop, because Freisler is shaking his head. 'I meant what *really* happened.'

'Go on.'

'It wasn't you.'

'No?'

'No, it was those two ... *idiotisch.*'

I blink, shocked. It's not like Freisler to offer any form of criticism. 'What do you mean?'

'Hecht's played it down. He had to. *Barbarossa* had been green-lit. Any criticism of Seydlitz ...'

Would have meant the cancellation of his project ...

I nod my understanding. 'So?'

'So it endangers us all. That level of incompetence, I mean. It undermines what we've been doing.'

'But surely ...?'

'When they killed those Russians, they tripped all kind of alarm wires. The Russians sent in quite a few of their agents to have a really close look to see what was going on. It got quite hairy back there for a time. And you know what they were looking at?'

'What?'

'Seydlitz. They paid him a lot of attention. You know how they do. One of their men will be sitting at a nearby table in a bar, listening in, while another one will be standing outside in the street as he comes out. It's how they work. They get to know our men really well.' Freisler smiles; a cold, wintry smile. 'Luckily we have me. And the Russians don't have a clue who I am.'

But you *know who* they *are* ...

'So why are you telling me? Why not Hecht?'

'Hecht's busy. Very busy. Besides, I wanted to alert you.'

'Alert me?'

'About Seydlitz. I've an instinct for these things.'

It's almost ironic. 'You think him unsound?'

'No. Seydlitz is immensely sound. He would do anything for the *Volk*. He's clever and resourceful and his project – Barbarossa – is a good one. It had a good chance of succeeding. Only the Russians know now who he is, and he can be headstrong. The killings ... I can't help thinking that we'll pay for them. *How*, I don't know, only—'

'Did they bring them back?'

'The two that were killed? Of course they did. They may have three times as many agents out there, but they don't waste men for nothing. Besides, it was easy for them. Just a minor change in Time. Why, that very evening I was drinking with them like they were old friends.'

I stare at Freisler a moment, trying to understand him; wondering if I've got him wrong. Then, with a small dismissive shrug, he goes over and takes a book down from the shelf. As he turns back, he glances at me. 'That's it,' he says. 'All I've got to say.'

'Ah. Only I thought ...'

But it doesn't matter what I was thinking. Freisler has said his piece and – in a manner reminiscent of Hecht – he has dismissed me. But maybe that too is part of his game: to remind me that he's closer to the centre of things than I am, however it might seem.

'Oh,' he says, as if he's suddenly remembered. 'Your friend Ernst was asking after you. Wanted to know if you had an answer.'

Do I imagine the cold smile that flickers across his lips, or is he really such a bastard as to know already and enjoy making a taunt of it?

'*Thanks*,' I say, emphasising the word. 'And thanks for the warning. I'll sleep on it.'

17

Ernst is in my room when I get back, but one glance at me tells him more than he wants to know.

'Hecht said no, didn't he?'

'Yes. He feels you aren't ready yet.'

Ernst slumps down into the chair. 'Shit!'

'I'm sorry.'

'I know. Only it's so unfair.'

I don't want to argue, so I change the subject. 'You'll never guess who I've just been speaking to.'

'Who?'

'Freisler.'

'*Freisler?* That bastard!'

'Oh come. He's not the friendliest of men, but—'

'But what? Those eyes of his, the heavy lids, it's like he's shielding his soul. Preventing you from looking in and seeing what a vacuous bastard he truly is. They say he does all of Hecht's dirty work.'

'Someone has to.'

'Sure. But he doesn't have to like it so much, and it doesn't mean *I* have to like *him*.' Ernst stands, agitated now. 'So what did the *Jagdhund* say?'

I smile at my old friend's relentlessness. 'He says he has a feeling – an *instinct* – about Seydlitz. He thinks we should watch him carefully. Oh, and he thinks that maybe the Russians have singled him out. They were very interested, it seems.'

Ernst nods thoughtfully. He knows what it's like to have the Russians single you out.

'You should keep an eye.'

'I shall.'

'But right now ...' Ernst grins. 'Right now I could do with a drink.'

18

Ernst stares at me, his eyes gleaming. 'So ... when will the first report come back?'

'Within the hour. That is, if Hecht isn't studying it right now.'

'Ah.' Ernst looks thoughtful. He strokes his close-shaven chin, then shakes his dark unruly mop of hair. I know him so well that I can tell there's something he wants to say – something he maybe wants to ask – but he doesn't quite know how.

'What is it?'

'Nothing, it's ... nothing.'

'No?' But I leave it. Ernst is like that. He takes his time coming to the point. There's nothing rash about him, nothing ill-considered.

We're in the North Bar. Not that it's north. Direction is arbitrary here in the *Nichtraum*. Yet we need a sense of it, and so where we sit, on a balcony overlooking the pool, is deemed the polar north.

'I hear Klaus is back,' I say, filling the sudden silence. 'How's he getting on? And how's our old friend Nevsky?'

Klaus Kubhart is Ernst's replacement back in thirteenth-century Russia, his *protégé*. Ernst trained him up, taught him everything he knew about the era, then sent him back.

'Klaus is fine,' Ernst answers, wiping froth from his upper lip. 'He's doing well. As for Nevsky ... he's just as foul-mouthed and gargantuanly conceited as when you last met him.'

I take a long sip of my beer. So it is with heroes. Theirs and ours. Some are genuine, others painted so to suit the purposes of history. But Nevsky is one of the worst I've come across. To the Russians he's a demi-god, the saviour of their nation from the Swedes and the Teuton Knights, but then they've never met the man in person, were never forced to spend an evening in his odious company.

Of such men and women is the Chain of Time compounded. If there's a human type, then that type has been a king, their faults, like their virtues, exaggerated by the power they wield. I have seen them all: priests and sadists, pedants and visionaries, the lazy and the psychotic, adventurers, hedonists and nihilists, the corrupt and the cynical, the feeble-minded and the iron-willed, gluttons and simpletons, schemers and cowards and oh so many more.

To find the weakest among them is our task, for through such men might history be changed.

Yet history is not just the tales of individual men; there are tides and currents, and while the strong man might swim and the weak man flounder, it is usually to men of little consequence – your average swimmer – that Chance hands the poisoned chalice of kingship.

Of this and other things Ernst and I converse, as we so often do. It's nothing new, yet it's good simply to be there with him. Silence would suit as well, for we have been through much together, Ernst and I. We owe each other lives.

'So when is Klaus going back?'

Ernst looks away, embarrassed by the question. Yet he must have known it would come. 'Later,' he says quietly. 'He came back to pick something up.'

'Ah.' But I don't press him. He knows why I asked. Knows why I want to go there with him, only ...

Only there are some things we simply cannot talk about.

'How's Frederick?' he asks, and I laugh. It's been some while since I've been back in 'my era'.

'Did I tell you? I had to stop some bastard taking a pot-shot at him.'

Ernst grins. 'A Russian?'

'No. An Austrian, damn it!'

We both laugh. Time is the strangest thing: just when you think it's set, so it flows and alters. Small, subtle alterations.

Ernst finishes his drink, then stands. 'I'd better go. I have to see Klaus before he returns.'

I look up, overeager. 'You want me to tag along?'

He shakes his head. 'No, Otto.' Then, smiling: 'I'd best go now.'

'Then take care. And when you need me ...'

'I know.' And he turns and leaves, quickly, before he can change his mind.

19

I'm in my room, alone, lying on my pallet bed, reading Lermentov's *A Hero of Our Time* when a messenger comes from Hecht.

It's Leni, one of the younger couriers.

She hands me an envelope, then leaves.

I peel it open.

Inside is a wafer-thin file and a handwritten note.

Normally Hecht would have sent a typescript – it's not his practice to let us see our fellow agents reporting to camera – but this time he clearly wants me to. Which implies that he wants me to observe Seydlitz himself, not just what he says.

I walk over to my desk and switch on the lamp, then pour myself a drink and settle to the report, slipping the tiny slither of plastic into the viewing slot.

At once Seydlitz appears on screen. His is sitting in a chalet-style room, sparsely furnished, with a view of forest through the open window behind him. He's wearing evening dress, a high white collar and a black bow-tie, loosened now, so that he looks very much of that time. Indeed, with his ash-blond hair and grey eyes, his square jaw and perfect bone structure, he looks the perfect Aryan – a regular young god – but has he fooled them? Have they accepted him at face value?

One last detail. On the table, to the left of the picture, is a packet of cigarettes, a blue packet with the name prominently displayed. Beside them is a small cream-covered flip-book of matches – the kind restaurants give to their customers. I smile. Whether it's stress, or just part of the disguise, Seydlitz has become a smoker.

But before he's had a chance to say a word – even as he takes a breath, ready to launch in – I freeze the image.

You see, for a moment I think I must have glimpsed something – a shadow, maybe, or the hint of someone else in the room with him – yet tracking back I find nothing. Seydlitz is alone.

I let it run.

Seydlitz speaks in a hushed yet awed voice:

'Time hangs in the balance. I know that. Earlier, as I walked down the corridor, guards in dress black saluted me. Perhaps they sensed the urgency of my mission. If I failed to convince the Führer ... But I could not think of failure. I had to succeed.'

He glances aside, as if getting things clear in his head, then resumes:

'When I entered the room, Hitler was standing with his back to me, still mulling things over. He'd read all the reports and knew now that what I told him at our last meeting had come about. Despite which, well, finally he turned. His vividly blue eyes searched my face for some final sign that this was all a trick, some elaborate form of treachery.'

Seydlitz shakes his head.

'It's so intense, that gaze of his, so ... penetrating. Yet I don't think he saw anything. "It is true, then, Herr Seydlitz," he said. "Does it all come to nothing?"

'"Yes," I said.

'He stared at me a moment longer, then, abruptly, he looked away, smashing his right fist into his left palm.

'"There must be something!" he said. "Some way of changing it." He turned back to me, his eyes wide, filled with a strange, unfathomable pain. "There has to be!"'

Seydlitz moves back slightly, the momentary intensity draining from him. There is the faintest smile, quickly gone. He is enjoying this.

'We were not alone, you understand. I mean, I'd scarcely been aware of the others, but they were there, standing against the walls to either side, like shadows, listening and looking on, saying nothing. Himmler and Rosenberg. Ribbentrop and Ley, Goebbels, Bormann, Speer, Goering and Funk. Hess, of course, had fled a month back, just as I'd said he would.'

He reaches up and removes his tie, then undoes the top two buttons of his shirt. He's sweating now.

'Hitler was still watching me, the same intensity in his eyes, his head slightly lowered. I could see that this frightened him, perhaps more than death itself. Yes, and he'd changed since our last encounter. He looked at me now as if he saw the figure of Fate itself come down the years to reveal to him the futility of his endeavours.'

And with good reason, I think, noting the date of the report. It was the evening of 21 June 1941. In the morning German troops would cross the border and invade Russia. Operation Barbarossa would begin.

Seydlitz clears his throat.

'I told him: "Already things are changing. Today, for instance, you, my Führer, wrote a letter to Mussolini. In it you said to him: 'Whatever *may come now, Duce, our situation cannot become worse as a result of this step. It can only improve."*

'*I saw the effect that had on him. He blanched and his mouth fell open. Every tiny little thing was adding to my authority; each tiny revelation undermining his certainty. In time he would be mine entirely – dependent on me.*'

I smile. Seydlitz is a big man, broad-shouldered and heavily muscled, yet sharp, like a figure from the *Nibelungen*. I could imagine the scene, Seydlitz's strong, resonant, orator's voice filling the low, raftered room of the Wolfensschanze, while outside the summer day was dying and the gloom of the East Prussian forest pressed closer, making the room seem cold despite the fire.

In my mind's eye I could picture Hitler there, in the dead of winter, alone in that room, studying the maps. They would tell a different story then.

Seydlitz smiles.

'*I was hard, unrelenting. "But it will not improve," I said. "Though you come to the gates of Moscow itself, you shall not enter them, for when the snows come, they will find you naked."*

'*As I said, it was harsh. But Hitler responded in kind. He faced me squarely, his chin raised, defiant yet in the face of Fate. "What do you want?"*

'*"For myself," I said, "nothing, but for my people . . . I want everything. For them I want the future."*

'*Hitler laughed sharply. "The future?" Even so, I saw it had touched a chord. "And who are your* people?" *he asked.*'

Again Seydlitz pauses. That last word – *Volk* in the tongue he would have been speaking in the ancient German of that time – was heavily, almost ironically emphasised. This was clearly important to Hitler. He was alluding, of course, to his concept of the *Herrenvolk*, the chosen race not of God but of the evolutionary universe itself.

Seydlitz reaches out and takes a cigarette from the pack and, striking a match, lights up. He takes a long draw on it, exhaling the smoke in a long, satisfied breath before continuing.

"*The Germans,*" *I said.* "*The Volk.*"

'*It was clearly what he wanted to hear. He stared once more, searching my eyes, and then he nodded. His hand made a small gesture of acceptance. I had him.*'

Seydlitz's hand makes the gesture. He looks away, grinning now, clearly pleased with himself, then faces the camera again. Smoke from the cigarette trails up between his fingers.

"*On the evening of October sixth,*" *I said,* "*the first snows will fall. General Guderian will see it and notify you. But long before then conditions will have made your advance difficult, and by the second of December, the advance will falter outside Moscow. Some of the Fifty-Eighth Division will reach the outskirts, but they will fall back.*"

'*I looked from Hitler to Goering. This much was reiteration, but I could see how much it impressed them.*

"*Then,*" *I said,* "*on the sixth of December the Russians will counter-attack. On the seventh the Japanese will attack the US naval base at Pearl Harbor. These two events will determine the whole course of the war.*"'

Seydlitz draws on the cigarette. His eyes slip to the side as he remembers.

'*Hitler was watching me very closely by this stage, glaring at me, his whole will opposed to what I was saying. I could see from the tension in his body that he would have liked to have struck me or flown into a rage. Only he believed me. It was frustration that made him clench his fists. What I'd shown him could not be disbelieved. There was no way of knowing – of anticipating – such things.*

"*Your machine,*" *Hitler said, stepping closer.* "*What it sees ... is it fixed?*"

"*No,*" *I said.* "*It can be altered.*"

'With that, his whole expression changed. A smile came to his lips. It transformed the intensity of his stare into something almost demonic.

'He fixed me with that stare. "And you can change it?"'

Seydlitz looks down at the cigarette thoughtfully.

'"I know how to act," I said. "How to influence the outcome of events."

'Hitler seemed pleased. "You've done this?" he asked.

'"Yes," I said.'

Only it's a lie. Seydlitz doesn't know for certain how to change events. None of us do, when it comes right down to it. But he can try. He is there to try.

He leans in closer, relishing his role as narrator:

'"We have made plans," I told him. "Changes of emphasis. Innovations. Tactical variations. Things that will have their effect."

'Hitler stared back at me, his suspicion momentarily naked. Then he smiled. "And what is your role in this, Herr Seydlitz?"

'I laughed. The time for modesty was past. They understand few things, these early men, but they understand them well. Greed. Power. The survival of the strong.

'"I want to govern Russia," I said. "I want the German Ukraine. In return I will help bring you victory. I will advise you ..."'

Seydlitz pauses, remembering something:

'I saw how Goering looked at me, then away. That's one man I'll have to deal with in the not-so-distant future. But Hitler ...

'He stood there, looking at me pensively, and then he smiled – a smile of recognition and understanding. "And when the snows come?"

'I met his eyes. "This time we shall be ready for them."'

20

'Well?' Hecht asks. 'You've seen his body language. What do you think?'

I tear my gaze away from the shining image of the Tree and meet Hecht's eyes.

'I think he's enjoying himself. He seemed relaxed. Confident. Why? Do you still have doubts?'

'No ...'

But Freisler does, I finish for him in my head.

'He's doing well,' I say. 'Much better than I thought, if you want the truth.'

Hecht smiles. 'He's very capable.'

'Yes ...'

There's a moment's silence, then Hecht nods. 'Okay,' he says. 'You can go now.'

I stand.

'But Otto ...'

'Yes, Meister?'

'Keep an eye. I'll send you the summaries.'

21

Seydlitz had gone back further to hatch his scheme, back beyond the beginning of that century. Officials had been bribed with freshly minted gold, and perfectly forged documents were entered into the records of the US government: nationalisation papers; certificates of marriage and birth. All this to establish his team's credentials – the 'reality' of their existence. In the Twenties they obtained passports, travelled, met those who, later, they would need to meet again. And so on through the Thirties, stretching their group existence thin – sufficient to create the fiction; enough to satisfy the prying eyes of Himmler's agents when, eventually, they came to look.

And so Seydlitz was twice-born in the records of this world;

once in the Indiana of 1896, and again in the Berlin of 2963. What vast gulfs separated those times. Otto, studying the files, knew how it felt. When Seydlitz walked the streets of Columbus, Indiana, back in those distant days of his first birth, he no doubt found it exhilarating simply to stroll beneath an open sky on a spring day, the sun on his bare arms. Like heaven.

He entered Germany through neutral Sweden in the autumn of 1940. France had fallen by then. Hitler was in the ascendant. Russia and the United States had yet to enter the arena. Great Britain was alone in holding out against the Führer. In such circumstances his mission seemed possessed of little attraction. Why should Hitler listen? What could Seydlitz offer that destiny – in Hitler's mind – had not already granted him?

Nothing that Hitler did, it seemed, could go wrong. Each step he took raised him higher. Destiny, surely, meant to raise him higher still – maybe to the very pinnacle itself? So he thought. And soon, Seydlitz knew, he would lose touch with the reality of Germany's situation. His sense of destiny would, piece by piece, destroy what he had built. The Fatherland, the *Volk* itself, would be sacrificed to Hitler's sense of his own greatness.

Unless they could stop him. Unless they could undermine his confidence *before* he ceased listening to conflicting views.

Seydlitz had studied him long, watched him on film and read of him until he could sense the thought behind each look, the feeling behind every gesture. Hitler was a consummate actor, a master of the art of self-delusion. In his speeches he would work himself into a state of total belief – as credulous, as much a victim to his creative manipulation of the truth as the least of them who watched and listened, their eyes agleam, their lips shaping echoes of his words. But he was also cunning, paranoid, utterly ruthless.

In the summer of 1941 the fantasist and the realist were

delicately balanced in his nature, but after the snows nothing would be the same again – that balance would shift ineradicably. Hitler would become a recluse, hidden away in the Wolfensschanze, Hitler's Wolf's Lair, his military command post in the heart of the Mazurian forest; refusing to acknowledge the fact of his defeats; talking endlessly, repetitively of the victories of the past and dreaming of the miracle to come.

He did not know it, but Seydlitz was that miracle: the future come to greet him. He was Hitler's fate, his destiny, the *deus ex machina* that would change the very shape of history and bring about the Dream.

Stettin, where Seydlitz landed, was a cold, suspicious place. As an American national he was at first treated politely if not warmly by the local SS. What was he doing there? What did he want? Who was he going to meet? This was expected.

'I have a meeting with Herr Funk,' he said.

Things changed at once. Walther Funk was President of the Reichsbank and Minister of Economics. The SS officer looked at him, noting that he spoke perfect German and that his name was Seydlitz. An honourable *Prussian* name. Hostility was replaced by respect, even by a degree of obedience. A telephone was brought and he made the call.

Funk's secretary hesitated, then put him through. In a minute or two it was achieved. Funk had received his letter and remembered him. Funk was busy, yes, but he would see him.

Seydlitz smiled and handed the phone across to the officer, letting him confirm the details. There was no real secret to this business. No doubt Funk did remember him. It had been at Cologne in '35. Funk had been running the *Wirtschaftspolitischer Pressedienst* and acting as contact man between the Nazis and big business. Seydlitz had gone out of his way to impress him with talk of his company's vast wealth and his admiration of the Reich.

But this was not why Funk had agreed to meet him. Germany needed foreign currency badly, and he had promised much in his letter.

Funk, he knew, was unimportant in himself. He had replaced the capable Schact – Hitler had appointed him in the interval at the Opera House – and had taken on a subordinate role in the Nazi machine. But Funk was his entry. Funk would introduce him to others who, in their turn, would bring him to Hitler.

He spent the winter in Berlin, the real Berlin, not the claustrophobic *Nichtraum* – the 'no-place' – he remembered from his own, personal past. This was a very different city. The spirit of the New Order hung over the place, transforming its massive boulevards as well as its old world streets. He walked down the Unter Den Linden with its imposing buildings and its massive sculptures. Standing beneath Rauch's magnificent equestrian statue of Frederick, he felt a thrill pass through him. Here was the Dream. Here, in the purity of this vast and magnificent architecture, was the very seed of the Reich.

That winter was a busy one for Seydlitz. He met Julius Streicher, the whip-bearing Gauleiter of Nuremberg. Streicher and Funk introduced him to the Foreign Minister, Ribbentrop. By December, his name had been mentioned to Hitler. In the first week of January, Goebbels came to see him. By then more than five million dollars had entered the Nazi coffers – all of it perfectly forged, none of it distinguishable in any way from the real thing – such was proof of his friendship to the Party and to the Führer. Goebbels sounded him out. Unlike Streicher or Funk he was a clever, perceptive man. Goebbels came meaning to see through Seydlitz, but went away strangely pleased with him, wondering how he might fit him into his propagandist schemes.

He first met Hitler in the February of 1941, in Berlin, at the Opera. It was Wagner, naturally. *Das Rheingold*. Afterwards there was a small reception. Seydlitz entered late, accompanying Ribbentrop. There the introduction was made.

'You enjoyed the opera?' Hitler asked, extending his hand and smiling.

Seydlitz smiled and bowed his head in salute. 'I was moved, Führer.'

He released Hitler's hand and met his eyes. Hitler was watching him, smiling, nodding. Then he gestured towards the nearby table. 'Will you have a drink, Herr Seydlitz?'

Seydlitz shook his head. 'Thank you, but no, Führer. I do not drink alcohol. Nor do I eat meat.'

He saw how Hitler's eyes lit at that. It pleased him greatly. 'Then we have much in common, Herr Seydlitz.'

'I hope so, for I would dearly like to serve you.'

There was no weakness in the words, as if to serve Hitler were the natural channel for the strong. This too pleased Hitler inordinately, flattered his ego beyond the superficial phrases of such as Ley and Ribbentrop. He glanced at Goebbels and gave the slightest nod, as if to confirm something they had discussed earlier, then he looked back at Seydlitz, his intensely blue eyes filled with a sudden, almost passionate warmth.

'We must meet again, Herr Seydlitz. I would like you to be my guest at Berchtesgaden. We must talk.'

At that Hitler nodded curtly and turned away. It was done. He had gained access to Hitler. That was the easy part – the hardest lay ahead.

22

In ancient Rome it would take a full six weeks to spread the emperor's writ throughout the empire. By the eighteenth century, news from Far Cathay would take six months or more to make its way to Europe. By the beginning of the twenty-first century, however, communication was instantaneous. News arrived as it happened. When the Twin Towers fell, the world watched it happen live.

We differ in but one respect. Our news is from the Past.

Seydlitz has been gone a mere eight hours subjective, yet already word of his great enterprise comes back to us.

I shower, then return to the latest report. Hecht has been busy, dispatching agents to assist, sending advice, attempting to fine-tune the venture. But essentially Seydlitz is alone. On his shoulders lies the fate of all. And to my mind, he's doing well. Whatever Freisler might think – whatever his *instinct* – Seydlitz has done a masterful job so far. He has Hitler in his pocket.

We can but wait, as the changes begin – a new branch sprouting on the Tree above Hecht's desk: a single glistening thread of brilliant light.

Hecht himself is in conference with the *Genewart* – or so we call that shadowy presence. Hans Gehlen was his real name, when he was properly alive. He was the genius behind Four-Oh; this *Nichtraum* or 'no-space' bunker – Neu Berlin – that lies outside the normal laws of the universe. He has been dead two centuries, yet his 'presence' – his *Genewart* – lives on, encoded in the gaseous centre of the great AI that runs the *Nichtraum*.

Some knowledge must await its proper time. We knew, as long ago as the end of the twentieth century, of superstrings and Q-balls. It was mere theory then. They said there were twelve dimensions, ten of Space and two of Time: seven and one *folded in* – 'hidden', one might say, from human perception. Yet it took eight centuries for the right man – Gehlen – to come along and transform that theory into practice.

Q-balls. For centuries they were as rare as the mythical unicorn, but then Hans Gehlen arrived and, with a stroke of genius, found a way of entrapping one of those dark nutshell universes. Travelling at over a hundred kilometres a second and containing 10 to the 22nd power particles, Q-balls zip through anything, even the burning heart of stars. Forged in the white heat of the newborn universe, they are incredibly stable yet also incredibly difficult to capture. One thing, and one thing alone can slow them down – a neutron star.

By the twenty-eighth century, black-hole technology had progressed to the point where it was safe, the accidents of earlier years forgotten. Tiny black holes, smaller than a pin-head, had been created and maintained and, as an energy source, had replaced all other forms. Yet it was not until Gehlen came and captured a Q-ball in the core of an artificial neutron star that its full potential was made plain.

Entering the neutron star, the Q-ball would begin to eat away at it, slowly destabilising it, until – wham! – a supernova would be born.

But not for ten million years. Moreover there were useful side effects. As the Q-ball burrowed into the heart of the neutron star, so it would spit out tiny blue flashes – Cerenkov radiation. These sprays of brilliant light were *pions* – particles traveling faster than the speed of light. Time travellers, no less. It was Gehlen who finally harnessed them, and who gave us the technology to use them.

Unfortunately, the Russians learned our secret, and in the war that followed ...

But that's another story. Gehlen himself is dead, yet we have use of him. Hecht will sit with his shadowy presence night after night, discussing matters and seeking advice, continuing the war we lost two centuries ago.

I switch on the viewer. At once, Seydlitz's face fills the screen. I sit back, listening again, enjoying his explanations, knowing that this is warfare, thirtieth-century style, for as much as not a single shot is fired. Or, as my old friend Frederick once termed it – 'War by other means.'

23

In the three weeks between their first and second meetings, Seydlitz had no further contact with Hitler, but Goebbels came to visit him. This time Seydlitz sounded *him*, used Goebbels to forward *his* purpose.

'There is a machine,' he said, introducing the topic, 'unlike any other machine ever built. It *sees* things.'

Goebbels frowned, a half-smile on his lips. 'I don't follow you. Sees what?'

'Things yet to be. Events blind to normal sight.'

Goebbels laughed. 'What kind of game is this, Herr Seydlitz?'

'No game. Look here.'

He handed Goebbels a sheet of paper. It was a photographic copy of Basic Order No. 24, *'Regarding Collaboration with Japan'*, signed by Adolf Hitler and dated 5 March 1941. That date was three days off.

'What is this?' Goebbels asked. Then, looking sharply at Seydlitz: 'How did you get this?'

'The machine. Hold on to that for three days and see what happens. When the order comes, check it against what you have. Then come and see me again.'

For a moment Goebbels simply watched him, and Seydlitz knew that the whole venture was balanced on a knife's edge. Then he folded the paper, put it in his jacket pocket and stood. 'All right,' he said. 'For now I'll play your game. But when I see you next, you will explain this fully, understand?'

'I understand, Herr Goebbels.'

On the sixth Goebbels returned. Seydlitz gave him copies of newspapers dated a week ahead, photostats of documents relating to the secret discussions with the British, none of which had yet happened at that time. He gave him a separate sheet of quotations from various people – things they would say in Goebbels' presence in the next few days. This, more than anything, would convince him. Seydlitz could imagine him standing there, amazed to hear the words uttered, as if to a script.

When Seydlitz saw him next it was at Berchtesgaden. Goebbels met him at the station and they drove together up to the Berghof. The last few days had changed Goebbels. You could see that at once. He looked at Seydlitz now with a mixture of wonder and fear.

'Your machine,' he said, staring out away from Seydlitz as they sat there in the back of the Mercedes. 'How much can it see? How far ahead?'

Seydlitz did not look at him, but kept looking at the magnificent scenery of the Bavarian Alps, conscious that none of this existed in his time.

'Five years. After that things grow uncertain.'

Goebbels nodded. In the driver's mirror Seydlitz could see him frowning deeply, trying to accommodate this new fact. He could sense how keyed-up Goebbels was, so full of unasked questions.

'Does Hitler know?' he asked, turning slightly. 'Have you mentioned this to him?'

'I've …' Then he laughed; a strange little high-pitched laugh. 'How do you mention something like this, Herr Seydlitz?' Goebbels looked at Seydlitz directly, challengingly. 'But you knew that, didn't you? That's why you approached me first. Because it isn't a thing to be mentioned, is it? You have to prove it – show how potent this "seeing" is – before the mind can accept it.'

Seydlitz nodded.

He had not been wrong. Goebbels was the key. His belief would make it easier for Hitler to believe. And with belief would come change.

The Führer met them on the steps and ushered them into the house, taking Seydlitz's hand firmly, warmly, then touching his shoulder.

'It is good to see you again, Herr Seydlitz. There are so few men of culture left in the world. So many little men, destroying life with their putrid visions.'

Seydlitz laughed and quickly agreed. It had begun. In the next few hours he would come to know at first-hand what others had reported of Hitler: his tendency to lecture; his refusal to listen to another, conflicting view. But Seydlitz played him with genius. Whenever Hitler paused he would insert a comment that both confirmed and illuminated his argument and Hitler would seize on it with an almost childish glee. Seydlitz pampered his hatred of modernism in art, gave him evidence of the superiority of Aryan culture, and fostered his anti-Semitism with instances from history. They talked all afternoon, and when it was time for dinner, Hitler was delighted with his new friend, beaming openly as he led Seydlitz to his chair.

'We are exceptional men, Herr Seydlitz, are we not? Is it not right, then, that destiny places us at the fulcrum of history?'

It was too perfect, too opportune a moment to be missed. Seydlitz nodded and took his seat, then broached the subject. There would be no better time than this.

'Barbarossa will fail,' he said. 'In October the line will be halted, at Leningrad in the north, at Rzhev, Mozhaisk and Orel in the centre, and at Stalingrad, Grozny, Pyatigorsk and Maikop in the south.'

Hitler's smile had gone. He stood there by his chair, staring at Seydlitz as if he had suddenly changed shape. Across from them Goebbels was watching, equally intent, his eyes going from Seydlitz to Hitler.

'What?' Hitler said after a moment. 'What did you say?'

Seydlitz reached into his pocket and pulled out an envelope, then handed it across. In it was a report from General Guderian, from the Russian front, dated late October 1941.

Hitler took out the report. Seydlitz saw how his face twitched as he read it, noted how his left leg and left arm trembled when he was excited by something – advance signs of the savage disability to come. Hitler looked up abruptly from the report and glared at Seydlitz, then threw the paper down. There was spittle on his lips.

'What lies are these? What vicious game is this, Herr Seydlitz?'

Seydlitz had prepared himself for Hitler's anger; even so, its sheer, elemental force was unexpected. It was like facing the figure of Hatred itself. He rose from his seat and bowed deeply, as a soldier bows before his commander.

'Forgive me, Führer, but it is how it will be,' he said. 'I have built a machine that sees the future.'

Hitler laughed at the absurdity. Then he looked to Goebbels. 'Did you know of this, Joseph?'

Goebbels nodded, but you could see how intimidated he was, how reluctant he was to own up to what he knew for a fact. For a moment it was even possible that he was going to deny Seydlitz. Yet he *did* believe, and in his sharp but devious mind he could imagine what defeat in Russia would mean.

'It's true,' he said, softly at first, then, much louder. 'Herr Seydlitz has proved it to me beyond all doubt. His machine sees into the future.'

Again Hitler laughed, but there was no humour in it. 'Have you *all* gone mad? Even you, Joseph?'

He turned away, a look of sheer disgust on his face. Then he turned back. 'We cannot *see* into the future, we can only *make* the future!' And he hammered his right hand into his left palm as he said this, glaring at Seydlitz defiantly.

'Let me prove it, Führer. Please! For the sake of us all!'

The sneer grew more excessive. He shook his head in a gesture of finality, but it was all or nothing now and Seydlitz risked his fury, pressing on.

'In my bags I have further documents. Maps, newspapers, secret documents, transcripts of conversations. All of them copies of things that do not yet exist. Look at them. Examine them. See if these things come about. And meanwhile put me under house arrest. Under armed guard. Then, on the twenty-first of June, at Wolfensschanze on the evening before the Russian invasion, see me again.'

Hitler was looking away from him now, staring directly at Goebbels. 'This proves it to me. We attack Russia in May, not in June. The man is raving.'

But Goebbels shook his head. 'Listen to him, I beg you, Führer. If he's wrong then no harm is done. But if he's right ...'

Hitler stood there a moment, glaring at his Propaganda Minister, then he seemed to relent and soften. Goebbels was, after all, his oldest friend. They had shared this journey since the early Twenties.

'There will be a coup,' Seydlitz said. 'In Belgrade. On the twenty-seventh of March. Ten days later you will strike hard to avenge this outrage. The operation will be named Retribution. You will crush the Yugoslavs. Then you will turn and face Russia. But only then.'

Hitler laughed scornfully, but met his eyes again. He had calmed down, but his eyes were dangerous, incensed even by the sight of Seydlitz. 'A coup? In Belgrade? They wouldn't dare.' He shook his head exaggeratedly. 'And yet you see all this as if it has happened.'

Seydlitz nodded. 'As though it were all in the past.'

For a moment longer Hitler stared at him, then he waved him away impatiently. 'Put him under house arrest.'

Guards came to his summons, took Seydlitz by the arms.

'You are a fool, Herr Seydlitz. But I will humour Joseph here. I will look at your evidence. And when I know it for the garbage that it is, I will have you killed. Understand?'

Unsmiling, like the soldier that he was, Seydlitz bowed his head silently. Hitler's threat meant nothing now. He had won. Day by day the evidence would mount, until, when they met again at Wolfensschanze, Hitler would be his.

24

Seydlitz was in his rooms in Friedrichsfelde when the summons came. It was 6.15 a.m. on the morning of 21 June 1941. More than one hundred and fifty German, Romanian and Finnish divisions were waiting on the Russian borders, complete with nineteen armoured divisions, twelve motorised divisions and air cover of 2,700 planes. Three great armies under Generals Leeb, Bock and Rundstedt. Great but fragile, for none of them was equipped for a winter campaign.

He had an hour to get his things together before they came to take him to the aerodrome for the flight east. This in itself was different. Historically, Hitler had been in the Chancellery in Berlin on the night of the invasion, Goebbels entertaining some Italian guests at the Schwanenwerder. But not this time.

25

'Otto, come ...'

I follow Hecht out, along the broad, central corridor that leads directly to the platform. There, in that great, domed circle, surrounded by the buzz of our technicians, we wait. The women look up from their screens expectantly. It is not often that Hecht comes to greet an agent at the platform, but everyone here knows how important this is.

Seydlitz will appear any moment now, returning for the first time since he boarded ship in Sweden.

There is to be a meeting – one final consultation before he goes back. Hecht looks at me and smiles. He does not need to tell me to say nothing. That goes without saying. Things are more complex than normal. While *we* know what has happened, Seydlitz does not. In his time-line he has yet to meet Hitler; has yet to have that fateful meeting in the Wolfensschanze. In his own personal time-line, Seydlitz has yet to send his report back. And that could prove dangerous. To prevent the possibility of time paradoxes, he must go to that meeting without prior knowledge of its outcome.

Oh yes, it happens sometimes. From our viewpoint, here on the very edge of Time, our knowledge of the Past is not always sequential. Yet we must deal with it as though it was. Harsh experience has taught us so. Play games with Time and Time can play wicked games on you. Ask Hans Gehlen. Or what's left of him.

There is a sudden pulse in the platform, a crackling in the air as ions spark and tiny flashes of electricity pass across its surface. Then, with a sudden surge of power, Seydlitz begins to appear. I put my hand up, shielding my eyes, as a tiny circle of intense light – the focus – jumps into being, and in a fraction of a second, Seydlitz himself takes solid form, ribcage and arms only visible at first, then pelvis and head and legs, the whole thing sprouting, fleshing out from that single, brilliant point, blood vessels and nerves, muscle, bone and inner organs visible for the briefest instant as the focus bleeds light into the living body, slowly fading with a dying flicker.

As Seydlitz blinks and looks about him, I realise that this could well be the last time it will be like this. This is not just some pawn's move in the Great Game but a bid to take their queen, maybe even to checkmate the king itself. As the repercussions of his scheme begin to take effect, so this all would change. I shiver at the thought of it. If all goes well, the circle will be broken and Berlin – *our* Berlin – will cease to exist. And we with it. But that would be a small price to pay for such a victory. Neu Berlin might die, but Europe would live, the *Volk* be saved.

As the force shield comes down, Seydlitz looks across at us and smiles. From the thirty-two long, low desks about the great circle of the platform comes a murmur of greeting. Seated at those desks, the *Volk*'s technicians – all of them women, many of them heavily pregnant – smile back at him, pleased to see him safely home.

Objectively he has been gone less than a day; subjectively it has been close on eleven months.

Someone throws a cloak about him, another hands him a drink. One of the women gives him a hand and helps him down.

'How goes it?' Hecht asks, as if he didn't know.

For a moment Seydlitz finds it hard to understand what Hecht has said. His ear has grown too accustomed to the old tongue. The Anglicised ergot we speak is very different, more American than German, the bastardised product of a thousand years of change. Hecht repeats the question.

Seydlitz smiles. 'I've met him. Got him to listen to me. And I am to see him again tomorrow. At Wolfensschanze. I think he'll listen.'

Hecht nods. There is sadness as well as hope in his face. For Berlin there are possibly only a few, small hours remaining, whatever happens. If Seydlitz's scheme succeeds it will wink out of existence – or exist only in the memories of those who have gone back.

Seydlitz is clearly disoriented. After the open skies and freedom of the Past this place is acutely claustrophobic. I know from experience what he is thinking: how had he stood this? How could any of us survive like this, cooped up like prisoners in this air-tight hell?

Walls are everywhere. Four-Oh is the last bunker, the last gallant outcrop, fighting against the Russian enemy that surrounds it on every side and in every dimension. Each day, each hour, almost every second, quantum missiles hammer into our defences, homing in on the platform's carrier signal, slowly weakening our force fields bit by tiny bit, breaking down our mighty resistance. Clever, subtle missiles, like the probability worms, which burrow into the very fabric of the *Nichtraum* itself, destroying the bonds between moments.

Things we don't feel or hear, but which are there all the same.

We have bought time – each tiny change has guaranteed our survival and extended it – but all about us lies the darkness, and a map drawn red from Atlantic to Pacific.

Maybe that is why Hecht has decided on this final cast. Nothing small this time. Instead a major change, for whatever results can surely be no worse than this slow attrition, this gradual wearing down.

Seydlitz looks about him once more, noting the brave, familiar faces that surround him. These are his people, his *Volk*. For them he has gone back. For them he has striven to change the destiny of the Reich. For if the Reich fails a second time then there is nothing.

Yet it is hard, standing there, not to feel doubt. In spite of all we have done – both here and in the Past – it all seems so very fragile. One wrong decision, one moment's tiredness, and it would all be gone. As if it had never been. History would forget us.

Seydlitz stays an hour. Friends come and wish him '*Stärke*' – 'strength'. Not 'luck' or 'love' but 'strength'. Such is our world – the world he now goes back to change.

26

On the morning of the twenty second – the first day of Barbarossa – Seydlitz held a conference. There were six of them: Hitler, Goering, Goebbels, Himmler, Bormann and himself. The projector was set up in the Map Room and a screen hung in front of the Graf portrait of Frederick the Great. Elite members of the *Shutzstaffel*, Himmler's SS, stood outside, alongside Hitler's personal bodyguard, Ratenhuber, guarding the doors, ensuring no one entered. Inside, four of them sat in a staggered line facing the screen. Seydlitz at the projector just behind them. At his signal, Goebbels dimmed the lights and returned to his seat. A moment later the beam from the projector cut into the darkness. The screen lit up, forming flickering images.

And so he began showing them, for the first time, the future he would now set out to change.

Seydlitz kept his comments brief and to the point. Several times, at Hitler's order, he froze the image and wound it back. He could sense that Hitler was still reluctant – that part of him refused, even now, to believe in what he was seeing. It was hard for him – harder than for any of them – for it struck at the very core of what he thought of himself, the Man of Destiny. This was the outcome of *his* vision, *his* failure. But Seydlitz could not present it as that. He knew Hitler too well. *This is betrayal*, he had to say. *This is what will be unless we act*. He had ready a list of traitors and their crimes.

The images were simple but effective. The Russian snows. Transport and soldiers floundering in the mud of the sudden thaw. Zhukov's Siberian regiments driving the Wehrmacht back. Then on in time – to General Paulus surrendering at Stalingrad. Burning tanks in the Tunisian desert. The British liberating Athens. The failure of the U-boat campaign. The sky dark with American bombers, Dresden a single burning pyre. The landings in Normandy, the gallant Rommel thrown back. Then, shocking in its juxtaposition, the Map Room where they sat, devastated after Stauffenberg's assassination attempt on the Führer. Black American troops sitting in an amphibian vehicle, crossing the Rhine, grinning into the camera. Berlin in ruins, the Chancellery a pile, Hitler Youth detachments fighting a last-ditch battle against the Russians. Then Mussolini, bloodless, hanging from a meat hook in the Piazzale Loreto between Gelormini and Petacci, his mistress. Goebbels' body, charred but still recognisable, beside those of his wife and six children. Goering, sat in the dock at Nuremberg, Judge Robert Jackson pointing across at him.

And nowhere a single sign of hope. These were images of annihilation – of a Dream reduced to nightmare. When the lights came up again Seydlitz went to the front and looked at them. Goebbels, beside the light switch, was ashen. Bormann looked down at his feet. Goering was tugging at his collar as if it was too tight and staring away distractedly. Himmler, however, was looking to the Führer, waiting to be told what he should do. There was a kind of hopeless trust in him, a deficiency of character. Seydlitz had kept back his death.

Hitler was silent for a time. Then he stood and turned his head towards Seydlitz. His eyes, at that moment, were filled with a bitter hatred.

'You were betrayed,' Seydlitz said calmly. 'The Jews, your generals, even some of those you trusted best – they betrayed you. What you have seen is the chronicle of their betrayal.'

Hitler narrowed his eyes, but said nothing. Seydlitz took the list from his pocket and handed it across. It was detailed. Names, dates, arrangements. More than five hundred names in all. Not all the traitors – not Himmler, Goering, Rommel – but many who would surprise him. Hitler took the list and opened it, watching Seydlitz all the while. Then he looked down, studying it.

'What is this?'

'A list, Führer. Of traitors.'

Hitler looked up sharply, then back at the list, flicking through the pages, stopping now and then, his eyebrows going up, his face registering unfeigned surprise, even pain. Many of the leading figures of the Reich were listed. Abruptly he folded the sheaf. His hand was trembling now and his face was red with anger. His arm shot out to his left, holding the list.

'Heinrich! Take this and copy it! Then act on it! At once!'

Himmler took it, then bowed in salute and clicked his heels. In an instant he was gone from the room. The repercussions would begin at once.

Seydlitz had been careful in selecting that list. None of those who would lead the Wehrmacht to the gates of Moscow were named. Nor were those whose treachery lay more in Hitler's failings than their own. But in one single swoop he had rid the Reich of most of its major doubters and schemers. It was a beginning. But there was much more to be done. It was not enough to prune the tree of state, they had to stimulate new growth, and do what no one before Seydlitz had ever managed: to change the mind of Hitler.

Seydlitz faced him again.

'Though I was born in another land, I am, before all, a German. And as a German I recognise that the destiny of my people is bound inextricably with the destiny of the Führer. My machine has seen much that is ill. But the illness lies not with destiny but with a betrayal of that destiny, in the poverty of others' little lives.'

Seydlitz let that sink in a moment; saw how they all watched him, waiting to hear what he would say next.

'How can a leader lead if those whom he must trust – must, because he is but one man, however great, and mortal in spite of all – how can he lead if they are false, if the information they provide him with is false, if their advice is false? How, in the face of such overwhelming falsity, can a leader lead?'

Hitler was nodding. The trembling in his left arm had almost gone. Seydlitz could see that his words were working, the spell drawing him in.

'The policy of legality served us well in gaining power in Germany. It was a tactic born of genius. To use against our enemies that which they valued most. To see through the democratic sham and grab the reality of power.' Hitler was nodding more strongly now, smiling at Seydlitz; his eyes, which only moments earlier had burned with anger, were now filled with fervour. Seydlitz had studied him well. Now his long hours of study reaped their dividend. He played him as Hitler had once played others, as indeed Seydlitz had played him once before, after the opera that time, weaving a spell of words about him, binding him fast to the Dream.

'What was legality if not the pacification of our enemies until we were strong enough to strike at them? An exploitation of their intrinsic rottenness? What was legality if not the means to our necessary destiny?'

Hitler laughed. 'Indeed, it was so!'

At his side the others joined his laughter. The mood had changed. It was time to strike.

'What then will it be in the years to come, but a means by which the Führer will unite the continent of Europe in a single Reich, from the Atlantic to the Urals, from the Arctic circle to the Mediterranean!'

Goering spoke. 'What then of Mussolini? What of the Italians, the Spaniards?'

Seydlitz looked directly at Hitler as he answered. 'Are not the meetings at Hendaye, Montoire and Brenner eloquent enough? These southern Europeans are rotten through and through. There is something weak, something *corrupt* in their very nature. But while we need them we can use them. In time, however, our use will have ended and then we shall pay them for their rottenness.'

Seydlitz knew that Hitler would not be quite so pleased with this little speech, even as he nodded. Seydlitz knew that Franco had bested the Führer in the discussions at Hendaye and kept Spain out of the war. At Montoire, the Vichy-French had wriggled out of any real commitment to the Reich. And at Brenner Hitler had confronted Mussolini with his duplicity in attacking Greece without consultation. It was no secret that this trilogy of failings had irked Hitler all winter. Seydlitz's reminder was the opening of an old wound, cruel but necessary.

'You said you knew ways,' Hitler said. 'Ways of changing the future ...'

There was suspicion in those vividly blue eyes. Suspicion and an element of pure dislike. He was a man who would have no rivals, and in all he did Seydlitz seemed to set himself up as rival to him. In this, as in so much, he needed to be devious. He needed to make these schemes – like Manstein's for the invasion of France – seem Hitler's own.

'My role is simple, Führer. My task easy. I must help the leader lead. I must clear away the falsity in those surrounding him. I must pave the way for victory. For destiny.'

Hitler laughed, amused at Seydlitz despite his suspicion. 'By killing traitors? Is that all of your mighty scheme?'

Seydlitz shook his head. 'You have already shown us the path. It is already written, in *Mein Kampf.* Our enemy is Russia. We must crush the Russians at any cost. But to do so we must avoid a war on two fronts.'

Seydlitz took a breath, then said it. 'We must pacify the Americans.'

27

He began a new routine. Each morning at six he would leave his chalet and walk the forty metres to the Wolfensschanze, past the armed SS guards and into the Map Room. There, Hitler and he would go through orders and consider the reports from the front. At first he suggested few strategic changes. Then slowly, taking care to make each change seem as though it had sprung from Hitler's mind, he began to manipulate the war.

At first Hitler was loath to take up Seydlitz's suggestion regarding America. Despite all the evidence, he continued to see them as a weak, divided nation.

'So they are,' Seydlitz would say. 'But when Japan attacks, something will happen to them. Their pride will be hurt and they'll respond. The challenge will make them strong.'

It was this argument, much more than the 'fact' – documented and presented long before – that eventually persuaded him. Ribbentrop was sacked as Foreign Minister and Admiral Raeder, a less abrasive, more honourable man, was sent to Washington to ensure the peace. Raeder's appointment was a temporary move, but effective. He would be needed later, when the U-boat offensive began in earnest, but in July and August of 1941, as German troops drove the Russians back relentlessly, he successfully wooed the right-wing elements of American public opinion. The Tripartite Pact, less than a year old, was dramatically dropped. Without a word of explanation, Japan ceased to be an ally. The effect in

Washington was considerable. Roosevelt summoned Raeder. Through an interpreter Raeder explained that Hitler did not want war with either the United States or Britain. Russia alone was his enemy. There were many Germans in America, he went on to say. It would be a tragedy if German should have to fight German. Roosevelt remained sceptical, but his certainty had been shaken. Hitler called off his U-boats and cut all derogatory references to Roosevelt from his speeches. It was an old game and he enjoyed it.

Dr Todt, the Armaments Minister, had been on the list of traitors. This was a fabrication and ended Todt's life ten months earlier than otherwise. In his place Hitler appointed Albert Speer. From the first Speer's influence was marked. New factories were opened in the conquered Russian territories. Fuel dumps were established. New tracked equipment was hastily manufactured to designs Seydlitz provided. Winter clothing was stockpiled in warehouses close to the front. When the snows came this time they would find the German army well prepared.

The fleet was moved south, from the Norwegian coast. Two divisions were spared to strengthen the Italian push on Egypt. Revolt was fermented in Iraq and in Egypt itself. The bombing of British cities stopped and all efforts returned to destroying their airfields. Each move strengthened Germany's position and brought them one step closer to success.

And all the while Seydlitz had his men moving back and forth through Time, reporting back to him on the progress of their machinations. Up ahead – in the time to come – things were slowly changing in their favour, but still the major thing remained the same: when the snows came the Russians would halt the German advance and throw them back. From that moment the war would be lost. Their actions – small as they were – had extended the war into the early months of 1947. Even so, defeat was inevitable.

Early on Seydlitz had been forced to show them the 'machine'.

It was a fake, of course, primed with a few gobbets of information his men had prepared elsewhere, but its focus was real enough. Seydlitz told them there were two such machines, focusing on the future. The other was somewhere in Spain, hidden where they would never find it. That was not liked, but it was understood. Hitler even smiled when Seydlitz told him.

'You are a cautious man,' he said.

Seydlitz nodded. More cautious than he knew.

The big changes came in August. Instead of sending the Centre Army south, Hitler ordered General Bock to press on to Moscow. On the seventeenth there was a major engagement thirty kilometres south-west of the Russian capital, and two days later Guderian swept into the city. There followed a week of hand-to-hand and street-by-street fighting. But by 28 August Moscow had been taken. Bock dug in, then sent Guderian and Hoth, his two *Panzer* commanders, north to help the attack on Leningrad.

On 30 August Seydlitz accompanied Hitler on his first visit to Moscow. There, in the Kremlin, Hitler took a march past of his triumphant army, standing where Stalin himself had stood only four months earlier.

Stalin had fled, but he had not got far. Seydlitz's men had traced him and found him, and in a small village eighty kilometres east of Moscow they ambushed him. On the morning of 2 September, they woke Hitler at five and presented him with the body.

What did the future look like after this? Moscow and Stalin had both fallen. They had cut the head from the Russian bear, but would the bear fall? Up ahead they saw the counter-attack, led by Zhukov. There was still the possibility of failure. But then, in mid-September, Leningrad fell and Zhukov himself was taken.

For Seydlitz these were heady days, and while they unfolded there was a kind of camaraderie between Hitler and himself. But in the aftermath of Leningrad, as in the north they dug in and looked to the south for further victories, a sour note slowly crept in.

Among the small but elite group surrounding Hitler – those who knew Seydlitz's role in events – things had changed. Subtly, almost imperceptibly, the power base had shifted. Goebbels was closest to Seydlitz, perhaps, but there were others who looked to him first and Hitler after for their lead. Goering was effusive in his praise, while Himmler, ever the follower and never an innovator, balanced precariously between obedience to the Führer and deference to Seydlitz.

For all that he did to defuse this situation – for all his humility, self-deprecation and pampering of Hitler's monomaniacal ego – Seydlitz could not wholly deflect Hitler's jealousy and suspicion. Memories of what Hitler had done to Strasser and Rohm in 1934 haunted him, not because he feared for his own life, but because his death might mean the failure of the whole scheme. Seydlitz had always been a rival, and though he might claim – and rightly – that such plans were Hitler's alone, espoused as early as 1924 in *Mein Kampf*, Hitler only had to look about him to see what they truly thought. Even Bormann, the most loyal of his acolytes and his private secretary, looked on Seydlitz as a saviour.

Up ahead things had improved beyond recognition. The East was secure. Continental Europe was Hitler's. Britain was a satellite. The Middle East was steadily being conquered. But in the present things were coming to a head. What if Hitler decided Seydlitz was dispensable?

On the evening that Kiev fell – the first evening of snow, in late October – he had his first argument with Hitler. They were in a field camp outside the city. News had just come of the surrender of a Russian army of almost one and a half million men. This, even more than Moscow, was the height of their success. This was victory – the capitulation of the last Russian forces west of the Urals. As Seydlitz heard the sober words of the report he felt both joy and sadness. The Russians had been beaten – the age-old threat finally defeated – but up ahead, in 2999, Berlin, *his* Berlin, had, he was certain, ceased to be. His exile was complete. This now was home.

He turned to Hitler and looked at him. Hitler was staring down at his hands, which were clenched one over the other. There was no sign of surprise, certainly nothing of the elation one might have expected him to feel at such a moment. Instead there was the merest nod of his head. Then he looked up.

'So it's done,' he said. 'Just as you said, Herr Seydlitz.'

Seydlitz did not move. Hitler's eyes seemed to hold him there, intense, his anger and hatred suddenly so raw, so naked, that Seydlitz knew he had come to a decision.

'You have done it all,' Seydlitz said, letting nothing show in his face. 'You have done more than any man has ever done. More than Frederick. More than Napoleon. More than Alexander or Caesar.'

But they were empty, fatuous words, for all their truth, and Hitler knew it as well as he.

Hitler turned away. 'I am tired, Herr Seydlitz. You will excuse me?'

It was so odd a thing for him to say that Seydlitz knew he would need to be careful that night. Unless he acted he would be dead before morning.

That evening he jumped forward to the world of 2999, and jumped back almost instantly.

He had jumped on to a platform, without walls, suspended in the darkness of space. Beneath him – a hundred miles below where he stood suspended – lay a planet. *Earth?* A lifeless world, anyway. A smooth, iced globe surrounded by a thin, rarefied atmosphere.

Afterwards, as he lay there on the floor of his tent, gasping for breath, his limbs trembled, remembering what he had seen. His throat was raw from the single breath he had taken, his eyes felt burned, and his skin seemed to prickle with an unnatural heat.

What had happened? What in Urd's name had happened?

He had only moments to speculate. Even as he lay there two men came into the tent and stood over him. He knew them both – knew why they were there. Heinrich Himmler and Reinhard Heydrich. Each held a pistol.

He tried to speak, but the bitter cold had done something to his vocal chords. Instead, through stinging, watery eyes, Seydlitz looked up at them and smiled.

Tell Hitler this, he thought. And jumped.

28

Hecht smiles then switches off the screen. Above him, the Tree of Worlds glows brightly in the shadowed room.

'It goes well.'

'But what he saw ...'

'Don't worry, Otto. It isn't finished yet. The days ahead ...' He falls silent, as if he's said too much.

I meet his eyes. 'I thought it might—'

'Become reality? No, Otto. Look.'

I look. The great trunk of the World Tree glows a crystalline white, like a thick column of ice-cold water falling, perpetually falling from the dark into the dark. About that trunk, a cluster of smaller, finer threads branch off, like tiny colourful lightning bolts, snaking out then up, bending back upon themselves until they almost reach the crown. Almost ... for about the great Tree's crown is a tiny circle of darkness. Not a single thread crosses that dark ring, nor can it, for if one did ...

I imagine it. Imagine reality becoming something other than itself.

'But why?'

'Be patient, Otto. All will come clear.'

He reaches over, hands me the latest report.

I smile. Seydlitz might think us all dead, but he has not forgotten his duty. He has not neglected his reports.

'He's still there, then?'

Hecht nods, but says no more. And so I stand and, leaving that place, return to my room, my head buzzing, wondering if, when the change finally comes, I will remember anything of this.

29

When the snows came they were ready. From the safety of a room in Heidelberg, Seydlitz read the reports in the newspapers. The counter-offensive by the Siberian divisions was turned back and routed at Kolomna, ninety kilometres south-east of Moscow. Hitler's armies – warmly clothed, well-fed and housed, their tracked vehicles coping with the heavy snows – held the line and in many places extended it. Saratov, on the Volga, fell in the last week of December, Stalingrad a month later. When Gorki fell in the second week of February the war in the East was finally and irrevocably decided. The Russian generals capitulated at Kazan, ceding all of the land west of the Volga to Germany. Hitler was pictured on the newsreels, standing on the banks of the Volga, looking outwards and smiling. Behind him Goering and the generals looked on, smug, knowing they had achieved what Napoleon had only dreamed of doing.

That was the public face of things. Other events were already in motion. Garrisons were being built all along the Volga and throughout the conquered territory. Himmler's extermination of the Slav intelligentsia and the Jews was under way. Already many divisions were heading back west, preparing for a new campaign.

Scydlitz's small dream of ruling Russian Europe was dead. Nonetheless, he rejoiced that the bigger Dream lived on, applauding each triumph of the Reich. When Japan finally attacked the USA at Pearl Harbor on the last day of February 1942, he held his breath, but Hitler, true to his plan, held back from a declaration of war and surprised Roosevelt with an open letter of sympathy and friendship – a letter much quoted in the American press, who played down its hypocritical condemnation of his former allies. Audaciously, Hitler offered the Americans five of his best divisions to wage war against the Japanese. It was his own touch, and played cleverly upon the racial antagonisms newly awakened in the American nation. Roosevelt refused, but his refusal won him few friends, except in Britain.

For Seydlitz the winter was a hard one, not because he was materially uncomfortable – he had stashed clothes, papers, and sufficient money in a wood near Mosbach – but because of that glimpse he'd had of the world to come. Settling in Heidelberg, he quickly re-established contact with his men, meeting them at the buried *focus* – effectively a miniaturised platform – just outside the town. In the months that followed, while the Reich grew and prospered, they began their tentative exploration of the years ahead.

In the short term, all seemed well. The policy of pacifying America worked beautifully. While they trounced the Japanese in the Pacific arena, Hitler invaded Britain, and, after a bitter, frustrating campaign, finally took it. By the end of 1943, Italy, Romania, Hungary, Bulgaria and Sweden had all been assimilated peacefully into the Reich. Then, in the summer of 1944, Hitler attacked and conquered Spain in eight short weeks. Turkey followed before the year was out.

Europe was his. The Middle East was next. Then Africa. On 20 April 1949 – his sixtieth birthday – he proclaimed himself

Emperor of Greater Germany, holding the coronation ceremony in his new capital of Linz, amid Wagnerian pageantry that made the old Nuremberg rallies look tame.

Then, somewhere in the middle of 1952, there was a hole in Space-Time itself. A vast, unfathomable maelstrom in the fabric of reality. And after? – nothing but darkness, ice, the falling snow.

They lost three men tracing the edges of the flaw, but estimated its epicentre at or around the middle of June 1952. Somewhere there it had happened, whatever it was, and its effects had distorted Time both on and back. There was no way to tell what had happened: no way to anticipate the immediate cause. Even so, *something* had caused it, and Seydlitz knew that if they looked hard enough they would find it.

At first he suspected treachery. Irrationally, Seydlitz believed it was the Russians, pre-empting them, outguessing them maybe in a game through Time. But when he calmed down, he realised how ridiculous that was. They had seen ahead – seen the total, irreversible defeat of Russia, even before Seydlitz's experience at Kiev. It had to be Hitler.

They began their search at the end of 1944, gathering information from throughout the Reich. Slowly, painstakingly, they combed through 1945, looking for something that might provide an insight into what had happened in '52. Seydlitz was looking particularly for developments in weaponry – for something big enough and advanced enough to cause what they had seen up ahead. Only later, when it grew clearer what it was, did he realise that he had been looking in the wrong direction.

It wasn't Hitler after all. It was Roosevelt.

30

It was early morning – sometime after two – and Paul Joseph Goebbels was alone in his bedroom, seated before the dressing-table mirror, removing his tie. His evening jacket lay on the bed behind him and as his fingers reached to unfasten the stud at the back of his neck, he yawned.

Seydlitz appeared silently, into the shadows at the back of the long, high-ceilinged room. He stood there a while, out of sight, watching Goebbels, then stepped out into the light, and stood there directly behind Goebbels, where he could see him in the mirror.

Seydlitz watched his face, saw him start, his eyes widening further as he recognised who it was. That moment's naked fear turned into something more complex, more calculated. Goebbels turned and faced Seydlitz, looking down at his hands, finding them empty.

'Max?'

'How are you, Paul?'

Goebbels lowered his eyes a moment, then looked back at him 'Things go well enough, Max.'

He could sense Goebbels' suspicion, his uncertainty. They were almost tangible. But behind them was something else. A warmth, a degree of respect that remained intact. Slowly he smiled. 'Where did you go, Max? Where have you been?'

'Here and there. Is the Führer well?'

The smile tightened. 'In good health.' He hesitated, then added, 'I have orders to kill you if I see you. We all have.'

Seydlitz nodded. 'I understand. There is only one Führer, eh?'

Goebbels looked at him sadly. 'I liked you, Max. I suppose I still like you, but ...' He shrugged.

Goebbels was unarmed, but there were guards outside the door.

He had only to call out. Even so, he waited, knowing that Seydlitz must have a good reason for coming to him.

'You must warn the Führer. Tell him not to antagonise the Americans. He must wait before he presses them on the Jewish question.'

'Why?'

The tie still hung loose about Goebbels' neck. His dark hair, slicked back from the forehead, shone in the lamplight.

'They have a secret weapon. Unimaginably powerful. Something we cannot fight. So powerful, in fact, that they do not know how harmful it is themselves.'

Seydlitz shuddered, thinking of the hole in Space-Time only three years in the future.

Goebbels looked away, then shook his head. 'It may be so, Max, but I can't help you.'

'What do you mean? This is important, Paul. If they use it – and they will – it will mean the end not just of the Reich, but of mankind!'

Goebbels laughed. 'Tell that to Hitler, Max. Germany *is* mankind, remember?'

There was a sourness in him Seydlitz had never seen before.

'What's happened, Paul?'

'It's nothing,' he answered, but his expression said the opposite. 'Just that Hitler wouldn't listen even if I told him. He hears nothing I say these days. He—' Goebbels looked away, as if in sudden pain at the thought of it, then continued. 'He remains loyal. I am still, outwardly, Minister of Propaganda. But I have no influence with him. You understand, Max?'

'Why?'

Goebbels looked at him and smiled sadly. 'Because I liked you, Max. And because I was the one who brought you to him.'

Seydlitz went cold, understanding suddenly what he should

have known before. He had been the great rival to Hitler, and all those that liked him were therefore traitors.

'I'm only alive, I think, because he saw that film of me. At least, of my corpse. The thought that I had stayed with him when all the others were gone. That I was willing to die with him and for him.'

'Then there's no hope.'

Goebbels was silent for a time, staring down at his hands, then he looked up again. 'You've seen this weapon used?'

'Yes,' he lied.

Strangely, Goebbels laughed. 'You know, when we took Spain, Hitler had them scour the country for the other machine. The one we had – your one – never worked again after Kiev.'

'It never worked anyway.'

'What do you mean? The documents. The films – they were all false?'

'No. They were real enough. But they didn't come from the machine.'

Goebbels was looking at Seydlitz oddly now.

'You see, I've not been looking at the future at all. I've been studying the past ...' And, putting his hand to his chest, Seydlitz disappeared.

31

If Hitler would not listen, then there was only one solution – they would destroy the weapon before it could be used. A direct assault was likely to be difficult and possibly dangerous; instead they made their investigations, then went back fifteen years and killed all of the scientists involved. The weapon would never be built.

They were celebrating when the first of their men came back from up ahead. 'It's still there,' he said. 'Unchanged.'

Seydlitz shook his head, for the first time conscious that this might not be as simple as he'd thought. When the second man didn't return, they went back. The scientists were dead, but the weapon still existed, as if it was anchored to the epicentre, its existence guaranteed by that vast rupture in Space-Time up ahead.

'It's hopeless,' one of his men – Ritter – said.

Seydlitz turned and struck him. 'Nothing's hopeless! Remember how we were in Four-Oh? Remember how hopeless *that* seemed? But we defeated them, didn't we?'

Ritter touched his bloodied lip and nodded. There was no more talk of hopelessness.

There had to be a way out – some way of changing it all. For a time his mind refused to see it, and even when it did he shook his head. It was far too drastic.

Looking at his men Seydlitz knew this was something he would have to do alone. He could not ask one of them to do it for him. He would go back and kill Hitler. Kill him before he was ever born.

32

It was late in the season. An icy wind blew across the Waldviertel from Poland, a north-easterly that set up a fierce howling through the trees surrounding the village. Seydlitz had been walking most of the afternoon and it was growing dark as he came to the out-skirts. It was a remote, uncultivated place, even for that year, and he shivered as he stood there, looking across at it in the twilight. Two dozen houses, a church, an inn, and at the back of all the forest, dark and primeval.

Few travellers chose to come this way.

He had been walking to the side of the track, avoiding the deeply rutted mud at the centre. Now, as he came into the broad, central street, he had to cross and recross, avoiding the huge puddles that had formed. The houses seemed well kept: sturdy, wooden buildings that served as barn and stable as well as home. On his left as he passed, in a space between two houses, a man was unharnessing a horse. He stared at Seydlitz openly as he passed – as if he were a thief – and watched him until the wall of the house obscured him. Even then he stepped out on to the street, clearly wanting to see where Seydlitz went. So it was here. Strangers were not welcome. The people here were simple, hard-working peasant stock, Czech in origin and suspicious by nature. They spoke a mixture of Czech and German, though neither with any grace, and talked of the capital, Vienna, as though it were in another country than their own.

Seydlitz walked on, conscious of how odd he seemed, walking in out of nowhere to this godforsaken place. The village was Dollersheim. The year was 1836, and ahead of him – only metres away now – was the inn where he hoped to meet the man he'd come to see, Johann Georg Hiedler, an itinerant miller and the supposed grandfather of Adolf Hitler.

Three open wooden steps led up to the inn door. He climbed them and tried the door. It was locked. He knocked and waited, turning to smile at the villagers who stood there watching him. There were five of them now, just standing there, staring at him, wondering who he was and what he wanted. He knocked again. A moment later there was the sound of a bolt being drawn back. The door swung open.

The landlord was a short, balding man with a cast in one eye. He turned his head to one side as he looked at Seydlitz, then, in rusty German, asked him what he wanted.

'A room, a meal, a beer.' Seydlitz saw how the innkeeper looked him up and down, trying to estimate what kind of man he was, then he put out his hand.

Seydlitz smiled and took two large coins from his leather purse.

'Here,' he said, placing them in his palm. He watched him test them with his teeth. Silver thalers. Far more than his upkeep would cost. Satisfied, the man nodded and stepped back, letting Seydlitz pass.

Five hours later Seydlitz was sitting in the corner of the smoky room, his feet up on a stool, a pewter tankard in hand. Across the table from him Johann Hiedler was leaning forward, Seydlitz's sketchbook open on his knees, his steiner forgotten for the while.

'These are good,' he grunted, looking up at Seydlitz, his vividly blue eyes smiling. He wiped at his moustache and then took another swig of his beer. 'Very good indeed. You have real talent, Herr Friedrich.'

He was stouter than his grandson, but the eyes, the mouth were the same. Not only that, but those gestures – which had grown so familiar to Seydlitz from those morning conferences at the Wolfensschanze – were here in embryo, as it were. The same movement of the hands above the paper, the same abrupt and yet sweeping motions that had so infuriated General Halder more than a century on. But this was a slovenly, complacent man – his whole posture spoke of a certain weakness and inattention. There was no sharpness to him, no intensity. Like a poor copy he sat there, bloated, double-chinned, more like a man of sixty than one of forty-four. Yet here was the man whose seed contained the destiny of Europe. Seydlitz looked at him and almost laughed.

'They are all right,' Seydlitz said, non-commitally. 'In my studio in Dresden is my real work. Oil paintings. Landscapes mainly.'

Hiedler nodded, watching Seydlitz carefully, impressed by his lies. The sketches had been done by one of Seydlitz's men – copied directly from the notebooks of the German romantic painter, Caspar David Friedrich. For his cover he had stolen the details of Friedrich's life, but the man and his work were of no real interest. Like Wagner it was a tool – a means of getting what he wanted. It was enough for Seydlitz that they did their work: put Hiedler at his ease and explained Seydlitz's clothes, his accent and his presence there in that remote place.

'I drew when I was a younger man.'

Hiedler closed the pad and sat back, his loose, fleshy lips forming a smile. 'I believe I too could have been a painter, if circumstances had been different.'

Seydlitz smiled and bowed his head slightly. In this too Hiedler was like his grandson, boastful and vain. But there the similarity ended, for his ambitions – his dreams – were small and uninspired.

A woman came to their table, bringing a jug of ale. Seydlitz put his hand over the mouth of his cup.

'No more for me, thanks. I must be up early tomorrow.'

But Hiedler had no such qualms. He thrust his glass at the woman and waited while she poured.

Seydlitz had not looked at her – was conscious of her only as a dull brown shape beside him – but then Hiedler spoke to her.

'Will you be staying here tonight, Maria?'

Seydlitz looked up. She had a plain, almost severe face, the nose small but sharp, the lips thin and pinched. Her long auburn hair had strands of grey in it and was tied back in a single plait. He knew at once who she was.

She looked at Seydlitz before she answered Hiedler. 'I am.'

For a moment longer her eyes rested on him, and then, with a brief glance at Hiedler, she backed away. There was a faint colour in her cheeks.

Hiedler leaned forward. 'A good woman that Maria. Her father was an ogre. He beat her.' Then, lowering his voice, 'And maybe other things too, eh?'

Seydlitz joined his laughter, liking him even less, but glad that it was so. It would make it so much easier to kill him.

Later, as he climbed the stairs, he thought of the woman. It would be best if he killed her too, just to be sure. But now that he'd seen Hiedler he was certain in his mind that he was the father of her child. Or would have been. Kill him and it ended. There would be no reason for Roosevelt to use his weapon.

33

The bed was lumpy and uncomfortable, but Seydlitz slept soundly and woke with the dawn. For a while he lay beneath the rough blanket, thinking about the day ahead, then he smiled and sat up, drawing back the heavy curtain.

Outside it was bright but cold. Ice rimed the edges of the puddles and filled the rutted tracks. Faint flakes of snow drifted slowly from the sky. The first snow of winter.

He dressed, then sat on the bed and checked his weapon thoroughly. It was a nice job, a Honig. Its eight, needle-fine chambers would fire a tightly focused beam. He placed it carefully in his shoulder holster, then buttoned his jacket.

He greeted Hiedler, who was waiting for him in the room below, like an old friend. He found him at the table they had shared the evening before, an empty bowl in front of him. Seydlitz had arranged with him that he would take him to the sight of an old ruin in the woods. Hiedler had seen such a ruin sketched in his pad and had mentioned that there was one only a few miles from the village. Seeing his opportunity Seydlitz had asked him if he would take him there. Hiedler had agreed at once.

'Did you sleep well, Herr Friedrich?'

'Very well indeed, Herr Hiedler.'

He waved aside the offer of breakfast. 'I would as soon get going. If it's as you say, then I would like to get a full day's work.'

Hiedler nodded. 'I have prepared everything. Maria has packed us lunch.'

'Good. Then I'll get my coat and we'll be off.'

On the way Seydlitz talked to him, sounding him about his life, getting a good idea of the kind of man he was, but offering little about himself. Hiedler's was a dull, uneventful life, lacking in even those small things that give a life its quality. Even so, he seemed content, even self-satisfied. If he had only been born into a better family …

Seydlitz smiled and nodded, detesting him. Then, at last, he brought the talk round to Maria.

'The woman at the inn. Is she the innkeeper's wife?'

Hiedler laughed and stopped, turning to face him. 'Maria?'

They were on a steep hillside, a dense wood to their right, pastures falling away to their left. It was darker now and the snow was falling heavier. Flakes rested in Hiedler's dark, fine hair. 'Kurth is a fool. And not just a fool.' He laughed again, his wet mouth falling open as he tipped his head back. 'He can't get it up. You know?' Again he laughed. 'He had a wife, but she ran off. Maria helps him out now and then, that's all.'

'Oh?' Seydlitz looked surprised 'She's not married, then?'

Hiedler's eyes narrowed. For a moment he seemed to glare at Seydlitz, then he relented, and turned his head to one side. A strange, lecherous light came into his eyes. 'You want to know the truth?'

Seydlitz frowned. 'What do you mean?'

In answer Hiedler pulled off his right glove and thrust it in Seydlitz's face. 'That's her,' he said. 'Her smell.' It stank of her – was ripe with her most intimate scent. 'All last night I had her. In the room next to Kurth's.' He grinned ferociously. 'He lies there listening to us, unable to sleep for the sounds coming through his wall.'

He laughed ferociously, then pulled his glove back on.

Seydlitz had gone cold. This changed things. He had hoped to spare the woman, but now – now she too would have to die.

'Isn't that risky? I mean, what if she falls pregnant?'

Hiedler shook his head. 'There's no danger of that. She's much older than she seems. Thirty-nine, would you believe?' He laughed. 'No, I could fuck her until the seas froze over and there'd be no chance of her swelling out!'

They walked on. Where the land dipped they went down, to the right, following an old path that was now grassed over. Through the trees Seydlitz could see the dark outline of a ruined building. Tall arches and soaring buttresses, the stone black against the snow that now lay over everything.

Coming out from the trees, he stopped on a ledge of rock, looking down into the clearing. 'It's beautiful,' he said, for the first time meaning what he said. 'But what happened? Why did it fall?'

Hiedler clambered down and then looked up at him. Behind him fallen stone littered the snow.

'Impudence,' he said. 'They meant it to last a thousand years.'

Seydlitz shivered and turned his head slightly. The irony was discomfiting. *So why did it fall?* The thought returned more strongly. He began to climb down, feeling a sudden wrongness to things.

He was halfway down when he heard the noise above him. He turned, one hand holding on to the outjutting slate, and looked up. Above him stood the woman. She was looking down at him and smiling. In her hand was a gun, a large-mouthed Spica.

She had appeared from nowhere.

He put his hand to his chest and jumped. Or tried to. Nothing at all. He was still standing there, the rocky outcrop cold through his glove, the woman above him.

She laughed. 'Poor boy,' she said. 'You poor, poor boy.'

Behind him Hiedler also laughed, but it was not the foolish, self-complacent laughter of before. It was sharper now, more wicked.

Seydlitz clambered down and faced him. The slackness had gone from Hiedler's face now. With one hand he beckoned Seydlitz on, while in the other he held a Spica similar to the woman's.

Russians.

'What have you done to me?'

The Russian smiled. 'We borrowed you for a time. While you were sleeping. Maria drugged you.'

'And this?' he indicated the ruins, the woods on all sides.

'A game,' the Russian said. 'An entertainment. We're filming all of this, you know. It will be a great success back home when we show it. The last stand of the Third Reich. Its final defeat.' He chuckled, enjoying himself. 'The look on your face was wonderful.'

Seydlitz stared at him, not understanding.

'I've seen this already. Heard myself say all this many times before. It's an odd feeling, you know, being here, doing these things and saying these words after having seen them so many times.'

Seydlitz was silent, trying to understand. They must have cut the *focus* from his chest. Cut it and healed it. Which meant that they had had him in their charge for months, maybe even years. And all the while he'd slept – or thought he'd slept – in Herr Kurth's room. There was a sour taste in his mouth, a tightness in his stomach, but he wasn't beaten yet.

'I don't believe you,' he said.

'Have it your way.'

Seydlitz circled him, watching the Spica, afraid that he would fire it before he had a chance to use his own weapon.

'You gave yourself away,' the Russian said. 'Time after time you skimped. Only did half your work. Enough to get you by and no more. And you thought it would do.' He sniffed his disgust. 'You *amateur*, Seydlitz.'

The Russian was silent a moment. Then, surprisingly, he sat down on one of the piles of stone and lowered his gun. 'Like this,' he said. 'You didn't stop to think why there should be a ruin here, in Austria. All the ruins are north, in Puritan Germany. Here the Reformation never happened. The Catholic monasteries were never sacked, never fell into ruin.'

'So where are we?'

He laughed. 'Russia. And this – like the village – is all a sham. Convincing, but a sham for all that.'

Seydlitz looked across at the woman. She still stood there on the ledge, but her gun was out of sight now. Seydlitz moved slowly to his right, closer to a low wall, keeping both of them in sight.

'It was amusing, watching what you did. We learned much from you. That business in '52, for instance. A bugger of a thing to happen, eh?' The Russian slapped his thigh and laughed. 'There you were, all the while warning Hitler against the dangers of provoking America, against a war on two fronts, quoting *Mein Kampf* at him, and all the time forgetting that there are no fronts in Time. No fronts at all.'

Seydlitz drew the Honig. The Russian looked at it and smiled, while the woman actually laughed. He threw it down.

'You understand, then, Herr Seydlitz?'

Seydlitz nodded. 'So what now? You know what happens. What do I do?'

'You came here to kill me, didn't you? Then, when you'd done that, you were going to go back for the woman.'

He hesitated, then nodded.

'Speak up!'

Seydlitz took a deep breath, then wiped snow from his hair and brow. 'Yes. So what is this? A trial?'

'Not quite.'

The woman was climbing down. She came across and stood there at the Russian's side. She seemed tense suddenly, awkward.

'Come on,' she said. 'Let's get it over with.'

They went round past the towering, half-ruined chancel of the ersatz monastery, picking their way between vast chunks of fallen masonry. There, against the massive wall, stood a cottage. Light shone from its single window. Smoke rose from a hole in its roof.

'There,' the Russian said, pointing towards it. 'Inside. The woman will join you in a while.'

Seydlitz turned to look at him, but he had turned away and was talking to the woman now in Russian. Seydlitz hesitated, then did as he was told.

Inside was a single large room, sparsely furnished. A peasant's dwelling. A fire burned in a brick grate, but the walls were wood and wattle. It was a Slavic dwelling, primitive, inferior. He looked about it, feeling an aversion for its crudeness.

As he stood there the woman entered. She glanced at him once, then closed the door and crossed the room. With her back to him she began to undress. When she was naked she slipped between the sheets of the bed and called to him.

'Why?' he asked. 'Why should I?'

'Because you must. Eventually. Oh, we've played this out thirty times and more, but you will. I know you will, because I've seen it.'

Seydlitz shook his head. He understood none of this. What was it? One final humiliation? Did they think that he couldn't get it up?

She laughed softly. 'You, Seydlitz, are dead. But in me you'll live on. In my child.'

'You've seen this?' Seydlitz laughed. 'I can't believe it.'

'He's tall, like you. A strong man. A leader like no other.'

Seydlitz shivered. It was as if they knew his deepest, most treasured dream. He stared at her, his mouth open, shaking his head slowly.

'It's true,' she said, sitting up, letting the sheets fall back to reveal her breasts. Not an old woman at all, but a girl. A young, attractive girl. Seydlitz looked at her and felt a trembling pass through him.

My child. My son. A leader like no other.

'No,' he said. 'This is a trick. A game.'

'No game,' she answered. 'This much is for real. This much will remain unchanged.'

'What do you mean?'

'This is the last of it. The tying of ends. The circle mended. Only the file to remind us of the cost of meddling.'

Seydlitz hesitated. He had looked at her face in another light and found it plain, but now he saw its strength, its beauty.

'I would have killed you.'

'I know,' she answered. 'It doesn't matter. Only this matters now.' And, smiling, she drew back the cover. 'Come, Max. Undress and join me here. Your son awaits creation. Destiny calls him.'

Seydlitz shivered violently. *Destiny* . . .

'Yes. Now come. I want you.'

34

Seydlitz lay there, watching her dress. Outside, in the twilight, the snow fell heavily. Inside, the flames of the fire cast flickering shadows everywhere. He watched the light's pattern on the smooth skin of her back as she stooped to lift her skirt up over her legs and waist. Her breasts hung free, part in light, part in shadow, and her eyes, when she looked at him, shone with their own inner warmth.

For the first, and perhaps for the only time in his life, Seydlitz was relaxed, at ease. Desire – all desire – had been quenched in him by her, and he looked at last with eyes freed from the wanting that had shaped his life. *You, Seydlitz, are dead*, she had said, and he had no reason to doubt her. But this was not defeat. His seed lived on in her. Even now it was growing in her, forming their child, their son.

'What will you call him?'

She had fastened her bra and pulled on her jumper. Now she was pulling on a pair of socks – long socks, thick and woollen – that reached up to her pale and slender thighs.

'I called him Joseph.'

'Not Max, then?'

'No. Nor Adolf.'

Her smile was tighter now. She pulled on her long leather boots, then reached for her coat. 'I guess I should thank you, really.'

'Thank me?'

'For spreading the seed.'

'I don't understand.'

'You weren't meant to.'

He leaned up on one elbow. 'Do I just wait? Will someone come for me?'

She fastened her coat then looked at him. 'No. No one will come now.'

The gun was in her pocket. She took it out and pointed it at him. It seemed too large for her hand. A man's gun.

Seydlitz sighed, watching her. No, there was nothing in her eyes. What warmth there'd been had been only the warmth of satisfaction – of a job well done, a victory achieved. There was no love, no caring there. Those too had been illusory. But what had he expected?

'Go ahead,' he said. 'Get it over with.'

She nodded. 'I'm sorry. Perhaps I should feel more. I love my son, and what I see of him in you I also love. But you're not him, Max Seydlitz. You never could be him. And anyway, you have to die. This has to happen.'

Seydlitz said it for her. 'You've seen it.'

She nodded. 'Our son will be a Russian. And not just any Russian. *The* Russian. The architect of our modern state.'

Her face lit with pride. 'A strong and powerful man. A hawk among men.'

Seydlitz stared at her, stunned. Chkalov, that's who she meant. His son would be Joseph Maksymovich Chkalov, otherwise known as Yastryeb, 'the Hawk', Grand Master of Time and rival of their own Grand Master, Hecht.

'Impossible,' he said, his voice a whisper. But she was shaking her head.

'I took him back. Two hundred years. Back to when it all began. That's where I gave birth to him. The rest' – she smiled – 'is history.'

'I still don't understand. Why me?'

'Your DNA. It's special. One of our analysts noticed the similarity. How closely it resembled Yastryeb's. And then we noticed others, among the young agents you were sending out into Time. Germans, but not entirely German. Your seed, Max. Your sons.'

Seydlitz opened his mouth to say something, then saw what she meant. He looked appalled.

'You understand, then?'

'Russians? I've been fathering Russians?'

The gun was still pointed at him. 'It's not quite as simple as that. But it was there, among the repeated sequences in chromosome eight. A copy-cat pattern. Like ours, *very* like ours, but one which your platform still considered German. What I believe you'd call a permitted code. That's what we used.'

'Used?'

'To identify those we could—'

He lunged at her and, as he did, she shot him, knowing he would lunge, one bullet to the head, one to the heart. Making sure. Completing the circle.

'—turn,' she said, finishing what she had begun, a sharp and sudden pain in her face, seeing the mess she'd made of him.

She threw the gun down and half turned, seeing Lavrov in the doorway where he always was. Yes, and now it began. Sixteen hours they had. Sixteen hours to do all that they needed to get done.

She looked at him one last time, then stood. 'He's all yours,' she said, knowing from having watched herself a hundred times that these were her last recorded words.

Sixteen hours.

Part Three
Berlin, 1759

'In short, anything can be said of world history, anything conceivable even by the most disordered imagination. There is only one thing that you can't say – that it had anything to do with reason.'

– Fyodor Dostoevsky, *Notes From Underground*

35

I am asleep when the summons comes. Ernst's soft *suden Deutsche* voice fills the room.

'Otto! Wake up! Hecht wants you.'

I rise and dress, still half in my dream of her, the room silent about me, the single night-light on the far wall revealing the contents of my room.

I am not one to acquire much – most of what I need is in my head – but I do keep certain little luxuries, gleanings from the shelves of Time: books and tiny statues; coins and photographs and, oh, trivial things, but meaningful to me. Sometimes I think that it's not even for the things themselves, but to try and mask the truth of how we live. Not that I was ever one for evading the truth. Outside, I know, is a vacuum, and no ordinary vacuum at that. To cross a single micron of its vast emptiness, one would need to slip sideways and back a thousand times.

But no riddles now. Hecht awaits me.

Dressed, I go to the door and punch out the code for Hecht's apartment. Our doors are not what they seem. They do not open on to some contiguous space, rather they link to whichever portion of this *Nichtraum* – this 'no-space' – we desire to visit. None of it actually exists. Our dwellings are like soap bubbles, only folded in, like Russian dolls. And the doors transport us. At a touch of the pad we transform the topography of Four-Oh, linking rooms that were previously unlinked. At least, that's how it seems. Just as we travel in Time, linking one unrelated spot to another, so do we travel here. And if the doors ceased to work, then we'd be trapped.

Right now, it hisses open. In front of me lies the briefest of corridors; bare and functional, designed for one purpose only: to get me across this bubble universe of ours to Hecht.

Hecht is sitting at his desk. Busy at his screen, he does not acknowledge me at first, and when he does it is with that strange half-smile of his, as if, in that single glance, he has already all he needs to know.

Hecht is the oldest of us. How old nobody knows, yet old enough to have taught three generations at least. Old enough to have seen a thousand minor changes and to have been changed a thousand times.

And yet still himself – Hecht, 'the Pike'. His stubble-short silver hair seems to glisten in the overhead light, his grey eyes to fasten on me as he speaks.

'Ah, Otto, we seem to have a problem.'

His voice is soft and the words seem innocuous enough, yet something in the way he says them makes me go cold. Besides, it is not his way to summon you from sleep. Rarely does such urgency move him. After all, we have all of Time and Space.

He is wearing blue today – the blue of an early winter sky. His bare arms on the desk are strong and thickly haired, his hands the hands of a blacksmith, the fingers interlaced.

'A problem?'

He nods, and as I wait for him to spell it out, I can feel my own heartbeat, feel the pressure of its quickened pulse against my chest.

Above Hecht is the Tree. Some of its branches are clear, others faint, yet all except the central trunk seem frail – the merest threads of possibilities – as if, at the blink of an eye, they might disappear.

Hecht's eyes never leave mine. He watches me as if to gauge something from my reaction.

'We've been infiltrated.'

'What?'

'Seydlitz. He didn't return. Not in person, anyway.'

I don't follow, but he continues anyway. 'We've arrested three in his direct genetic line, but that still leaves five unaccounted for. They're out there somewhere, doing mischief.'

'*Eight?*'

'Yes. They used Seydlitz's DNA to infiltrate our bloodlines.'

'Ah ...'

Then this *is* serious, for our whole security system – the very way we travel in Time – is determined by our DNA. We use its information as a code, the best there is. But now the Russians have stolen it and used it against us.

Eight of them. My mind reels. We've been infiltrated before, but never on this scale.

'Why didn't we spot this before now?' I ask, conscious even as I say it that this is Hecht's direct responsibility.

'Because we weren't looking for it,' he answers. 'We'd been making the assumption that if they were born here, then they would be German, right down to the smallest strands of their DNA. I mean, our women never leave Four-Oh, and the only men they sleep with are *our* men, so it seemed safe to assume that there wasn't a problem. Seems we were wrong. Mind, it didn't help that the variations in chromosome eight were extremely marginal.'

'But these men ... they're still our agents, yes?'

'Ours and theirs.'

'I see. So where precisely is the danger?'

'We don't know.'

I consider this a moment. 'Sleepers,' I say, and Hecht nods. 'So why didn't Yastryeb activate them before now?'

'My guess is this. That they were planning something big. Maybe something to do with the platform of Four-Oh itself. Why else would they turn our men? What other use could they have?'

'Yes, but why not activate them? Why wait for us to discover them?'

Hecht shook his head. 'I don't think they did. My guess is that they thought they had more time. Time enough to put together something imaginative and bold, something that would damage us irreparably. Maybe even eradicate us.'

'And you think they'd go along with that? I mean, the Russians may have turned them, but to make them take that next step, to harm their own. After all, they were born and bred as Germans ...'

'I know,' Hecht says, and there is the slightest hint of dismay in his voice as he says it. He, like me, I'm sure, is surprised – shocked may be the better term – at how patient, how long-term the Russian planning has been in this regard. We'd always considered them more impulsive than that. More spur of the moment.

Only now that they *had* been activated, maybe we'd see Yastryeb adopt some ad-hoc scheme. Something that could shake the Tree. After all, why waste the opportunity? And maybe that is why Hecht is troubled by this. Because for once we're not in control.

Sixteen hours, I think. It's not a long time when you think of it, but experienced agents can cause a lot of damage in that time. The thought of that makes me ask the question I've been wanting to ask since I was summoned.

'So just who are they?'

'Of your operatives? Gruber ...'

'No.'

Hecht pushes a pair of genetic charts towards me, studies of the repeated sequences in chromosome eight which form the genetic fingerprint of a man. At first I don't see the similarities, and then I do, and nod.

'What did they do? Clone him?'

'Nothing so complex. Seydlitz always liked women. All they needed was to trick him into sleeping with one of theirs.'

'And you think that's what they did?'

Hecht's smile is bleak. 'I know it for a fact. The Russians even made a file of it.'

That, too, shocks me. A file ...

But I realise something else from what Hecht's said. The 'three' must already have been interrogated. I sigh, wondering who they are, and if any of them are good friends. We are a small community, after all.

Before this latest war there was another war, fought – at first – with more conventional weaponry. That war – in its first, long phase – lasted all of eighty-seven years, and at its end only a handful of survivors remained – in the 'no-space' bunkers of Neu Berlin and Moscow, the command staffs and their families. Thirty-one families, in our case, seventy-eight in theirs. And from those narrowed bloodlines all of us now derive.

I meet Hecht's eyes. 'How did they get their orders?'

'In the field. Each one of them was contacted the very first time they jumped back.'

'But that isn't possible. How could they know where to be or when?'

'Krauss told them.'

I stare at him, incredulous. '*Theodor* Krauss?'

Hecht shakes his head. 'No, thank Urd. Phillipe.'

'Ah ...' I have a vague image of a man; tall, blond-haired and broad-shouldered. A lot like Seydlitz, now that I come to think of it.

'And the damage?'

But Hecht only sighs, and I realise that he doesn't know. The damage is being done right now, and he needs us to rectify it before the game is lost and the branches of the Tree blink out one by one.

Time. There is never enough time.

36

The platform is ready, its massive concave circle vibrating faintly as if alive. As I step into the room the women look up from the surrounding desks, their eyes anxious. They know that I may not return this time.

So it is sometimes. But this is much more serious than usual. I am the third operative to depart. Two more will leave after I'm gone. Yet will any of us return? Not if we're too late. Not if we can't undo the damage that is even now being done.

I have been busy between times. Hecht gave me Ritter's report to read and a copy of the Russians' file. Where he got the last, I don't know, but they are both sobering documents. Freisler was right, after all. Seydlitz *did* get careless. Hecht blames himself. He thinks that the very directness of Seydlitz's project may have alerted the Russians, but Freisler and I know otherwise.

Meanwhile Time has healed itself. History is as it was. The river flows on. All except for that huge gap in Space-Time in the middle of 1952. That is still there, for some reason, though the main current of Time appears to flow about it, like a river about a rock. And we're not sure why. Some changes take on a permanency, others don't. Some alter the river's course, others merely dam it for a while.

And sometimes – and these are perhaps the worst instances – it changes and our perceptions and memories change with it, so that there seems no change at all. That is, until a traveller returns from the past and finds us so.

Those are the times I fear. To lose something – or someone – and not to know.

I have come straight here from a conference – Hecht and the five of us. He wanted to see if we could discern any pattern to events. Aside from the obvious, that is. Of the five who are out there, not a single one is in charge of a major project. They're all cadet operatives, learning their trade in the field before taking on new projects of their own. It's how we all start, helping others to carry out their schemes while learning all we can about those Ages in which we travel.

Beyond this, what? Gruber is patient and careful – meticulously so. Of the other four, there is the same divergence of character one might expect from any group of young men.

The eldest is twenty-eight, the youngest twenty-three. None of them has any longer than four years' experience in the field. Anticipating things, Hecht had the genetic charts of all the dead operatives over the past four years checked out. Of those, another fifteen carried variants of Seydlitz's distinctive genetic pattern.

Murdered, he thinks. Killed because they would not switch sides and betray the Fatherland.

But the big question is, how will the Russians *use* them? What scheme have they hatched to get at us through these 'sleepers' in our midst? Or is the damage already done?

Hecht thinks not. It is a characteristic of Time that while one can travel back a long way, one cannot travel forward a single nano-second beyond the Now. In that sense, Time has a ceiling. It is as if we are in a lift that is moving slowly upward, but down the shaft of which we might plunge at any moment. A hole so deep one might fall for ever.

In Hecht's opinion, the Russians' plan will have been triggered the very moment Seydlitz went missing. Until then, they would not have risked removing the foci from their chests, for as soon as they did, those agents would vanish from our tracking screens, alerting us. But unless they remove them and substitute their own – a lengthy process that can take anywhere between twelve and sixteen hours – what possible use can they be?

No. Things are happening now – right now – but in the Past.

Our job then is to locate our missing operatives and bring them back. Or, failing that, to kill them. It isn't a pleasant thought. I like Gruber. Yet as I stand there on the platform, waiting to jump, I find a matching coldness in myself. If he succeeds, then I die, and all my friends with me.

And if I die, who will look after Katerina?

37

The room is locked. As I look about me, I remember how things were and note that nothing seems to have been disturbed. My books lay open on the desk to the right of the bed as I left them, the old brass candlestick I bought in Konigsberg spattered with melted wax. My black leather boots rest on the floor to the left, dry mud still clinging to them, while my green velvet smoking robe hangs from the back of the tiny walnut wardrobe.

In the corner, tucked away, rests my leather travelling case, a white cloth belt acting as a strap.

It is the evening of 27 July 1759, and the sun is shining in through the leaded window of my Potsdam apartment. But what I am most aware of is the smell.

Someone has been in my room. I can smell the faint odour of their cologne, like a dark ink stain in a bowl of crystal clear water.

Smell. It always hits you powerfully when you jump back. Its richness can be overpowering at times. This time, however, the smell means something.

Gruber. Gruber has been here.

It takes a moment to assimilate. As my pulse slows and my lungs become accustomed to the richer air, so my thoughts clear.

Getting in here was no mystery. Gruber had a copy of the key.

Until today there was no reason not to trust him, but now I know what he is.

There could be a bomb here somewhere, or a device to trap me.

I decide not to touch a thing – not even to look – and, turning about, I open the door and slip out, locking the door and then walking down the stairs, careful to make no sound, pausing on the turn to listen before hurrying to the door and out on to the street.

My clothes are of the Age: a long brocade jacket and a three-cornered hat, knee-length boots and britches. And, as this is Potsdam, capital of Prussia, and the style is distinctly military, so the cut and colour of my clothes is simple too: blues and greens, with a plain black hat. I blend in. And little wonder. I have spent years here in this place.

Church bells are ringing for the evening service. Even here, in free-thinking Prussia, religion is still important, and people stroll in their best attire, enjoying this most beautiful of evenings.

I see it all, but am distracted. Where is Gruber? That's what I want to know. That's why I hurry now, as if late for the evening service.

Gruber's rooms are on the other side of town, near St Nikolai. He'll not be there. He'd not be that stupid. But I have to check.

His landlady squints out at me from the darkness of her hallway, then grudgingly lets me pass. She knows me as Gruber's friend, nor is there any reason for her to suspect otherwise, unless he's told some tale. But it seems not. I am allowed to go up. The door is locked, but again I have the key. I hesitate. What if there's a bomb? I fling it open, trusting to fate. Of Gruber there's no sign, but it's clear he was in a hurry. Clothes are strewn all over the place, and the contents of a bag have been emptied out over the floor. And there on the bed ...

I walk across, then crouch, sniffing at the stain on the cover. It's blood. Gruber's blood, no doubt, where they cut the focus from his chest. Indeed, after a moment's search, I find the tiny, delicate circle lying there among the debris. It looks like the very finest of filters, its ridged edge like the milling of an ancient metal coin.

They would have had to have done the crudest of operations on him – the most basic of repair jobs – but they will need to buy themselves time if they're to replace it with their own. It takes twelve hours minimum to fix a new focus, sixteen max – it needs to grow into the nerves, to integrate with the whole of the body's nervous system, especially the brain. Get it wrong and you might arrive at your destination missing a hand, a leg, or even your head.

I straighten up and look about me. There is a second smaller room just off to the left behind a pair of doors. I go through. Inside is a card table and four chairs. Two empty wine bottles and three glasses clutter the table. And cards. I can almost see them there, playing endless hands of cards, seeing out the night, awaiting the moment when they'd have to act. No doubt a messenger was sent, the very instant that the focus was taken from Seydlitz's chest.

I smile and reach into my pocket, drawing out the skin-tight gloves. Pulling them on, I pick up the cards and slip them into the transparent bag.

As ever, I have come prepared. I knew I would find this, or something like this. To take Gruber they would have to have come here in person, and that meant that they would leave traces. From those traces we can put faces to them, reconstruct their appearance from their genetic code. Saliva, sweat, skin particles – anything will do. And the results are good. Ninety-eight per cent accurate, or thereabouts.

Because it will help to know who I'm looking for. Gruber they'll hide away. But they can't all hide. Not all of the time. And if I know what they look like it will give me an advantage. That is, if Gruber hasn't already given them *my* likeness.

Gruber and his new friends will be armed, but that doesn't worry me. If I find them I'll give them no chance to use a weapon.

But before then I need to trip back.

38

They are waiting for me at the platform. Inge takes the samples and hurries off, and while I wait, Urte comes across and asks me how I am.

I have not seen Urte in almost a month. She's almost half my height, but she always seems somehow bigger than her physical size. Her grey eyes smile up at me.

'Will I see you later?'

'Sorry?'

'Have you forgotten?'

For a moment I wonder what she means, and then it hits me. We have an appointment for that evening. This thing with Seydlitz and Gruber had driven it from my mind.

'No,' I say. 'I shall be there.'

Either that, or I'll be dead. But I do not say that. I stand there, awkward now. And, sensing that, she smiles and nods and walks away, leaving me wondering how she manages to do that to me. After all, she is only half my age.

I walk over to where Zarah is sitting, hunched over her monitor, and ask her how things are. She looks up at me, distracted momentarily, then gestures towards the screen.

'He's still there. For the moment.'

She is speaking of Klaus, Klaus Heusinger. He has gone back, too, to take out Schwarz, another of the turncoats. They are out there right now, somewhere in the late twenty-fourth century, in the Time of the Mechanists. At any moment he might return. Or things might change.

In an Augenblich, I think. *In the blink of an eye.*

If a single one of us fails, we all fail. If a single one of them is successfully operated upon by the Russians, then we have lost, because then they can infiltrate us before we know what's happened and can thus penetrate our defences. Right now, however, all five are suspended in their timestreams, subject to the normal flow of Time. Until the Russians can place foci in their chests they are vulnerable. And so we must hit them now. There will be no second chance.

If you're clever, you might have spotted a paradox of sorts in there. If they could operate, then they would have done, and we would have lost already, so this wouldn't actually be happening. Only it doesn't quite work like that. Timestreams have this peculiar property of running twice: first time without interference, and only then, second time round, with their changed characteristics. For instance, the day *before* Gehlen invented his first crude time machine, no one had ever travelled back in Time. Time was pure. No one had tinkered with it. There were other dimensions and secondary universes, certainly, but there were no links between them. Only when Gehlen started things rolling – made his first trip back, eighty-five years into the Past – was the timestream sullied.

Inge returns and offers me a pair of files. 'There are three separate DNA strands, Gruber excluded. Those are the first two. The other's new, so it'll take a while to process.'

I open the first of the files and study it.

His name is Nemtsov – Alexandr Davydovich Nemtsov – and the generated image shows him to be a large-built, heavily muscled man. They've made him thirty in the picture, but he could be anywhere between twenty and fifty. Dark eyes, dark hair and a large, long nose. Not a handsome man.

I push the picture aside and look at the report. Nemtsov has crossed our paths on two previous occasions, once in the twenty-third century, and once late in the twenty-fourth, during the last days of the Mechanist Kings. According to this he killed one of our agents, but on neither occasion did we get a good look at him, so the image *could* be wrong. Unlikely, but …

He's clever, this one. Good at his job. But this seems to be the earliest he's ventured back, and I note the fact, hoping it might help. If he's not familiar with Frederick's period then he might just fuck up. It's possible.

The other one is Dankevich.

I look up at Inge and laugh. 'You're kidding!'

She smiles back at me. 'No. It's your old friend. Guess they needed someone who knows the Age.'

True. But Dankevich! I had shot the bastard twice, the second time fatally – but that didn't mean that it wasn't the same man. When you travel in Time, things don't always happen sequentially. What was *my* past was probably *his* future. But at least I knew one thing: I wouldn't die this time round, not if Dankevich was there, because if *I* died, then who would shoot *him*?

I grin then close the file. It's time to get back. Time to find Gruber and close him down.

39

I return to Potsdam. It is still the evening of the twenty-seventh. A single hour has passed since I was last here, but the shadows are lengthening, and the streets are silent now. At the Black Eagle tavern, the innkeeper, Muller, tells me he saw Gruber earlier in

the company of two men: a big, dark-haired man and a weasel of
a fellow.

Dankevich.

They bought several flagons of wine, then left.

'How long ago?'

Muller shrugs. 'Two hours, maybe three?'

I thank him with a silver thaler, then hurry to Taysen's stables
to the west of the town. As I walk between those neat, Prussian
houses, I start trying to think like them. Gruber and I were here
for one reason only: to save Frederick's life.

In seventeen days' time, Frederick will take on the combined
armies of Russia and Austria at Kunersdorf, eighty kilometres east
of Berlin. It will be a fateful battle, and Frederick's forty-eight
thousand men – almost half the strength of the enemy force – will
be soundly beaten. That much we cannot change. But we can keep
Frederick himself alive. Two horses will be shot out from under
him on the battlefield, and two musket-balls will penetrate his
cloak. The second will kill him. Unless the snuff-box that it hits on
the way – a flimsy silver thing, barely capable of deflecting a shot –
is replaced by something sturdier.

Historically I knew I had already succeeded. Frederick *had*
survived. But unless I actually made the swap, he would not. And
then ...

It was simple, really. If Frederick died, so too would Prussia,
partitioned off between its three great rivals: France, Austria and
Russia. Not a square mile of it would survive, and without Prussia
there could be no Germany.

Because Frederick had lived, catastrophe was turned into
ultimate victory, for though only eighteen thousand of Frederick's
men survived that bloody encounter, by the end of the month
Old Fritz would gather together a brand-new force of thirty-
three thousand men and, in an act of heroic defiance, steel

himself to fight one final battle on the open field before Berlin.

He never had to, of course. His defiance proved enough. Both the Russians and the Austrians withdrew. Prussia was saved, and so, a century further on, its greatest chancellor, Bismarck, would create the German Confederation.

So history functioned. With a little help from us.

As I came into the street where Taysen's was, I looked up past the walls of the town towards the royal palace. Sanssouci rested on the hills above the town, a marvel of rococo architecture, its elegance understated, like its owner.

He was a wonder, Old Fritz. For six years now he had taken on the rest of mainland Europe and held them off. And not merely held them off, but beaten them soundly on numerous occasions. He was an inspiration to us all. Prussia, a country of four and a half million souls, had faced a coalition whose joint population was over ninety million, and whose combined armies were at least six times the size of Prussia's own. In the space of nine months, between November 1757 and August 1758, Frederick had crossed a thousand miles of Central Europe and defeated his three main rivals one after another – the French at Rossbach, the Austrians at Leuthen, and the Russians, finally, at Zorndorf. Each time the odds were heavily against him, and each time he emerged from the battlefield the undisputed master. To have won a single one of those battles was remarkable, but to have triumphed in all three ...

There was no king to match him in all of Germany's long history, and I had met them all. But the long struggle had cost Prussia dear. To arm and feed his armies, Frederick had bled his country white. There was barely an animal to be had in the whole of Potsdam, or so Taysen told me as we sat in his office sharing a tankard of beer.

Taysen is an old friend, but this once he says he cannot help.

'I'll pay well,' I say. 'Whatever you ask.'

He gives the faintest smile. 'If only it were that easy, Otto.

You see, I've sold all my horses. Yes, and for a good price. Your friend Gruber—'

'I need a horse,' I say. 'If you can get me one ...'

I place a heavy bag of silver thalers on the table before him.

'Otto, I ...' He shrugs apologetically, but his eyes look longingly at the bag of silver.

'There must be *one* horse left in Potsdam, surely?'

The notion gets him thinking. He reaches for his beer and downs it, then stands. 'Wait here,' he says. 'I'll see what I can do.'

Thus it is that, twenty minutes later, I am riding north-west towards Berlin on a horse that previously belonged to a captain in the Bayreuth Dragoons. The man, Taysen tells me, was drunk, else he'd never have contemplated the deal, but my only concern is not to be taken as a thief.

Besides, I have other things on my mind. Like where Gruber is. I go to Nauener-Tor and ask the gateman if he's seen a party heading out on to the Berlin road – merchants, not soldiers, with pack horses, maybe – and he says yes, they passed not an hour back. Four men in a hurry. And he thought it odd, because they had three spare horses with them, and horses being at such a premium, and there being no wares on their saddles ...

I thank the old man and ride on, hastening my pace as darkness falls. If I were them I'd find lodgings in Berlin – in one of the poorer quarters, maybe – and do the operation there. But they'll know I'm after them.

Or someone like me.

40

There are a dozen inns on the road and I am forced to stop and check each one, but my instinct is that they've headed straight for Berlin. If I were them, I'd try to lose myself in some back-street lodging house and do the operation there, but I know from experience that it's a mistake to try to outguess the Russians. They rarely do the expected. The only thing I'm certain of is that Gruber cannot jump – not yet – and they won't leave him here, so until they're settled somewhere they'll move fast and try to lose me.

Of course, it's possible that they left the Berlin road and doubled back in the dark, but it's unlikely. This is *Angerdorfer* country – farming villages. There's not a major town for more than fifty miles, unless they make for Brandenburg, and why go there? Besides, Berlin is on the way to Kunersdorf, and, if my hunch is right, they'll not waste the chance to make a double strike: at us, through Gruber, and at Frederick himself.

It's after dawn when I reach the Schloss Bridge to the west of the medieval town. The royal residence dominates the skyline on the other bank, but it's of no interest right now. Frederick has not been to Berlin these past six years. He's south of here. Until three days ago he could be found on a lonely farm in Duringsvorkwerk, catching up on his correspondence, but having heard of Marshal Saltykov's victory at Paltzig, he'll have broken camp immediately and will be marching north, towards Frankfurt-an-der-Oder. In four days' time he will reach Sommerfeld, and four days after that he will arrive in Frankfurt itself. It's there I plan to meet him. But not until I've dealt with Gruber.

The gate is open and has been for an hour, and when I ask the gatekeeper, he tells me that four men entered the town at daybreak. It would appear that they have let the spare horses go, for the man makes no reference to them when I question him. I leave him with a thaler in his hand and gallop on, down the Schlossfreiheit with its tall and massive buildings, then out into the open space before the Schloss itself.

Berlin, even in this age, is large, and I barely know where to begin my search, but I'm certain they'll head for one of the poorer, less reputable parts of town. I stop and look about me. There are stalls out already. I dismount and walk across to one that's selling *Bouletten*, and purchase several of the spicy meatballs that are Berlin's culinary specialty. I'm hungry, but that's not the reason why I choose this particular stall. It's well placed, on the corner of the two main thoroughfares, with a good view of the entire square. The vendor is a big man in his forties, with an untrimmed hedge of a moustache, and as I chew on one of his delicacies, I ask him if he saw four travellers pass earlier.

He's been here since first light, hoping to catch the early trade, and he remembers the men well. He even describes the fourth of them: a tall man, quite young and yet completely bald, with the look of a priest about him. He says they went south, down the Bruderstrasse.

I thank the man with a coin, then walk my mount across the cobbled square.

I should be hurrying, only I've a good idea now where they've gone. Berlin is, and always has been, a twin city, and here, to the south of the Schloss, begins its other, smaller half. This is Colln. Where I'm walking now is the nicer, more respectable part of Colln, but to the south, where the town nestles in a curve of the River Spree, is a huddle of streets that spill out on to the river front.

Berlin is a cosmopolitan place, even in this century. You can find a colony of French Huguenots to the south-west in Martinicken, near the Kleine Tiergarten, or Bohemian Protestants in southern Friedrichstadt. There's a Jewish quarter in Kreuzberg, and smaller gatherings of Poles and Slavs and Dutch to the east of the old town. All add to the flavour of the place, yet none of these has such an influence on Berlin's character as its soldiers. Right now they are a hundred miles away, marching to Frederick's order, but in peacetime up to twenty thousand might be found quartered throughout the city. It is why Berlin is a city of whores. But while the soldiers are away, the landlords must find other lodgers, the girls other sweethearts.

I stop at the north end of Fischerstrasse, looking down that long, narrow street. The facing rows of tall, four-storey houses seem to lean in towards each other, soot dark and close enough to touch, their wood-framed windows opened outwards. It's a shabby, grimy place and its inhabitants dress to match. I have a gut instinct that they're here, but I could be wrong. They could be anywhere. But then, why head south from the Schloss? If they were looking for a place to the east of the city, they would have carried on along the Konigstrasse, out past the town hall and the police headquarters.

Mind, they could be heading towards the Kietz ...

I need to be careful now. For all I know one of them is keeping look-out, trying to spot me before I can spot them. It's cat and mouse. And there's the problem of where to stable my horse.

I smile, knowing suddenly what to do. If I find where they've stabled their horses, then I'll find them.

It takes me half an hour, but the time's well spent. They're here in Colln, or not far away. Until they can operate on Gruber, they'll need their horses, just in case they have to make a quick escape. There's no quicker way of travelling in these times.

Having stabled my own horse, I call the ostler to me and, slipping him a few coins, tell him I'm one of Frederick's spies, working for the Marquis D'Argens, and that I'm trailing the four who came in earlier.

Like everyone, he knows D'Argens by reputation, and the mere mention of the name is enough to persuade him to help me. He takes me over to the stall where their horses are and, as I walk about them, he tells me what he knows.

The big man, Nemtsov, appears to be their spokesman. It was

he who paid the ostler, he who gave instructions concerning the horses. The other three were silent, the 'priest' eerily so.

'I knew,' he says, with a self-satisfied smirk. 'I just knew they were up to no good.'

I notice blood on one of the saddles – Gruber's blood, no doubt – and turn and ask the man if one of them seemed hurt.

He shrugs. 'Maybe.'

But I know he doesn't know, and that worries me a little, because Gruber would be hurting by now, and it *would* show.

I leave the stables and move swiftly down the street. They could be anywhere in the vicinity, but there are ways of narrowing down the search.

In these days before advanced communications, everyone seems interested in everyone else's business. I walk across and, doffing my hat and bowing, greet them.

'Ladies. I'm looking for some friends.'

There are giggles and blushes, but one of them, more forward than the others, meets my eyes, a flirting smile on her lips.

'And what would these friends of yours be like, master?'

She's a working girl, up early for her kind, and from her clothes I'd judge she's far from Berlin's finest.

'Four men,' I answer her. 'A big man and a priest. A small, dapper little fellow, and one other. Young. Dark-haired.'

There's a moment's consultation, and then the girl puts out her hand. I smile and place a silver thaler in it – a real one, not one of Frederick's debased 'ephraims'.

She stares at it round-eyed, then looks back at me and grins. 'Are you sure these friends of yours can't wait an hour? That is, if you've another like this.'

But I am not tempted. I want Gruber, and I need to find him soon.

'Another time,' I say, and smile back at her pleasantly.

'A shame,' she says, 'for you look like a fine gentleman.'

'And no clap-ridden soldier!' remarks one of the others, and they all begin to giggle once more.

'Well?' I ask. 'Am I to know where my friends are lodged?'

In answer she smiles and turns and puts her arm out, like an actress on the stage. 'Right here,' she says, 'on the third floor, above old Schmidt.'

And even as I look up at the window, I see one of them – the bald one – and know that I've been spotted.

The girl's smile changes to shocked surprise as I push past her, drawing my gun. The stairs are inside, to the right of Schmidt's stall, and as I hurry up them I can hear urgent voices coming from above.

But even as I turn on to the first-floor landing, there is a familiar hiss of air behind me and I whirl about to find Nemtsov there on the steps below. He raises his gun, but I'm much quicker than him. The beam catches him through the temple and he falls back with a cry.

I turn back in time to see the priest's bald head duck back from the landing above. I hear the soft thud of a grenade drop on the stairs close by and, without thought, throw myself at the door to my right. It gives, and I am halfway across the room when the thing explodes.

I pick myself up and stagger to the window. The house is on fire now, the old wood burning fiercely on the landing. There's no way out the front, so I open the shattered window and clamber out, then drop into the cluttered backyard.

I move back, looking up at the backs of the old houses. There is a rickety wooden fire escape two houses down, and if they were to get out on to the roof they could make their way across to it. Even as I watch, I hear the roof hatch crack open and see the bald one's head appear.

I fire off two pulsed beams at him, but he scrambles behind the chimney stack, and neither hits the mark. Brick dust and scorched cement showers down. The angle's awkward and I really need to get higher. Not only that, but I'm vulnerable where I am. A single shot could pick me off.

I run inside, making my way through a dank, dark basement room and out into the shop. Schmidt is standing there, looking up the staircase, his face distraught, wringing his hands in anguish. The whole top of the building is now on fire, and a crowd is slowly forming. A bell is clanging some way off, and as I step out on to the street again, the working girl points me out and yells. 'That's him!'

'It's okay,' I shout back, putting my hands up defensively as the crowd looks to me. 'They're Russians … Russian spies!'

But it's far from okay. I knew they'd fight me, but I didn't expect them to risk Gruber's life – not in so cavalier a fashion.

I move back across the street, looking up at the rooftops again, trying to get a glimpse of them, but there's nothing. Even so, they will have to come down. The fire is already spreading to the surrounding buildings, and while the Russians can jump, Gruber can't, and I'm pretty sure they won't leave him to his fate. Yet even as I start forward someone grabs me and pulls me about. I find myself staring into the angry face of a soldier – a captain by his uniform.

'Who are you?' he demands gruffly. Behind him stands the ostler. 'Klaus here tells me you work for D'Argens, but I've never seen you before. I think *you're* the spy, my friend!'

I try to pull away, but his grip is firm, and I decide to plead with him.

'You've got to help me. If they get away, then we're all done for. There's a man in there, Gruber – he's about to betray us all!'

It's the truth, and something of my conviction must get through, because the captain loosens his grip.

'My name is Behr,' I say. 'Otto Behr, and I *do* work for D'Argens, only you won't have heard of me because I've been away, in Silesia, trailing these Russian bastards.'

There's a scream. I turn to see that one of the women is hit – burned by the beam of a Russian gun. There's a sudden stench of burned flesh.

'Get them out of here now!' I yell at the captain, hoping he'll respond. And he does. The tone of authority in my voice does the trick. He's Prussian, after all. Yet even as he tries to urge the crowd to leave, two more are hit.

There's screaming now, and panic in the crowded street. The very nature of the wounds – huge gouges of exposed and burning flesh – scares them. I use the moment's chaos to escape and run towards the second house down and kick my way inside, gun raised, ready to brazen it out.

And stop dead, astonished.

'Otto. It's about time you did something useful.'

It's Freisler. He puts a finger to his lips. There are hurried footsteps coming down the stairs. As a figure appears on the landing, Freisler raises his gun and aims, then lowers it again.

It's an old woman, moving with the haste of someone half her age. She's in a state of undress and not a pretty sight, but fear has clearly triumphed over vanity. She sees us and freezes, but Freisler waves her down, giving her his most reassuring smile, and she hurries away, the door slamming shut behind her, leaving Freisler and I alone in the silent house.

'How did you know?' I ask quietly.

'You came back and told us,' Freisler answers, not looking at me. 'You had a bit of trouble. We thought we'd change that.'

'Trouble?'

'They shot you.'

'Ah ...'

'But you got back.'

'Ah ...'

'But that won't happen this time.'

There's a creak on the stairs. Someone is coming down, slowly, carefully, step by step. Freisler gestures to me to go across and crouch beneath the stairs. I do as he says. This is my place, my time, but I am used to taking orders, and this is not a time to argue.

I glimpse his boots first, beautifully polished leather boots. He hesitates, then leans forward very, very slowly, looking down towards where I am crouched.

And I burn him, straight through his right eye. He makes a shocked, strangled noise of surprise and tumbles over. We don't expect to die, we time travellers, but we do. And sometimes more than once.

I wait a second or two, listening to the silence, trying to make out if Dankevich is up there too, but there's nothing. He's probably still on the roof, with Gruber.

I go up quickly. The 'priest' is lying on his back, a pool of blood beneath his head. Dead. At least, in this time-line. And maybe dead for good, unless they act to change things.

I call down quietly to Freisler and he joins me after a moment.

'Bobrov,' he says, looking at the man. 'A real nasty bastard. He's killed a good dozen of our men.'

I look at Freisler and blink. Something's wrong, but I can't pinpoint it. Besides, we need to deal with the others. I look to Freisler and gesture up the stairs with my Honig.

'You first or me?'

'Age before beauty ...'

And so I let him go ahead.

There's no sign of them on the next two floors, which leaves the very top of the house. There's a strong smell of burning now and the street outside is full of smoke. The flames will spread to this house in a while, but for now we're safe. Besides, we can always jump.

Freisler steps out from one of the rooms and looks to me, then glances up the stairs. 'Something's wrong.'

'Wrong?'

'They're good, the Russians. Better than us, most times. But this … it's not their style. You found them too easily. And two dead with two shots. You're not usually that accurate, are you, Otto?'

It's true. He's right, and suddenly I know what I missed.

'Bobrov …' I say. 'We've a file on him, right?'

'Right.'

'But the fourth man, the other Russian, he wasn't on our files. Inge couldn't give me a likeness.'

Freisler stares at me. 'So?'

'So there are more than three of them here. And those spare horses …' I bang my hand against my forehead. 'Damn! They've switched him! They've bloody well switched him!'

But it doesn't matter. All that matters is that we get out of there at once.

'Jump!' I yell. 'Just jump!'

And even as I say it, there is a distinct click and the air begins to glow.

But I'm gone, even as the centre of Berlin erupts.

41

Hecht is waiting for us at the platform. I jump through first, Freisler a moment later. His hair is singed, his clothes steaming, but he's alive.

'Shit!' he says angrily. 'Think quicker in future!'

'What happened?' Hecht asks.

I glance at Freisler, then answer him. 'It was a trap. I followed them to Berlin, but they must have made the switch on the way. They've a team there. Six men at the very least.'

Hecht looks down. We both know we can't afford to match the Russians man for man.

'You and Freisler go,' he says. 'I'll see who else I can rustle up. If any of the others return early, I'll send them through. Where will you be?'

'Potsdam,' I say without hesitation. 'This time I want to be there when the messenger arrives.'

42

But it's not as simple as that. Every jump necessitates a careful calculation. Even when we seem at our most cavalier and jump to safety, there's always a pre-planned destination – a bolt-hole, if you like. That's how it works, and the women at the tracking screens make sure it does. They keep an eye on us. They know just where and when we are for every second of our time back there in the Past. And when we need, as now, to go to such a place and such a time, it is they who work out how to do it. With a little help from the machines.

There are a lot of factors involved, and in the early days it was very hit and miss. Agents were sent back into the sides of mountains, into mid-air, even into lakes. We lost a lot that way. But as the years have passed they have got very good at what they do.

It's not just a case of calculating how far back and to what point on the earth's surface we need to jump, there's also the fact that the planet is revolving not only about its axis, but about the sun, which is itself slowly drifting out from the centre of a slowly revolving galaxy. Everything is in constant motion, which is why our calculations have to be updated nanosecond by nanosecond to keep the Time-grid accurate. That grid registers the position of the jump platform in absolute terms. Wherever we are right now is forever zero, zero, zero, zero. Hence *Four-Oh*. And from Four-Oh every point in Time and Space has its own four-dimensional grid reference. Those references change moment by moment yet the machines keep track. If I need to go back to a certain place, they can get me there in the blink of an eye – they're that fast.

And if that seems complex enough, there's a second factor to be taken into account. Nothing inorganic can make a jump. Only living matter can be transported back and forth through time. Which means that if I don't want to find myself back there, buck naked with only my dick in my hand, I have to take back artefacts that are made of living tissue.

Again, it's no real problem. We've had centuries of doing this. The clothes I wear back there, the money I spend, even the gun I carry, are made of my own DNA – marvellous fakes that our experts spend much time and care producing from moulds they make back in the Past. What's more, the use of it makes it easier to screen who jumps back to the platform. Any Russian landing there would find himself fried in an instant.

Or so it was, until yesterday.

I go to the workshops to see Hans Luwer. He is alone in his workshop for once, none of his other selves about. Hans is our artefacts expert and has a bag of goodies waiting for me: guns and knives and bombs. And two other special items I requested. One is an ornately jewelled snuff-box, specially strengthened, the other is a copy of Fénelon's *Les Aventures de Télémaque*, in the 1699 original edition – Frederick's favourite book. Both are gifts for Old Fritz, and like all else they're made of my DNA, but you wouldn't know that, not unless you owned an electron-microscope. They look and feel quite real.

I thank him and turn to go, but he calls me back.

'Otto, would you do something for me?'

I can see this is awkward for him, and I'm not sure why.

'Of course. What is it?'

'Just a note. To a woman I met. I— the address is on it.'

I take the sealed envelope from him and slip it into my pocket. Hans has been back with me a number of times, to do his own research into coinage, clothes and the like, but this is the first I've heard of the woman.

'I thought she deserved some kind of explanation,' he says, not meeting my eyes.

I smile sadly. 'Not the truth, I hope.'

He looks up. 'Oh, no! No, I … Shit, Otto, why is it so difficult sometimes?'

I reach across and hold his arm a moment and he nods, thanking me for my understanding. Then I turn and leave, wondering how many more of us have these little secrets.

43

I am outside, further down the street, concealed in a shadowed doorway, when Dankevich emerges from the house. He looks up and down the road, then gestures for Gruber to come. I see my erstwhile friend, hunched, clearly in pain, step out, Nemtsov at his back, holding his shoulders, keeping him upright.

I could take the three of them out right now, but I want to know what else is going on. This is my patch, my little segment of history, and I don't like the fact that the Russians are here in force. If I can kill all six of them I will.

That is, if there are not yet more of them.

The fourth of them – a short, neat man with jet black hair – is the last to emerge. He looks right across at me, but I know that I'm too well hidden. Unless, of course, he's got night lenses in. It's a possibility, but then why would he not react on seeing me?

Unless that too is part of the game.

You see, nothing is ever straightforward in Time. If we both did the same old things, time and again, it would soon become predictable. And though the aim is to win – to eradicate the enemy – there is also a feeling, and I know I'm not alone in this, that the game is of itself a satisfaction, and a deep one at that.

I like to outguess them, to prove myself not only quicker and tougher, but also smarter than they are. They outnumber us three to one and they are good – Yastryeb has trained them well – but we're better. We have to be simply to survive.

I let them get some way ahead, then follow, keeping to the shadows. They are going to Taysen's, of course, to buy up the last of his horses, and I could have waited there for them, but I want to be there when they link up with the others – to see exactly what's going on.

Freisler is waiting at the Nauener-Tor, just outside the north wall of the town, among the trees. He has the horse I purchased from the captain of dragoons. If the Russians double back, he'll see that and pursue them, otherwise I'll catch up with him on the Berlin road.

Their business with Taysen takes but a moment. Nemtsov goes in alone and emerges with a big grin on his face and seven lead reins in his big right hand. Dankevich and the other go across to help him with the horses, but Gruber holds back.

I get a glimpse of his face in the light and see the pain there. But whether it's a physical thing or something deeper, some malaise of the soul, it's hard to tell, and I wonder just what made him switch. Is the blood tie really that strong? Or did they work on him with drugs and propagandist talk until he buckled to their will? If so, I didn't notice any change in him. Yet change there must have been.

Nemtsov helps Gruber into the saddle, then mounts his own horse. In a moment they are gone. I hurry after, trying not to look suspicious. But the big garrison town is quiet now and I reach the gate without incident.

Freisler is waiting for me among the trees outside the town wall, and I climb up into the saddle behind him. He tells me that the Russians have gone straight on, and so we follow at a canter, but we have barely gone two miles when Freisler slows and, half turning to me, puts a finger to his lips.

He's right. There are voices in the darkness up ahead. We jump down and, tying the horse to a tree, walk quietly, silently, towards them.

The road climbs, then dips towards a village. As we stop on the ridge, we can see, not two hundred metres away, a group of men standing in the centre of the muddy track. Two of them carry lanterns, and by their light I can make out six figures. Bobrov is one of them, and there beside him is Dankevich. The two who are holding the lanterns look vaguely familiar, but it's too distant, the light too patchy, for me to make them out properly, but that's not what worries me.

Freisler says it for me. 'Where's Gruber?' he whispers.

'He's there somewhere,' I say quietly, only half convinced. 'He must be there.'

But I can't see him. There are raised voices now – a disagreement. They're different from us in that way, too, these Russians: we know what we have to do and get on with it, but the Russians ... the Russians love to argue. As Hecht says, they've a dozen generals for every foot soldier.

Nemtsov, particularly, seems very heated. He makes an angry movement of his head, then leans in and pokes one of the newcomers in the chest. There's a moment's stunned silence and then the other draws his gun. Nemtsov laughs and turns away, as if it's of no consequence, but when he turns back there is a gun in his hand too and he fires it point blank. The Russian drops like a sack.

'What the ...?'

Freisler, for once, seems shocked, but my own thoughts are going in another direction. The Russians like to set traps. The bomb in Berlin was one, so why should this not be another, a fall-back, just in case the first one failed? Only what are we meant to believe, and how might it work to their benefit?

There are shouts, threats, another shot. Another Russian falls.

Games within games. But what if it's true? What if Nemtsov *has* just shot two of his own men? What's going on here?

I think back to the first time I pursued them down the road. There was no sign then of a scuffle. No bodies by the roadside. But then, I was a good hour or two behind them, and they would surely hide their dead among the trees.

And how does this help them in the least? If the four go to Berlin, who's Gruber with? Not with the dead men, that's for sure.

'Look!' Freisler hisses.

It's Gruber, staggering across, pleading for them to settle things. One hand clutches his chest, and even as we watch he falls to his knees and keels over.

It has its effect. The Russians stop arguing at once. Nemtsov looks about him, then gestures to the two dead men. He says something I can't catch and there are nods all round. Then, with a strange unanimity of purpose, they disappear, one after another, vanishing like soap bubbles into the air, the two corpses following a moment after.

There's a moment's strangeness. Vision swims. The air itself shimmers. And then it's gone.

Silence. The call of an owl. Freisler touches my arm. 'Come on,' he says. 'Let's take Gruber now.'

But he has barely uttered the words, when we glimpse lights among the trees up ahead and hear their laughter, coming down the road ahead of us.

A game. It's all a bloody game to them.

44

They split up outside Berlin, in Spandau, two of them heading south with Gruber, the others travelling on, to Colln and Fischerstrasse.

Freisler leaves me there and goes to report back, while I trail the southbound party. They're heading across country now and I have to stay closer than I like simply to keep in touch, but after a while they change direction,. Heading east towards Furstenwalde and Frankfurt.

Their actions surprise me. Gruber is clearly in a bad way and, unless they can operate on him soon, he's liable to die. When I catch a glimpse of him, it's like looking at a ghost, he's so pale. And his eyes ...

I can't get over how he looks. Not like a zealot at all, but like a condemned man, haunted by his betrayal. And that altercation earlier – what was that about? Was Nemtsov merely making a point, knowing that all he had to do was jump back and change events? If so, it was not how we Germans would behave.

And what were they arguing about? Whatever it was, it's settled, and Gruber – looking half-dead himself – now rides with two men I saw shot dead before my eyes not six hours past. Then again, I shot Nemtsov myself, only an hour before that.

These dead who can't stay dead, they worry me.

It's midday when they finally stop. We are still in dense woodland. I dismount and tie my horse to a tree, then go to investigate.

The two Russians – the ones Nemtsov shot – are very much alike. One is the man I first glimpsed coming out of Gruber's apartment, the other could be his twin, but for the duelling scar on his left cheek. They talk quietly, ignoring Gruber.

As for Gruber, he seems in a kind of trance. They have given him a plate of food – meat, bread and cheese – but it rests beside him on the ground, untouched. I could shoot him right now, but I hesitate. There's something in his face. And besides, I want to know what the Russians are planning. So long as they're not operating on him, I can afford to wait.

For a while I listen to them, picking up the odd word, the odd phrase. It all seems harmless enough. Chit-chat mainly. I speak Russian fluently – like a native – but theirs is heavily accented, and it gives me a clue as to where they're from. There's Mechanist jargon thrown in here and there – odd words that jar – and that's where Nemtsov was operating. So maybe these two are Nemtsov's men, and maybe he was making a point as to who was boss.

Maybe ...

I jump, then jump straight back. A moment later, Freisler appears beside me, homing in on my grid-reference.

He nods towards the Russians and mouths a word.

Now?

I shake my head and he puts away the gun. We could take them. It would be fairly easy, in fact, only I know what would happen. Kill them and the place would be swarming with Russians.

No – tell it right. The place would be swarming with Russians *right now*, merely because we intended to kill them. We would never stand a chance. They would hit us before we even knew they were there. But as it is ...

I gesture towards my left and begin to make my way back, making no sound, knowing that Freisler is behind me. Back at the horsc, I unfasten the saddle-pack, take a couple of packs of food and hand one to Freisler.

'Any news?' I ask.

'They've got Locke.'

'Is that all?'

'It's a start.'

Then there are still four loose, Gruber included.

I meet Freisler's eyes. 'Did you *see* Gruber?'

Freisler nods. 'He doesn't look a willing man.'

That's true, but I hadn't thought of it that way. Putting my food aside, I tell Freisler to stay where he is, then go back.

Gruber is exactly where I left him, only he's looking down now, staring at his feet. There's misery in his face. Not anger or a desire for vengeance, just misery. I see, and know, without a shadow of a doubt, that he is being coerced.

I go back, keeping my thoughts to myself. If I say what I'm thinking, then Freisler will want to discuss it. He always does. He's like Hecht in that; he thinks you can pick at a problem. But I trust to my back-brain. I like to let a problem stew inside my head until an answer comes.

The Russians move off after a while, and we follow, keeping some way behind them, listening to their voices drift back to us through the trees. And all the while I'm thinking about Gruber. If this isn't voluntary on his part, then precisely why is he doing it? What possible hold could they have over him? Like all our agents, Gruber's single, and as far as I know there's no one in this age. But then, that's precisely what I thought about Hans Luwer.

In fact, I'm so immersed in my thoughts that when Freisler pulls up the horse and turns to me, I'm at a loss as to why.

'What?'

And then I hear it. Silence. Not a whisper of a voice. The ancient wood seems to sleep around us.'

We jump down, and while Freisler ties up the horse, I draw my gun and crouch, searching the surrounding woodland with my eyes. It's possible they've doubled back; that they're watching us even now. The hairs on the back of my neck stiffen as I peer out into that maze of branch and leaf, craning to see some shape, some sudden movement among the trees. For a moment the sense of threat is overpowering, yet as the seconds pass and Freisler joins me, I start to think.

What would you *do, Otto? How would you handle the situation?*

Whatever they plan to do with Gruber, they need to make him theirs – to put *their* focus in his chest. To do that they need time, true – and that's what we've been obsessed with so far – but what else do they need?

Simple. A place to do it in, and the right equipment.

All along I've been assuming that they'd take shortcuts; that they'd get him to some hideaway in one of the towns and do the operation there. But why? They have had years to prepare for this.

No wonder they're playing with us. No wonder they're so relaxed about it all.

'Come on,' I say to Freisler and stand. 'It's here somewhere.'

He stares at me. 'What are you talking about?'

'Don't you understand? They're not going to a town. They're going to do it here.'

'But this is a *forest*!'

True. And what better place to hide something away? Even so, we search for the best part of an hour before we find it.

'Urd protect us!' Freisler murmurs as I come and stand beside him, looking across the clearing at it.

The place is well camouflaged. Were you not looking for it, you might take it for a rocky outcrop. Young trees have sprouted all about it, disguising its shape, but there's no doubting what it is. A bunker. The Russians have built themselves a bunker here – and for a single purpose.

'They're in there.'

Freisler looks to me and nods. 'You want to fight them?'

I smile, then shake my head, for once admiring Freisler's no-nonsense spirit, but he's not thinking straight. If I were them, I'd make sure the place was well defended, particularly when they needed it most – that is, while they were operating on Gruber. We haven't seen any yet, but I'm pretty certain there will be cameras and guns, computer-operated and primed to shoot at whatever came close. Yes, and I'd mine the surrounding area, just for good measure. Because while I was operating on Gruber, I'd not want to have one eye trained on intruders. It's a complex job, and they'll not want to botch it.

There's no point in trying to get in there. The place will be defended like a fortress. But that doesn't matter. I already know what to do.

'Come,' I say to Freisler. 'Let's get back.'

45

As Klaus and Gunner operate the digger, I set the charge and check the timer. We've come back thirty years, to May 1729 and, as I thought, there's no sign yet of the bunker. If I were them, I'd not want to leave it there too long, either, lest someone stumble on it accidentally.

It won't take long to make the bore-hole. The earth here is soft and at this time of year it yields easily to the excavator. We go down forty feet, just to make sure, then plant the charge and seal the hole. When the Russians come they'll not suspect a thing. They'll build their foundations directly over it.

Finished, we jump back to Four-Oh. Then, alone, I jump back to the clearing, this time to July 1750.

It's there, just as I guessed it'd be from the age of the young trees I'd seen growing on its slopes. Those trees are mere saplings now, dotting the bare earth that covers the bunker. I move cautiously, yet I know I won't be seen. Why? Because if I *was* then I'd not be able to do this at all. If they'd seen, they'd know, and they'd come looking for me. And so, unwatched, I make my way inside and see what they've prepared for Gruber.

Inside, there's a simple lab facility with an operating theatre and living quarters for six agents. To set this up, they'd have had to bring things through bit by bit over a number of years, and it's clear they're far from finished. There are no defences yet and the cupboards in the operating theatre are bare. But someone has been staying here. There's food in the cold-store and a change of clothes in one of the drawers.

Satisfied, I jump out of there and then instantly jump back, to two fifteen on the afternoon of 28 July 1759.

The clearing is exactly the same as I remember it. It is barely ten minutes since Freisler and I jumped out of here, though in subjective terms I have been gone the best part of four hours. I count to ten and Freisler appears beside me, shimmering out of the air like a ghost.

There's a rustling in the branches to our left and I turn abruptly, tugging my gun from my pocket, but it's a deer, a young buck. He stands there, staring across at Freisler and I from twenty paces away, his head held proudly upright, his antlers displayed. In that instant I meet his dark amber eyes and smile, even as the whole of the clearing in front of us begins to lift into the air with a tremendous roar, as if some sleeping giant has woken in the earth.

The startled deer turns and bounds away, even as the sky begins to rain earth and splintered wood. And as it does, so Freisler and I jump back.

46

Back at Four-Oh, the celebrations have begun in earnest. Finding that first bunker was the breakthrough. After that it was just a question of finding the others, then going back and blowing each of them.

Hecht is delighted with me. It was such a simple, elegant solution, and the best part of it is that the Russians probably don't know just how we hit them. What's more, they never will, for immediately it was done, we sent back agents to make small changes to each of the five time-lines, well back from the period we were dealing with.

I know what you're thinking. What difference does that make? Only that, by making those small yet subtle changes, each of the time-lines containing one of the bunkers was shunted off into an alternate branch of history. Side-lined, if you like. And now, if the Russians go back, they can't access those histories, not without discovering how we made those changes and when. And if they can't access them, they can't get at their agents, and their agents will remain dead, along with the traitors.

History is like that. Beside the great trunk of the Tree of Time lie countless other ghostly branches – the remnants of endless experiments to change and shape it. Sometimes one of those experiments works, and the ghost becomes reality – a switch is made. The sap flows elsewhere. But that doesn't happen often. You can even travel to those other worlds and see the effects of your what-ifs, but you need to be careful always to come back to the point at which you entered that otherness. Step even a foot to the side and you can be lost.

For ever.

While I'm celebrating, Urte comes up to me and, gently stroking the back of my hand, asks me if I've remembered our appointment. Although it was only this morning, her time, for me it's been a long time since I spoke to her – almost three days subjective – and I'm tired. Even so, I know my duty.

'Half an hour,' I say, and she slips away, grinning, as if I'd promised her the world. But now my mood is darker, and I wonder just how much use to her I'll be.

I stay another fifteen minutes, then get a detoxifier from Zarah. She asks me what I'm doing later, and I tell her I've an appointment with Urte, and she nods, as if it's okay, but I know Zarah is sweet on me, and I'm sad I can't reciprocate. Oh, I'll sleep with her when it's my turn to see her, but for her that's not the same, and I think I understand just what she's feeling.

Urte is waiting for me in her room. As the door hisses open and I step through, I see that she's made a real effort for tonight. There are sweet-scented candles and, in the far corner of the long, shadowy room, she's filled a bath.

I smile at her, though I feel little like smiling. Though it's my duty, I don't have to be unpleasant to her. It's just that I can't do this like I used to. It used to be ... what? Recreation, I guess you'd call it, and I used to enjoy the physical side of it, but now – since I've known Katerina – I find it very hard. Each time is a betrayal.

Urte is naked. She has a nice body, and as the door hisses shut, she slips from her bed and comes across to me, taking both my hands in hers.

'I'm glad you came,' she says, looking up into my face, and I find myself at once feeling guilty. Guilty because she clearly wants me and, try as I might, I know I don't want her. I just can't give her back all the love she seems to want to give me.

Not that this is about love. This is duty. How we maintain our bloodstock.

Urte is one of the most intelligent of our women, She's our astrophysics specialist, though what she doesn't know of higher maths and electrical engineering isn't worth knowing. In any other time or place she would be considered a Meister. A mere *Frau* she is not. But like all of us she has no choice in this. We serve the *Volk*.

She leads me across and, as I undress, she sings softly to herself, watching me all the while. Naked, I wait for her next move and, as I thought, she takes my hands again and climbs into the bath. We sit there, facing each other.

'You're a real hero, Otto. You know that?'

'Yes?'

But I don't feel like it. I feel like a man who has just killed an old friend.

She leans closer and plants a soft kiss on my chest, just beneath the hollow of my neck, then places her hands gently on my shoulders. It's pleasant, yet I have to fight the urge to pull away; to climb from the bath and run from there.

I close my eyes. 'I'm glad it's over.'

'Mmm ...' And her lips move down, her tongue now playing at my nipples. Yet if she senses my reluctance, she doesn't show it. Or maybe she thinks she can simply win me over. I am a man, after all. And in a sense she's right. I've never failed yet. I've done my duty by the *Volk*. Once a week since my eighteenth birthday I've done this, each week with a different woman. It's how, in this small community of ours, we attempt to diversify the gene pool. Just how many children I have from this is hard to tell. Hecht knows, I'm sure, but we are not allowed to. All of the children are *our* children; all of the women *our* women.

I try to think that way right now, but it's hard to. I liked Gruber, and the thought of him having died in that explosion haunts me.

I keep seeing the misery in his face, and I'm conscious that I don't know why – that I didn't even attempt to find out why.

Even so, my cock grows stiff, my body responds to her gentle ministrations.

It's late when I wake, and for a time I wonder where I am. I roll over and find that Urte's next to me, her eyes closed, her tiny, compact body on its back, her small breasts barely prominent. For a moment I am somewhere else, and the sense of loss makes me almost want to cry, only what's the point? It's no use trying to change things.

'Otto?'

Her eyes are open now. She studies me a while, unconcerned that I do not answer her.

'Otto ... why can't we women go back in Time?'

I laugh. 'You want to, then?'

She nods, her eyes never leaving mine, and I realise that this matters to her.

'Because it's dangerous.'

'The Russians send *their* women back.'

'The Russians are barbarians.'

She's silent a while, then. 'You know, sometimes I feel ... degraded.'

'What?'

'*This!*' She laughs at the reaction in my face. 'Oh, I like you well enough, Otto, and in other circumstances ...' A shivering sigh passes through her. 'It's just so unfair, being a brood-cow.'

'But ...'

Only I don't know why she's raised this right now. It's how it is. How it's always been with us. The men go out and back, the women stay at home. That's the German way of things. As for the Russians ... well, the Russians *are* barbarians. They kill each other for fun, then resurrect themselves.

151

I make to say something, but she interrupts. 'You want to fuck me again, Otto? You know, I'd rather like a child of yours.'

47

Back in my own room I try to sleep, but it's no good, there's all eternity to sleep. So I go to Zarah and she gives me something to keep me awake for a couple of days, and then I visit Hecht. And so it is that, two hours after leaving Urte's bed, I am standing on the platform once again, a knapsack on my shoulder, waiting to jump.

I am going to see Frederick, to give him the snuff-box. I have to, otherwise none of it means a thing. Frederick dying would mean a *big* change, a major re-routing of the Tree, and I can't allow that.

As I step into his tent, Frederick looks up from his map table and smiles at me.

'Ah, Otto, where have you been?' Frederick has the bluest eyes you've ever seen. They dominate his lined and careworn face and are – so I've come to learn – the absolute barometer of his mood. He is forty-seven years old, yet he looks a good ten to fifteen years older, an impression that his unkempt uniform does much to enhance. Yellow snuff stains cover his unwashed indigo blue coat – what, in his youth, he called his '*Sterbekittel*', his 'shroud'. Nowadays he never changes from it. Even at court he wears this patched and shabby uniform. Only on his mother's birthday does he take it off and wear 'mufti'.

Still smiling, he beckons me across, then stabs a finger at the hand-drawn map.

'Saltykov's in Frankfurt, and Daun is marching north to meet him. I mean to cut them, Otto, and bring each one to battle separately.'

Frederick is much smaller than me – five two to my six foot

– yet he dominates the space surrounding him. Like Urte, I think, and wonder briefly what she'd make of this, for Frederick is our hero. As much as Frederick Barbarossa, he is Germany, though if you were to say that to him he would laugh, and curse the Saxons for pigs and dogs, and tell you what a barbarous language it was. No, Frederick speaks only French, as now.

And so I answer him. 'You think they will attempt to link their forces, then?'

His eyes seek mine. 'Assuredly. Saltykov is still licking his wounds from last year's battle at Zorndorf. If what my spies say is true, the Empress Elizabeth would prefer him not to sustain a second bloody nose.'

I nod, but we both know that it is only half the story, and that Frederick's words, as ever, contain an element of bravado. Zorndorf was a terrible confrontation – as fierce as any in this bloodthirsty century – and both the Russians and the Prussians came away from it with a new respect for the ferocity of their opponents. Neither side, I know, wish to repeat the experience. Yet Frederick seems determined to force the issue.

His flute stands in one corner, propped up against a music stand. Nearby is a small shelf of books: Tacitus, Horace, Sallust and Cornelius Nepos in French translations, Rousseau, Racine, Corneille, Crebillon and Voltaire in the original. Nothing German.

This is a complex man, an icon of the Enlightenment, and a friend of that impish monkey Voltaire; a man whose private art collection includes works by Rubens and Watteau, Titian, Corregio and van Dyke. Yet he is also a king steeped in the blood of his own people, a man who has lost one hundred and twenty generals in battle, and who has been in the thick of ten of the most terrible battles of the century.

An honourable and untrustworthy man, full of contradictions.

'So how have you been?' he asks, turning from the map.

'Not too well,' I say, sticking to the tale I have invented for myself here in this time and place. 'My chest ...'

He nods sympathetically, for if Frederick understands one thing it is physical suffering. He is troubled by his teeth and has gout in both his feet. Moreover, the cold, damp weather bothers him and causes him arthritic pain in his hands and knees.

'We are plagued, you and I, Otto.'

'So we are. But there are spiritual compensations.'

I remove the knapsack from my shoulder and open it up, then hand Frederick the first of my two gifts.

He studies the leather-bound volume a moment, squinting at the binding, and then his eyes open wide with delight.

'Fénelon! His *Telemaque*! My God, Otto, where did you get hold of this? When my father destroyed my library ...' He stops, lost for words, then reaches out and holds my arm affectionately. 'Thank you, dear friend. This is indeed a valued gift.'

'And this ...' I say, and hand him the tiny gold snuff-box.

Frederick laughs. For that moment his smile and his eyes are as clear as a summer sky. 'You know me too well, old friend. Why, this is beautiful. Is it Dutch?'

'Russian,' I say, and he laughs with delight.

'Russian, eh? Then they can do more than just drink and fuck and fight?'

'Oh, sometimes ...'

And we both roar with laughter and he claps his right arm about my shoulders, even as two uniformed men step through the flap into the tent. Frederick turns to them, still grinning.

'Friedrich ... Hans ... come in ...this is my old friend, Otto. Otto Behr.'

Friedrich and Hans ... I almost want to laugh, for these are none other than Seydlitz and Zieten who, since the deaths of Keith and Winterfeldt, have become Frederick's chief advisors.

154

Seydlitz, yes, but not *that* Seydlitz. This is his historical pre-decessor, the man who, almost single-handedly, won the day at Rossbach and was subsequently promoted to the highest rank by Frederick for his valour. Seydlitz is an elegant, attractive man. Zieten, by comparison, is an amiable thug, a man who would fight you for a wager, or even for the sheer hell of it. Both stare at me now, suspicion in their eyes. They have heard of me, for sure, but this is the first time we have met.

'Is there news?' Frederick asks, releasing me, a sudden sobriety changing his whole face, giving it that cynical, trouble-plagued expression that was so often noted by observers.

And so they talk, discussing the latest news. Most of it is rumour and hearsay, dangerously inaccurate. Many of Frederick's spies, I know for a fact, are double-agents, paid by the Austrians to provide him with false information. And as they lean over the map, I realise I could surprise all three by telling them exactly where Daun and his Austrians are right now, and what instructions he carries from his Empress. But that might lead them to think *me* a spy, and so I hold my tongue, knowing that this part of it is unimportant in the greater scheme.

You might think me cold. By not saying what I know, Frederick will lose Kunersdorf and thousands of men will die who might otherwise have lived. Indeed, Kunersdorf would not happen at all – Frederick would intercept Saltykov's Russians at Gorlitz, to the north and, despite the odds, beat him. But he would die there, taken by a party of Cossacks, who would cut his throat and strip him naked before leaving him on the battlefield.

I know because I have seen it. I have stood on that terrible battlefield, the screams and shouts echoing in my ears, and watched as fate snatched away all hope, even in the hour of victory. We have tried to make that change, and each and every time it ends the same: the Prussians win, but Frederick dies. Each death the kind of death we can't undo. Only by losing at Kunersdorf, by suffering the very extreme of adversity, can Frederick, and thus Prussia, survive.

History is like that, sometimes. Things seem fated. There appears to be but a single path. Which is why the snuff-box that now rests in Frederick's pocket is so important. Yet if it *is* fated, then you might ask why I go to such lengths to get it to him. If History wants it so, then surely History will provide.

Not so. This is what we call the 'fallacy of inaction theory'. I know that Frederick will live, that the musket-ball will strike the strengthened snuff-box. That is what happened, after all. But I also know that it happened *only* because I interceded, and I know that because our experts analysed the snuff-box and saw what it was made of.

DNA. *My* DNA.

Circles, I know, but one I must complete. Inaction is not an option.

I am about to leave, to make my excuses and go, when Frederick turns and looks to me.

'Otto, you know the Russians. What do you think is in Saltykov's mind? Do you think he'll try and march on Berlin?'

This is awkward, for I know precisely what is on Saltykov's mind. Not only that, but I have seen with my own eyes his mistress Elizabeth's detailed instructions to him. She doesn't trust the Austrians – not completely – and is worried in case Daun decides not to link up with her army, but stay where he is in Gorlitz, near the Elbe. Their alliance is one of mutual suspicion, and only a joint hatred of Prussia holds it together. What's more, she is afraid – and rightly so – of extending her supply lines further than she has to. Last year's retreat from Zorndorf proved more costly than the battle, and she is loathe to repeat the experience, hence Saltykov has been warned to be cautious.

'He might,' I say. Then, pushing him – for I know I must – I add, 'Unless you prevent him.'

Frederick beams, his blue eyes shining at me. 'Exactly! And now that Finck is here, we should move at once. Word is that Loudon has crossed the Oder and joined Saltykov in Frankfurt. They have a combined force of seventy thousand to our fifty, but we'll do what we did last time – ferry our troops across the Oder north of them and establish a bridgehead. From there we can outflank them ...'

Frederick stops, looking past me, even as the sound of the commotion reaches my ears. There are raised voices, threats and curses, and then a young captain – barely twenty if he's a day – bursts into the tent and, sweeping off his hat, bows before Frederick.

Frederick strides across, his face deeply lined with concern. 'What is it, man?'

The captain glances at me, then answers. 'We have captured an intruder, your majesty. A friend of Herr Behr.'

Frederick looks to me, but I am too shocked to respond. Hecht said nothing about sending anyone else in after me.

'Otto?'

I shrug. 'I'm sorry, I—' And then I gasp, as Gruber steps into the tent, his arms held securely by two soldiers.

'Otto,' he says, his eyes pleading with me. 'Otto, you have to help me.'

48

I have them tie him to a pole, then have them leave me.

Frederick was curious, naturally, but he has known me long enough to trust me, and so did not insist on being here for the interrogation. I have explained only that Gruber was captured and, so I thought, killed. But I say no more than that. How could I? After all, it was I who killed him. Or so I thought.

I look at him now and sigh deeply. 'Hans ... what in Urd's name happened?'

He tries to look away, but his head is tightly bound and he can't turn it. There is shame in his eyes. Understandably so, for I was his friend, his *brother*, and he betrayed me.

'They're after me,' he says, his voice quiet against the noises from the camp outside. 'They took him, and now they're going to kill me.'

'Took who?'

'Adel.'

'I don't understand.'

'I have a son, Otto. A little boy. Six he is. Just like me. He—'

'And they took him, right? The Russians?'

Gruber nods.

So that was it. I can see it all at a glance. It's like Hecht said. The Russians take blood hostages. Nothing else could have turned him.

'Who was the mother?'

'A Russian.'

'You knew she was, when you slept with her?'

'No. No, I ... I fell in love, Otto. She—'

But he doesn't have to say. I know. I know all too well how it is.

'So tell me. How did you get out? We blew that place sky-high.'

Gruber almost smiles. 'So I saw. And it saved my life. I ran, you see. Tried to get away. And they came after me. They cornered me and were about to shoot me, and then the bunker blew. I knew it was you, Otto. You always were the smart one.'

But I don't want his compliments. I want to know what the Russians are up to. I'm about to ask another question when Gruber speaks again.

'I knew they'd failed. Knew it as soon as I saw you following us.'

'You saw?'

He shrugs. 'I thought I glimpsed you once. Through the trees.'

'And the others, the two Russians, they didn't know?'

'Those two!' Gruber almost spits his contempt out. 'They were brothers. Alexi and Mikhail Kondrashov. Nemtsov hated them. They were the weak links, or so he claimed. Corrupt, lazy, and they drank. More than was good for them. Nemtsov wanted them dead, but Yastryeb overruled him.'

'The argument – when Nemtsov killed them.'

Gruber's eyes meet mine for the first time, surprised. 'You saw that?' He looks away again. 'Yes, well … it seems Nemtsov was right. If they'd not fucked up you'd have never known.'

That's true. If they'd been more alert they'd have known we were trailing them, and then, perhaps, we'd never have found the bunker, and they'd have won. And I'm surprised for once, because I thought Yastryeb was better than that.

'So what now?' Gruber asks, glancing at me, trying to gauge my mood.

Again I sigh. This is hard. Much harder than the first time.

'I can't let you live, Hans. Hecht wouldn't let me. You'd always be suspect. There'd always be the chance that you were still a "sleeper", playing the long game. You talk of Yastryeb. Well, I don't believe he'd make such an elementary mistake. He's not such a fool.'

'Then what?'

'I don't know. This has a … diversionary feel. I think Yastryeb is playing a deeper game.'

Gruber is watching me. His blue eyes plead with me. 'We were friends, Otto. You could let me go. No one would know.'

I could. Only then the Russians might capture him again and we'd be back to square one.

'You see, I thought maybe I could go back. Save the boy.'

'The boy's already dead.'

I watch him deflate and wish I'd not had to say that. But it's probably true. The Russians don't tolerate indiscipline, after all, and they don't make idle threats.

I swallow, my throat suddenly dry, then draw my gun. 'I'm sorry, Hans.'

But he hasn't finished.

'I know about your woman, Otto. The one in Novgorod. Does Hecht know?'

Hecht doesn't know. At least, I don't think he does. Then again, it isn't Hecht's business. Not really.

'It's one thing taking lovers, Hans, another to betray your blood.'

'I didn't *want* to, Otto. Urd knows I love you all. But the boy ...'

And now his voice breaks and tears begin to flow. I'm moved, but I still have to kill him. It's my duty.

Yet even as I raise my gun, a cry of surprise comes from outside the tent. I turn, then hurry out, just in time to see something small and fleshy vanish from the air.

Locators! Shit!

The two guards are standing there, their rifles out before them, as if under attack, but there's an unnatural fear in their eyes. And little wonder.

I whirl about, just as another two – no three! – materialise in the air, in a circle, not a metre away from me. Each is a tiny gobbet of flesh, rounded and opaque, like a gouged eye. For a full twenty seconds they hover there, rotating slowly, giving off a hissing, crackling noise, like meat on a spit, and then, with the tiniest pop, they disappear.

Beside me the two guards moan and cross themselves, their eyes almost bulging out of their heads with fright. But those were no works of witchcraft, those were locators: the means the Russians use to test out a location before sending in a man. Those tiny, ugly gobbets of flesh are expendable. They measure air pressure, temperature, oxygen content. And if they jump into something solid, that's measured too. Send a man in without first using them, and the likelihood is that he'll die.

'Shit!'

I turn and run inside. Taking the knife from my belt, I slice through Gruber's ropes, then hand him the knife.

He stares at me as if I've gone mad.

'The Russians, Hans. The fucking Russians are coming!'

It shocks him into action. 'Here?'

'Yes, they've sent locators.'

'Shit!'

Yes, deep shit. And I know who they're after. Not me, and certainly not Gruber. They're after Frederick.

I hold Gruber's upper arms a second and look into his eyes. 'Help me, Hans. Help me save him and I'll try my damnedest to help you get the boy back.'

'But you said—'

'I know what I said. But I don't know for sure. And you don't know. And there might be a way. Shit, we'll find a way …'

And Gruber nods, and gives me the faintest smile, then turns, even as the first of the bastards comes in through the flap.

49

Frederick gets up slowly from beside the second corpse and turns to me.

'Who were they?'

'Russians,' I say. 'The ones who took Gruber.'

Frederick nods, then looks to his *Flugeladjutant*, von Gotz, who is standing just behind me. 'I don't understand. How did they get through? Did the guards see nothing?'

'They're very good,' I say quickly. 'Three of Bestuzhev's best.'

'Bestuzhev-Riumin? He's in charge of security now for the Russians?'

'No, but there's a special corps ...'

Frederick stares at me a moment, then lets out a sighing breath. 'Otto, what's happening? What aren't you telling me?'

I hesitate, then decide to tell the truth – or half of it, at least. 'They were assassins. They meant to kill you.'

He gives the briefest nod, as if he already knew, then gestures to von Gotz to take the bodies away.

We were lucky. If I hadn't stepped outside when I did, they'd have nailed us. As it is, Gruber is hurt, his left arm badly burned.

But Frederick isn't finished. 'This other matter, the manifestation. You saw it, Otto?'

I shake my head, denying it. 'I saw nothing. Nothing at all. I can only think—'

Frederick frowns. 'What?'

I laugh, as if embarrassed. 'That they were *enchanted* somehow.'

I almost said mesmerised, but Mesmer is yet to be born and hypnotism is way in the future.

'Enchanted?' Frederick laughs, amused by the idea. He is a rational man, after all. 'No matter – but I will find out who's responsible for letting the bastards through!'

'One thing,' I say, as two guards enter the tent to take away the first of the bodies. 'You should burn them.'

Frederick stares at me, surprised. '*Burn* them?'

'You didn't see what they did. In one village ...' And I shudder and look away.

Frederick nods, as if he understands, then looks to von Gotz again. 'Do as he says, Carl. Burn them.'

50

You might ask why. After all, they're dead. *They're dead and they're still here.* Normally the Russians take their bodies back. So why not this time? My guess is that they planned to wait a while, then call them back and send in live agents in their place. But not if there *are* no bodies. Not if their foci are destroyed in the flames.

No. These dead were going to stay dead. Dead for eternity.

Alone again, I laugh with relief. But it was close, and, if I know Yastryeb, he hasn't finished with us yet. No. These were only his opening gambits. It is beginning to feel like he's sounding us out, testing us, looking for our weaknesses, because he knows, just as I do, that Frederick is the key. Not Hitler, nor Peter, nor even Nevsky, but Frederick.

I walk across and stop, looking down at the dark patch of blood on the sandy ground. Something is nagging at me. Something about the whole situation.

What *was* Yastryeb up to? What did he want? When he went to sleep at night, what did he dream?

In essence, the scheme he had concocted was a simple one. He'd had five chances – five separate possibilities – of getting one of the 'turned' agents back on to the platform. Once there he could have had them jump back ... to Moscow Central. And then he'd know *precisely* where we were in Time and Space. Four-Oh would become a number – a grid reference on the Russian map, and once there ...

I laughed, astonished. So *that* was how ...

If you live with a problem day after day, year after year, eventually you stop looking for an explanation. It's how things are, and you get on with life. But for years now we have been suffering a prolonged sub-space bombardment, wondering how they knew where we were, when all the time ...

They've already done it! They've already sent an agent back to the platform. Only ...

I squeeze my eyes shut, trying to work through the logic of it.

Only why aren't we all dead?

And I laugh once more, amused by the paradox inherent in the answer.

Because I thought of it just then.

I jump back and summon Hecht. He comes to the platform and I tell him what I've been thinking, and he nods and turns to Zarah.

And he organises it there and then and sends someone back to when the bombardments first began, along with the blueprints for our defence system. And so we survive.

Put it down, once more, to the fallacy of inaction theory.

If I'd not thought of it and told Hecht, then it would never have happened. But I had to, and it did, and here we are.

I jump back, arriving only seconds after I'd left. Only Gruber is there now, inside the tent, his left arm bandaged, in a sling. He smiles then draws a gun from his waistband.

51

'Was it true, about the boy?'

Gruber nods. 'I've a dozen of the little bastards. These Russian women ...' He laughs unhealthily. 'But you know that, don't you, Otto? They're like animals in bed.'

I know nothing of the kind – only that I made a mistake. I should have killed him when I could. Oh, I could jump right now, but I need to stay and find out what's going on. If I jump, what then? Gruber stays here, armed and within striking distance of Frederick. And so I stay, to keep an eye on him.

It is the ninth of August and Kunersdorf is three days off. I can't keep awake that long, not even on what Zarah gave me, but that doesn't matter. If something doesn't happen soon, I'll have to jump back and get some help. That is, if we're not stretched too thin already.

Which sets me wondering. Is that Yastryeb's plan? To keep us busy and stretch us thin, almost to breaking point, while somewhere else, on some other part of the board, he makes the move he's been thinking of all along?

It would explain these endless subterfuges, these time-consuming distractions he has thus far thrown into our path. But one thing doesn't make sense. Why, when he sent that first 'turned' agent back to the platform, did he not also send a bomb? It wasn't difficult to do, and he could have destroyed the platform in an instant.

Yes, but we would have rebuilt it.

Maybe. But it would have bought him time. Time in which to make a dozen different moves. A dozen deadly changes to reality.

I look at Gruber thoughtfully. 'Was it you, Hans?'

'Me?'

'Who went back. To the platform.'

He laughs. 'Urd, no. That was Krauss. He's worked for them for years. His father ...'

But I know the story. Krauss's 'father' – that is, the agent Krauss believed to be his father – was abandoned in an alternate timeline. He might have been saved, only, well, it might have cost us three, maybe four agents to get him out, and there was no guarantee we could.

How simple it is, after all. But no one would have guessed. Not for a moment.

'He killed himself, you know.'

'Did he?' But Gruber seems unconcerned.

And it strikes me that he's waiting for someone. He has been told exactly what to do, and this is part of it. I look into the barrel of his gun and shake my head.

'Put it down, Hans.'

'What?'

'The gun. Put it down. You know you won't use it.'

'Won't I?'

'No. Because you'd have done it by now. Who's coming, Hans? Who wants to see me?'

The surprise in his eyes is almost comical, but I know I've guessed right.

'Nemtsov,' he says. 'He said to keep you here.'

'I see.' But the truth is, I don't. I was expecting Yastryeb himself. Perhaps to gloat and tell me it was all over. But no. It was only Nemtsov. Only the messenger boy.

'What have they promised you, Hans? What was your price?'

That riles him, but he's trained well enough not to let it show in his voice.

'I get to live.'

'You're that confident, then?'

Gruber laughs, but there's a hardness in his face now. 'You're doomed, Otto. There's just so many more of them than you, and that'll count in the end. Because they're every bit as good as you. And Yastryeb, well, Yastryeb will crush you, you'll see.'

'And that's it, is it?'

Gruber nods, and I laugh and really anger him.

'You're a fucking fool, Otto. A bloody idealist. Can't you see we can't win?'

'*We?* I thought you were *them*.'

The gun trembles, then he lowers it. And as he does, so Nemtsov shivers into being beside him.

'Herr Berr ... I've heard so much about you.'

I smile. 'I've killed you, you arsehole. In Berlin.'

166

'You think you did.'

And that might be true. After all, there's no mention in history of a nuclear explosion taking out the centre of eighteenth-century Berlin.

Nemtsov is a bear of a man, complete with a bushy black beard that seems to sprout from the base of his neck. I imagine, naked, you would not see an inch of flesh on him, only a lush dark growth of hair, like the primeval Russian forest.

'So what do you want?'

He grins and takes a letter from his pocket. It's sealed with red wax, like some ancient document. A nice touch, I think, and take it from him.

'For me?'

'No. For Hecht. It's from Yastryeb.'

'And you want me to give it to him, right?'

Nemtsov nods.

I turn the letter, then lift it to my nose and sniff. It smells old and musty, as if it's been kept in a box for a century or more.

'How can I trust you, comrade? This could be a weapon.'

'It could. But it isn't.'

'So you say.'

'Then test it. I'm sure you have ways.'

He knows we have, and he knows that I'll deliver it. But I want something more from this exchange.

'What's he like, your master?'

'What's it to you?'

'Just that I'm told he has a weakness for young girls.'

Nemtsov's eyes widen and his nostrils flare. It's true what they say about these Russians. They *are* more passionate than us. But that passion can be a weakness. It can get in the way of clear thought.

'Go fuck yourself, Herr Behr!' And there's a kind of mocking, childish sound to the way he pronounces the last two words. But sticks and stones ...

I slip the letter into my pocket, then smile at the two men facing me. 'So? Is there anything else I should know before I go back? Any other little messages you'd like me to carry with me?'

'Just this,' Nemtsov says, and glances at Gruber, a sudden gleeful look in his eyes. 'We'll see you in three days ...' And with that, both he and Gruber disappear.

I stare at the blank space in front of me, shocked. Gruber ... has gone.

'Oh shit!'

And I jump, not knowing what I'll find.

52

The place is silent. Eerily so. There's no sign of damage, but then, there doesn't have to be. The mere fact that there's no one there makes me think the worst, because there's *always* someone there, day and night, every day of the year.

I step down off the platform and look about me. Expecting what? A tiny pile of ash here, another there? But there's no sign of a struggle, no evidence that anyone's been here, except ...

That's it. The absolute silence. The lack of even the slightest tremor. The bombardment has stopped. That constant sub-level trembling has stopped. Gone is that faint pressure in the ears, the ever-present smell of oil and burned plastics, so subtle that it can only really be detected now, in its absence. The desks glow softly, the screens alive and tracking still. I walk across and look at one.

'Otto ...'

My name, uttered in that silence, is enough to make me jump

and turn. It's Hecht. He stands there by the portal, facing me, one hand extended.

'You have a message, I believe.'

I should know by now not to be surprised by anything Hecht does, but this surprises me. How could he possibly know?

'It stopped,' he says. 'Shortly after we acted. Yastryeb must have grown tired of the charade.'

I stare at him, wondering if that's really how he views it. After all, if a single one of those nano-worms had penetrated our shields, we'd all be dead.

I hand him the letter. He unseals it and unfolds it, then gives a brief laugh. 'The bastard wants us to surrender. He says we're finished.'

'Then why not finish us?'

'Precisely.' And Hecht makes a ball of the ancient paper and lets it drop. I ache to read it, to see exactly what Yastryeb has said, even to glimpse his handwriting, but I show no sign.

'Where is everyone?'

'Having a rest. It's about time, wouldn't you say?'

'But ... who's tracking our agents?'

'No one. They're back here.'

'All of them?'

Hecht nods, then gestures for me to follow. We go through, into his room. I sit across from him, cross-legged.

He's silent for a moment, contemplating something, and then he looks at me and gives that faint, enigmatic smile of his.

'You want to know what's going on, don't you?'

'It might help.'

'It might. Then again ...' He hesitates, then sits forward slightly. 'As I see it, we're at something of a stalemate. Anything we do, they undo, and anything they do, *we* undo. It's cat and mouse out there, but who's the cat and who the mouse? Or, to put it another way, Otto, we're too well matched. This thing could go on for ever.'

There's something about the way he says this that makes me curious. 'What's happened?' I ask. 'I mean, to you.'

Hecht looks at me admiringly. 'Very perceptive of you, Otto. I wondered if you'd notice.'

'Well?'

He folds his hands, then sits back again, closing his eyes. 'I met myself today. My future self.'

'Ah ...'

'Yes, ah ...'

'And what did you say to yourself?'

Hecht's eyes flick open. 'Which self would that be, Otto?'

'Your future self. What did he tell you, other than that Yastryeb was full of shit?'

Hecht laughs. 'You want to know?'

'Yes.'

You see, it isn't often that we visit our own selves. It's not encouraged. Our future selves know too much – who died and when, and who did what – and it's not always best to know that kind of thing. It's hard enough living with the rest of it, the changes and the dead who aren't dead. So future-Hecht must have had a damn good reason to visit himself. One hell of a good reason.

Hecht is smiling that smile again, which makes you think he's mocking you, but instead of telling me, he shakes his head.

'No, Otto. This once I'll keep it to myself, if it's all the same to you.'

I sigh. Maybe it's best that I don't know what's going to happen. Then again, if Hecht is alive up the line, then things are probably all right.

'I'm tired,' I say.

'Then get some sleep. Or go visit Zarah. I'm sure she'd like to see you.' And he smiles, as if he knows something that I don't.

But I don't want to see Zarah, however much she wants to see me. I want ...

To sleep. It hits me now. The drug is wearing off, much sooner than I thought it would. Maybe it's the stress – that business with the Russians – but suddenly I am dead on my feet. I stand and nod to Hecht, then turn and make my way across. But no sooner am I in my room, than I am gone, lost to the void, an atom, endlessly circling.

Endlessly, endlessly circling.

53

And wake, on my feet, a battle waging all about me, the blue coats of the Prussian grenadiers packed densely to either side, their bayonets fixed.

A sword swings wildly past my right shoulder, a flash of silver in the acrid, smoke-filled air, and I step back smartly, half-crouching, knowing that I'm in real and mortal danger.

This happens. I do have blackouts. But rarely like this.

There's no time for that, however. I have two options: to jump straight out of there or to fight.

I choose to fight.

It's scorchingly hot and the air is filled with the shouts and screams of men, the thunder of cannon fire and the whistle of musket-balls. But where we are, on the Muhl-Berge, the battle rages fiercest, cold steel deciding the issue. It is early afternoon, and the battle is barely an hour old. I know this because of where we are, among the Russian trenches, where four battalions of Frederick's finest men – his grenadiers – are causing havoc, slaughtering the demoralised Russians to a man.

I draw my sword and parry a low thrust from one of the few

Russians who has the stomach for the fight. Many are just letting themselves be bayoneted. It is sheer carnage where we are, but I know that this phase of things won't last much longer. Even as we cut our way across the great hump of the Muhl-Berg, Saltykov is redeploying his men in a new line of defence just beyond the sandy little valley called the Kuh-Grunde. From there the combined Russian and Austrian batteries will take their toll of our forces, turning potential victory into bloody defeat.

But that's to come.

The Russian falls, shot from close range by one of my fellows, and I am conscious suddenly that I am in full Prussian uniform, the rough cloth unfamiliar, but I recognise it at once as that of the thirteenth infantry regiment. I look about me and see, far to my left, his sword drawn, encouraging his troops, Major-General August Friedrich von Itzenplitz. He will die today, but right now he grins like a demon, sharing his soldier's bloodlust.

I know precisely where I am. I have walked this battlefield a dozen times or more, and even stood on the escarpment beside Frederick, watching as the battle unfolded. But this is different. Never, in all my years, have I been in the thick of the conflict.

I am dressed as a captain, and I wonder how and why. There's a gun tucked into my belt, too, a replica, made to look like a pistol from this age. And slowly, piece by piece, it comes back to me. This is Hecht's plan, not mine.

As the action begins to die down and the platoons reform, I make my way across to Itzenplitz and, saluting him, request permission to seek out Frederick and give him the news of our success. He smiles and bids me go, then calls me back to thank me for serving alongside his men. And I realise there and then that I must have volunteered for this only last night – and as I leave, making my way through the ranks, the soldiers cheer me and slap my back, like I'm a hero.

I find Frederick up on the Kleiner-Spitzberg, to the east of Kunersdorf village. Already he has made several major mistakes. His men are exhausted after their long overnight march, and the terrain is not to his advantage – there are long ponds stretching all the way along between our forces and the Russians, and now Frederick has marched his men another six miles simply to attack his enemies on their best fortified flank. Things are going badly wrong. The cavalry are arriving in dribs and drabs and the Kuh-Grunde is about to become a massive killing ground. But when I report to him, he seems elated by his early successes and keen to press his 'advantage'.

It is not my role to talk him out of it, but for once I'm tempted. I have been down there, among the dead and dying. I've seen the suffering first-hand. Many are dying of the heat and thirst, their wounds untended, their loved ones far away, unaware of their fate. And there's more to come. A whole afternoon of suffering.

Ten thousand men will die today, while another thirty thousand will carry the scars of this battle for the rest of their lives. And for what?

For a gamble. Which is all this is, after all. One mad cast of the dice against the odds. For even Frederick can see what is happening. Only he doesn't want to. He thinks sheer will and Prussian grit and *luck* will win the day. But he forgets Zorndorf. His enemy did not run that day and they will not run on this. Four hours from now it will be his troops, shocked and bloodied, who will be staggering from the field of battle, a defenceless mob, mortally afraid of being captured and transported to Siberia.

But I keep my mind to the task. It is Frederick who matters now, wrong as he is, evil as this day's work of his will prove, for without him we do not exist.

I stand close to him, watching as he gives his orders. Finck is to attack with his eight battalions from the north, struggling across the swampy ground to be slaughtered, while the Hauss battalion under von Kleist, a cultured man of letters, will be cut to ribbons by the Russian batteries, Kleist himself mortally wounded.

It is a butcher's shop, and even from this height we can hear the screams of the dying and the wounded. But worse – far worse – is to come. Frederick has yet to commit his main army. Only then will the battle turn. Only then will the true horror of things be revealed.

I stay with him as things develop, witness to his moods. Elation and despair, anger and brute frustration war in his face. News comes of Seydlitz's failure to penetrate the Russian defences, and of the bullet wound to his hand. Then, as the afternoon wears on, we learn that Major-General Puttkammer, a favourite of Frederick's, is dead, shot in the chest. All is gloom.

Late afternoon sees us up on the Muhl-Berge, Frederick encouraging his army on. But they are fleeing now, their discipline finally broken, and though Frederick attempts to make a stand with six hundred men of the Lestwitz regiment, the battle is already lost and he knows it. It's here and at this time that Frederick is in danger. One horse has already been shot out from under him, and now a second receives a musket-ball in its chest.

This is the moment. This is the reason I am here. To watch over him at this cusp in men's affairs. To ensure that he survives these coming minutes.

As the horse collapses, von Gotz rushes across to help the King from his saddle. There is no let up in the battle. The air is filled with deadly metal. Shaken, Frederick looks to me, smiling weakly, as if to reassure me, then turns, taking the reins of von Gotz's horse. He allows his *Flugeladjutant* to help him up into the saddle, then lifts his head and looks about him.

The grey horse turns, lifting its head proudly, as if it knows it now carries a king, yet even as it does, so Frederick slumps, then slides to his right, tumbling from his mount. There's a cry of despair and a dozen men come running to help. They huddle around the fallen figure of the king, and as I look down past von Gotz's shoulders at Frederick, I see with horror that there's blood on his coat.

'*Mein Gott!*'

I turn and look and there, not ten paces from me, dressed in the plain blue coats and orange waistcoats of the Diericke Fusiliers, are Nemtsov, Dankevich and Bobrov, and, just behind them, Gruber. They grin as they raise their guns once more.

And this time I jump and jump back moments earlier, Ernst at my side, Klaus over to my right, Freisler just behind the Russians.

Two hours have passed subjectively – perhaps the longest two hours of my life – spent closeted with Hecht, arguing about just how and why and *when* we'd deal with this, for there's every chance this is a trap – a way of sucking in our forces in one final, make-or-break confrontation. After all, the Russians *know* that we have to respond – that we can't let Frederick die. But anything we can do, they can do.

It's a gamble, but what else can we do?

He gives me Ernst because – well – because I *plead* with him to let me have Ernst there at that moment. Because I trust no one half as much as I trust Ernst.

And so we step from the air, four against four – even odds for once – and open fire with our replicas. No mussel-loaders these, but modern high-tech lasers, made to resemble their ancient counterparts.

Nemtsov falls, dead again, and Bobrov staggers, blinded, then topples in a heap. I glance across and see that Klaus is down, and as I look back, so Dankevich aims his weapon at me.

I watch him die, not by my hand but – with savage irony – by an ancient musket-ball which strikes him square in the temple and carries away the top half of his skull.

Breathless, I turn full circle, waiting for others to appear, but that's it – no one else is coming to this fray. Ernst is okay, and Freisler. And there, not twenty yards away, is Frederick, mounting von Gotz's pale grey horse. Safe now.

I turn back, looking for Gruber. At first I don't see him, but then I do. He's also down, lying there on his back, groaning.

I walk across to him.

Gruber stares up at me, blood and spittle on his lips. The wound to his chest is a bad one. He's been burned deeply and he's ebbing fast, but as he sees me he smiles, as if he's won.

'Here,' he mouths, and I kneel, leaning close to make out what he's saying.

'Your Katerina ...' he says, then coughs. 'And Cherdiechnost ... The Russians *know* ...'

And so he dies. But I feel a fist of ice about my heart. They *know*? Urd protect me, let it not be true!

Part Four

Katerina

'*Te spectem, suprema mihi cum venerit hora,*
Et teneam moriens deficiente manu.'
'May I be looking at you when my last hour has come,
And dying may I hold you with my weakening hand.'

– Tibullus, first century BC

54

Katerina. Let me tell you about Katerina.

The day is freezing cold, even for March in that northern latitude. Novgorod in winter *is* cold, with the wind coming off Lake Ilmen and the frozen Baltic, but this day is bitter even by its severe standards. Ice clings to my lashes and brows, and as Ernst and I make our way to the merchant's house, we pull our thick furs close about our necks and hunch forward, taking care not to slip on the snow-covered logs that constitute the main street.

Novgorod at this time – and we are speaking of 1237 Anno Domini, or Year 6746 by the old Orthodox calendar – is a sprawling metropolis of thirty thousand souls. But it is still a frontier town. Few of its buildings are made of stone. Like Moscow, it is a town built of wood, a product of the primeval forest that covers all these northern lands.

But before you get things wrong, Moscow in this Age, important as it is, is little more than a military outpost. Novgorod is the capital of the north, a thriving city-state with massive colonies between the White Lake and Lake Kubenskoe – in the *Zavoloch'e*, 'Beyond the Portage'. It was to Novgorod – or, to be pedantic, to *Gorodishche*, the old town, just to the south, known also as Holmgarthr and Nemogardas, that the Varingians, later called the *Rhos*, or *Rus*, first came a full five centuries ago, from their homelands in the Aland Islands and central Sweden. The same men who, in time, became the grand princes of Kievan Rus'.

For its time, this is a massive city. Only the cities of ancient China are larger. Twenty-five *volosti*, or districts, sprawl across both banks of the Volkhov river, each a small town in itself. We are heading for the west bank, the *Sofiyskaya storona*, or 'cathedral side' as it's known, the great square church of St Sophia, with its golden cupolas, looking out across the river to the eastern bank, the *Torgovaya Storona*, or 'Trade Side'.

This is not my first visit. For two years now I have been cultivating contacts in the town, posing as a German merchant from Lubeck. This is Ernst's project, and I am only one of four agents helping him, but Ernst confides in me, and I repay his confidence by aiding him as often as I can.

That is why I am there that day, walking at Ernst's side as we cross the narrow wooden bridge that spans the turbulent Volkhov, heading up past the onion domes of St Sophia to see the merchant.

Mikhail Razumovsky is a relatively new contact, a rich boyar with trading links in Scandinavia. Ernst met him a week ago through a mutual friend, and they got drunk together. The invitation to supper came three days back. And so it is that we struggle against the wind that whips the snow up from the logs, even as the sun begins to set.

I pause on the steep path that leads up from the river, seeing the raw beauty in the day. The sun is a low, orange circle balanced on the dark edge of the world. Beneath it, huge bars of red-gold light lay on the rooftops and on the patchwork of lakes and rivers beyond. But it is the forest that awes me most, for it stretches all the way to the horizon, covering the land so densely that the night seems to well up from its dark and endless reach.

There is no darkness like the darkness of northern Russia, and when night falls one can believe that the world is in the grip of some force far older than Man.

Two blazing torches light the wooden gateway to our host's residence. Razumovsky himself comes out to greet us, a tall man with a bushy black beard and fierce dark eyes. He embraces Ernst, slapping his back like they are the oldest of friends, then leads us across the frozen courtyard.

We are expecting a small, private meal with our host, but we are not alone. A dozen or more faces – heavily bearded, some familiar, others not – grin back at us from about the long table as we enter the room. A huge log fire blazes in one corner of the room, crackling fiercely, its smoke rushing up into the ceiling gap, yet the men still wear their heavy furs at table.

'Ernst!' one of them, a big man with an impressive bright red beard calls out. 'Come! Sit with me!'

The table is stacked high with food and wine. There's meat enough to feed a small army, let alone this gathering. This is not the 'supper' we were promised, but a feast – a *bratchina*.

I look to Razumovsky and smile. 'We have not met before, Mikhail. My name is Otto.'

And, taking off my gloves, I shake his hands firmly and then embrace him, holding him close a moment, as is their fashion.

Razumovsky grins. 'I'm glad to meet you, Otto. You speak our language well for a *Nemets*.'

'I try,' I say, then let myself be led to a place beside my host.

Ernst is deep in conversation with the big man. I don't recognise him, but Ernst clearly knows him well.

Razumovsky leans close, speaking to my ear. 'I didn't know your friend, Ernst, knew the *tysiatskii*.'

I look again, surprised. So the big man is Novgorod's military commander, second only to the *posadnik* in the civil administration of the town. The two men work with the prince to govern Novgorod and, like him, are elected by the *veche*, the council of boyars.

I look around the table, reassessing the situation. Far from being a simple supper, Razumovsky has gathered together a small yet impressive group of men. Five of them, at least, I know to be on the *veche*, and of the others, at least two are merchants of considerable wealth. I smile and nod, acknowledging each in turn, then look to Razumovsky.

It is not their way to be direct, and so I do not ask him what the purpose of the gathering is. Instead I ask a simple question. 'Your family, Mikhail ... they are in good health?'

Razumovsky grins at the question, his poor, yellowing teeth showing through his thick black beard. 'Most well, thank you, my friend. Indeed, you will meet them in a while. They would have greeted you ordinarily, but we were not sure when you would come, and besides, Masha is supervising the slaves. But here now ... here they are!'

He stands, and a moment later all about the table rise to their feet as two women enter, small trays of drinks held out before them. Heads bow respectfully, and I lower mine in accord with their custom. Yet as I raise it again, I look across and meet her eyes ...

And catch my breath, for there, before me, is such a beauty as I've never yet beheld. Her eyes are like the bluest of lakes, and yet so deep ...

And in that single, fateful moment I am lost to her. I do not even know her name, only that, in that instant, her soul has touched mine, and fused.

She looks down, blushing, even as her father goes to her and, grinning with pleasure, parades her for his fellow boyars.

I stand there, unable not to stare, conscious that if any there were to study me, they would see at once my fixed attention on her. Even so, I cannot help myself. I drink in the sight of her.

'Ernst, Otto, may I present my eldest daughter, Katerina.'

Katerina. The very word seems to glow with special meaning. Yet now I feel embarrassed. I look away, flustered, disturbed by the suddenness, the very strength of what I am feeling.

'And this,' he continues, 'is my wife, Masha.'

I look back and see how the girl is staring at me now, her eyes wide, questioning. *What has happened?* she seems to ask. *Who are you and what do you want of me?*

Yet even as our eyes make contact, she quickly looks away.

Her eyes – I speak as if she is but a pair of eyes. But it is so. Her hair is dark and lustrous, her figure the full figure of Russian womanhood. A beauty she is, without doubt, yet it is her eyes I fall in love with.

'She does you credit, Mikhail,' one of the guests – Vavilov, I think it is – cries out. 'She'll make young Oleg Alekseevich a good wife!'

Her eyes find mine. There is shock in them now and pain, the very mirror of my own, for in those brief, few seconds I have both found and lost the woman of my dreams.

'So she will!' Razumovsky crows, his self-satisfied grin seeming to mock me. 'The banns are to be read next week in St Sophia's, and the wedding will follow in the spring.'

He puts his arm about his daughter's shoulders and squeezes her to him, oblivious of her suffering. 'May they have many children!'

Goblets are raised, and all about that table a dozen bearded faces grin broadly as they robustly echo Razumovsky's hideous words.

'Many children!'

55

I can remember little else of that evening Only that my heart has been torn from me. On returning to our rooms in the Peterhof, I lock my door and refuse to talk to Ernst. He knows that something has happened, but what it is, he can only surmise. I am no lover, after all. If anything I have a reputation for being a cold fish when it comes to love. Besides, he's drunk, and far from capable of riddling it out.

'Otto … what is it?'

But how can I answer? It seems ridiculous even to me. Do I know this girl? Then how can I say I am in love with her? Besides, there are strict rules – laws more than guidelines – to which we travellers must adhere, and the most important of those is not to spill our seed anywhere in the past. Things can be complex enough without messing up the gene pool.

And if sex is forbidden, how much more so love?

I know my duty. My duty is to forget the girl and get on with things. I am not here to fall in love. I am here to help Ernst undermine the current Prince of Novgorod, Alexander Iaroslavich. But I am hurting so badly I cannot focus on my duty. All I can think of is that I have met someone, and that that someone – Katerina – seems to want me as much as I want her. To no avail. For she's to be married shortly.

I should have gone back, right then. Jumped back to the platform and confessed to Hecht. They might have treated me, erased my memory of her, perhaps, or cured me by some subtler means. Yet I do not want to be cured. It is as if some strange sickness has overtaken me. Wherever I look I see her eyes, staring back at me, as naked in their love for me as mine for her. And even when I close them, there she is.

Such nights are endless torment. Dawn finds me sitting on my bed, staring at my hands, the situation unresolved. I want to go to Razumovsky and tell him how I feel about his daughter; to throw myself at his mercy and beg him to break off the engagement and marry her to me. But the man would only take that as an insult, and then Ernst's long-worked-at schemes would be undone.

No. Directness is not an option. What then? Be sly? Pursue the girl by covert means?

I know what that would mean. It would be dangerous, for it would mean defying all that this society believes in. A young woman like her will be protected from all suitors but her future husband. Why, even to glimpse her, as I had glimpsed her, was a privilege allowed only to the few. Most of the time their women are kept well out of sight of prying males, in the Byzantine fashion, closeted away inside the *terem*, where only women are allowed to venture.

The day is barely an hour old when Ernst comes and knocks upon my door. I unlock it, then sit again.

'Otto? Are you all right?'

I look up at him, then shake my head. 'I'm not well, Ernst. I need to go back.'

Ernst sighs, then sits beside me. 'I didn't think you were. You barely touched your drink last night.'

I smile faintly. Ernst smiles back, then places his hand on my shoulder. 'Can it wait half a day? There's something I have to do, and I really do need your help.'

'I don't know ...'

'I have to see Razumovsky again. I told him that you were far more important than I'd first made out. I said that you were the representative of certain trading concerns from Utrecht, and that you could get him silver. I would have briefed you last night, only ...'

I look down. The last place I need to go this morning is Razumovksy's, for she is certain to be there.

'Okay. But I leave, once we're done?'

'Of course!' And he slaps my back, Russian-style. 'Good. Then grab your furs. It's bloody cold out there.'

56

The place looks different in the daylight. Less magical. What's more it smells, though faintly, thank Urd. These houses are all the same, an enclosed stockade with a single gateway and buildings to all four sides of the main courtyard which doubles as a rubbish dump. In summer the place would stink worse than a farmyard.

Razumovsky's steward meets us and leads us through, into the same huge room where we sat last night, only cleared now, the table against the far wall, the benches stacked away elsewhere.

I sniff the air, as if to get her scent.

It's several minutes before Razumovsky finally makes an appearance. He's in his shirtsleeves despite the cold. He looks to have been washing, for even as he greets us a servant brings in his jacket and a thick fur hat, which he pulls on.

He looks at me differently this morning, as if I have been concealing something from him. Yet he doesn't seem displeased. If anything, he's more respectful.

'I'm told,' he begins, glancing at Ernst, 'that you can get us silver.'

I meet Razumovsky's eyes – brown, not blue – then reach into the deep pocket of my furs and bring out the heavy cloth bag Ernst gave me and hand it to the merchant.

With what seems indecent haste, Razumovsky goes to the table and, untying the mouth of the bag, spills its contents out on to the surface.

Twenty tiny ingots of pure silver, each stamped with the symbol of the town of Utrecht.

He looks up at me and grins. 'If this is pure …'

'It's pure,' I say. 'Take one and test it.' I smile. 'I trust you, Mikhail.'

He nods, then slips one into the pocket of his jacket. 'Okay. But just how much silver can you get?'

'How much would you like?'

He laughs, as if I am playing with him now. Then, seeing that I'm serious, his eyes narrow. 'I need to—'

'Ask?'

'Yes.'

There's a moment's silence – the silence of mutual understanding – between us, and then he grins again and takes my arm firmly. 'I think, dear Otto, we shall become good friends.'

And, turning, he shouts into the darkness of the passageway behind. 'Oleg! Bring us more wine to celebrate!'

Turning back, he grins and nods once more. 'Such good, dear friends ...'

57

If there is one thing these Russians can do, it's drink. We pull out a bench and sit and talk and drink. And so the morning slowly passes. Yet Fate, which has thrown me back into Razumovsky's house, has one further twist for me that morning. Two hours have passed and, feeling light-headed, I stand and beg Razumovsky's excuse while I go to empty my bladder. I know the way. Twice the previous evening I had sought out the crude pit at the back of the house.

As I stand there on the wooden boards, pissing down into the hole, I think of her. No less romantic place could there be for such thoughts, yet she fills my mind, as she has done all morning. Even as Ernst, Razumovsky and I talked, I was wondering all the while just where she was in the house – whether above me or to the side, whether to my left or right – as if that knowledge were the most important thing I might possess. I had hoped – vain hope, I know – that she might stray into the room, to see her father, perhaps. Yet as the hours passed I'd grown resigned. I was to be tormented. To be this close, yet be denied the sight of her.

I button up and step out into the dark, narrow corridor, but I have not gone three paces when I hear the soft rustle of cloth behind me. I turn, my hand going to my belt to seek my knife. Yet I know who it is. I utter her name, the word the merest breath.

'*Katerina?*'

She comes close, a dark, mysterious shape in that stifling darkness, then leans yet closer and whispers in my ear.

'Don't say a word. If my father were to know …'

The smell of her is intoxicating; not perfume, but her own sweet bodily scent. I close my eyes, savouring the softness of her breath upon my neck. And then, heaven itself, her hand brushes my arm and seeks my left hand, her fingers lacing with my own.

'Tomorrow,' she whispers. 'In the marketplace after morning service. In the lane beside the cathedral.'

And saying that, she squeezes my hand and lets it go, moving back into the darkness.

I stand there a moment, as if bewitched, then put my hand to my face, smelling it, seeking even the faintest trace of her, my skin tingling from the touch of her.

Sweet Urd, I think. *Oh gods protect me!*

But it is far too late. I know now that I'll not go back.

Tomorrow. I shall be seeing her tomorrow.

58

But Ernst has other plans.

Back at our rooms, he tells me what he's arranged for that afternoon. We are to jump forward six years, to a specific date and time. There we'll make a detailed note of circumstances before returning here. It's fairly routine. We often do this, to measure just how the changes we are making are affecting history. Only this once I do not want to know, because *she* will be there. Katerina. Six years older. And I will learn just how she's filled those years.

If I dare ask.

I should have done it then. I should have told Ernst and let him solve the problem for me. No doubt he would have sent me back, taken me off the project. But I will never know. And why? Because I didn't tell him.

And so we jump back to 2999 and the platform, and then jump again, to Novgorod, but this time in the summer of 1243.

The town has barely changed, though without its winter coat it seems transformed. There is a bustle to the place, as well as a stench. Traders from Denmark and Sweden, Finland and Germany, Byzantium and the Bulgar kingdom crowd its streets, their carts piled high with the produce of a dozen different cultures: silks and spices, jewellery and furs, glass bracelets and beautiful, colourful necklaces, woollen cloth and tubs of wax, carved bone and leather goods, pottery and – most rare of all – silver; oriental *dirhams* mainly, but with a scattering of ingots from the west.

Ernst looks about him as we push through the crowd, seeking a face he knows, but there are only strangers here.

He turns to me, yelling above the noise. 'Razumovsky's!'

It's what I feared, yet at the same time I am compelled to go. I cannot stop thinking about her, not for a second. To not know what has befallen her – that's an impossibility. I *have* to know. And yet I fear it. Fear the hurt I know is in store for me.

As we climb the steep, log-lined thoroughfare, between those endless, windowless wooden houses, I imagine what I'll find. There will be children – four at least, maybe five – for that's a woman's role in this time and place. But what of her? Will her eyes still shine? Or would the drudgery of marriage have aged her – worn down her soul until the light in her was doused?

The place has barely changed. Razumovsky's sign – a red boar's head – has been carved and then painted on a rounded shield and hung beside the gate. Otherwise all is as I remember it.

Ernst bangs loudly on the gate, then turns and smiles at me.

'Next time we come, we'll see a change, eh, Otto? Razumovsky doesn't know his luck! He'll be able to pull this shit-house down and build himself a palace with what he makes from us!'

But I am only half listening. The truth is I feel sick just thinking about what lies ahead.

The gate creaks back.

'Masters?'

It is the steward, Oleg. The last six years have aged him badly, bent him like an old man. He blinks at us, then stands back, letting us pass.

'Is your master home?' Ernst asks.

'He is, merchant. If you would follow me.'

The place stinks, but no more than any other in the town. Even the prince's quarters stink at this time of the year. Yet it reminds me once more of how crude this age is, how uncivilised. And not merely its dwellings, but the people, too.

Mad. I have to be mad even to think what I am thinking at that moment. Yet I cannot stop myself. I can feel her fingers interlaced with mine, feel the soft warmth of her sweet breath on my neck, and know I am lost.

Razumovsky takes his time appearing, and when he does it's clear that he's drunk. Bleary-eyed, he stands in the far doorway, swaying slightly, staring in at us as if looking at two strangers. He gives a grunt. 'Oh, it's you. I wondered when you'd show your pasty faces.'

Ernst seems taken aback. 'Mikhail?'

But Razumovsky doesn't seem to care. He comes across and sits, kicking out at the dog that's lying under the table. It runs from him, yelping.

Razumovsky wipes his mouth, then turns, looking back at his steward. 'Oleg! Bring me a drink!'

As Oleg scuttles off, I look to Ernst. 'Maybe we should come back. When he's not ...'

'Drunk?' Razumovsky stares at me, his red eyes challenging. 'If you'd had my misfortune, you'd want to stay drunk.'

'Misfortune?' Ernst takes a step towards him, but the merchant raises his hand as if to fend him off. The drunken slur has gone from his voice. Now there's only bitterness.

'Since that arrogant bastard beat your fellows on the lake nothing has been the same. His faction rules here now. And woe to those who once opposed them. What trade I had has vanished, like the sun in winter.'

'Prince Iaroslavich?'

Razumovsky sneers. 'Nevsky, as they call him now.' He turns his head and spits. 'Curse the day his mother bore him!'

'And your daughter?' I ask.

Ernst looks to me, puzzled. It's such a non sequitur, that even I am surprised that I've asked.

Razumovsky stares at me, then shrugs. 'I do not see her, trader. Her husband ...'

I understand, or think I do. The husband is part of the triumphant faction. To mix with Razumovsky – even as his father-in-law – would not be wise, and so Razumovsky does not see his daughter.

'Does the marriage go well?'

This time Ernst glares at me. 'Otto!'

But Razumovsky laughs. 'She hates the little cunt. Why, it's said—'

He stops dead, realising he is saying far too much. But I am intrigued now.

'What is said?'

'Nothing,' he snarls, getting to his feet. 'Not a damn fucking thing! Now if you gentlemen will excuse me ...'

'Wait,' Ernst says. 'I think we can help you.'

'Help?' Again the merchant laughs, but this time there's bitterness etched deep into his face. 'The only way you could help me would be to kill that fucker ... yes, and all his men. I'm leaving here, trader. Finding some place where his word isn't the law. Vladimir, maybe. Or Kiev itself.'

'Kiev has been sacked,' I say. 'The Mongols rule there now.'

He grunts, then sits again. Reaching out, he picks up his tankard, then drains it. Wiping his beard, he looks at me again. 'You asked about my daughter, trader. Well, you could do me one favour, if you would.'

I glance at Ernst, then nod. 'Name it.'

'I would send a note to her. Her mother ...' He hesitates, awkward now. 'Her mother misses her.'

But I can see that it's not his wife but he himself who misses her.

'If you'll have her write a note, I'll do my best to deliver it.'

'Write?' Razumovksy laughs, and I realise as he does what I have said. Barely anyone can write in this Age. Why, Razumovsky himself is barely literate.

'And Katerina, your daughter, she would be able to read this note?'

Razumovsky nods exaggeratedly, beaming with pride. 'The priest taught her. Old Alexandr. He'll write the letter for me. I'll go to him now, if you'll wait.'

'We'll wait.'

As soon as Razumovsky has gone, Ernst turns on me. 'Otto, what are you doing?'

'You want information?'

'Yes, but …'

'We'll get nothing from him. But his son-in-law … He'll know what's going on. That is, if it's as Razumovsky says it is.'

'Maybe …'

'No, Ernst. Trust me. The daughter's the key.'

I am persuasive, but I am also lying. For once I do not care what's happening in Novgorod. We are there to change it, after all. No, I want one thing only: to see her again, and to find out how she is.

She hates the little cunt …

The words had almost made me laugh with joy. But I had to play this carefully. If Ernst even guessed what I was thinking …

59

Oleg Alekseevich Kravchuk meets us at his door and welcomes us like long-lost relatives. He is indeed a little man, a good head shorter than his father-in-law. What's more he has the kind of eyes that never settle. They take little sips of sight, then move on, as if fearing to let you see inside.

Shifty, I think, and know why Katerina would come to hate him.

'Come in, sit down. You gentlemen will have a cup of wine?'

Ernst looks to me, then turns and bows and smiles. He knows the game. But this once he's at a loss to know just why I'm acting thus.

I look about me, seeking some sign of her, but when someone does come, it isn't her, only a young slave girl – a Turk by the look of her – whose sultry familiarity with her master tells me all I need to know.

This is a house in turmoil; an unhappy, selfish place, the product of a small man with his small wants. And I look to Oleg Kravchuk and hate the man with a vehemence I have never felt before. If I could, I would kill him for what he's done here.

Ernst makes to speak, but I talk over him.

'Kravchuk. I need to speak to your wife.'

He stares at me, shocked and outraged. This is not how a guest behaves. But I don't give a shit. All this will change. I'll make it change. So what I say here doesn't matter. Only I do need to know. I need to see her.

'Careful what you say,' he begins, the quietness of his voice itself a threat. But I am not to be threatened by such a toad as Kravchuk.

'You heard me, Kravchuk. Bring her now!'

And I draw my gun.

Ernst makes a small noise of surprise, and takes a step towards me, but I warn him off.

'Don't interfere, Ernst!'

Yet I realise, even as I point the gun at Kravchuk, that he doesn't have any idea what I am aiming at him. He has never seen a gun and never will again, after today. And so I fire the thing, burning a dark, round hole in the floor beside his feet.

And he yelps and crosses himself, as if suddenly I've changed into an ogre. This is dark magic indeed, and he knows now he's in peril.

'Bring her!' I yell, and point the gun directly at his face. 'Have your slave girl bring her straight away.'

Ernst is shocked. 'Otto – what the fuck are you doing?'

But I ignore him. I am driven now. The madness is like a tidal bore, filling me, sweeping me along. I *have* to see her. To discover what she has become without me.

Kravchuk's eyes are out on stalks. He trembles as he gestures to the girl. She too is terrified, yet she does what she is told and, running from the room, calls out her mistress's name.

'*Ka-ter-i-na! Ka-ter-i-na!*'

I look at Ernst and see how fixedly he's watching me.

'It's fine,' I say. 'All this will be undone.'

But it's not that that's worrying him. I can almost see what's going through his head, and I know I'll have to deal with this just as soon as we get back. But right now there's only one thing that I need.

It's mad. Even *I* know it's mad. Urd help me, I hardly know the girl. Yet instinct is driving me on, as if naught else is important. She is the centre. She and she alone.

I hear her footsteps come and then she's there. Older and much larger than she was. Careworn and dowdy now. Yet when her eyes meet mine I know her. As if I have known her since the first day of eternity.

'Otto ...'

I smile at her, then raise my gun and fire, and Kravchuk falls. Dead. Dead like he's never lived. And in the silence that follows, I look at her and say the words I know I've said a hundred times to her.

'Wait for me, Katerina. You know I'll always come for you.'

And jump. Back to the platform.

60

I tell Zarah nothing, only that I have to go back: back to the moment before I first arrived. While she's making the calculations, I go to my room and quickly write two separate notes, then, pocketing one of them, return to the platform.

Zarah smiles at me. 'Are you ready, Otto?'

And then I'm there, back in Novgorod, ten minutes before Ernst and I will shimmer into being in this room.

Only now we won't. Not in this reality. For if I change but a single thing, then that strand of time in which I kill Kravchuk will be shunted off into non-existence – into a shadowy realm, inaccessible, unless I were to come and change this back again.

And why should I do that?

I go to the table in the corner, then take the note from my pocket and place it where I know I'll see it, my name boldly underscored in jet black ink.

I stare at it a moment, wondering for once if it will be enough, then jump back.

To find Ernst waiting for me on the platform. Like me, he wears thick Russian furs.

He grins and holds my arm familiarly. 'Otto … I wondered where you'd gone.'

For a moment I have the strangest feeling that there's something wrong – that there's something I've forgotten. And then I smile:

'Okay,' I say. 'Let's go fuck with Nevsky's head.'

61

The note surprises me. I read it through, twice, then hand it to Ernst. He reads it and shrugs.

'I guess you have your reasons, Otto. But it's most unusual.'

It is indeed, and I wish I knew more about what happened, but I trust myself. Kravchuk, it seems, is the key. If we can discredit him …

We go to Razumovsky's, and it's there that it happens. I fall for Razumovsky's daughter, Katerina. And find myself once more, alone in my room, staring at my hands, cursing fate for showing me the woman and then taking her from me.

Only there's the note.

I stand then walk across. I pick it up again and read it through, trying to get some clue from it, only there's nothing in the words, not even a hint. Yet I do know one thing: all of this has happened once before. And then something went wrong. Something to do with Kravchuk. Something I've been warned not to repeat.

You must stay calm, it warns, but already I'm finding that difficult. It's Kravchuk, you see. For now that I know he's to marry Katerina, I've come to hate the man. It's irrational, I know, but I can't help it.

Nor can I tell Ernst what I'm feeling.

Her eyes. For a time I see nothing but her eyes. And then I snap back to the now.

Think, Otto, think.

I need to find out all I can about Kravchuk. What he does, who he is, who he knows. Only then will I know what to do about the man.

Only I dream of her, and when I wake – Ernst hammering on the door – it's her I want to see.

We go to Razumovsky's, and we give him silver, and we sit and drink, and later, as I step out from the midden, Katerina comes to me and promises to see me the next day, in the street beside the cathedral, and my heart skips a beat at the thought of it.

Only Ernst has other plans.

We go forward six years and meet Razumovsky again. He's annoyed with us and bitter at his fate, but he directs us to Kravchuk, giving us a note to deliver to his daughter.

We're on our way there when it hits me.

I stop dead, then turn to face Ernst. 'I'm sorry. I have to go back.'

He stares at me strangely. 'Why?'

'In case I left something.'

'Another note, you mean?'

I nod. And it is possible, after all. It's how I do things. Only this business with Katerina and Kravchuk has thrown me. I'm not thinking straight.

'Go back to my room,' I say. 'I'll meet you there.' And, stepping into a side alley, I jump.

This time Hecht is there. He wants to know what's going on.

'I don't know,' I say. And it's no lie. 'But I might have left myself something.'

He comes to my room with me, and waits while I read the second note. Only this one's no more useful than the first. All it says is *'And don't take a weapon.'*

Hecht reads it and smiles. 'Brief and to the point, I'd say.'

I hand him my gun and he nods and says 'Good luck.' And I go back.

Ernst is waiting for me. Stretched out on my bed and sleeping. I wake him and tell him what I found.

'Maybe you killed him,' he says.

And we both laugh. It's preposterous, but it sets me thinking. What if I did go there and argue with Kravchuk? What if it came to blows? And what if, in the heat of the moment, I'd had to shoot him, to defend myself?

It was possible. Possible but unlikely.

Yet the note had been specific.

We set off again, to Kravchuk's, sweating in the mid-afternoon heat. Kravchuk greets us personally and ushers us through, welcoming us like long-lost relatives. He's a tiny little man, a good foot shorter than Razumovsky, and his eyes are shifty, yet he seems genuinely pleased to see us.

'Come in,' he says, 'sit down. You gentlemen will have a cup of wine?'

Ernst glances at me, then bows to Kravchuk, accepting his kind offer. Meanwhile, I look about me, seeking some sign of her, yet when someone comes, it isn't Katerina, merely a young slave girl of Turkish descent, whose familiarity with her master tells me all I need to know.

She sleeps with him. I can see it by the way his eyes linger on her too long. You might say it is *his* business what he does, yet all I can think is how hateful the little toad is, because I know instinctively that his pleasure is bought at his wife's expense. At Katerina's. This is a house in emotional turmoil; an unhappy, selfish place – the product of a small man with his small needs.

I feel the sudden impulse to challenge him in his own house, to demand to see Katerina and talk to her alone, yet even as I go to speak, Ernst beats me to it.

'I hear you're doing well, Oleg Alekseevich.'

Kravchuk smirks at that and gives a little bobbing nod of his head.

'I do all right, thank you, Herr Kollwitz. Enough to feed my wife and daughters.'

The words chill me. A tiny spike of ice is driven into my guts. *Daughters. He has daughters, then.* But what was I expecting? A wife's a chattel here. One might beat her and even kill her, and no one would interfere. At most her relatives might come knocking on Kravchuk's door, seeking compensation, but the law would do nothing. So making her do precisely what a wife was *meant* to do, and bear him children ... what was so terrible about that?

Yet the thought of him going near her drives me close to madness. I am so jealous I want to choke him with my bare hands.

'Would you prefer wine, gentlemen, or beer?'

I let Ernst answer, not trusting myself to speak, and when the girl returns I take the solid silver goblet and join Ernst in a toast to the man, stiffening my features into the rictus of a smile. But Kravchuk's attention is on Ernst.

'It's a few years now since we've been in Novgorod,' Ernst says. 'Things have changed.'

'*Changed?*' Kravchuk gives a disarming laugh. 'If you mean that things are better run than before, then that's true. Under Nevsky, the town is flourishing.'

It seems the truth. Yet we know for a fact that only a select few are benefiting from this recent upturn. For most, the burden of the Mongol tribute lies heavy. And who is it who's responsible for raising that levy? None other than Prince Alexander Iaroslavich himself – or Alexander Nevsky, as he's known. The people's hero.

'Will you stay for dinner?' Kravchuk asks. 'I have friends coming tonight. You might wish to meet them.'

Ernst looks to me, then nods. 'That is most kind, Oleg Alekseevich. We have some business to transact this afternoon, but later … yes, that would be good.'

Ernst and he shake hands, then toast again, as if the very best of friends, while I look on, longing to crush the man.

Outside, I have to stop and lean against the wall, I feel so faint.

'Otto? What's the matter?'

'It's okay,' I say, fending him off. 'It's just the heat.'

I feel as though I've walked through a furnace. My shirt is soaking wet and clings to me. Salt stings my eyes. Yet Ernst is dry as a bone.

'I can't come,' I say. 'Tonight, I—'

'You must,' he answers. 'Kravchuk's expecting us both, and we won't get a better chance to find out what's been happening here. Besides, you've a letter to deliver.'

I stare at him, shocked, then take the letter from my pocket. 'I—'

'Forgot? I know. I was wondering if you had, or whether you were just biding your time. After all, you can't just go barging in, demanding to see such a man's wife. There are ways …'

Yet that's precisely what I'd wanted.

I shake my head, then start to walk again. Away from Kravchuk's house. Away from Katerina and her daughters. And the thought of it makes me want to cry. Only I can't tell Ernst that or he'll send me home.

Tonight. What new depths of misery will tonight bring me?

62

The table's laid for a feast. There's more wealth on display than in a dozen neighbouring households. No wonder Kravchuk hires guards. And, seeing it all there, I begin to wonder just what Kravchuk's trade is, and realise that I know practically nothing about the man.

Ernst had suggested going back and finding out, but that kind of thing is risky – more risky than going forward. A few inadvertent changes and the whole picture could be different. Besides, we don't need to be so specific. We need a far more general picture of events.

As it turns out, we've met four of the guests before at Razumovsky's, all those years – those few hours? – ago. They remember us but vaguely, and that's no surprise, for in this time-line we have barely begun our work. Once again the talk is of Nevsky and the new affluence. There's no mention of the levy, or of the Mongol threat, and certainly no reference to Nevsky's part in policing the bought peace. And when I talk finally of the great victory on the ice, they seem to glow with pride at the reminder, and mock Ernst and I gently, for we are *Nemets* – Germans – after all.

Our enemies. But they do not know that. They think us friends, concerned more with coinage than with the currency of blood.

But we will humble them.

We feast and drink, the roars of laughter from the Russians like a constant gale. But for me it is an hour and more of terrible antic-ipation, until finally, when I have ceased to expect it, she steps into the room, her two infant daughters clutching her legs.

Silence falls about the table as I turn to look at her. She is older than I remember – a good deal more than six years, it seems, have passed in her face, and she has put on weight. She looks somewhat dowdy and careworn, her hair unbrushed, yet when she turns and looks at me, I know her, as if I have known her since the first day of eternity.

'Otto ...'

And she almost smiles at me. Then, abruptly, she looks down and, gathering her daughters in her skirts, makes to turn and leave the room. But I am on my feet and call to her.

'Katerina ...'

She stops, her eyes averted. Afraid of me now. Every eye but hers is on me now. But it is Kravchuk who answers me.

'Herr Behr – what is this?'

'I have a letter,' I say, looking at her, not him. 'A letter from her father.' And I hold it out towards her.

She looks up and meets my eyes again, and what I see there dismays me, for I see that he has broken her. Destroyed whatever spirit she once possessed. Even so, she looks at the letter longingly.

'Here,' I say gently. 'Take it.'

Kravchuk stands, his chair scraping back, his goblet clattering to the floor.

'Give me that!'

I swallow, then take a further step towards her, willing her to take the letter, but Kravchuk snarls at me.

'I said *give* it to me! *Now!*'

I turn and stare at him. He's trying to act big in front of his friends, but something in his voice gives him away. He wants to be stern, but there's a slight edge of hysteria to his words. And so

I slowly walk across and, giving him the slightest bow, hold the letter out for him to take.

He snatches it and rips it open, slowly mouthing the words to himself. And then he laughs and, turning to his friends, gives a mocking smile.

'The nerve! The old fool wants to meet her! Well, fuck that! He's meeting no one. Least of all my wife.'

And he crumples the note and throws it into the fire. I hear Katerina's cry of dismay, then see her begin to run towards the flames, yet even as she makes to pass his chair, he turns and lashes out, catching her about the side of the head.

My hand goes to my belt, but the gun's not there. Yet even as I take a step towards him, my arm raised, I see her get up from the floor. Her face is dark, her eyes ablaze. Someone shouts a warning, and it's only then that I see what's she's holding.

The burning log strikes Kravchuk directly in the face. He screams and falls back and as he docs, so two of his servants rush forward, pinning Katerina's arms, while another goes to help his master. But Kravchuk beats him off and, standing, pulls out his short sword.

The sharpened edge winks red in the firelight.

She struggles, pulling an arm free, then glares at her husband, defiant now. One eye of his is closed, and his hair still smoulders, but from the look in his face I can tell that all thought of pain's forgotten now. He simply wants to hurt her.

'I never loved you,' she says quietly, triumphantly almost. 'It's *him* I loved.'

And she points at me.

Ernst stares at me, astonished, but the room's in sudden turmoil. Men make to grab me and drag me down, but I pull away, even as a woman servant gathers up Katerina's daughters and takes them, kicking and screaming from the room.

Ernst jumps, his warning to me fading in the air, but I'm not going anywhere. I lash out at one of them, then duck, trying to get at him. But I'm too slow. As in a dream I see him grab her hair and tug it back, exposing her pale white throat.

'Nooooo ....'

Arms grab me, hold me, stop me moving forward.

'*Katerina!*'

But the word is barely formed when Kravchuk turns and glares at me, and draws the glistening blade across her throat.

63

I sit on the platform, my head in my hands. A crowd of women surrounds me, concern in every face. Zarah lifts my chin and looks at me, but I turn my head aside.

'Noooooo ...'

I am in agony. Somewhere, in some other universe, she is dead, her throat cut by that half-man Kravchuk, her children grieving, just as I grieve for her now.

I sit there and sob like a child, and they hold me and try to comfort me, until Hecht comes and, waving them away, sits beside me, his arm about my hunched shoulders, his soft and quiet voice speaking to my ear.

'What happened, Otto?'

The words come shuddering from me, as if on jagged strings.

'The bastard killed her.'

'Killed who?'

'Razumovsky's daughter.'

'Ernst says ...' Hecht hesitates. 'No matter. So what are you going to do?'

I know the answer. At least, I know what Hecht wants me to

say. But that's not what I'm thinking. I want to jump right back there, my gun in my belt, and burn a hole between that bastard's eyes. I want to see him fry. And I want her to live. I don't want her to die. Not in any universe. But I say what I'm expected to say.

'We go back,' I say quietly. 'Get Nevsky. Concentrate on that.'

'Good,' Hecht says. 'For a moment ...'

I meet his eyes, a question in mine.

'No matter,' he says once more. 'Focus on Nevsky. The woman ...' Hecht sighs. 'They all die, Otto. You can't prevent that.'

And I know it's true. Only I want her to live. I want it more than ...

Well, more than life itself.

I look down at my hands, knowing that I've got to go back. I've got to change it.

Yes, but how?

Tomorrow, she said. She was meeting me tomorrow, in the lane by the cathedral. I look up at Hecht and nod. 'I'll be okay,' I say. 'I just need to rest for a while.'

64

Only I hardly sleep at all. I keep seeing it – that awful, helpless look in her eyes. And I burn to make it not so. Never have I felt this urge so powerfully. But I know I must take care. Ernst is sure to have said something to Hecht, and if Hecht thinks for a moment that this might get in the way of me doing my job, then he'll pull me from the project.

And I can't allow that. I have to see her again.

So when Ernst sends a message, I take my time, as if I'm unconcerned, and when finally I get there, he looks at me quizzically.

'Otto, where have you been?'

'Sleeping,' I say. 'It was a shock, that business. I guess ...'

And then I shrug and smile. 'Hecht's right. We need to focus on Nevsky. If we can build on those contacts we've made ...'

I see the relief in Ernst's eyes, and know he's been worrying about me. Yet even as he begins to spell out the next stage of things to me, I find myself only half listening, some part of me transfixed by the thought of seeing her again.

And so we go back. To Novgorod, in the winter of 1237, and there, in the tiny lane beside the cathedral, I stand in the shadow of that great white-painted building, its golden onion domes raised high above me into the blue, as I wait for her to come.

It's bitterly cold, and I am not quite sure when the service will end, but I know that I would wait for ever just for a single glimpse of her.

You're mad, I tell myself, time and again, as I pull my furs closer about my neck and stomp my leather-booted feet, trying to keep warm. Nor do I know quite where this madness leads, only that it must have meaning. If not, then why feel such painful intensity?

I ponder that a while, as if I can make sense of it, then give it up. If Hecht is right, then everything's genetics – cell calling to cell – and all our human instincts just a means our DNA have found for propagating themselves at the expense of other 'lesser' strands. We're but the vehicle that they use.

If so, then powerful genetics are at work here, for each single cell of mine cries out for each of hers. Or so it feels.

But now the great wooden doors swing open, and slowly the congregation – the great and good of Novgorod, in their fine furs and expensive trappings – emerge from that warm, candle-lit, inner darkness out into the snow and the cold mid-morning glare.

I crane my neck, trying to get a sight of her, but it's hard to make out who is who among that fur-clad throng. But then a small group breaks off and begin to walk up the side of the cathedral, directly towards me.

I step back into the shadows, not wishing to be seen if it's not her. And it seems as if I'm right, for the small party passes me by, talking among themselves. I step forward once more, gazing down the lane towards the milling crowd, trying to make out Razumovsky, and even as I do, so I feel a hand on my shoulder and turn to find her there before me.

White fur rings her perfect face, framing the dark curls of her hair as she looks up at me from those deep blue eyes.

'*Katerina* ...'

The word's a breath, pluming in the air between us. Her eyes quiz me once more, their tiny, darting movements making me catch my breath. It's as if she sees the whole of me in that moment. And then she smiles. Such a smile as lights a thousand years.

'Who are you, Otto? What do you want?'

And I want to tell her everything. Only I know she'll think me mad. So I say what's in my head and watch her smile turn to wonder.

'I want you, Katerina. I want you for ever.'

65

We do not kiss. We barely even touch. There is that one brief moment, and then she is gone, hurrying to catch up with her maids before she's missed. Yet in that instant we are pledged to each other. For all time.

'Well?' Ernst asks, when I return to him. 'Did you make contact with him?'

'He wasn't there,' I lie, as if I'd bothered looking for the *posadnik*. 'We'll have to go to his house.'

Ernst sighs but doesn't question me. I've never lied to him before, and there would seem no reason why I should be lying now, so he accepts what I've said. Only I don't feel comfortable with it. Ernst is my closest friend, and I hate such shabby subterfuge. But what other option have I?

To give her up ...

Only that's not going to happen. I know that now. It's the only certainty I possess right now. I have no plan, no way of making her mine, only an absolute and unshakable belief in Fate. She *will* be mine. How, I do not know, but it *will* happen.

I could look, of course. See if and how and when ... or so you think. Only it isn't so. Right now she isn't mine, she's Kravchuk's. To have her I must act, must sully the timestream. To gain her I must triumph over Kravchuk. But how? How can I manage that without first killing the little weasel?

Oh, I want to kill him. How could I not, having seen him murder her? But I am not that kind of man. Or so I think. For I am learning things about myself. Things I never guessed.

Ernst and I agree to visit the *posadnik*; to knock at his gate and seek an audience with the great man. It's rather more direct than Ernst likes, but there seems no alternative. No one's offering us an introduction. Why, even Razumovsky's shy of it. And without gaining the *posadnik*'s friendship, there's no way we can get to Nevsky.

And that's the next stage of Ernst's plan.

We take expensive gifts to bribe his steward.

And so it is that we find ourselves inside his palace. A palace made of wood, of course – more fort than castle – yet with a touch of grandeur for all that, for this is a powerful man. He rules alongside the prince – both appointees of the *veche*, the council of boyars that rules Novgorod.

He greets us sullenly, never leaving his big, carved wooden

chair, as if he's little time for such as we. We are only traders, after all. And *Nemets*, too, come to that. He sees us as an unfortunate necessity. Beyond that … well, his distaste is evident in the way he looks at us, like we're the lowliest of insects. But that doesn't matter. We could buy the likes of him ten times over. That is, if we wanted to alert the Russians.

They're here. We know they are. After all, it is as much in their interests to defend Nevsky as it's in ours to bring him down. That's the nature of the game. But who their agents are and what their strategy – that we do not know.

The *posadnik* is a thin fellow of indeterminate age. His bright red beard suggests an aristocratic background – these are *Rus*, after all – yet I know for a fact that his grandfather was born a common man.

'What do you want?' he asks disdainfully.

'Forgive me, my lord,' Ernst says, bowing low, 'but these are dark, uncertain times, and—'

'*Uncertain* times?'

We have his full attention now.

'I mean, what with the horde …'

He stares at Ernst fiercely. 'We are a long way from Kiev.'

'But not from Moscow. Word is it was burned to the ground. With not a single house remaining. In such circumstances …'

The *posadnik* leans right forward in his chair and points at Ernst.

'Enough! Now state what you want or leave!'

It is blunt enough, and I almost laugh at his pomposity, only we need this man.

Ernst nods, then says it outright. 'I wish to purchase a letter of protection. From yourself, my lord. To allow us to travel to Vladimir.'

He sits back, happy now he knows what hold he has over us.

'I see. Well, you ask a lot, trader. In these times, as you say …'

But these are only words. What follows is a haggle, as common as any in the marketplace, and when we finally settle it's at a price far lower than we were prepared to pay. Ernst bows and wishes the *posadnik* health and many children, and promises to bring the silver by the following morn. In return, the *posadnik* will prepare a letter for us.

But why Vladimir? Because that's where Nevsky is right now. Beside his father, Yaroslav, who's such a popular man, his servants will poison him, a dozen years from now.

It will be another three years before Prince Alexander Iaroslavich is appointed Prince of Novgorod, but ours is the art of preparation, and right now we aim to sow the seeds of future circumstance. We must meet the man on numerous occasions, such that when we finally need to act, the prince will trust us, maybe rate us as his friends.

It is snowing as we leave the *posadnik*'s house, and the town, spread out below us, seems almost magical. I have seen many sights over many centuries, yet this, I have to say, is truly beautiful. A feast for the eyes. Or is it something else that makes me think so?

I turn to Ernst and hold his arm a moment. 'Go on back,' I say. 'There's something I need to do.'

'Otto?'

'I'll be all right,' I say. 'An hour at most.'

He nods reluctantly, then reaches out and holds my upper arm. 'Take care, Otto. This is a dangerous Age.'

Yes, and quite wonderful, I think. And I turn away and in less than twenty paces I am lost to his sight.

But then you know where I am headed. To Razumovsky's.

I reach there as the man himself is about to set out.

'Otto,' he says, 'what can I do for you, my friend?'

'It's Kravchuk.'

'Kravchuk? What of the man?'

'I'm sorry to impose like this. I mean, I know the man is to become your son-in-law, but ...'

Razumovsky stares at me oddly. 'But what?'

'It's just that I've heard things. In the taverns. And Ernst and I were about to do some business with him, and I thought ...'

'What have you heard?'

I sigh heavily, as if I hate saying what I'm about to say, then launch in. 'I'm told he's dissolute.'

Razumovsky laughs. 'Aren't all young men? But when he's married ...'

'I'm told he keeps a mistress. A Turkish woman. And that he beats her.'

Razumovsky's mouth opens then closes again. He quickly walks across and closes the door that leads out to the passageway, then comes back, standing closer to me. When he speaks again his voice is quieter than before.

'What he does is his own business. But I thank you, dear friend, for bringing it to my attention. It cannot have been easy for you.'

'I was in two minds ...'

'Yes, yes, I'm sure.'

'And so I went to the priest at St Sophia's and I told him what I knew, and he told me that if it troubled my soul so much I ought to come and see you, Mikhail.'

He nods solemnly, my mention of the priest enough to convince him now that what I've done is right.

'Well,' he says, after a moment. 'What a business, eh?'

'Only I thought you might have known ...'

He looks at me a moment, just the slightest flush of anger in his face, then shakes his head. 'You think I would have let her marry him if I'd known? What kind of man do you think I am?'

'Then what's to do?'

He sighs, then sits, putting his hands in his head, and I truly feel sorry for doing this to him.

Only it *is* true, in a way.

Kravchuk *will* be a bad husband to his daughter and he *is* dissolute.

It's just hidden by the years.

But I hate having to lie, even if it's for a good cause.

Razumovsky looks up at me, bleary-eyed. 'God help me, Otto. If this is true ...' And he stands and paces the room a moment before stopping and looking to me again.

'I guess I could buy him off, only ... well, a promise is a promise.'

'And what does she think?'

'*She?*' He laughs, then sits again. 'She's not been well. Not since the other evening. She stays in her room all the while, pacing back and forth. The only time I've seen her is when she came to church with us this morning.'

I almost smile, but that would give the game away. Instead I spin another lie.

'Maybe I can help.'

'Help? In what way, my friend?'

'I was a healer once. Back in Lubeck.'

Razumovsky stares at me, then shrugs. 'I don't know, Otto. It's just, well, what am I to do about Kravchuk? If I had known ...'

'Confront him,' I say. 'Give him a chance to clear his name. I'd say that was the fairest course, wouldn't you?'

His eyes light at that, and he stands and slaps my back. 'I shall. And I'll do it right away. Oh, and Otto – will you be here when he comes?'

'Do you think that's wise, Mikhail?'

'Who knows what's wise when it comes to such matters. But I know something. I would welcome one impartial observer at that meeting.'

66

And so it is, that evening, much to Ernst's surprise, we are at Razumovsky's again, waiting for Kravchuk to appear. Razumovsky has given him no notice of why he's summoned him, and he clearly has no idea, for when he comes he's rather too cocky, thinking himself the certain master of this house. Which is something that, in all of this, I had forgotten. When Razumovsky dies, Kravchuk will inherit. So it is in this society. And Katerina would have no say.

I watch the little bantam enter the room, see his surprise to find me there. Ernst is in one of the back rooms, drinking wine while this matter is sorted out.

Kravchuk greets me cautiously, then turns to wait for Razumovsky, staring towards the door, ignoring me.

'So what is it you do?'

He almost twitches. 'I'm sorry?'

'I am curious. You seem a prosperous man.'

He half turns, but does not quite deign to look at me. 'I do well enough,' he says.

'So I see by your furs. Silver fox, is it not?'

He smiles this time and nods. 'I have several, actually. But this, yes, this is a fine fur.'

And expensive, I think. So what *does* he do? Something he doesn't want the world to know about, perhaps?

But I do not get to question him much more, for Razumovsky appears.

'Mikhail!' Kravchuk says, going to embrace him, but Razumovsky raises a hand, and Kravchuk steps back, confused.

'Mikhail?'

'There have been rumours, Oleg Alekseevich.'

'Rumours?' And now he turns and glares at me, as if he knows whence they've come. 'Rumours of what?'

'I thought you might explain yourself. About the woman you are said to keep.'

Kravchuk looks astonished.

'Well?' Razumovsky says, his dark eyes watching the smaller man. 'Will you not deny it?'

But it seems that Kravchuk's lost his tongue. He stands there staring at Razumovsky, and I realise with a start that it's true – it's actually true! My wild surmise was right. He *has* a woman that he keeps!

I laugh and both men look to me.

'Who is this fellow?' Kravchuk asks.

'A friend,' Razumovsky says. He's watching Kravchuk closely now. 'But you've not answered me. Or perhaps you have.'

Kravchuk laughs, but it's so lacking in sincerity it falters before the sound has died. His eyes move restlessly between Razumovsky and the floor. 'You know how it is, Mikhail. A man has needs.'

But it's a poor excuse, and not one Razumovsky is about to accept. This is his daughter's honour we are talking of, and if this news gets out and she still marries him, then he, Razumovsky, will be a laughing stock. Besides, he loves his daughter. He would not let her suffer the humiliation.

'You shit! You fucking little shit!'

And, without warning, Razumovsky swings his arm and smacks the little bastard straight across the chops with his open hand. It's a stinging blow, and Kravchuk cries out and buckles instantly, clutching his face.

'The wedding's off! I'd rather you married my neighbour's pig than had a sniff of my daughter!'

But Kravchuk is backing away. 'You cunt,' he mumbles. 'I'll get you, see if I don't ...'

But Razumovsky is not listening. He aims a kick at Kravchuk's departing backside, then picks up a chair and throws it after him, even as he runs across the courtyard towards the gate.

'And don't think of coming back, you little toad!'

But Kravchuk is not coming back, and inside I feel a joy that's inexpressible. He's gone! The little bastard has gone!

67

Only he hasn't. Kravchuk *is* a weasel, after all. And, what's more, he has friends in high places. The *posadnik* for one. And when Ernst and I visit the *posadnik* the next morning, Kravchuk is there, standing beside his chair, and I know that we're in trouble.

'Are these the ones?' the *posadnik* asks.

'They are, my lord.'

'Then I shall leave this matter to you.'

And with that, the *posadnik* stands and leaves the room. Kravchuk stares at us a moment, then grins and takes the old man's seat.

'Well, well,' he says. 'Fancy us meeting again so soon.'

I'm about to walk away, when Ernst brings my attention to the letter in Kravchuk's right hand. He holds it casually, as if it's of no moment, but we both know what it is. It has the *posadnik*'s seal upon it, after all.

'And how is your friend this morning?' he asks, after a moment's silence.

'My friend?' I ask, seeing that he's addressing me.

'Yes. That loser Razumovsky. I thought, maybe, he'd have a change of mind. Send me an apology. But the man appears to have no manners.'

I stare back at him, astonished by the words, but he's not finished yet.

'I'd try and reason with him, only such a man scarcely knows what's in his best interests.'

'Best interests!' But before I can say another word, Ernst grabs my wrist in an iron grip and glares at me. I fall silent, but I cannot help but show my hatred for the little creep as I meet his eyes again.

'I see you have something we want,' Ernst says with an icy calm. 'So tell us what you want for it, and we'll tell you if you have a deal.'

Kravchuk smiles. This is more his language. In his world, anything can be bought.

'That's good,' he says, waving the letter at Ernst. 'But I warn you, this doesn't come cheap. I had to pay my old friend the *posadnik* dearly for this privilege. However, there is one unbreakable condition ...'

'Go on,' Ernst says, his expression set.

'I want Razumovsky's daughter for my wife.'

'Never!' I say, but Ernst rounds on me.

'Shut up, Otto! You've no say in this! Understand?'

And when I go to say something more, Ernst slaps his hand across my mouth, then roughly pushes me back.

Kravchuk looks from one of us to the other and then smiles. 'I'd say your friend was sweet on the girl, Herr Kollwitz.'

Ernst turns and faces him again. 'I assure you, nothing is further from the truth. My friend will do his best to help you *reconcile* things with her father ...'

'I'm glad to hear that. I thought perhaps there would be *difficulties.*'

Too fucking true, I think, but I keep my face a mask. I want to kill the bastard more than ever, but that's becoming more difficult by the moment. Ernst wants that letter of protection. Without it he can't get to Nevsky, and without getting to Nevsky his scheme will never work. I know that and ought to be working hard to help him, only I'm in the grip of a jealous rage that threatens to unhinge me. The thought of going back to her father and supplicating for this arsehole fills me with horror. Ernst will have to do it. And even then ...

My mind races, trying to think of ways out of this, but I can't think of a damn thing. Kravchuk has the letter, and he has his condition. If we don't play his game, we'll find ourselves stuck here in Novgorod.

Oh, I know what you're thinking. We could jump direct to Vladimir, and fake the letter, but in the longer term that would cause more problems than it would solve. Vladmir is four hundred miles inland, beyond Moscow, and we can't just walk out of the forest. In Novgorod it's not a problem, but in Vladimir we must be known. That letter of protection is essential. Without it, we would be cast into a pit and left to rot.

And so I hold my peace and leave it to Ernst, even as I rage inside. Kravchuk will *never* have her! But can I prevent it? Not without ruining Ernst's plans.

I groan and Kravchuk looks to me.

'Eaten something bad, my friend?'

He laughs, and I swear to myself that I will kill the man.

68

Back in my room, Ernst slams the door and faces me.

'Just what do you think you're doing, Otto? Why are you being so bloody-minded?'

I look down, wanting to tell him just what I'm suffering, but I know I can't, because then I *would* be out.

'I'm sorry, Ernst. There's just something about the man.'

'I know. But it's not like you to let it get to you.' He pauses, then laughs, more at ease for seeing me so contrite. 'For a moment there ...'

'Go on ...'

'Well, just for a moment, I thought, well, that maybe Kravchuk might have been right. That you have a, well, a *thing* about the girl.'

His hesitations are telling. He's trying now to make a joke of it, but I sense he's half-convinced that Kravchuk's right. And he has every reason to think so. But now's the perfect time to allay those fears of his.

'That's nonsense, Ernst. Why, I've met her only twice and both times were in a crowded room, remember? I doubt she even noticed me.'

'Then why ...?'

I look a query at him, but he just shrugs. I know what he's alluding to, however. If there's nothing between us, then why did she say what she did in Kravchuk's house, six years down the line? And why, if she meant nothing to me, was I so shaken up by her death?

I have to make a gesture. To prove she means nothing.

'I'll go,' I say. 'I'll talk to Razumovsky. Persuade him to have Kravchuk back as his son-in-law.'

'You'll do it now?'

I swallow. It was not what I had in mind, but I nod.

'Good. But spin him some tale, Otto. Something that will convince him that it was all a misunderstanding. Tell him you've new information. You know the kind of thing.'

I do. Yet I am loath to use my verbal skills in Kravchuk's service, especially when it means handing my soul itself into his hands.

And that's the hardest part of this. For there's really no decision to be made here. If I do what Kravchuk says, I might just as well take a knife and slit my own throat. Not to have her – for her *not* to be mine – oh, my soul, that would be hell itself.

69

Razumovsky is pulling on his furs when I get there, a black look on his face.

'What is it?' I ask, and he almost growls his answer.

'It's Kravchuk. I don't know what's he's done or said, but that little fucker's meddling in my business. I've lost more trade in a morning than I could drum up in a month!'

That fills me with foreboding. Especially as I've the task of pleading for the man.

'You're sure it's him?'

He stops and looks at me, then pulls on his right boot. 'Who the fuck else would it be? No one says it's him, of course, but what other reason can there be? I kick the fucker out of my house and *this* happens!'

Razumovsky's not stupid, nor is he mistaken. This stinks of Kravchuk. But why is he doing this if he wants to be reconciled to Razumovksy? To show his power? To bring Razumovsky to his senses? If so, he's read the man completely wrong, for even I can see that all this has done is to enrage him.

'Listen, Mikhail,' I say, as I watch him pull on his other boot then stand, preparing to leave. 'I have to talk to you.'

But Razumovsky's barely listening. 'Not now,' he says, then turns and looks at me. Relenting, he reaches across and pats my shoulder with his massive hand. 'Make yourself at home, Otto. We'll talk when I get back.'

I watch him go, then slump on to a bench, relieved as much as dismayed by this turn of events. I sit there for a long time, trying to sort things out in my head, but nothing's resolved. What's more, this business with Kravchuk grows more mysterious by the moment. I had no idea he had such influence. But Kravchuk seems to be pulling the strings, and important men are dancing to his beck and call.

I walk over to the window and, lifting the thick cloth covering, stare out into the yard. It's strangely silent in the house. Outside the morning sunlight glistens on the snow. I take a long, calming breath, then turn, hearing the soft swish of cloth.

Katerina is standing there, on the far side of the room; her dress is the purest blue, her top a brilliant carmine red, with threads of bright yellow and green and blue sewn in. Her long, dark hair is braided in the old style, tied with tiny blue ribbons, and a silver necklace of tiny carved animals hangs about her pale white neck.

She is all I remember and more. For in the sunlight from the window she seems to glow, as if lit from within, and as I step towards her now, she smiles, and her eyes, which are the windows to her soul, seem to open to me, as wide as eternity itself.

'Katerina ...'

She hushes me, then quickly steps across to where I stand. I make to speak, but she silences me with a kiss.

And such a kiss. Our mouths as they touch seem to melt, and as we embrace, my hands at her neck, her arms locked about my back, so it seems that we have always kissed this way, since the first hour of the very first day of the world. And when our lips part, there is wonder in both our eyes.

To feel her pressed against me inflames me. Never have I felt this way with a woman, and I know, as I look at her, that she wants me. She stares into my eyes and speaks, her voice the softest lilt.

'I knew you'd come.'

She sighs, and my heart is moved so much by it, that I put my fingers gently to her brow, as if to calm a child.

She smiles, and then a cloud appears. She looks at me directly. 'What's happening to us, Otto? What strange enchantment is this?'

And again I want to tell her. Tell her that I have stepped from the air itself to come to her. But the truth is stranger than any enchantment, for I am unborn these many centuries, while she, in my time, lies in the earth, long dead, her bones turned to dust.

And yet we kiss and stare and touch, as if Time itself did not exist.

Oh, this is alchemy of sorts, but no words can encompass how I feel, standing there, holding her, looking back into those eyes. And so I kiss her once again, and the kiss becomes a flame, igniting us, and our mouths, which were so soft, press now with a hard and sudden longing that we can no longer deny.

But Fate denies us yet. There is a hammering at the outer gate, then shouts and voices arguing. She breaks from me, a sudden fear in her eyes, then turns and hurries from the room. I am left there, staring at the empty doorway, willing her back in my arms, but servants are everywhere suddenly, hurrying here and there, as men invade the inner courtyard, their voices raised.

'Where is he?' someone bellows. 'Where is the murdering bastard?'

And suddenly he's there, pushing his way through, beating off the hands that seek to grab him. As Razumovsky turns and looks to me, I see there's a dagger in his hand, slicked red with blood, and I know whose blood it is.

'Mikhail! Why, in God's name? *Why?*'

But I know why. And as he casts the knife aside, I put my hand up to my chest.

And vanish from the air.

70

Hecht stretches and draws his fingers through his stubble-short silver hair, then sits forward again, looking from Ernst to me.

'I must consider this,' he says. 'For now, do nothing. Carry on with your duties here. When I've thought this through, we'll reconvene, and …'

I go to speak, to interrupt him, but he stares me into silence. I bow my head, and he continues.

'And *then* we'll make a decision.' He looks to me, a certain sympathy in his cool, grey eyes. 'I know how frustrating all of this is. But Kravchuk's an unknown quantity. He could be a Russian agent.'

'Then why don't we find that out?'

'Otto. Be patient. This is unlike you. We have time. All the time we need. But we need to think it through. We can't afford to lose another one.'

This is true. Recently the Russians have pressed us on every side. And it would be nice to turn the tables on them. But that's not what's bothering me. I need to see her; to hold her once again and kiss her. Right now, every moment spent apart from her seems a moment of purest torment. But I can't say that. I can only argue necessity. Can only twist what I know to somehow get me there again, beside her.

If this were my project it would be easy, only it's not. This is Ernst's. When it comes down to it, he calls the shots, not me. Or, in this case, Hecht. I'm a mere foot soldier.

Hecht reaches into one of his drawers and brings out a chart. He studies it a moment, then looks to me again. 'I see you're down to teach, Otto.'

'Tomorrow,' I say, frowning, wondering if, in the confusion, I've got it wrong.

He consults the chart again, then nods. 'Ah, yes. Well, you could bring the session forward if you like. Leave you more time later on to help Ernst … when we've come to a decision, that is. In fact, there are other duties you could bring forward. You might as well free up the week.'

My mouth goes dry. I know what he's referring to and, yet again, I wonder if Hecht can read my mind. It's Zarah's turn next, you see. But that's three days away.

Unless I bring it forward.

'I'll think about it,' I say. 'I—'

'Yes, Otto?'

I nod, then stand. 'I'll think about it.'

But back in my room, I find myself restless, unable to settle to anything. I ought to be working – researching my period, or preparing my lesson for later on – but I can't do anything but think of her. My body tingles, just thinking of her.

I close my eyes, knowing that she's out there, a billion separate references on the grid. I could go to the platform now and jump to her, wherever in Time she is. Only I can't. Hecht won't let me. And so I pace my room like a caged animal, until Ernst's soft *suden Deutsch* voice breaches the silence.

'Otto. Come to the Map Room. Something's happening.'

71

I stare at it in wonder, then shake my head. When did it change? And why did I feel nothing? Or did I, and have I just forgotten the moment?

For the map now is almost purest red. Red from left to right, from top to bottom. Only in one small place is it black. Berlin alone remains.

I look to Hecht for explanations, and he shrugs. 'We don't know,' he says. 'Not all of it, anyway, but it looks as if it originates in the thirteenth century – at the time of the Horde.'

Or 1240. Which is precisely where we've just come from.

It's too much of a coincidence.

'You've got to send us back,' I say, and for once Ernst agrees. But Hecht's still looking thoughtful.

'It's something we missed. Something obvious.'

Ernst shakes his head. 'We took it all into account. You know we did. Fifteen years, I spent, checking out details. This ...'

But he can't say what 'this' is. None of us can. So we are going to *have* to go back.

'I just can't see how,' Hecht says, puzzled. 'I mean, how do you stop the Horde?'

'Assassinate Genghis Khan?'

'The Russians tried,' he answers. 'We outmanoeuvred them. But even those times they succeeded, they couldn't stop what he'd set in motion. The Horde succeeds, and so keeps Russia in check for the next two hundred and forty years. Without that ...'

He stops, as if he's stumbled on to the answer, and then he sighs. 'No, I just can't see it ...'

Which leaves only one thing.

72

We are back in Novgorod, Ernst and I, in the summer of 1237. That fateful summer, before I first met her. Only we're not here to make contact with Razumovsky this time. We're here to find Kravchuk. Because that's the only factor that changed. Kravchuk died and the map went red. But why? After all, history doesn't even mention Kravchuk.

Which, for Hecht, is reason enough.

'Not everyone who shapes history leaves a mark,' Hecht said before we left. 'And maybe Kravchuk is one such.' But I can't imagine how such a weasel of a man could possibly have made such an impact.

We arrive back in May, after the thaw, and begin at once, trying to track him down. We go to his house, only it isn't. It belongs to a man named Vyshinski, who has never heard of Kravchuk. Further investigations reveal that he's not alone. Not a single person we ask has ever heard of our friend. It's like he doesn't exist.

Only he does. And he's going to marry Katerina.

We jump forward a month, to a time of heat and fires. I beg Ernst to be allowed to call on Razumovsky, but he's against the idea.

'Not until we've tracked down our man,' he says, and I'm forced to rein back. Only it's three days subjective now since I last saw her and held her in my arms, and I'm going slowly mad. Or so it feels, for I want her like my lungs want oxygen. Like ...

But there are no 'likes' in love. It is itself. Pure. Perhaps the purest force there is.

Two days later and we've located Kravchuk in an inn to the south of the city, in an area dominated by craftsmen from Kiev and Vladimir, Pereiaslavl and Riazan.

We try to be discreet, not to draw attention to our interest in him, but somehow he gets to know, and so, on our third evening in town, he comes to us.

It's late evening and we are sitting at a trestle table in the corner of the smoky, barn-like inn, when Kravchuk enters.

'Kollwitz? I hear you've been looking for me.'

Ernst is seated across from me. As I look up, Kravchuk is just behind him. Ernst turns, to find a knife at his throat.

'So? What do you want?'

His accent is strange, like he's been away for a long time and is only now getting used to speaking Russian again.

I stand. Or try to. Strong hands hold me down. And now I notice them, standing in the shadows just beyond Kravchuk. Two men in strange, oriental attire.

Mongols.

I half turn my head and see another of them – the biggest of the three – just behind me. They are his hands on my shoulders.

'I want to trade,' Ernst says, as calmly as he can. 'I hear you have goods you might wish to sell.'

'Then you heard wrong. You think me a common trader, *Nemets*?' And there's a sneer in Kravchuk's voice as well as his face. But he puts the knife away, his point made.

He sits down beside Ernst on the bench and stares at me a moment, his eyes narrowed.

'Do I know you?'

'No,' I say. 'We've never met.'

But it's not true. I *do* know him. Know him for the sadistic little slug that he is. Only there's something more to him, I realise now, and his companions are the clue. They shouldn't even be here. Not for another year, at least. But they are. So what does that mean?

'So ...' Kravchuk begins, looking from one of us to the other. 'Who gave you my name?'

'A friend,' I say, nodding to Ernst who was about to speak. 'A certain Alexander Iaroslavich.'

There's a moment's reassessment in Kravchuk's face, then he laughs and shakes his head.

'You *know* the Prince?'

I nod, but I can see that Kravchuk's not convinced. What's more, Ernst is looking at me with a puzzled expression.

I lean towards Kravchuk, lowering my voice. 'So just what is the deal?'

Kravchuk stares back at me, stone-faced. '*Deal*? Who said there was a deal?'

'But your masters ...'

There's a sudden, tense stillness about the table, and I know I've said the wrong thing. This is a secret mission, and we seem to know too much. Kravchuk stands, then draws a finger across his throat. And as he does, I jump …

73

I'm bleeding badly. There's a three-inch gash on the right side of my throat and I'm conscious that if I'd left it another second I'd be dead. Ernst is untouched but he's angry and very confused. As Urte sees to me, sealing the wound with plasflesh, he stands over me, his hands on his hips, shouting down at me.

'What the fuck were you doing, Otto? You almost got us killed!'

'The Mongols,' I say, wincing as Urte presses down on the gash. 'The little fucker's working for the Mongols!'

'I don't care who he's working for, when you're back there you shut the fuck up! It's my project and the sooner you realise that, the better!'

I stare at him, shocked, then look away. Was I *that* out of order back there?

'Look, Ernst,' I begin, 'I'm sorry, but—'

But he's not listening to my apologies; not this time.

'You're out, you understand me, Otto? *Out!* You're a bloody wild card, and I can't afford you. I don't know what the problem is, and I don't want to know, but I won't have my project endangered by you.'

Everyone's gone still around the platform, listening, and though I know I ought to leave this and take it up again when Ernst is in a better mood, I'm stupid enough to fight him there and then.

'You can't,' I say. 'You *can't.*'

'Can't I?' And he turns and makes to leave, but I call him back.

'Look, I'm sorry, Ernst. I won't do it again. Only I …'

He turns, staring back at me. 'Only what?'

Only I can't say, because then everyone will know.

'Well?' he insists.

I push Urte away, ignoring the pain in her eyes, and get to my feet.

'Nothing,' I say. 'Not a damn fucking thing!'

74

Zarah comes to me that night. It's her turn, and I've no right to send her away, but I do. I can't do it, you see. I physically can't do it. And she's so bloody understanding about it that it hurts, so much so that I almost call her back. Only that would be a mistake, the way I feel.

For the best, I think, wondering whether I'm thinking now of Zarah or of Katerina. Only I'm not convinced that it is. In fact, I'm hurting so bad that I actually contemplate going to Hecht and throwing myself at his mercy. He'll understand. Surely, he will.

Which only goes to show how deeply this madness has got into me.

Leave it be, Otto, I tell myself. *There's no future in it.*

Ironic, huh? Only it's not. Because it hurts too damn much. I need her, like the Earth needs the sun and the soil needs the rain. And if Ernst says I'm out …

That galvanises me. I decide there and then what I must do to get back in. Hecht's the key, of course. If I can prove to him just how important this is, and how vital it is that I'm involved …

Yes, but that means undermining Ernst. And Ernst's a friend. The best I have. He was with me as a child in the Garden, and later on he roomed with me when we were boys at the Academy. A dozen times and more he's saved my life. Only …

Only I don't love Ernst. I love Katerina.

It sounds callous, even to me, but I have no choice. If I'm to see her again, I must take charge. I must overrule Ernst. And so I take out a pad and begin sketching out a plan to present to Hecht.

Not that it's hard, because this is what I'm best at – what my life has been shaped to do. To evaluate and make decisions. To seek out the right events and *act*. And I'm not just good at this, I'm the best. There's no other operative – not a single agent – who can analyse circumstance the way I do and see where to act and when. Ernst doesn't even come close, so that when I go to Hecht that following morning, Ernst has not even begun to think the problem through, whereas I ...

Hecht looks up and smiles. A smile of deep satisfaction.

'This is good, Otto. This is *very* good.'

I have it all, you see. Oh, not the fine details, but the broad strokes. I can see how Kravchuk worked it, and when and who with. It's only a question now of filling in the gaps. For he is, indeed, working for the Mongols. Using Mongol silver to buy off Russia's princes. To prevent them from forming a united front against the Horde, such that when the Great Khan's armies appear on the steppes, there will be no effective opposition.

I feel almost a sense of admiration at the scheme. It's so simple, after all. Only there's one big problem. For it to work, Kravchuk has to live. And every atom of my being cries out to kill the little toad.

But we'll cross that bridge when we get to it.

I'm down to teach that morning. It's a small class of six students, cadets in their late teens, and the subject's one of my favourites, identifying the patterns of history, but halfway through I find myself preoccupied and, rather than cheat them, I decide to involve them in my problem.

'Okay,' I say, looking about me at their eager faces. 'Let me float a hypothetical at you. What if, when the Horde invaded Kievan Rus' in the thirteenth century, the Rus' had been prepared for them? What if, when Batu's army had attacked Riazan in the winter of 1237, the other princes had rallied to Riazan's aid? What if they had defeated Batu outside Riazan and thrown him back across the steppes?'

Six hands go up. I choose a slender, blond-haired boy to the right of the group.

'Yes, Muller.'

The young man hesitates, getting things clear in his head, then begins: 'In the short term, things would have been very different. The Suzdalian reinforcements would not have been destroyed, and so Moscow and Vladimir would not have fallen to the invaders. Suzdal and Pereislavl would not have been besieged and there would have been no defeat of the depleted Russian armies at the Sit River in March the following year.'

'Good. So you're saying that from that first failure, all the rest follows?'

'Yes, sir.'

'That there would, in effect, have been no Mongol campaign that winter of 1237–38?'

'Yes, sir. It's clear – at least, from the historical record – that they reacted much too slowly to the threat and grossly underestimated the size of the Mongol army that was facing them. They clearly thought that the Mongols were merely another raiding party, like the Polovtsy, who they'd been fighting for the previous two centuries.'

I smile. 'And in the longer term?'

Muller shrugs. 'I think they would have crushed the Russians. Come back in greater force and finished off the job.'

'So you might think. But let's widen the net a little, and see what else was going on. The initial success of the Mongols in destroying the major power in the region allowed them to concentrate, for the rest of 1238, on subduing all of the minor powers. The

Polovtsy, the Circassians, the Ossetians of the northern Caucasus, and – perhaps most important of all – the Mordva and the Bulgars, who rebelled against their rule that year. You see, victory over Kievan Rus' – even as partial a victory as they attained – allowed them to consolidate at little cost. And when, two years later, they turned against Kiev itself, Rus' was so weak by then that, when the Mongols laid siege to Kiev, the Grand Prince abandoned his own people, and left them to their fate. If the princes had worked together …'

A hand goes up.

'Yes, Alpers?'

Alpers is a big, well-rounded boy with fine dark hair. His grey-blue eyes look puzzled as he speaks.

'Forgive me, sir. I understand what you're trying to say, but surely that's exactly the point. Even when the Rus' princes worked together, they failed. And would it really have mattered much if their conquest had been delayed a year or two? In the end it would all have worked out much the same.'

Again I smile. They've learned their lessons well, these young men. But like me, they've been making far too many assumptions in this one regard.

'I take your point, Alpers, but for once I want to challenge that. A question for you all. How long did that first Mongol invasion last?'

Haller's hand shoots up first and I point to him. 'Five years, sir.'

'And why did it cease?'

I point to Kubhart, who shrugs, so I ask Haller again.

'Because the great khan, Ogedei, died. And Batu had to return to attend the *khuriltai* in Central Asia to appoint his successor.'

'Good. So we might ask, how did the Mongols succeed? Was it purely, as is usually argued, because of brute force and superior military technique, or were there other, crucial factors involved?

We might note, for a start, that the Mongols did not campaign at all during the period of the thaw. Their campaigns were mainly winter ones, when they could ride across frozen rivers and ignore those natural barriers that, at other times of the year, would have held back their advance. And the most crucial of all their winter campaigns was the first, not only because it allowed them to create a power base in the Caucasus, but because it also instilled in the minds of their enemies the myth of their invincibility. There's no doubt that, in attacking Kievan Rus', the Mongols overstretched themselves considerably. Why, one only has to look at the failure of their campaigns against Poland and Hungary to see that their expansion was unsustainable. And so, I feel, it might have been in Rus' itself, had the princes cooperated, instead of bickering among themselves.'

Alpers raises his hand again, and I nod to him.

'But the fact is, sir, that they did, and the Russian cities fell, one by one, to the Horde. Even if they'd been delayed a year, it wouldn't have mattered much. They were far too strong for the Rus'.'

Or too clever.

But I'm suddenly convinced. More than when I visited Hecht earlier. Kravchuk is the key. His bribes, his influence, are crucial to the Mongol victory. By buying advisors and sowing the seeds of doubt, he's done as much as any Mongol army in the field. And it is our job to aid him, because if we don't . . .

I spell it out for them. The failure of the Horde, the great empire of the Khans falling apart in the space of eleven bleak years as internecine warfare rips it asunder, its demise as spectacular as its expansion under Genghis Khan. And into the vacuum steps a new, regenerated Rus', under a vigorous young ruler, Alexander Iaroslavich. No longer 'Nevsky', but 'the Great', a heroic leader whose forces cross the great plains of Asia and conquer China.

They laugh, as if I'm playing with them, but for once this is no jest. This is what has happened. It is history now, not hypothesis.

Unless we change it back.

I end the class, then spend the next three hours reading in the main library. Every book is different now, yet everything I read is familiar somehow. So it is sometimes. For this change is far from set, and the memory of what was is still strong in all of us. Thus it is that I notice the omissions. Under Alexander, Rus' grows strong, and his seed – the Riurikid dynasty – thrive in their new conditions, extending all the way into the current age, not ending in 1598 with the death of Ivan's son, Fyodor. There is no Peter, no Catherine, no Lenin and no Stalin, for all's transformed.

Minute by minute it grows stronger. Minute by minute *what is* takes hold, and *what was* slips from us. Yet we retain enough to know what we must do.

Hecht is waiting at the platform next to Ernst. Ernst can barely look at me, but that no longer matters. What matters is that we act and act quickly. And so we jump. Back to the moment before I went to visit Razumovsky. There, I meet myself in the snow-covered street and tell myself to go back to the room with Ernst and wait, while I walk on, answering destiny's call.

And so the circle's broken. For once there, I argue with Razumovsky, and keep him in the room, persuading him not to go and confront his enemy. And so Kravchuk lives and history's re-made.

Except I want him dead. Dead so he can't come back.

Or is there another way?

Razumovsky's daughter is there, above me in that house. And if he'd left, she would have come to me and kissed me. But that's all changed now. Now we have never kissed. And I ache to kiss her. Ache to have her in my arms. And so I offer him a deal. I'll recompense him whatever Kravchuk's cost him – ten times more, if need be – only there's one condition: his daughter's hand in marriage.

He stares at me, as if I've suddenly changed shape. 'Is this what it was about, Otto? Is this why you told me what you told me?'

I want to tell him the truth, even if it costs me, but I know I can't. This man is proud enough to kill, and I'm not so good a friend that he'll forgive me. And so I lie.

'Think, Mikhail,' I say, standing over him. 'Think what this will have done to her reputation. To cast off such a suitor as Kravchuk ... she'll not find it easy to find another, will she?'

It's a truth he finds unpallatable. 'Maybe so, but what are you, Otto? A *Nemets*. A mere trader. You could not pass for Russian even if you tried. And half the year you'd be away ...'

'And she could live here, with you.'

I see he likes the idea. Even so, he's far from convinced.

'You have no house, no servants ...'

'Then I'll make one, and buy some. I'm rich enough.'

'And bold.' But he looks aside, despair on his face, not joy. In a day he has gone from being a useful member of his community to becoming a pariah, and whatever I offer doesn't help change that. Unless ...

'Mikhail ... what if we were to become partners?'

He looks up sharply. 'How's that?'

'Trading partners. I have the goods, you know the markets. You see, I am limited by the Prince's decree as to where I travel. But you, you have no such restrictions. You could travel to Vladimir or Kiev itself. They say you can charge three times what they'll pay here in Novgorod.'

He nods, knowing the truth of it. 'And what of your compatriot?'

'Kollwitz? He'll do as I say.'

But I can see, even as I say it, how much Ernst will rail against this. He'll see it as another erosion of his authority. And rightly so. But I can't pull out. Not now. Because I can see that Razumovsky's half-convinced. If his business here has fallen apart, he's as well off trying some other avenue of trade.

'Well?' I ask.

'All right!' he says, and standing, grins at me. He takes my hands, then pulls me closer, embracing me in the Russian fashion. 'All right! Let's seal it with a drink!'

And my heart exults, for she's mine. Katerina is mine.

75

Hecht stares at me then shakes his head. 'I'm sorry, Otto, but Ernst is right. We can't afford to get involved with this man, Razumovsky. It's Kravchuk we need to focus on. We need to keep the man sweet. And we really need to keep things quiet. So I'm sending Ernst back to change things again. He'll meet with Razumovsky alone and this time he'll say nothing about Kravchuk. We'll let things take their course, okay?'

'And Nevsky?'

Hecht looks to Ernst, who seems suddenly deflated. 'I've decided to put that scheme on hold. Nevsky seems to be an important figure in this other matter. If we undermine him, who knows what other damage we might do. No? We need to find out a good deal more about Kravchuk and his activities before we return to that.'

I keep the disappointment from my face. In fact, it's only when I get back to my room that it hits me. They're going to leave things as they are. Which means that Kravchuk will marry Katerina. And he'll father children by her, whereas I ... I won't even get to meet her.

The thought of it destroys me. I lie on my bed all afternoon, unable to raise myself. It's as if I've died, only if I'd died there'd not be this pain. And it doesn't cease. The torment is endless. Until, eventually, I can take it no longer and I get up and go to the gym and spend an hour pushing myself to my limits.

Evening finds me in Kurtz's Bar in the recreation area. There's a dozen or more people scattered about the place, but no one I'd call a friend. Besides, there's something about my body language that discourages them from coming across.

I'm on my fifth whisky when Urte comes and sits with me.

'Hi,' she says.

'Hi.' But I can't even force a smile, and she sees that.

'You want to talk?'

I stare back at her coolly. 'No.'

'You sure?'

'Completely sure.'

'Only I ...'

I wait, and eventually she finishes the sentence.

'Only I couldn't help noticing what's been happening.'

'And what *has* been happening?'

She looks down. I've already done enough to rebuff her, but she's sticking it out, and I realise that she must like me a lot. Not that it matters. Not that anything matters right now.

She reaches out and touches the scar at my neck. It's almost healed, but it's still tender.

'It's the only one that shows.'

'What?'

She smiles sadly. 'Look at you, Otto. You're a classic, you know that? Walking wounded. A bullet to the heart, endlessly repeated.'

My mouth is suddenly dry. I go to speak, but she shakes her head, then turns and orders two more whiskies. Doubles.

We end up in bed, of course. Where else is there to end? But it's not for sex. No. I let her comfort me. I let her hold me while I cry, never saying a word, never explaining a thing. Only she knows, I'm sure. Or guesses. And when I wake, she's gone. Only there's a note beside my bed and the lingering smell of her perfume in the air.

'*Otto*,' it reads, '*follow your heart. Love Urte.*'

76

For the next two days I try to keep myself busy, catching up on my work, but my heart's not in it. People leave me alone, like they know something's wrong. I send in a request to go back and visit Frederick, but my note comes back stamped 'REFUSED', and no explanation. I know I need a break, maybe even a mind-clean, but the thought of losing her – even the little I have – fills me with dread. This is indeed a form of madness, for I would rather have the memory of her – torment that it is – than nothing.

And so I persevere, into a third day. A day of reckoning.

77

It begins as any other day. I wake from dreams of her and roll on to my back and groan. For a while I lie there, my eyes closed, listening to the silence. And then I sense it. Something's changed. Something's happened in the past, and everything is different again.

I go to see Hecht, only he's not there. At the platform they don't seem to know where he is, but then, suddenly, he's there, jumped back from who knows where, his hair smoking, his clothes on fire.

I help put him out, then stand there, waiting for him to say something, but all he says is: 'Briefing. My room. Now.'

'What's happened?' I ask, before he can say a word. 'I felt the change.'

His eyes widen. 'Did you?' And he sits. For a time he's silent, thinking some problem through, and then he looks at me, his mind made up.

'I want you to go back, Otto. To Novgorod. Ernst is missing. I think he may be dead. He was ... *compromised*.'

I wait, and Hecht explains.

'You were right, Otto. Kravchuk *is* an agent for the Mongols. And Nevsky's definitely on his payroll. But something else is happening. I think Yastryeb has made a move.'

'And Ernst?'

'We lost contact with him, and when we activated his focus, nothing happened. He didn't come back. That's why I went in, to see if I could find him. I jumped to his last known location, but he wasn't there.'

'How long was he in there?'

'Two months subjective.'

'And what do we know?'

Hecht spells it out. Ernst jumped back twice, to report on things. On the second occasion, Hecht felt he seemed nervous, but as Ernst made no reference to any threat, he let it pass. What he'd learned confirmed our suspicions. Kravchuk was one of a network of Mongol agents sent in before the invasion. Each carried letters from the Great Khan, offering generous terms should the recipient prince come to an agreement with the Khan. But those letters were to be handed over only once other, more covert negotiations had been concluded. They were to 'sound out' all of the princes of the ruling Riurikid dynasty and certain princes – those who it was felt would be willing to listen to the Great Khan's inducements – would then be targeted. Each agent was given the means to 'buy' whoever they needed to gain access to those princes. Kravchuk's target was 'Nevsky'.

'So what's Yastryeb's involvement?'

'I don't know. But they've agents there. Ernst saw one of them. A fellow named Alekhin.'

'I don't know him.'

'No. But it seems he's an expert on that period. A big, heavily bearded man. Fits in perfectly with his surroundings. The interesting thing, however, is where Ernst saw him.'

'Go on.'

'He was in Nevsky's entourage. Part of his *druzhina*, his comrades-in-arms.'

I take in the significance of that. To get that close to Nevsky means he would have had to have stayed *in situ* for a long, long time. Years, maybe even tens of years.

'A bodyguard, you think?'

'Maybe. And maybe not the only one. Ernst was going to try to find out.'

'Do you think they know about Kravchuk?'

Hecht shrugs. 'I don't know, but I'd guess no. If they knew, they'd have had him killed, don't you think?'

It's what I'd do if I were them.

'And the fire?'

I indicate his charred clothes, and he nods. 'When I couldn't find Ernst, I went back to your rooms. I was only in there five minutes when the whole place went up.'

'Yastryeb?'

'Who else? Unless someone's invented the grenade four centuries early.'

'So how did they know you were there?'

Hecht smiles, and it's like the sun on a winter's day. 'That's what I want you to find out, Otto. That's why you're going back.'

78

Back again, to the summer of 1237.

I arrive at the town gates, a heavy pack on my shoulders, and pay the toll. Inside, I make my way quickly through the packed streets, the mid-morning sun making me sweat beneath the rough clothes I'm wearing. Hecht has told me to find a room, then seek out Kravchuk. He wants me to be Kravchuk's friend, to win his trust and be his confidant, but I've another plan. I know that Kravchuk's been here only three days – not time enough to make friends – but time's limited, and I want to be sure.

Razumovsky stares at me doubtfully, then has his steward search me for a knife. The fact that I know his name makes him wary of me, for he's never heard of me, and he deals with many *Nemets*. Moreover there have been troubles with the Germans lately. The Livonian Brothers of the Sword have merged with the Teutonic Order and are pressing all along the north-west border of this land, so strangers are highly suspect, and I'm a stranger. Even so, he does not shirk his hospitality, and as I sit there, so his servant brings me a beer, and we drink a toast to his family.

'You have a family, trader?

'No. But I am looking for a wife.'

Razumovsky grins. 'A good German wife, I suppose.'

'Not at all. I mean to settle here, in Novgorod.'

'To settle?' His eyes take on a thoughtful cast.

'That's so. I plan to buy a plot of land in the Peterhof and build myself a house. Nothing grand, you understand. Nothing as grand as this, anyway.'

Razumovsky smiles at my compliment.

'But who knows,' I say. 'I have contacts back home in Stuttgart. Men who know me and trust me, and would welcome an agent in this town. If all goes well ...'

He studies me, his right hand pulling at his beard, and then he stands. 'You have the means to do this, trader? To buy land and set up home here?'

'I do,' I say. 'And call me Otto, please, Mikhail.'

He nods, then tilts his head a little. 'And you say you are looking for a wife?'

'She must be young,' I say, 'and pretty. And she must come from a good household. I'll not marry one who doesn't. Oh, and she must be of the Orthodox faith.'

This last surprises him. 'You're Orthodox?'

'Not yet. But I plan to convert. I want to put down roots here, Mikhail. Novgorod is a growing town, and I want my sons to be a part of it.'

This impresses him and sends him into a second bout of thoughtfulness. He looks at me, then nods to himself. 'You have your eye on a young woman, Otto?'

'No one in particular. But your friend Chernenko told me you would be sure to know someone.'

'You know Chernenko?'

I do, only he hasn't met me yet. Not in this time-line. But I will rectify that later. Even so, it does the trick.

'Look,' he says, putting his arm about my shoulder. 'There is a girl, but, well, it's delicate. Maybe we could talk some more. Over dinner, perhaps?'

'Dinner?'

He nods and grins at me. 'You'll be my guest, I hope.'

'I'd be delighted. Only ...'

He narrows his eyes. 'Only what?'

'You see,' I begin, as if this is awkward for me. 'It's not that I don't trust the people I am staying with, but, well, all of my worldly goods are here, in my pack. If I had somewhere I could store it. Somewhere it would be safe ...'

Razumovsky beams. 'Look no more. You can leave it here, my friend. There's no safer place in the whole city.'

I look embarrassed. 'You're very kind, but ...' I pause, then, going to the pack, pull out the top item, and, stepping over to the table, open up the plain white cloth in which it's wrapped.

Razumovsky's eyes open wide in astonishment. 'Mother of God!'

'It's beautiful, isn't it?' And I hand him the silver dagger with its jewel-encrusted hilt, and watch as his eyes drink in the beauty of its workmanship.

'Who made this?' he asks.

'A friend.'

'A good friend, or did you pay him for it?'

I meet his eyes and smile. 'Oh, I paid him. One hundred thaler.'

Razumovsky's eyes wrinkle with calculation. 'One hundred? And it's worth ...?'

'Five hundred. Maybe a thousand. The jewels are real, not paste.'

In fact, they're made of my DNA, but they're good enough to fool anyone in this Age. And there are other things beside. I show them to him, one by one, and know, as he hands each back, that his mind has been busy calculating.

'*There is a girl ...*'

And I smile and accept his kind offer of a room.

'Tonight,' he says. 'We'll talk some more tonight.'

79

I have washed and dressed, putting on a long shirt of the finest linen and a deerskin jacket, long leather boots and a hat of soft kid. Dressed so, I look more like a prince than a trader, and Razumovsky greets me with a respectful bow before turning and introducing me to his other guest.

Who smiles, and stands, and offers me his hand.

Kravchuk.

Razumovsky sees nothing, but Kravchuk notes the hesitation, and there's a sudden question in his eyes.

'You know me, trader?'

I smile, trying to disarm him, but my pulse is racing and I find it hard to breathe.

'No,' I say. 'No, it's just – you reminded me briefly of someone. A friend.'

He accepts that, nods, then grasps my hands and shakes them. But I am still surprised to find him here. When did he call? Or has he known Razumovsky a long time now?

I look to my host, as if seeking an explanation, but he seems unaware that there's a need. It seems, however, that he's told Kravchuk about me.

'I hear you are from Stuttgart, Otto. It's a very pleasant town.'

It is, but I have never been there. Not in this century. And so I shift the subject, to my fictitious travels in the Asian heartland, and find Kravchuk staring at me thoughtfully, as if maybe I know him after all.

He says little, not wishing to betray whence he's come, and so I change the subject once again.

'They say the *veche* here are unhappy with their prince.'

Kravchuk's eyes go to me, then he looks away. But Razumovsky laughs. 'If it were possible, we would have no prince at all! But it will be a cold day in hell before Kiev *imposes* one on us!'

He leans toward me, about to say more, when there's a movement in the doorway behind him. He turns and grins.

'Ah, Masha, Katerina ...'

The two women of the house enter, each carrying a large wooden tray stacked high with food. There's ham and chicken, cheese and pickled fish and more besides.

I look on, amazed, falling in love with her again. Yet for a time she does not even notice me, but goes about her task, helping her mother set the table. And only when she's done and turns, a half-smile on her lips, do our eyes finally meet.

I watch as her lips slowly part with the shock of recognition. There is a moment's naked panic in her eyes, and then she looks away, colour forming at her neck and in her cheeks.

I am a stranger to her, yet now – and I can see it clearly from where I stand – her heart beats quickly beneath the bright blue blouse she wears.

'Gentlemen,' Razumovsky begins, stepping between the two women and turning, an arm about each, 'let me introduce my wife, Masha, and my daughter, Katerina.'

And I make to step forward, to take her hand and kiss it, but Kravchuk is there in front of me, bowing low before her, his hat removed.

'Katerina,' he says. 'What a delightful name ...'

80

It is an evening hardly to be borne. It is not simply that the man is odious, it is the fact that Razumovsky can't see through his boasts and flattery and glimpse the little slug he really is. In fact, by the evening's end, I have come to think Katerina's father a total fool. Even so, I try one last, vain time to speak to him alone about his daughter's hand, only to have him raise it at the table.

'Hark, Oleg! Otto here wants my daughter's hand!'

Kravchuk stiffens, then looks at me challengingly. 'He is no Russian, Mikhail,' he says coldly. 'And Russians should marry Russians. It is not good to mix the blood.'

I stare back at him, furious. I want to kill him, only I've no weapon on me. Besides, it's Razumovsky's decision, not his.

I look to my host and realise just how drunk he is. Bleary-eyed drunk. Can't-hold-your-head-up drunk. He just wants to fall over in the corner and sleep.

'Wha—?'

'I said,' Kravchuk begins, but I cut him short.

'Don't interfere. Hear me? You say another word, I'll kill you.'

'You'll what?' And Kravchuk laughs, and reaches across to take another chicken leg. 'Kill me, my arse! You're all hot air, you Germans. As full of shit as a pig's intestines!'

I stand, glaring at him. But he's not even looking at me. It's as if I'm of no consequence, and I feel the urge to tell him that I've killed him once already – burned a hole in his fucking head – only he'd think me mad. So I leave before I do something I regret. Only as I go to step into the street, someone catches my arm and I turn to find her there, wrapped in a cloak, a shadow in the darkness by the gate, and she says the words I sense she's said a hundred times or more.

'Who are you?'

And I answer her with a kiss, and then I take her hand and lead her out into the darkness of that thirteenth-century night, away from Kravchuk and her fool of a father. And she asks me where we're going, and I say I don't know, just away, and I realise that I have left all of my belongings behind, but it doesn't matter. I have the only thing I need with me. The only thing I value. And when we stop, beyond the bridge, beneath a cresset lamp that burns fitfully in its metal cage, I take her face in my hands and kiss her once again and tell her that I love her, and her eyes, the image of which are burned into my soul, shine back at me in that wavering light as she smiles and softly laughs.

81

As the dawn's light fills the room, I wake to find her there beside me, naked, her dark hair spread across my pillow, and I know that I must have died and gone to heaven, for I have not ever seen such beauty.

I watch her for a time, content to see her sleeping there beside me, the memory of what we did in the night filling me.

Razumovsky would kill me if he knew. But she is no longer his. She is mine now. My wife. For all eternity.

And I know that I have crossed some Rubicon of the soul, but it matters nothing. All that matters lies beside me now, her warmth, her sweet reality my compass and my anchor for all time. And I know now what I sensed that very first time I saw her, that nothing will part us now. Nothing.

Even so, I must go and see her father.

She wakes, and her eyes, opening to me, are filled with love. We kiss, and that kiss reminds us of the night, and she and I begin again that sweetest game of all, that game of mouths and tongues and fingers, and our bodies press hard, as if to merge, my need and hers a single, growing force, until she cries out, her body arching under mine, and I groan and feel my seed course into her.

Afterwards she lies there, crying quietly, and I ask her why, and she tells me it's because she has never been so happy. And I am struck with awe that she is mine. Wiping her tears away, she lifts herself up on to her elbow, looking down at me, a strange intelligence in her eyes.

'How do I know you, Otto? Where is it that we've met? And how, then, did I ever forget you? For surely I must have. It's just that it seems … *unnatural*.'

I almost laugh and tell her everything: that I hail from a time so distant that more than fifty generations separate us … Only I don't, for I know that such knowledge would frighten her. And, having won her so completely, I fear to lose her now. Yet she seems to sense something. It is as if she *knows*. But knows what?

'The priests who taught me,' she says, one finger gently tracing the length of my jaw, making me shiver at the touch, 'they claim that everything is pre-ordained. That God alone has set our destiny. Only being here with you I begin to question that. You and I ... it's like we were fated. I'm not even sure what I mean by that, only ... I *knew* you, Otto. Knew you at first sight. One moment nothing, and the next ...'

She leans closer, lowering her face to mine, her lips to mine, her breasts warm, like silk against my chest. Yet even as I turn and reach across to caress her face, there is a hammering at the door.

'Behr! Come out! Come out, you bastard!'

I look to her, seeing the fear in her eyes, and try to reassure her. 'It's okay,' I say softly. 'It'll be okay.'

But I know I'm in trouble, and while normally I could just jump right out of there, I cannot leave her. That's Kravchuk's voice, and if he's come, he'll not be alone. He'll have his Mongol friends with him.

'Get dressed,' I tell her. 'Then go over to the corner. They'll not harm you.'

'But Otto ...'

My voice grows hard as the hammering comes again. 'Do as I say! We'll be all right.'

She dresses hurriedly, and once she's ready, I go to the door and draw the upper bolt.

Kravchuk is there, of course, and his three friends. He stares at me, surprised to find me naked, then steps inside and sniffs the air. A cruel smile appears on his lips.

'Oh dear ... Our friend Razumovsky *won't* be pleased.'

I face him squarely. 'What do you want, Kravchuk?'

'I want your bollocks, trader. I want them on a string about my neck.'

And he steps aside, to let his goons come at me. And they're good. There are few fighters throughout history to equal the Mongols for their savagery. But I am trained for this. I've been trained since I was four – turning and kicking and punching, using my hands and feet as lethal weapons. This much is pure instinct. And as the last of them falls, clutching his crushed manhood, I turn to Kravchuk and smile.

'You want to cut them off yourself, Oleg Alekseevich?'

The worm swallows and backs towards the door. He's drawn his knife, but he has no confidence in using it. It trembles in his hand.

'Are you sure you don't want to try?'

And I want him to make a move, so I can throw him down and choke the life from him. But he's seen enough and, throwing down the knife, he runs for it.

I watch him go, then take a shuddering breath. For a moment I stand there, swaying, coming down from that peak of intensity, my body relaxing after the adrenalin rush. And then I turn, remembering her.

She's watching me, like she hasn't really seen me till that moment. And as I step towards her, she flinches, and I say:

'It's okay, Katerina. It's only me. We're safe now.'

And her face seems to break, and tears come, and I hold her, like a father holds his child, until the storm has passed and she gives a shuddering sigh against me.

'Who are you, Otto? Who are you *really*?'

82

Razumovsky is out with a host of his friends, searching the back streets of Novgorod to find his daughter, but his wife, Masha is there when we call at the house, and she greets Katerina with a single look that takes in everything. She knows. But then, I'm not about to deny it. I plan to brazen this out. What I know is that Razumovsky as good as promised me his daughter until Kravchuk turned up. But now things are different. He might kill me, but he'll find it hard to find another husband for his daughter, now that I've stolen her away. Word will go out. And, after all, it's better for her to have a live, rich husband, than a dead one who's worth nothing.

Or so I hope. For I know that Razumovsky is a passionate man, and would as soon kill a man as listen to reason. He's done it once before, with Kravchuk, and he could just as easily do it to me.

And so we wait, while a servant runs off to find his master and give him the news that we're here. Eventually he comes.

I am standing there alone when he steps into the room. His friends are behind him, but he turns and waves them away. This is for him to deal with alone. Turning back, he shoots me a fierce look, as if I'm in for it now, yet what he says surprises me.

'You're a cool one, Otto Behr. To come back here, after what you've done.'

I wait, not saying a word, and he speaks again.

'So? What am I to do? Kill you? Or make a son of you?'

And he smiles, and I realise that, even as he's searched the streets, he has been thinking. And maybe – for it's likely in a town this size – he's also heard what I did to Kravchuk's friends. And maybe that too has set him thinking.

'I'll make her a good husband.'

'That we'll see.' But he doesn't seem aggrieved now. After all, if I marry her, then no harm's done. Even so, when he takes my hands, he squeezes them a little, just to show me who's the master here.

'Father,' I say and bow my head to him, then turn, as Katerina enters, looking first to her father and then, her eyes wide with delight, to me. She rushes over and clings to me, and I look past her at her father, who now stares at me, puzzled by this.

And I know what he is thinking at that moment.

Who are you, Otto Behr? Just who are you?

83

Hecht's mad with me, but that doesn't matter. Now that she's mine, I can focus on the rest of it.

The map's still red, you see, which means that Kravchuk and his fellow agents have failed. But now that I've bested him, I can put that right. Now that he knows who's master, I can be his ally.

You'll find that odd, perhaps, yet it's so. Now that she's mine, my animosity towards the man has gone. He's lost that contest, but he needn't lose the game. In fact, we need him to win.

But first I have to find him.

Leaving Katerina with her father, I go to the east of the town, the *Torgovaya storona*, to the rooms where Ernst and I unearthed him first time round. He's not there, but I'm told by the innkeeper that he did return, not an hour back, and left almost immediately.

So where's he gone?

I jump back an hour and wait and watch him go inside, then, less than two minutes later, leave hurriedly. I follow, keeping well back, as he makes his way to the western gate. There he waits, pacing back and forth, as if he's meeting someone.

Ten minutes pass, fifteen, then someone comes. I recognise the man from the first time we visited Razumovsky's house. It's Ernst's friend, the *tysiatskii*, Novgorod's military commander. Kravchuk talks to him a while, huddled close, talking to his ear, his whole manner urgent, and then the *tysiastskii* turns and hurries away, leaving Kravchuk alone once more.

I wonder just what's happening, and how the *tysiatskii* knew he'd be there, when the town's bells start to ring.

I turn, looking back over the roofs of the houses and see the reason why. There is a fire down near the river, in the direction of the Peterhof – the foreign quarter. I watch for a while, seeing the dark pall of smoke swirl upwards in the morning sunlight, then turn back.

Kravchuk's behind me, no more than ten paces away. As I turn he stops, looking at me uncertainly. I don't know what he intended – to surprise me, perhaps – but I can see he's still afraid of me, and so I put up my hands in a gesture of peace.

'We've no need to be enemies,' I say. 'I've got what I came here for.'

He doesn't answer, so I continue.

'I could help you, Kravchuk. Smooth the way for you. Get you introductions. Even help you find a wife.'

Anyone, I think. *Anyone but Katerina.*

He wets his lips, then shakes his head. 'I don't need your help, trader. I've friends of my own.'

'You mean Batu's men?'

His eyes widen with surprise at the warlord's name. He didn't think that anyone here in Novgorod had ever heard that name before.

'Oh, I know what you're doing, Kravchuk. But it doesn't matter. You and I want the same thing. For the Horde to be victorious. That letter you carry from the Great Khan. I'll help you deliver it. I'll help you get it to Alexander Iaroslavich.'

This is too much for him, however, and I can see he's torn

between running and staying to fight me. Only he's seen what I can do, and he clearly doesn't rate his chances.

'How do you know all this? Who told you?'

'It doesn't matter,' I say. 'All that matters is that I know. Everything. And I'm willing to help you.'

But he's still suspicious. Up until a moment ago I was a deadly rival, so why should he trust me now? Only I'm saying all the right things.

'Your friend, the *tysiatskii*, where has he gone?'

Kravchuk glances to his left, then to his right, as if he suspects some trap; as if, while I've kept him talking, I've brought up men to surround him. But it's only his paranoia.

'I don't know what you mean.'

'I saw you, talking to him. And then he hurried off. Why?'

But Kravchuk's not about to say.

The smell of burning is stronger and the great pall of smoke has risen so high now that it starts to block the sunlight. Kravchuk glances toward it, then looks back at me.

'Tonight,' he says. 'At Razumovsky's. We'll speak then.' And he turns and hurries away, back towards the river. Towards where the fire burns fiercest.

84

That evening, Razumovsky holds a great feast, announcing to his astonished friends that I am to marry his daughter just as soon as I've converted to the faith. A massive cheese is brought out and laid upon the table, its ritual slicing symbolising our *obruchenie* – our betrothal – and later a priest arrives and takes me aside and tests me, and, satisfied with my responses, says I am to be baptised into the Russian Orthodox faith tomorrow at dawn. In fact, things are moving so fast that I forget about Kravchuk until, returning to the feast, I see him, seated quietly at one corner of the great table, the big Mongolian at his side.

Talk at the table is of the great fire that swept the Peterhof that morning. The inn I was staying at was among those buildings destroyed, and I thought, perhaps, the Khan's men might have perished in the conflagration, but I can see that one at least survived, and so I go across and, standing before Kravchuk, bow to him in greeting.

'I see you've got what you wanted,' he says tonelessly.

'It would seem so.'

I look to the Mongolian, trying to gauge what his response to me now is. He seems okay, but these men are fiercely proud, and he'll not forget what I did to him earlier, so I give him the slightest bow of respect.

'You want to talk?' Kravchuk asks.

'Not here,' I say. 'Outside.' And, as the Mongolian makes to accompany him, I add, 'Alone.'

The Mongolian shakes his head, but Kravchuk places a hand on his arm and nods.

We step outside, into the warm darkness of the evening. The courtyard stinks, but we ignore it. Kravchuk is first to speak.

'You said you could help me? How?'

'I can get you introductions. Meetings with the men you want to see.'

He laughs. 'You're a *Nemets*. You don't even know these people.'

'Oh, I do. Much better than you think. And I also know that you're in danger. There are agents here – Rus' agents – who want to kill you.'

That makes him think. 'They know who I am? What I'm doing here?'

'Yes.' But the truth is I don't know. I'm only guessing now. I am assuming that the Russians got to Kravchuk. That they worked out what was going on.

'It's like I said earlier. I want what you want. I want the Horde to succeed.'

'And is that why you're marrying a Russian?'

I smile, but he doesn't see it in the darkness. We are but voices.

'Expediency,' I say, not wishing to let him know just what I feel. Not wishing to give him any power over me. 'If I'm to function here, then I need to blend in.'

'I see.' And he does seem to understand that. After all, it's what he's doing. Even so, he's not entirely satisfied, and now he asks the crucial question. 'So who are *you* working for?'

'Can't you guess?'

He hesitates, then, quieter. 'The Poles? The Livonians?'

I lower my voice, as if I don't wish to be overheard. 'No. But close. I report to the Grand Master himself.'

It's a half-truth, and I'm proud of it, makeshift as it is.

'I see,' Kravchuk says, and there's a new respect in his voice. 'I should have guessed.'

'Maybe. But now that you know, there seems no reason for us to be enemies. You and I, we want to bring these barbarians to their knees, no? To humble them. What better way than to undermine their princes, eh?'

And he laughs. A soft and quiet laugh that sounds like genuine amusement. And I begin to laugh also, and when Razumovsky comes out to find me, he finds Kravchuk and I arm in arm, laughing together, as if we're drunk.

'Gentlemen!' he says, putting his arms about us both. 'It's good to see you two becoming friends! But come inside now. Come! It's time for the toast.'

We return inside, and there is my beloved, her single plait, the symbol of her maidenhood, unplaited now, the lace *kokoshnik* removed from her head. As I step towards her, so she holds out a heavy gilded cup. There has been no time for a *devichnik* – a maiden's party – but she has bathed, as is the tradition, and now she offers me a drink of her bathwater. In another time, another age, this might seem ludicrous, but here this is seen as an almost magical rite, a throwback to their ancient worship of Lado, the fertility god. I take the goblet reverently, cupping her hands gently in my own, and sip, my eyes smiling at hers all the while, drinking of her, knowing that by this time tomorrow she will be mine.

85

I am up an hour before dawn, preparing myself. First light finds me kneeling in the front bench of St Sophia's, Razumovsky at my side, the tall, dark-bearded priest six paces distant, praying to the altar before he turns and beckons me across. There is the smell of burning incense, the flicker of candles in golden sconces. All goes well, and within the hour I step from the church, the taste of wine and communion bread strong in my mouth. Razumovsky looks at me and grins, then strides on in front, leaving me to catch up.

The wedding is to be that afternoon, in St Sophia's, and invitations are hurriedly sent out. I find the haste of it almost indecent, but Razumovsky's not to be denied. Now that he has me, he wants to keep me and make sure. He doesn't want me rushing off on some trading venture, only to find his unwed daughter swelling out, the townsfolk gossiping.

Not that I'm against the idea. Oh Urd no. I want her more than anything I've ever wanted, and the thought of marrying her that afternoon is like a dream. Indeed, it is my dream. Only Ernst is still missing, and I've not a clue yet what the Russians are up to. And Hecht wants me back.

But he can wait. This once they all can wait.

And now the hours crawl slowly, as if Time's an uphill gradient, and when the bells of the town sound for the midday service, I wonder just how it can be that the seconds can drag so, such that they seem a good twice their normal length. And, of course, I am not to see her yet, not until the ceremony, and as some one is always calling in to congratulate me and bring me presents, there is no way I can slip back and visit Hecht.

And so I wait, and wait some more, until the hour comes and, dressed in my finest clothes, I accompany Razumovsky's steward to the church.

It's only then that I realise I've no one to give me away. It ought to be Ernst if anyone, but, looking across at the hastily filled benches, I spot one face I've come to know too well. Kravchuk.

Impossible, I think. But someone will have to do the job. Besides, there's a kind of irony to this. Before I changed things, my bride was his. So maybe Fate intends this.

I walk across and, whispering to his ear, ask him if he will stand in for my father. He straightens, looking strangely flattered by my request, then nods and, standing, follows me back across.

And so we stand there, Kravchuk and I, at the head of that great aisle, as the incense burns and the choir moans its strange, alien refrains, and my love, my darling Katerina, walks towards me, her arm in her father's arm.

Slowly she comes as in a dream, her dress, hastily adapted from some party gown, seeming to float across the dark stone floor, her hair, braided with silver chains, flowing out from the *pokoinik* – the marital veil – she wears. And as she draws parallel to me, her eyes meet mine and smile, like the promise of an everlasting summer.

I am bewitched. I have never seen such a glorious sight. As we stand there, she to the left, I to the right of the priest, each of us holding a lighted candle, so I understand that all of my life, all of my travels throughout the length and breadth of Time have led to this one, single moment. This is the centre of it. The focus. All else leads to or away from here, like the hub of a great wheel.

We exchange rings – *obruchei* – and then join our right hands as the priest places a lightweight crown on each of our heads, then switches them, blessing us with incense and wishing us 'a peaceful and long life' and 'children and grandchildren to fill your house with abundance and beauty'. All this transpires, and yet for me the service passes in a daze. Somnolent, I say the magic words and make her mine. *Till death do us part.* And even Kravchuk's presence there – a man I've killed, a man I've seen kill her – does not affect my happiness. Indeed, his presence seems to be the seal on things, for if the wedding has his blessing, then surely nothing can unbind this.

Even so, as I turn, Katerina's arm in my arm, and face the congregation, my smile is tempered by the knowledge of Time's inconstancy. If I could win her from the very teeth of Time, then what's the chance of keeping her? What tricks and twists might yet unbind this moment?

I cannot bear the thought. A cloud crosses my face. But Katerina seems not to notice. She beams with happiness at my side, and, looking at her, I cannot help but feel that this was *meant*.

The great table's set once more, stacked high with food, a regular *bratchina*. And as I drink the first of a dozen toasts, the room packed with Razumovsky's friends, so my darling is taken off, to be prepared for her bridal bed, and the thought of it is more intoxicating than any wine, and I long to be there, alone with her, and not here in this stifling room with these endless, foul-smelling, bearded, grinning men.

An hour passes, and I find I'm feeling drunk. It's hard to deny Razumovsky and, as he fills my goblet once again, I look about me, wondering when she'll be ready.

Yet even as I turn, there's a commotion in the doorway and the crowd parts to reveal the *tysiatskii* and several of his men in full armour, their swords drawn, and I wonder what in Urd's name is going on. As the noise dies, so he takes out a scroll and unfurls it and, clearing his throat begins to read, and even as he does, his men push through that throng and lay their hands on me.

Razmovsky stands there, shocked by what he's hearing, staring at me in open-mouthed astonishment, even as I struggle to break free. But it's done now, and I know exactly who has done it. Traitor I am, according to the *tysiatskii*'s words. An agent of the Teutons. I turn my head furiously, looking for him, and find him, smiling in the corner, and curse him, and tell him I'll cut out his heart and feed it to his lifeless mouth. But Kravchuk merely laughs, his wet mouth showing red as he raises his silver goblet in a toast.

'To you, Otto! To you!'

86

I am clapped in irons and thrown into a dark, damp cell beneath the *tysiatskii*'s palace. It would be easy to jump right out of there, only I'm curious to see how they'll proceed, and what they know, and so I bide my time. Even so, I am in torment, for I had hoped this night to be in Katerina's arms again, as her husband, staring down into those beautiful eyes as we made love. The thought makes me wonder how she's taking this, and what her father's said, and my heart breaks once more thinking of her sorrow. And then, because there's time to think of everything, I wonder just why Kravchuk acted as he did.

It's clear I misread him. Whatever else is going on, it's clear he considers me a threat – a factor to be eliminated. More than that, the man truly is a slug. I bested him and so he takes his vengeance on my wedding night. And maybe, just maybe, he has designs on her still. Maybe he'll try to have the marriage vows annulled.

The thought horrifies me. I groan aloud, and the guard, hearing it, mistakes it for despair and laughs and begins to taunt me. But his words can't touch me. Nothing can touch me now, for I have lost the world.

I doze and wake to find them over me. There's two of the fellows. They haul me up between them then throw me against the wall. I'm winded, but they've only just begun. One of them strikes me with the back of his hand, and then the other brings his knee up into my balls. The pain's excruciating, but I still don't jump. If I can get to see the *tysiatskii*, if I can get him to listen to me for a moment, maybe I can set things right again.

The beating goes on for several minutes, and then they stand back, chuckling, enjoying my discomfort. I look up at them, then, pulling my chained hands up to my mouth, wipe away the blood. I climb to my feet, then face them, uncowered. My whole mouth stings and I know it's beginning to swell up, but I can still talk.

'I must speak with your master. There's been a mistake ...'

But they only laugh, and the bigger of the two, a surly looking fellow, kicks me back against the wall.

'You'll speak to us, *Nemets*. And you'll say "Master", understand?'

'I *have* to speak to him ...'

This only angers him. He runs at me and throws a punch, and though I turn my head, it hits me squarely on the lower jaw and I feel the bone crack, and the pain's so great that I slump against the wall, almost blacking out. And I know now that I'm never going to get to see the *tysiatskii*; that there's never going to be a hearing, and that I'm going to die in this awful, stinking cell unless I jump. And as the Russian stands over me, raising his fist ready to beat my bruised and bleeding face to a pulp, so I raise my eyes to his and spit full in his face, blood and saliva mixed.

Go tell your master that ...

And jump.

87

Zarah's angry with me – much more than Hecht was last time out. When she comes to see me in the care ward, she lectures me for a full half hour and, when I refuse to tell her what's really going on, warns me that she's going to do her best to get me grounded before I get myself killed. I'm touched by her concern, but there's no way she's going to stop me going back. She's like a mother and a sister to me and, if she had her way, she'd be my lover too, but that doesn't mean she can dictate to me.

I've kidney damage and partial damage to one of my testicles. Nothing they can't fix, but it means several days' rest before I can go back. In terms of the Past, that doesn't mean a thing – I can drop back any time I want – but it makes me restless in the Now. I don't want to lie there and recuperate, I want to get back to thirteenth-century Novgorod and kick seven shades of shit out of Kravchuk.

To change the subject, I ask about Ernst and whether there's been any trace of him, and in doing so I learn something that Hecht neglected to tell me first time round.

'That's right,' Zarah says, combing back her short blond hair with her fingers. 'He jumped back and disappeared immediately. We thought that maybe his focus was faulty, and wasn't showing a signal, but when Hecht jumped back there was nothing. Not the slightest trace of him. And that's not right. It's like he never was there. Only he *was*.'

'Has this happened before?'

'Never.'

'And Hecht doesn't have an explanation for it?'

'No.'

Then it's a mystery. And maybe I'm the one to solve it. I look at Zarah. 'Where's Hecht?'

She shakes her head. 'No way. You're getting some rest.'

'I only want to talk.'

'Yes, and try to persuade him to let you go back before you're ready to.'

'He's not that stupid.'

'No? He's a man, isn't he?'

And I almost smile at that. But I'm not leaving this. 'Just tell him I want to speak to him. If he's too busy …'

But Hecht isn't too busy. He would have come before, only Zarah didn't inform him that I was back, let alone that I'd been beaten up. He stands at the end of my bed and studies me.

'Nice bruises, Otto. They go with the scar you got last time.'

I'd forgotten that, but now my fingers find and trace the three-inch scar on the right side of my neck.

'Kravchuk again,' I say. 'Or his friends, should I say.'

And I tell Hecht the story. Or some of it, anyway. Nothing about Katerina.

'The problem is,' I conclude, 'that if I let Kravchuk live, he always – and I mean always – seems to get the drop on me. Yet if I don't …'

'The map turns red.'

'Precisely.'

'Then become Kravchuk.'

I stare at Hecht then laugh. But it's a brilliant idea. I could go back, find out where and when he first made contact with the Mongols, eliminate him, and set myself up as their agent in his place. That way there's never a conflict. That way I can kill Kravchuk, marry Katerina and keep the map from turning red, all at the same time.

The only trouble is that it's going to take time to set up. Maybe more than I can afford. After all, I've Frederick to look after. And it's clear Hecht thinks so too, for after pondering a moment, he says: 'Maybe someone else should take this on, Otto. Someone with some background on the Horde.'

Normally I'd not argue. It makes complete sense, after all. But I'm not in my senses. Not where Katerina's concerned.

'It won't take me long,' I say. 'I've some background already. And I'm the only one who knows who our contacts are in Novgorod now Ernst is missing. I know what's going on there. A new agent, well, they'd have to start again, from scratch. Besides, I know Kravchuk. Know his weaknesses.'

It's enough. Hecht nods. 'Okay. But first you get some rest. I'll bring you whatever you need on the Horde and their social organisations. Who's who, where they're based.'

He stops, then smiles. 'You know what?'

'What?'

'I think we're doing this the hard way, Otto. We want to find out Kravchuk's movements, right? Where he went? Who he met?'

'Right.'

'Then let's not bother following him around. Let's take the bastard prisoner, pump him full of drugs and let him sing.'

I smile. 'Okay. I'm game. I'll make a list of things I'll need to ask.'

'Good. And one other thing.'

'Yes?'

'Try not to get in trouble this time, Otto. It's upsetting the women.'

88

I'm all ready to go, when I have an idea ... about Ernst and what happened to him.

That's the beauty of having to rest up. Because while the body's relaxing, the mind goes into overdrive.

I go to Hecht and ask him to send me back to precisely the point where Ernst disappeared, only fifteen minutes before he 'arrived'. And before I go, I visit Hans Luwer in his workshop.

As I enter, all nine of Hans look up and, lifting their spectacles from their noses in an identical manner, say:

'Ah, Otto ...'

There is only one Hans, of course, but the man has much to do and this is how he copes, jumping back and forth through Time. Multi-tasking.

'Here,' says the third of him, seated slightly down the work bench from where I'm standing. 'I finished it an hour back.' And he hands me the camera I'm about to ask him for.

'Thanks,' I say, and then, because I must – to complete the loop – I hand him the rough sketch I've made for him and he stands and nods and wanders off, heading for the platform.

'So what's happening in the world?' Hans asks, his eight mouths working as one.

'Ernst Kollwitz is missing, and I'm trying to find out where he's gone. He disappeared.'

'Ah ...' And again the sound is echoed from eight mouths, as Hans looks to himself, as if, between his selves, he might come up with an answer.

I stay and talk a while, then head back to the platform. Zarah is there, still angry, and she glares at me as I climb up. Even so, she cannot help but wish me luck, as she checks the readings.

And then I'm there, in the clearing in the forest, where Ernst and I have come so many times.

In roughly five minutes Hecht will come through, and I don't want him to see me there, mainly because he didn't. Then, ten minutes later, Ernst will come through. Or rather, he won't.

I move into the trees, setting my camera up well back, out of sight, but with a clear view of the centre of the clearing.

Minutes pass, and then the air in the clearing shimmers and Hecht steps through. He looks about him then, like a thief, moves stealthily into the trees on the far side.

I wait, looking at the timer on my wrist, and as the fifteen minutes pass, so I see the slightest ripple in the air ...

And nothing. No sign of Ernst at all. Only the vacant air.

I watch Hecht step out and look about him. He crouches, studying the ground, then, frowning, puts his hand to his chest and disappears.

But I already know I have the answer, and, picking up the camera, I walk out into that space and, touching my chest, jump back.

89

Only three of the thirty frames catch it, but it's clear. Ernst did appear in the clearing. But just as quickly he vanished, into another dimension.

The question is how?

Hecht's puzzled, staring at the prints.

'It's some kind of trap, set off when he jumps through. The question is how did they know when and where he'd come through?'

'They didn't.'

Hecht looks at me. 'What?'

'They didn't have to. I reckon he had it on him, like some kind of mine. They must have made it of his DNA. It would be easy enough to take a sample from him. Some special device, triggered only when you jump back through time.'

Hecht considers that, then nods. 'Okay. So where is he?'

I look about me. 'Some place like this, I reckon. A no-space place.'

'Then how ...?' But Hecht sees how. He smiles, and stands and says, 'We'll get a team on to it straight away.'

And I know that Ernst will be okay. But meanwhile I've got to go and see Kravchuk and ask him a few questions.

90

Kravchuk shrieks when he next sees me, and tries to run. Only there's nowhere to run. The door to his room is locked and he'll need to get past me if he wants to unlock it.

I raise the gun and fire, then watch as he tries to pluck the dart out of his neck. He struggles for a time, then his hand falls away and he slumps on to the pallet bed. I kneel beside him.

'Oleg ... Oleg, can you hear me?'

He rolls over, on to his back, and smiles up at me, his eyes unfocused.

'Oleg, I've some questions I want to ask you. About your visit to the Great Khan.'

And so I learn it all. How, as a young boy, his father and his uncles took him to Samarkand where he first set eyes upon the Mongol Horde, and how those ferocious warriors had fired his imagination. Kravchuk's father was a Bulgar, who traded in furs, which the Mongols loved to have. He was a particular friend of the Mongol leader, Subodei, who, though born a mere blacksmith's son, had risen under Temuchin to become the commander of a 'Thousand', a Mongol army.

He had spent the next two decades among the Mongols, learning the Uighur language of the conquered Naimans, which Temuchin – Genghis Khan – had adopted for his people, and subsequently served as a *bichechi* – a secretary – to General Subodei.

I listened, fascinated, as he spoke of the great *khuriltai* of 1228, held at the thousand-tent encampment on the Kerulen River, deep in the heart of Mongolia itself. It was there, as I knew, that the *Mangqolun ninca tobchan* – the 'Secret History of the Mongols' – had its origins, and it was there that he saw, for the first time, all of the great names from Temuchin's campaigns – veterans now, their teeth black, their hair grey – as each evening they stood up and, in the flickering blaze of an open fire, recounted their tales of battles they had won and brave deeds they had witnessed or enacted.

And strangely, as he spoke I came to understand how this man might have been won to their cause, how, listening to those old men, he might have longed to be a part of it, however small, and how, when the chance came to serve his master, Subodei, and even the Khan, Batu himself, Kravchuk had leapt at it, eager to prove himself.

'I went to Karakorum,' he says, a glow of wonder in his face, 'to Ogodei's great palace, and saw the silver tree. Oh, it was beautiful. And the women ...' He laughs. 'But things were changing. They were growing soft. You could see it. All those riches they had won for themselves. Once they used to wear the skins of dogs and were a fierce, proud race, but now ... now they wear silks and furs and carry pockets full of jewels, and they grow fat and dull.'

'Then why serve them still?'

'For what they were. And what they yet might be.'

It is a good answer. It is why I serve *my* people. But there is something else I need to know before the drug wears off, and I ask it now.

'So, now that I am out of the way ... will you marry Razumovsky's daughter?'

Again he laughs. 'The deed is done. Or good as. He's promised me her hand – once the annulment's passed by the church elders.'

His answer chills me. I had thought for a moment that I might let him live. But now ...

I have all the answers that I need. All that remains is to kill the man. But still I hesitate. I do not like to kill in cold blood, nor is there any honour in cutting the throat of a drugged man. But if I leave him be, he'll marry Katerina, and that can never be. I have seen him slit her throat with not a flicker of remorse in the bastard's eyes. So now I steel myself, and draw my knife, remembering that.

Then jump, before the image of him smiling, his blood pooling beneath his head, haunts my nights.

91

And jump back, three nights later, outside the Razumovsky house.

Hecht's working on my list; sending in researchers to find out where and when's the best time to slip into Kravchuk's skin. Subodei is a problem, naturally, because he knew Kravchuk for so long, and he'd notice straight away if it was me pretending to be Kravchuk. So we need to find some point at which I can become him, and such things take time. So here I am, at Razumovsky's once again, less than a week after my wedding supper and the events that followed.

I ignore the gate. There's no chance that Razumovsky will invite me back with open arms, not after what I've done. Like all of them now, he thinks me some kind of enchanter – a man who can cast a spell and step out of the air. The truth, of course, is far stranger. But right now I'm not interested in Razumovsky. I need to see her. To let her know that I'm not what they say I am. And to let her know that I still love her and will come for her.

Only I've got to find a way inside.

It's dark. Only the faintest sliver of moon shows through the thick cloud cover. I climb in over the back of the stockade, then crawl up one of the roofs and drop down into the narrow space between two buildings. It's pitch black down there, but there's a door at the end, and it's unlocked, so I listen a moment, then slip inside.

And stop, getting my bearings clear in my head before I proceed. If I remember rightly, she's to my right and up a floor, but where precisely I'm not sure.

It's late, but there are still noises in the house: voices; the creak of a door being opened somewhere to my left. Fortunately there are no dogs. Razumovsky hates dogs, and I am grateful to him for once, for the last thing I want is to set a dog barking.

A sturdy set of wooden steps – more ladder than stairs – leads up, and I climb them quickly, then turn and stop, feeling with my hands.

Bare wooden planks give way to a door frame. I find the latch, and slowly, very slowly, push back the door. In the faint light from the window I can make out the bed, a big, carved, wooden bed, and in it Razumovsky and his wife, their snores filling the room, bass and treble.

I close the door silently, then move on down the corridor. She's here. I know she's here. Unless, of course, they've sent her away.

The thought stops me dead. What if they have? What if she isn't here at all?

I tiptoe on, searching the walls with my hands until I come to another door. I open it, and there, like heaven itself, she lies, her cloth-shrouded figure picked out in silver by the crescent moon which now shines forth from between the parted clouds.

I close the door behind me, then walk across, looking down at her from the foot of her narrow bed.

My wife. My Katerina.

And yet I fear to wake her – fear to see not love but horror of me in those eyes – and yet I must, and so I gently sit beside her and, reaching out, brush her forehead gently with my fingertips.

She moans, a soft, sweet moan, then turns the slightest bit, the cloth moving down to expose her perfect breasts. And now I am enchanted, for there's true magic in what is between two lovers. Magic beyond all Time. And I ache to kiss each sweet, soft bud and make her cry out once again as she did in the night beneath me, but I know this is neither the time nor place for that, and so I cover her and, brushing her forehead gently once again, softly call her name.

'Katerina, Ka-ter-i-na ...'

Slowly she wakes, and as her eyes adjust so she sees me. She smiles, but then, as she remembers what has passed, her eyes fly open.

'Otto ... what ...?'

She sits up, reaching out to me, barely conscious of her naked-ness beneath the cloth. There's fear in her eyes, true, but I see it's fear *for* me, that *I* might be discovered.

'I must go,' I whisper, thrilled by the touch of her hands against my upper arms, the womanly scent of her, her very closeness. 'But I had to see you. Had to let you know I'd come for you.'

Her eyes search mine a moment, looking for the truth of that, and, satisfied, she smiles. But then, once more, a sudden serious-ness grips her, and she looks away.

'Did you ...?'

'Kill Kravchuk, yes? It was he who did it. Who came between us.'

She looks at me, then nods, no blame in her eyes. 'Otto?'

'Yes, my love?'

'Take me away from here. Somewhere where no one can find us. To the ends of the Earth.'

Or the end of Time …

I swallow, moved by her words, then lean forward, brushing her lips with my own, fearing to do more, meaning to leave right there and then before I find I can't, but she reaches up and, holding my face between her hands, kisses me softly, fully on the mouth … the sweetest, most intoxicating kiss I've ever had – sweeter than any she has yet given me. And I know, there and then, that she is mine for ever. Nothing can change that. Neither Time nor Death.

Katerina. My darling Katerina …

Part Five

To Asgard

'I agree that man is an animal predominantly constructive, foredoomed to the art of engineering, that is to the everlasting and increasing construction of a road – *no matter where it leads,* and that the main point is not *where* it goes, but that it should go somewhere.'

– Fyodor Dostoevsky, *Notes From Underground*

92

Hecht is waiting for me at the platform. I make to step down, but he jumps up and takes my arm.

'No time, Otto. Something's happening.'

And we jump. Back to the clearing in the forest. And there – the merest suggestion in the air; the palest, most spectral of presences in that moonlit space between the trees – is Ernst, suspended like a chrysalis.

I stare, horrified, for the look of pain on his face is almost beyond imagining. It's as if he's been buried alive. Or crucified. Those eyes ...

'How long has he been like this?'

My voice, in that strange, twilit place, is a whisper. We are alone there, except for the silver-grey boles of the trees and the stars and the full moon hanging over us like a watchful eye in that sable, cloudless sky.

'A week or so. But it's growing stronger by the day. I brought a team in ...'

'*And?*'

'They're not sure, but they think it's because there's not enough energy to sustain a genuine no-space.'

'There's a power source, then?'

'Yes, but it's anchored somewhere else.'

'Have we any idea *where?*'

'No, but Zarah's doing the calculations. She thinks it's up the line somewhere, possibly in the mid-twenty-eighth.'

I look back at Ernst and shudder.

So that's it, is it? A man-trap, laid in Time. And every bit as savage as its ancient iron counterpart.

'Why isn't he dead?'

Hecht's voice registers his disgust. 'They're feeding him air – just enough to fill his lungs.'

'Then he can move?'

'No. They've paralysed his motor cortex. But his lungs and his heart are still functioning. They clearly want to keep him alive.'

And in torment. I groan. Poor Ernst. Poor bloody Ernst.

'So what are you going to do?'

Hecht smiles. 'I'm sending you in, Otto. Just as soon as we know where the power source is.'

'The anchor?'

'Yes …'

'But what of Kravchuk? I thought …'

But I leave it there. This is more important, I realise. Because if the Russians have found a way of trapping us – of doing *this* to our agents – then we may have lost anyway, whatever happens to Kravchuk and the Horde. Looking at Ernst, at his haunted, pain-filled, unblinking eyes, I know that he wants to be put out of his misery, that anything, even death, would be preferable.

'You'll say nothing, Otto, to the other agents.'

'No,' I say distractedly. 'No, of course …'

It'll be our secret.

93

'Are you ready, Otto?'

I'm not, but I nod anyway. I've got everything I need in a small leather bag on my back.

'Good luck,' Zarah says, looking at me fondly. Behind her Urte and Marie are smiling, but their smiles are strained. They know what's going on.

So much for secrets.

'Burckel knows you're coming,' Zarah says, handing me a small package. 'These are his instructions. He's to read them, then destroy them.'

For once I'm surprised. Hecht said nothing. Nor do I know what's in the package. But I take it and pocket it without a word.

'Okay,' I say, stepping up on to the platform. 'Let's get going ...' And in my head, I add: *for the sooner Ernst is out of there, the better ...*

I'm hoping Zarah's right – that she's pinpointed the precise location of the power-anchor. If so, and I can switch it off, then Ernst is free. And maybe, if the timing's right, I can undo all of his suffering. Nullify it.

Only there's a paradox here. If Ernst has been trapped that long, then maybe I've already failed, because if I'd succeeded ...

I try not to think of that. Try to concentrate on my actions having some significance. On the *urgency* of my task.

Zarah brings her hand down on the pad. There's a moment's bright intensity. My whole being seems to implode upon itself, every cell, every living atom of me falling inward.

And I jump.

Into a darkened room. Into silence and the smell of sweat and oil. I step across and, draw back one of the thick, heavy shutters.

And stare out across the immense sprawl of Neu Berlin. It is the fourth day of June, 2747 AD. Night has fallen and the massive buildings of this energy-rich city sparkle like solid slabs of jewels against the dark, filling the skyline horizon to horizon.

I turn, looking back into the shadowed room. To my left is a low pallet bed. Beyond it, in the corner, is a small writing table. Shelves fill the whole of the wall facing me, floor to ceiling, while to my right ...

'Light,' I say, and at once a flattened globe lights and lifts from among the clutter on the floor, its growing illumination throwing my shadow across the room. I stare about me, astonished. The place is a mess. A real pigsty. The bed's unmade, the shelves filled to overflowing. On the bare floor in front of them are piles of unwashed clothes and books and papers, while in a large crate in the right-hand corner are a jumble of assorted machines – broken, it seems – and a whole miscellany of objects. I walk across, then crouch, sorting through the mess, not sure what I'm looking for, or what instinct guides me.

My eyes look along the shelves. It's a curious mixture of ancient and modern, fact and fiction, but again I don't really know what I'm looking for, so I straighten up and, stepping carefully over a precariously balanced stack of books, I go to Burckel's desk.

Burckel is a 'sitter'. He's been here in Neu Berlin these past eight years, never once jumping back. None of the locals would ever suspect he was a time agent. Burckel is just … Burckel. A scholar. Something of an eccentric.

There's an ancient ink pot here, made of carved crystal, and various papers, political pamphlets mostly, many of them in *ge'not*, the revolutionary language of this Age. The possession of a single one of them could lead Burckel to be put away for a long time, and there are dozens here. I push them aside, then reach to the back of the desk where, beneath several slender volumes, my fingers discover a big, leather-bound book.

It's a diary – Burckel's journal by the look of it – but I can't read a word, and not only because it too is written in *ge'not*. The handwriting is tiny, minuscule, so small, in fact, that my unaided eyes can make out only the vague shape of the tiny, carefully crafted symbols. It makes me feel uneasy.

Closing the book, I push it back beneath the clutter, then return to the window, looking out across the levels.

276

We're two miles up here, in one of the central stacks, facing south towards the Tempelhof.

Low down there's a steady stream of SWs – *Schweben-wagen* – the long black shapes of the flyers flitting along the air-paths, but the traffic's relatively light this time of night. I'm about to turn away when there's an explosion, loud yet distant. In its glare I glimpse figures on the rooftops of one of the massive apartment blocks across the way, maybe a mile distant.

'Otto? Is that you?'

I turn, facing the figure in the doorway.

'Albrecht?'

Burckel lowers his gun, then steps across and embraces me. It's some while since I last saw him, but he greets me like an old friend.

'How have you been?' I ask, noting how much older he seems than when last I saw him. He's my age, yet he looks a good ten years older.

'I'm fine, Otto.' And as he says it I notice the excited gleam in his eyes. And little wonder. He has been waiting for this since he first arrived. These next few days are crucial to our history, for these few small days form a historical cusp, and both we and the Russians know it.

'How are things back at Four-Oh?'

'Nothing changes,' I say, and we both laugh, knowing how untrue that is.

'Oh,' I say, remembering suddenly. 'This is for you. From Hecht.' And I hand him the packet, then watch as he sits on the edge of his unmade pallet bed and picks open the seal.

I watch his eyes. See the surprise that comes into them. He glances up at me, as if he's about to speak, then decides against it. He slips something beneath the mattress, then carefully folds the single sheet of paper and, taking a light-stick from his pocket, holds the flame beneath it. Then, when it catches, he lets the burning paper fall on to a patch of bare floor, stamping out the embers with his boot.

Albrecht Burckel is a small man. He has a neat, rounded head, shaven and polished, so that it gleams in the soft light from the lamp. He is compact, muscular yet wiry, like a certain kind of dog, bred for its tenacity. That same smell that permeates this room, permeates him. He is wearing a black one-piece of rough cloth, and on his bare right arm there is a number: *145-G-774-ACGT 1133*.

He sees me staring at it, and gives a grin. 'We'll have to get you one of these, Otto. That is, if you want to get inside the fortress.'

I roll back my sleeve, and show him. Hecht thinks of everything.

'Are you hungry?' he asks, and when I nod, he grins again, a boyish, almost innocent grin. Looking at him, you'd never think him capable of killing, yet he has, more than a dozen men in all. Russians.

'Leave your pack here,' he says. 'It'll be safe enough.'

We leave the room, turning right towards the lifts. At once the Mechanist world assails me. Both sides of that long corridor flicker and buzz with bright-lit images, images that, in their depth and clarity, seem as real as Burckel and I. Each panel seems a room, as if only the thinnest sheet of glass separates us from another, busier world. Yet that other world has no more reality, no more *depth*, than a picture drawn on the finest of silken screens. Creatures a pixel thick walk from panel to panel, keeping pace with us, like figures from an ancient bazaar, anxious to make a sale. Their clamour is muted this time of night – how else would people sleep? – yet my eyes, bombarded from all sides, seek refuge in the untenanted stairs beyond.

We reach the lifts. There are fast-tracks for the execs, but we take the cage, rattling up the levels in a packed, malodorous box of steel and wire, glimpsing the miles beneath our feet through the mesh of the floor, two hundred or more of our fellows crammed in there with us, slowly ascending to the bright lights of the uppers.

I'm conscious at once of how different Albrecht and I are; natural men, *Naturlich*, among the genetically sculpted people of this age. I try not to stare, to keep my eyes from meeting others', but it's hard. These people have been *changed*, adapted for their tasks. Such body shapes offend an eye accustomed to the normal human form. Yet it is we who are the odd men out. It's their world now.

As the lift halts at the topmost level and the crowd spills out, Albrecht takes my arm, holding me back until they're gone. They turn right, heading towards the great bridge that spans the stacks, but Albrecht takes me left, through the flicker and buzz of another, shorter corridor, and up a winding set of steps.

Neu Berlin is a city of two hundred and fifty million people, and nowhere is that more apparent than here, in the sprawl of the southern city. Yet it is not until we climb one final flight of steps, until, coming out on to a broad verandah, we turn and see the enclaves, directly north, there where the land has been raised and terraformed, that the real majesty of the place is revealed.

I walk to the edge, a vertiginous drop beneath me, and stare.

The city is a high-rise sprawl, stretching away for miles on every side, a densely packed mass of gargantuan, slab-like buildings, contrasted here and there by a slender spike or two, thrusting up like the spears of giants. To the north the spaceport glows orange, like a furnace, while to the left – north-west of where I stand – is the dark, distinctive form of the *Gefängnis*, the Guild's prison, its windowless outer walls the very symbol of abandoned hope. Just left of that, a half mile distant, are the ministries with their distinctive pyramidal shapes, and beyond them, in a belt that follows the river west, lies the industrial district, housing the unsleeping furnaces of Greater Germany.

It's an astonishing vista, and yet the eye only dwells on such details for an instant before being drawn to the fortress itself, to its mile-high adamantine walls, its massive central gate, its battlements and, soaring above it all, the nine great towers, the *Konigsturm* at the centre, dominating all.

Nothing surrounds that massive edifice for a space of half a mile. Nothing, that is, except a huge moat, a hundred metres across and fifty deep. And into that moat, its motion never ceasing day or night, falls a great curtain of water, such that the fortress seems to rise from a pure white bed of mist, above which stretches a massive bridge, its single span arching a mile towards a second, equally massive gate that rises from a great dark mound, there at what used to be the Brandenburger Tor. Across that bridge, at every hour of every day, a mass of humanity flows, the servants of the King, uniformly dressed in black.

Asgard. I stare at it and catch my breath, for there, beneath the waning moon, lies the dark fortress itself, the Dream made real, its massive heap of night-dark stone more like a mountain than a castle, thrusting up from the heart of the ancient city, tier after tier of its massive central tower climbing the star-studded blackness.

I have been here once before, long ago, back in my youth, back when this massive edifice of sculpted basalt was brand new, the terror and envy of the world, yet seeing it now I am astonished once more by its size, by the physical reality of it.

Like all else here it is made of *Kunstlichestahl* – 'false steel' – more plastic than metal, though equally tough. Yet fake or not, its solidity is undeniable. It is German in a way that few buildings in our history have been. A castle. A fortress. An *embodiment*.

'There it is,' Burckel says, coming alongside me. '*Das Hornisse-nest.*'

A hornets' nest, indeed. I laugh, then turn my eyes from those soaring battlements. Burckel is watching me, his eyes weighing and measuring me in a way that I might find offensive in another. But I am conscious of what Burckel has gone through here. The state's spies are everywhere.

I follow, keeping close as we cross the bridge and descend into the Tempelhof. The steps and narrow alleyways are crowded now, the press of humanity increasing steadily as we near the *Vergnüngungspark* – the 'pleasure-ground'.

And suddenly, as we turn a corner, there, ahead of us, at the foot of a broad flight of steps, lies Von Richthofen Strasse, its broad avenue packed with pleasure seekers, throbbingly alive with music and the glare of lights from endless bars and cafes, their balconies cascading with flowers and greenery, like this is Babylon.

The evening's warm. Pushing through that densely packed crowd, my senses are once again assailed, this time by a hundred different smells, some sweet, some foul. There's an air of intoxication, of dangerous excitement, but so it is in these places, whatever the century. My eyes, however, note the differences. These are, after all, a 'sculpted' people, hand-crafted, one might say, by the great geneticists of the King's dark fortress. Some have longer arms, some heads that seem too thin or too broad. Some are tiny, like arrested children, while others have great muscular backs and chests. And though there is great variety, one notices immediately that such differences are differences of *type*, not of individuals. These people have been bred for specific tasks. Among them, Burckel and I are the exceptions. Not that we are alone, but *Naturlich* like us are in a distinct minority here. I see only three, maybe four others as we make our slow way through the press.

We're halfway along when I stop, my eyes caught by something. Burckel comes back and, taking my arm, speaks to my ear.

'What is it, Otto?'

I gesture towards a row of men and women dressed uniformly in black leather, their heads shaved, chained to the wall nearby – or not *chained*, I realise, but *plugged-in*, lengths of flex looping from sockets between their shoulders to a panel on the wall behind. It's all very high-tech, yet they have the look of slaves.

'Ah ...' Burckel says. 'The *Stopsel* ...'

Plug-ins. Of course. And he quickly explains that these are for hire, for any purpose. You have only to pay the requisite fee.

I turn, looking about me, and see another row of *Stopsel* further down, and, just across from us, another. As I watch, someone slips five credits into the slot of one of the panels and, as the flex falls free, catches it, then leads his purchase away.

It's brutal, yet no more ugly than things I've seen elsewhere, in other times. People have always sold themselves. If anything, it is its honesty that shocks.

Burckel walks on, past endless noisy bars and seething clubs, then ducks inside, into the *Schwartze Adler* –the Black Eagle. I follow him in, looking about me. It's done up like an ancient bier-keller, with great wooden trestle tables and crudely carved benches. There are slatted wooden partitions and iron cressets on the walls. Large-breasted, blonde-haired *Frau*, in tight, dark pleated skirts and frilly white blouses move between the tables, carrying large trays of foaming steiners. But I alone seem to notice the anachro-nistic strangeness of it all, for there, at the centre of that great barn of a room, two men – great shaven-headed brutes in combat gear – fight hand-to-hand in a jungle glade while a throng of eager-eyed customers look on from every side.

We stand there, watching.

There's the whack and thud of blows given and received. The two combatants grunt and sigh and groan as the death struggle nears its climax. It seems an equal match, and then one of them – the Russian – slips in his blood and falls and suddenly the bout is over in a blur of quick and vicious blows. Blood spurts, a fountain gush of blood, and a great cheer goes up – yet even as it does, the figures vanish, leaving the stage empty, a single spotlight picking out the bare wooden planks.

'Upstairs!' Burckel yells into my ear, his voice rising over the mob's excitement, and up we go, even as another figure – a tall, broad-shouldered man in a white senatorial toga trimmed with mauve – appears from out of nothing at the centre of the stage.

It is the war. Despatches from the front. Or maybe it's all staged – done for the Tri-Vees in some studio close by. All the same, the crowd laps it up, a gleam of bloodlust in every eye.

Burckel buys us a table in the far corner, bribing the pale, worm-like waiter heavily for the privilege, a *Wache*, or 'minder' positioning himself at the entrance to our open-sided booth.

'It's okay,' Burckel says, noting how silent I am. 'You can say what you like. The *Wache* are all deaf mutes.'

'So they tell you.'

But Burckel shakes his head. He isn't having any of it. In fact, he's grinning now, and as the waiter returns, he seems almost drunk. Burckel orders for us both – pork, potatoes, sauerkraut, gherkins and some savoury potato pancakes, *Kartoffelpuffer*, of which he knows I'm particularly fond. But my mind's not on the food. I'm thinking that he's been alone here too long. Or maybe he's taken something. Whatever it is, alarm bells have started ringing. I've seen agents go like this before.

I wait for him to order, then lean in close.

'What's happening, Albrecht?'

'Happening?' He looks at me, all innocent, then laughs. 'I've asked some friends to meet us here.'

I stiffen. *'Friends?'*

'You'll see.'

I stare at him, then stand. I am prepared to jump; to up and leave, right there and then, but as if sensing what I'm thinking, he reaches up and holds my arm. His expression has changed, that inane grin gone; his eyes are serious now.

'No, Otto. Stay. *Please.* You'll like them. I promise.'

283

My eyes fix on his. 'No one is supposed to know that I'm here. I thought you understood that.'

'I know, but it's okay. They think you're a relative. A cousin from the south.'

'You've *told* them about me?'

He nods. 'Look, it's okay. I've known them years.'

I stare at him a moment longer, then sit. 'Friends?' I ask again. 'What *kind* of friends?'

'You'll see.' And he turns away, the smile returning. That same silly smile that made me want to draw my gun and shoot the fucker. He's lost it. I can see that now. But I wait. And soon they come.

'Albrecht! And you, you must be Otto.'

I look up and meet his eyes. He's a big man, his smooth skull glinting red in the tavern's wavering light. His smile shows perfect teeth. He has his hand out to me, in the age-old, unchanging gesture, but I ignore it. I don't know who or what he is, and until I do ...

Burckel senses my hostility and tries to smooth things over, but I am watching the newcomer, my eyes trying to find something in his, some clue as to who he really is, because I'm sure he's someone, whatever Burckel says.

A Russian agent, maybe. Or a spy. Working for the fortress.

The two men who are with him are smaller, less significant, and I'm aware of them only as background shapes.

'Otto,' Burckel says, half rising from his seat, 'this is Werner.'

Werner. It's a good German name. But I'm far from certain that he's German.

He sits, facing me, not fazed at all by my refusal to shake his hand. His two friends – genetically adapted, I note – seat themselves either side of him, but back a bit, letting him dominate the table.

'Well, Otto,' he begins, the smile hovering on his lips, 'I've heard so much.'

I say nothing, just stare at him blankly, angry that Burckel has placed me in this situation. But Burckel clearly doesn't think he's done anything wrong. If anything he's angry at *me* now, for being so intransigent, so bloody-minded.

'Don't mind Otto,' he says, smiling nervously. 'He's tired, that's all. The journey from the south ...'

'They say the war's biting hard down there.'

It's an invitation to break the ice, but I decline it frostily. There's an awkward clearing of throats, then Werner stands.

'Maybe we should go. Leave you two alone ...'

But Burckel seems anxious that Werner and I be friends. 'No, stay. Please. It's Otto's way, that's all. Don't mind him.'

And the readiness with which the three men sit again confirms it for me. Anyone else would have left by now, offended by my behaviour, but they're staying. Why? Out of friendship with Burckel? No. Something's fishy here. Smiling suddenly, I cast out my little net.

'So what do you do, Werner?'

There's the tiniest little blink of surprise, and then he smiles again. 'I'm a gene surgeon.'

'And these?' I indicate the two who flank him.

'They're mine. My children, you might say.'

It's unexpected. 'So how do you know Albrecht?'

He sits back, his right arm gesturing to our surroundings. 'We share a love of the old, I guess.'

I look about me, conscious of what a throwback to the Past this place is. Almost authentic, only the wooden surfaces aren't wood, just as the stone isn't stone, but *Kunstlichestahl*. But then, nothing's natural here.

'So how's business?'

There's the slightest hesitation before he answers, enough to suggest that he's carefully considering his words.

'You know how it is.'

I don't, but I can guess. Genetics are strictly controlled in this society, and if I remember correctly there are tight restrictions. In all probability our friend caters for the black economy. But I'm not going to ask. It does make me look at him again, however, and though he's dressed simply – black vest, black baggy trousers and black slip-ons – there's something *groomed* about him that suggests he's not short of money.

'And you, Otto? How's the history business?'

I smile, then look to Burckel. From his evident embarrassment I can see he's let slip far more than he ought.

'It's fine,' I say, and hope that's innocuous enough. But I'm worried now. Such indiscretion in an agent is bad. It puts all of us at risk. And if Werner *is* a Russian …

'Will you have a drink?'

The big man smiles, relaxing slightly. 'That'd be nice. A beer, please.'

'And your friends?'

But he shakes his head, and I reassess his relationship with his silent companions, reminding myself that this is, beyond all else, a world of masters and servants.

94

When they're gone, I quietly ask Burckel what the fuck he thinks he's doing, and whether he's had our friend Werner properly checked out. He says he has, but I don't believe him. In fact, I'm so sure there's something wrong about the man, that I'm half-convinced I ought to check him out myself. Only that'd be no help to Ernst.

It's then that I break the rules and ask Burckel directly what Hecht said to him.

'I can't say,' he answers, but he's having a hard time avoiding my eyes. I get the feeling that he wants to tell me badly, if only to make up for his other indiscretions.

'But you know why I'm here?'

He shakes his head. So I explain – about Ernst and the energy-trap and how we've traced the power-anchor to this point. And it makes me wonder just what *was* in Hecht's letter, because if he knew none of that ...

Burckel says he can help. He knows someone. He just has to make a call.

I wait, while he goes to make it. And while he's gone, while I'm looking about me, casually studying the people at nearby tables, it's then that I have my second shock of the night. There, seated not half a dozen paces from me is an unpleasant little weasel of a man who I last saw back in the twenty-third century.

Dankevich! Urd's breath! It's Dankevich!

I quickly turn away, lest he sees me through the latticed wall of the booth. But what am I going to do? If I leave he'll see me. And if I don't ...

When Burckel returns, I grab his sleeve and pull him down, speaking urgently to his ear. He blinks, surprised, then stares directly at Dankevich, clearly recognising him.

'Another friend?' I ask quietly, and he nods.

'He calls himself Schmidt,' Burckel says quietly. 'Andreas Schmidt.'

But there's no time for more. At that moment, Dankevich stands and, throwing down a couple of credit chips, turns and leaves. I'm up at once, but when Burckel makes to follow, I turn on him.

'Wait! I'll come straight back.'

I follow Dankevich out and almost lose him in the street, then see him duck down a side alley and force my way through the crowd, hurrying to catch up. Again, I think I've lost him, but then I see him hovering in the shadows just ahead, waiting, it seems, for a door to be opened. As it does, so the light reveals his features once again, removing any last doubts. It's Dankevich all right – the same bastard I killed. And though I knew he was here, the shock of finding him so close – there in that bar, at a table so near to me – has fed my paranoia to the point where I want to jump right out of there, before the whole damn scheme collapses.

Dankevich. What the fuck was Dankevich doing at that table?

But it confirms what I suspected. The Russians have targeted Burckel. *Surrounded* him with 'friends'. And I've jumped into this.

I turn and hurry back, but when I get there, Burckel's gone. I wait close on thirty minutes, then, when he doesn't show, I settle the bill and leave.

He's not in his room, nor has he left a message. But just as I begin to lose patience, he returns.

'This is ...'

'A friend?' I stare at the man. To my eyes he looks identical to the two goons Werner brought along with him. He's the very same type. There's probably a name for it, but I don't ask Burckel right then. My priority is to dig Burckel out of the mess he's got himself into.

'You wanted help,' the newcomer says. Statement, not question. I look to Burckel, but he's just grinning again, like he knows something I don't.

'It depends what you mean ...' I begin, then understand just why Burckel's grinning. This is his contact. His man on the inside. The one he made the call to.

He looks to Burckel. 'Is the room clean?'

'It was when I left.'

'Not good enough,' he says. So we leave the room and ascend, taking the stairs this time, avoiding people, until we're standing on that great ledge once again, staring out across the misted dark towards the fortress.

'So what can you tell me?' I ask, now that he's free to speak openly.

'Tell me first why you want to know?'

It seems a fair request, so I tell him. 'Albrecht and I ... we're *Undrehungar.* We want to overthrow those fuckers.'

'*Undrehungar* ...' He clearly likes the word. *Revolutionaries.* He says it a second time, then laughs.

'Albrecht I trust, but why you? How do I know ...?'

'That I'm *genuine*?' I shrug. 'You don't. You'll just have to take my word.'

'I don't have to.'

'No. But someone will. *Someone* will give me the information that I need.'

'Not everybody knows it.'

But he doesn't seem smug about it. Once more it's a statement of fact, and I begin to like our new friend.

'What's your name?'

He laughs, and I realise I'm not going to get a name. A name is something that could be tortured out of me, and then maybe *he'd* find himself in the chair, being tortured.

'Okay,' I say finally. 'Your choice. But I tell you this. There are other forces at work here. They want to preserve things as they are. They don't want to see this regime fall. They want to prop it up until it decays from within.'

'And who are these people?'

'The Russians.'

He laughs, and doesn't stop chuckling for quite some while, as if it really was amusing. And finally, when he has his voice back, he asks me why the Russians – our deadly enemies – should want to do that.

'Because they view things in the longer term.'

'Really? Then watch …'

And, as if on cue, there are a series of blue flashes on the horizon, far to our right, at the eastern edge of the great sprawl of Berlin. I'm puzzled at first, but then our friend hands me a VEU – a visual enhancement unit – and, slipping it over my eyes, I see just what those tiny blue flashes are, and understand. They're missiles. I see the bright detonations, hear – a moment later – the dull concussions. I watch for some while, seeing how they move oddly, erratically, with a kind of predatory malice, as if they're looking down at the streets below, searching out specific targets.

'See how they do that?' the stranger says. 'The idea is to terrify the populace. Bigger, faster missiles would be more effective, but those things do far more psychological harm.'

We watch as a swarm of cruisers launch from the fortress, swooping out like great winged insects, heading east over the city to engage the enemy missiles. It's quite a sight, and we're not alone on the rooftops as the battle commences. Two of the big lasers open up from the fortress, sending fierce beams of searing light flashing out into the darkness, the after-image so bright it seems scorched upon the retina. The air is sharp with the burning smell of ozone.

And then, with a suddenness that seems almost anti-climactic, it's over.

I turn and look at him. 'How often do they do that?'

'Attack us? Oh, most nights. Sometimes three, even four times. It's like they want to remind us that it's not all being fought out on Tri-Vee.'

Burckel, who has been silent all this time, now clears his throat. 'Well?' he asks. 'Will you help us?'

The stranger stares at me, his dark eyes considering, then turns away. 'We'll meet tomorrow. I'll give you a decision then.'

Why not now? I want to ask. But I can guess the answer. Our friend is not working alone. He wants to consult someone. A committee, maybe. *Undrehungar* – real revolutionaries – not fakes like us.

'All right,' I say, keeping my impatience in check. 'And if there's anything we can do for you ...'

'*You?*' He laughs once more, as if what I've said is just the funniest thing he's heard in years. And, as he walks away, I hear him say a single word, the irony heavy in his voice.

'*Undrehungar* ...'

95

Burckel is angry with me. He thinks I was heavy-handed. And maybe I was. Only I'm far more angry with him, even if I don't show it.

'You don't know just how long I've cultivated my contacts here,' he says, pacing the floor, the glow globe in the corner illuminating his angry face. 'You come along here and think in one day you know it all, but you fucking well don't! You don't know the first fucking thing about what's going on!'

I'm sitting on the bed, watching him pace. 'Have you considered the possibility that they're spies, or Russians even?'

He stops and stares at me. 'Of course I've fucking thought of it. I'm not stupid. Hecht didn't pick me for my stupidity.'

That's true. Only something might have happened. A blow to the head. Some drug slipped into his drink. Anything, in fact. And the result? One ineffective agent who only *thinks* he's in control.

But that's the danger with 'sitters'. I meet his eyes and give a tired smile. 'I'm sorry. We seem to have got off on the wrong foot. It's just ... I'm worried. About Ernst.'

That's also true, but it's not the whole truth. I'm worried about Katerina. About leaving that situation for too long. For while I could, theoretically, jump back there any time I wanted, I'm still uneasy. Uneasy, yes, and missing her. Missing her badly.

'So what do you want to do?' Burckel asks, happier now that I've apologised. 'You know, before the meeting tomorrow. You want to see the city?'

I shake my head. 'No. First I want to find out about the place Dankevich visited.'

'Dankevich?'

'Your friend Schmidt.'

'Ah...' He looks thoughtful. 'You're sure it was him – Dankevich?'

'I'm certain of it. I killed the little fucker.'

'Then ...?'

'Different part of the loop,' I say. Even so, it's disconcerting how often I've killed men, only for them to pop up once again. That's the trouble with Time: it's not sequential.

'You want to do that first thing tomorrow?'

I stand and shake my head. 'No. Let's do it now. After all, who knows what mischief that little weasel is up to.'

96

It's a little after two when we get back there. Von Richtofen Strasse is still busy, but there's not the dense press of bodies there was earlier. Tomorrow's a work day for most, and life can be hard in the eye of the fortress – even so, enough remain to make the night eventful.

'Ignore the jags,' Burckel says to me, steering me away from a group of young men who sway drunkenly together outside one of the bars. 'We don't want any trouble.'

'*Jags?*' But even as I say it, it comes back to me. It's a catch-all phrase for drunks and lowlifes and addicts.

The side alley is empty. Telling Burckel to wait for me on the corner, I walk along until I'm facing the door Dankevich went into. There's no sign, not a word to say what the place is, but I guess it must be some kind of club from the peephole in the door. And someone is clearly watching from the other side, for as I go to turn away, the door opens and a big man – he has to crouch to get out under the lintel – steps into the alley.

'What do you want?'

It's too late to say 'nothing'. He's seen that I'm interested. But I don't really want to go inside, not if Dankevich is still there. I just want to know what the place is.

'A friend of mine said you were worth a visit.' I hesitate, then, 'I'm from the south ...'

'Ah ...' And he looks me up and down, then nods to himself. These Berliners think they're a good ten IQ points above their southern German cousins, and have done since time immemorial.

'Your friend ... did he have a name?'

I'm tempted to say Schmidt, but if Dankevich *is* inside ...

'Look, if I'm not welcome ...'

There's a moment's calculation in his face and then he stands aside. It's not an easy thing for such a big man to do in such a small alley, but now I can't back out. I could walk away, only that would just draw attention, and I'm pretty sure they've got me on camera. And if they *are* Russians ...

As the door closes behind me, I stand there in that tiny ante-room, conscious of his sheer size, his bulk and height. I'm a tall man myself, but this brute's a good foot and a half taller than me. Not only that, but he has hands the size of dinner plates. And they look incredibly strong.

There's another door directly in front of us, and while we wait for it to open, I feel intensely claustrophobic standing beside the big man. He seems to loom over me – to fill the room about me. I can smell the brutish perfume of the man – his *scent*. It's an uncomfortable feeling, and I wonder again just what I've got myself into.

Even so, I have an answer. The club is called *Das Rothaarige* – 'The Red-Haired One'. The two words are on a plaque beside the inner door, beneath a cameo of a long-haired man.

Red hair. It makes me think. Of Barbarossa, the red-bearded king of early Germany, and of Hitler's Russian campaign, named after him. Yes, and of the Rus', themselves, named after the band of red-haired Scandinavians who formed Kievan Rus', back in the middle of the tenth century.

The door doesn't open. Beside me the big man grows restless. I turn, meaning to ask him what the problem is, and see he has one of those massive hands to his ear, listening to something in his head. He nods silently, then turns to face the outer door, speaking to me as he does.

'It seems your friend wants to come in too.'

'My friend?' But then I see what he means and I almost groan. Why can't Burckel leave things be?

The door swings open.

'Otto, I—'

The big man grabs him, pulls him inside, then slams the door shut.

Almost at once the inner door opens, to the smell of cigar smoke and cologne and the soft murmur of conversation, interlaced with electronic music. Nothing loud or intrusive, the kind of thing that you might expect in such a club at any time, in any century. Stockhausen's *Licht*, if I'm not mistaken.

It's a gambling club, I see that at once, nor is it very big. I turn to thank the big man, but he's gone. In his place stands another man: small, almost arrow-thin, a polite, yet genuinely friendly smile on his face. He would seem ordinary, but for his flame-red shoulder-length hair.

'Herren ...'

I return his bow, then note how he glances at Burckel.

'You should have said,' he says, returning his gaze to me.

'Said?'

'That you were Herr Burckel's cousin.'

Again, my heart sinks. Is there not one place that Burckel hasn't made waves?

'I wondered about the name ...'

Rothaarige smiles, then reaches up to touch the loose-hanging ends of his hair. 'It's not hair,' he explains. 'Not real hair, anyway.'

I wait for something more, but it seems that's all he has to say on the subject. 'You'd like to play, Herren?'

I turn and look around the tables. There are six big, hexagonal tables with blue electrostatic tops. They're crowded, a dozen or more players – well-dressed men, mainly – standing about them, but there's no sign of Dankevich, nor can I see any other familiar faces.

I feel in my pocket then shrug. 'My money, I—'

Rothaarige smiles. 'Herr Burckel's credit is good. What would you like? A thousand marks?'

It's more than a month's wages in this world, but the players in here don't look like working men.

'Okay. But that's all.'

He laughs. 'I'd heard you *suden Deutsch* were cautious.'

If it's meant to goad me, it doesn't work. Cautious is good. I only wish Burckel was showing more caution.

The truth is, I hate gambling and I want to get out of there as soon as possible, but leaving isn't an option. Not yet. I really need to know why our friend Dankevich frequents this place. Is *he* a gambler? If so, how can I use that?

But underlying all my thoughts is the feeling that I have made a mistake by coming here. Maybe a big mistake.

A young man appears at my side and hands me what appear to be ten six-inch iron-black plastic spikes. They're pointed at one end, flattened at the other, like ancient nails. Indeed, the similarity is so striking that I stare at them in my hand, until Rothaarige laughs.

'You've not gambled before, Herr ...'

He's fishing for my second name, but I ignore him. 'One hundred each?' I ask, and he nods, then ushers us over to the nearest table. The crowd move aside, allowing us a place, and, glancing down, I see that the blue glow of the table is an illusion. Marked out within the great hexagon is something I recognise instantly.

At the centre of the table are two diagrams, each circle in each diagram the size of a large coin. Some are brightly lit, some grey. The top one is the chemical diagram for the adenine-thymine base pair, white lines linking the represented atoms, while beneath it is that of the guanine-cytosine bases. Between them they make up the constituents of DNA and thus of life itself. *All* life. And there, surrounding them, forming a great circle at the edge of the table, is the double helix spiral itself.

Again, some parts of that great circle are lit, while others are dull, and even as I watch, one of the circles – representing a carbon atom – comes alive suddenly, and I feel excitement grow about the table.

'I call it the Game of Life,' Rothaarige says quietly to my ear, 'though the common herd know it as Spirals. You know it?'

I wonder what's best, to bluff, or show my ignorance. But I'm curious now, and he seems willing to explain.

'Each player buys his cards, one hundred a card, a minimum of five cards, maximum ten. Play progresses clockwise from the dealer. Each player chooses one card from his hand at each turn. And no huffing. If you *can* play a card, you *must*.'

I look about me, seeing how, in front of each player, there's a tiny glade of plastic spikes, like miniature pines, stretching out from the dark cushion at the edge of the table, and how, just beneath my hand, the table is mottled with tiny holes. Some of the spikes are lit, others dark.

'Should I buy my cards now?'

'I'm afraid that's not allowed,' Rothaarige says kindly. 'Not until this round is over. You see, the winner is the one who plays the last card. It would be unfair if you were to enter the game now, after so much has already been staked.'

'I see.' And I do, but only vaguely, and so he continues.

'There are fifty-nine circles in all, but one hundred and eighteen cards … two packs, essentially. The idea is to match a card in your hand with one of the circles on the table. You slip the card into the slot just there. Any player who completes one of the four bases gets a reward – one twelfth of the existing stake. Similarly, a player who completes one of the pairings is also rewarded – only this time one sixth of the total stake. The greatest reward, however, goes to the player who plays the final card. He claims a full half of what remains.'

'And the rest?'

'Goes to the house, of course.' Rothaarige smiles at me. 'Though not all of it. One third of the house's profit becomes the players' stake in the greater game, though they must continue playing if they want to lay claim to it. If they drop out … well …'

My eyes trace the great, circular double helix and note, once again, how certain parts are lit, others dark.

'I don't follow you …'

'It's simple. Whoever finishes one of the base pair can claim a matching pair on the outer spiral. AT or CG, or their inverse pairings. If they can then complete a minor groove, or even a major, they are rewarded further.'

'A minor being ...?'

'Four consecutive strands, a major six.'

'Ah ...' And, looking once more, I see how far any of the players are from such rewards. But the night is young and the players keen. I make a quick calculation and begin to understand why the small man laughed at my thousand. It would go nowhere in this game, not with more than eight players at the table.

I watch, seeing how the circles light up, one after another. There's a small cry of delight as one of the players, a stooped old greybeard, completes the Thymine base. A moment later, a dozen or so of the spikes in front of him – previously dark – light up, bringing a warm glow to his deeply lined face.

It's twenty minutes before I finally get to play. Rothaarige's gone now, but Burckel seems keen to help. He's played before and, as I'm handed my cards, he tries to take them from me.

I bat his hand away.

Burckel frowns. 'I was only ...'

I glare at him, then sort my cards and look to the table. I have ten cards – ten options on the board. I can see already how tactical this game can be, how, if one kept back two matching cards, one might win. Given luck. Only the point is I *want* to lose. To get out of there as quickly as I can.

I play, ignoring Burckel, making him sigh with exasperation.

'Otto, that was foolish ...'

I say nothing. Watch my ten cards dwindle to two, realising that the meagre little copse of spikes below me are all dark.

'You want to increase your stake?' Burckel asks. 'You can if you want, Otto. I—'

'*Albrecht.*'

He falls silent.

I play my penultimate card. There are eight players, and though three of them are unable to play – their cards are doubles of cards already played and therefore worthless – there are still eight unlit circles on the table, evenly distributed, two to a base.

The fun starts here.

I watch as the play moves away from me around the table. Cytosine is quickly claimed. Other circles brighten. The player two to my right joins those unable to play, his two remaining cards doubles.

There are two circles unlit in Guanine and I have one of them, the rare N9. I hold my breath as my neighbour slips his final card into the slot. There's the briefest pause while the machine registers the play, and then the unlit C1 atom on the Guanine lights and I know I've won.

Burckel whoops. This particular game may be over for us, but we've won back our stake. Not only that, but I've earned one strand in the greater game.

I speak to Burckel's ear. 'We have to go.'

'But you can't,' he answers openly, not caring if he's overheard. 'You have a *presence* now, on the outer spiral.'

'That's a loser's game, Albrecht.'

'I'll stake you.'

'That's not the point. We need to go.'

Rothaarige appears at my elbow and gently touches my arm. 'Well done, Otto. That was subtly played. Next time, perhaps, you'll—'

He stops abruptly, turning, as we all do, to face the hammering at the outer door. He seems concerned, and I wonder for the first time whether this is legal. Then I notice how his hair seems to ripple. There's the faintest light flowing through it, as if through fibre-optics, and as it does, so he seems to calm. Smiling his apologies, he walks towards the door, even as it opens.

Rothaarige is a small man, but he seems to make himself even smaller as he nears the door, cringing almost, apologetic. And then I see why. Coming through the door, literally having to squeeze through it merely to get inside, is a monster of a man, so big that I wonder how both he and the doorman managed to get into that tiny ante-room. He's masked, yet even so, all there know who, or rather *what*, he is.

'Welcome, Guildsman,' Rothaarige says, his voice unctuous now, his whole manner suddenly, strangely servile. Or maybe not so strange. The Guild of the Teuton Knights is not to be messed with.

The Guildsman turns, scanning the room as if for enemies, then fixes the small man in his visored sight.

'Is the room prepared?'

Rothaarige nods and bows low. 'Of course, Guildsman. If you would come with me.'

But as I glance at those close by, I see how every eye is now averted, as if the Guildsman is not there, and though I'm curious to see one of them, I do likewise. Yet maybe I've seen enough. He's like a piece of crafted metal, his armoured exoskeleton more insectile than human, his hands like massive instruments of torture. And his eyes ...

Mechanical yet human. The nearest thing to a machine, and yet alive.

Beside me, Burckel shudders, and as the door shuts on the far side of the gaming room, he murmurs something.

'What?'

Burckel looks to me, his eyes haunted. 'I hate those bastards.'

But he says no more. He's not allowed to. We both know what's to come, but of it we are not allowed to speak, not even to each other.

'Come,' I say, now that Rothaarige has gone. 'I want out of here. *Now.*'

A Teuton guildsman and a Russian agent, both frequenting the same club. As we walk back down the levels to Burckel's apartment, I ponder whether there might be a connection, and if so of what kind. Was the Guildsman merely a player, or was he there to meet someone – Dankevich, perhaps? Or was it just coincidence? Whichever, I don't mention any of this to Burckel. He, for his part, is annoyed with me for coming away before we'd had the chance to make a line of four, or maybe even six.

'You're a lucky man, Otto,' he says, as he turns the lock and pushes open the door. 'But you ought to trust your luck, not shun it.'

I follow him inside, making no comment, wondering just where the hell I'm supposed to sleep in this mess.

'I'm sorry it's so …' And then he laughs. 'I never was tidy. Even as a child, in the Garden. I—'

I stare at him, shocked. '*Albrecht!* Have you *forgotten?*'

'Forgotten? No, I …' And then he laughs again, but this time it's in embarrassment. 'I'm sorry, I'm not supposed to speak of that, am I? It's—'

Secret, yes.

I contemplate jumping right out of there at once, but decide against it. Burckel clearly doesn't know what he's done and I'm not about to panic him. Even so, I change my plans. Hecht needs to know about this, and soon.

I look about me for the makings of another bed, but there's nothing, only piles of clutter. Burckel, however, seems unperturbed. 'You have the bed,' he says. 'I'll make myself comfortable on the floor.'

'Are you sure?'

'Of course. And look – you have to forgive me, Otto. I've not been myself tonight. If I've been a little *indiscreet*, well, I'm sorry, only it's been so long since I've had company. Someone I can trust.'

It's only a small glimpse, but suddenly I see how vulnerable he's felt being here. And little wonder, really, for this is the most dangerous place of all. Here at the fulcrum. Here where it all begins.

'That's okay,' I say, softening to him for the first time. 'It must have been hard.'

'*Hard?*' Burckel sighs. 'You just don't know, Otto. You really don't.'

98

I hear his breathing change, and when the pattern of his snoring becomes regular, I get up and, careful not to knock anything over in the dark, make my way to his desk and find the journal.

I'm sure the answer's here. And so, clutching the heavy volume to my chest, I jump. Back to Four-Oh. Back to Zarah and Urte – and Hecht.

Hecht is surprised to see me. He asks me what I've got, and so I show him, and, because this is not a specialty of his, he calls in Lothar, our expert in *ge'not*, and, throwing up an image of the last page on a screen, Lothar reads a passage aloud.

The translation sounds awkward, the words like an ill put-together poem, but when I query this, Lothar just smiles.

'What you're hearing is just one level of it, Otto. In *ge'not* the words are paired, like the genetic bases they derive from – "twisted together", you might say. I would need to work on this a while to get the full meaning of it. It's heavily concept-based ... it works at a higher level than normal everyday language. I liken it to Chinese poetry. It doesn't have one single, defined meaning.'

'I see. Then to translate this whole volume ...?'

'Oh, I'll have it back to you within the hour. Our machines can do the basic stuff. But what are you looking for?'

I tell him and he hurries away, even as Hecht looks up at me again.

'What's happening, Otto? Why did you jump back so soon?'

'I think Albrecht's cracking up. His conditioning has gone. He ... mentioned the Garden.'

'Loki's breath!' Hecht rarely curses, so the words have added force. 'Wait here, Otto. Make yourself at home. I'll not be long.'

I watch him go, then turn, looking about me at the shadowed room. I have been here many times, but I've never been alone here and, more from curiosity than anything, I walk across and, calling for light, pour myself a coffee, then turn back, studying what's on Hecht's shelves. He might be back at any moment, but I'm certain he wouldn't mind. After all, he trusts me. I am his *Einzelkind*.

It takes but a glance to realise that the books here are sorted into four distinct sections. The first of these is familiar to me – classics of Russian and German literature, from that brief flowering of the novel, that Golden Age of literary endeavour. They're first editions, by the look of them: Pushkin and Lermontov, Gogol, Chekhov, Turgenev and Dostoevsky, Tolstoy, Pasternak and Gorky, Zamatin, Solzhenitsyn and Pelevin; Fontaine and Schiller, Goethe, Holderlin and Kleist, Nietzsche and Rilke, Mann, Hesse and Grass. There are others too, lesser writers, forgotten by the tide of history, yet not a single great work is absent, and, taking one from the shelf – Hesse's *Magister Ludi* – I open it and read the handwritten dedication:

'*To Hecht, with profound thanks and in eternal friendship, Hermann Hesse.*'

The ink seems fresh as yesterday, the book just off the press.

I smile, then pluck another from the shelves. They're all the same. In each one is a personal dedication.

Hecht *has* been busy.

To their right is a second section. There are novels here too, and histories, of individual men and of nations, yet not a single book is familiar. These are from alternate timestreams, documents from cultures that have ceased to be: that blinked out of existence as some *Zeitverandern* – some Time-Change – swept it all to dust.

The books here are mainly in German or Russian – the lives of so-called 'great men'. And so they might have been, but not in our time. No, in *our* world, these died, or never were, or were deflected from their paths to 'greatness' by some chance event.

I take one down – a study of Charles the Bountiful – and, flicking through, begin to read, then laugh with surprise. This is my period, my century – *Frederick's* century – and yet there's no sign of him anywhere in this account. In this world, Prussia does not exist, nor any of the minor German states. No, all is Frankish here, from the shores of Portugal to the Urals. The heirs of Charlemagne are rulers in *this* world. Or should I say *the heir*, for in this reality Charlemagne's son, Charles the Bold, had his brothers Lothar and Louis killed, and so there never was a division of the kingdom into three, no Kingdom of the Germans east of the Rhine.

I slip the book back, then move on. This next section – the third – is perhaps the strangest of all, for here are endless volumes written, it seems, in gibberish, or in code, or what might pass as code if I didn't recognise one or two of them from my travels. These once again are from alternate time-lines, only these are in strange, hybrid languages that only Lothar and his team could possibly read; worlds so far from the central flow of Time that our agents have but touched upon them briefly and withdrawn, bringing these trophies back.

You might ask how. After all, nothing that is not made of our genetic material can be brought back from the past. They would disintegrate the moment they appeared on the platform. And that remains the truth. Only we have built machines – *duplicators* – that can be taken back by agents and used to copy most of the smaller artefacts we need if we're to function in the Past: books, brooches and coins, maps and medals, weapons, jewellery and a hundred other necessary objects. Without them we could not function. Without them ... well, we might as soon jump back naked.

I drain my coffee and, setting the cup down, walk over to the final set of shelves.

These are different from the others; the shelves are much broader, and sub-divided into cubbyholes. Inside each cubbyhole is a set of ancient scrolls. Or not so ancient, for these too seem freshly made – the parchment new, or at most a few years old.

Again I smile. These I know about, for Hecht has sometimes leant me a 'book' or two from this part of his private library. They're in Greek and Latin for the main part, 'lost' works by the great writers of the pre-Christian era. Aristotle's complete *Dialogues* is here, along with 'new' works by Catullus, Seneca and Epicurus. Archimedes' earliest mathematical works are also here, next to poetry by Sappho and – a gem among many gems – Julius Caesar's private journals. And lurid reading they make, too.

But that's not all. Beside these works by writers known to Time, are others by authors whose work – unpublished, or forgotten – are easily their equal. The Genoan, Augusto Landucci's epic *Rebirth* cycle is here, for instance, written sixty years before Dante's *Inferno*, and easily its superior – just one of many classics that were suppressed or openly destroyed by rivals, or by the church, or simply lost through circumstance.

I take one down and, unfurling it, read a line or two. It's Virgil's *Juvenilia* – the complete and amended version.

I look about me at the shelves, wondering a moment.

So much lost. So much forgotten. So much endeavour to so little purpose. Yes, and so many lives gone to dust and not a trace of them. Those mute inglorious Tams.

I return the scroll to its place then turn to find Hecht standing there, his face strange, his eyes oddly distracted.

'Is everything okay?'

'Yes …' He stops and looks at me. His grey eyes are pained. 'I thought for a moment we were undone. If they had got to the Garden …'

The Garden is where our children are. Cut off in Time and Space from any harm. Not even Zarah knows its whereabouts. Only Hecht knows, and the machine. And without Hecht's physical presence on the platform, the path to that safest of all havens is closed.

'All's well?'

He nods. 'I've made changes. Reprogrammed the machine. Even so … the very fact that his conditioning's failed … It shouldn't be possible.'

No, and it's never happened before. But then, a lot's been happening recently that's not supposed to happen, and that doesn't augur well. We've kept ahead of the Russians for so long that we deemed it our right, as if History were ours, but now they've got the upper hand. Maybe it's sheer numbers, but they seem to have the jump on us at last.

As Hecht settles into his pit and begins to tap away at his keyboard, I tell him exactly what happened back down the line in Albrecht's time. Occasionally he tuts, or glances up, but mainly he listens until I'm done, and then he shakes his head.

'I think you're right, Otto. I think the Russians have surrounded him. But let's persevere. Find out what they're up to. It might prove crucial. Besides, we've no chance at all of saving Ernst unless Albrecht's friend can find the power source for us. Hang in there.'

Meanwhile, I'll rustle up some cover. And don't worry, Otto. You won't be alone in there, I promise you.'

'There's one other thing.'

'Go on.'

'I don't know enough about the Age. I feel *unprepared*. And I don't know how much I can rely on Albrecht to fill in the gaps. Maybe I should—'

Hecht cuts me off. 'I take your point, Otto, but there's no time. As soon as we know what's in the journal, I want you straight back in.'

I make to protest, to remind him that we've all the time in the world, but for once Hecht is adamant. 'Don't fuss, Otto. You don't need to know any more than you do already.'

I don't argue. Besides, most men know little of the Ages they inhabit. It's only later, historically, that they begin to make sense of things. But I like being in control, and this once I don't feel I've got a solid grasp on anything. *That's* what I want to say to Hecht. Only I don't know that I should. He trusts me, after all.

He meets my eyes. 'Is there anything else?'

'No.'

'Then go and see Lothar. I'll join you there in an hour.'

I realise I'm dismissed, and so I turn and leave, unhappy for once. Maybe that business with the Garden has got to Hecht, but I've never known him so off-hand. Not to me, anyway.

Lothar, however, is glad to see me. His team – himself and two assistants, red-headed young men who look as if they could be twins but for a difference of ten years in their ages – have already got a dozen or more pages ready for me to read.

I sit down at one of the long benches, among the piles of foreign dictionaries and lexicons that clutter the desks, and begin to read. The walls surrounding me are stacked high with yet more volumes, and there's the smell of coffee in the air.

Lothar leans across. 'The top line – the blue – is the literal trans-lation, the bottom – the red – the metaphoric commentary. The idea is to try and read the two in tandem. Of course, it's not as satisfactory as reading the original, but ...'

I try it and see what he means. He throws up an image of the first few symbols on a nearby screen. They look like ornate iron-work – the kind you see on the gates of eighteenth-century mansions, all curls and curlicues and delicate spikes – only so fine as to be almost mesmeric to the eye; more like Arabic than Chinese.

'You know how *ge'not* developed?' Lothar asks, and when I don't respond, he continues anyway. 'It sprang from the need to keep up with developments in genetics. The abbreviation stands for "genetic notation". It's a kind of shorthand for the basic concepts of genetics. Or so it was intended. Only by the time two or three centuries had passed there were more than fifty thousand separate characters, each one describing something highly specific. Most of them are derived, of course, from the basic one hundred and forty-two root symbols, and the whole language – if I can call it such – has been through three major revisions in its time, but the basic emphasis of the language – as a direct reflection of a single field of human activity, *genetics* – remains unchanged.'

Even as Lothar speaks, more pages arrive, fresh from trans-lation, numbered and dated so that he can sort them into order for me. I look through, half concentrating on what Burckel has written, half on what Lothar is telling me.

'At first *ge'not* was used almost exclusively by geneticists, but later ...' He laughs, and I look up. Lothar is smiling, anticipating his own story. 'You'd not believe it, really, Otto, but it took a poet – Angossi, an Italian! – to use *ge'not*, part pictorially but also for its metaphoric richness. You've heard of Angossi?'

Who hadn't? But I indulge Lothar with a smile, as if it's the first time I've heard all this.

'In Angossi's hands, what was mere transliteration became poetic flight of fancy. He organised the language into a new, fragmented form – much like what we see here in Burckel's journal. These are not so much sentences or paragraphs as ... well, how do I put it? The purest *ge'not* is a form of maths. It quite literally adds up. If it didn't, it wouldn't make sense. You see, every symbol has its own value, its own *weight*, and—'

I interrupt. 'Hold on ... how on earth do they ever use such a difficult language? I mean, if it's so varied, so rich in meaning and yet also so mathematically precise?'

Lothar chuckles. 'They don't. *Verwendung ge'not* – that is, "used" *ge'not* – is a bastardised form, based on the two thousand eight hundred and sixty symbols Angossi chose from among the totality. Considering what he omitted it's quite subtle really, though nothing like as expressive as it *might* have been.' He sighs. 'If only Angossi had been a better linguist. Still, it's got more clever over the generations – become almost a creole, if you know what I mean.'

I nod, then whistle to myself, as I read what Burckel has written at the foot of the page

'Have you read any of these yet?'

Lothar shakes his head. 'Not in the full sense of it. Words, phrases ... Why, what does it say?'

But I'm up out of my seat and at the door. I want Hecht to see this and I can't wait another hour.

99

I jump back, precisely to the point I left. Not a second has passed. Even so, Burckel senses I've been gone. He wakes and sits up in the darkness.

'Otto? Is that you?'

'It's me,' I say, and, sliding the journal back into place, I make my way carefully back to the bed.

'Did you go back?'

I hesitate, sitting on the edge of that narrow pallet bed, then decide to tell him the truth. Or part of it.

'Yes. I was worried. Especially about Dankevich.'

'I didn't know he was a Russian. But now that I do ...'

I don't like the fact that I can't see Burckel, but it's late and I don't want to put on the light.

'We'll talk in the morning,' I say. 'I'm tired.'

'Was Hecht angry with me?'

'Why should he be angry?'

'For letting slip about the Garden. I've been worrying about it ever since you pointed it out. Worried he might think me ... *unreliable*.'

It is precisely what Hecht thinks, but I don't say that.

'Go to sleep, Albrecht. We'll talk about it in the morning.'

100

Only we don't. We're woken just before dawn by a banging on the door that would wake the dead.

While I'm still struggling up from sleep, Burckel calls for light, then throws me a gun. Jumping up, he goes across to the door and peers through the peephole, then reaches for the bolt and draws it back.

It's Burckel's friend, the nameless one. The *revolutionary*. He tells us to get dressed quickly and come with him. He hands us each a pass, marked TEMPORARY ACCESS ONLY, and when I ask him where we're going, he just shakes his head and says:

'Don't speak. Not a word. And leave the guns. You won't need them where we're going.'

I don't like the situation – I don't like having to trust strangers in an Age I don't really know – but there seems little choice.

Out in the corridor he turns left, ignoring the distracting images on the walls, walking with a quick and easy stride.

But we don't go far. Coming to a small door set into the wall, we stop. It's another lift, I realise, a small, service lift. Our friend takes a flat octagonal piece of plastic from his pocket and places it in the slot. A small overhead camera scans him and accepts his ID. *Maintenance*, I realise. *Our friend works in maintenance.*

The door hisses open and we step inside. Standing there in that narrow, box-like space, I stare into Burckel's eyes, seeing not the slightest flicker of the madness I think may have overtaken him. In fact, he looks so sane that I have to remind myself of that slip about the Garden, yes, and that journal entry too. If he could say those things then potentially he could do anything – maybe place all our lives at risk. Only not just yet. The moment hasn't come. Albrecht Burckel has yet to be tested, and until he is, I need him, because he's my key to these people and these people are my key to freeing Ernst.

I have my orders, you understand. And one of them is to kill him once we're finished here.

Burckel smiles, but I haven't the heart to smile back. It would be cruel. And so he looks away, taking my seriousness for nerves or concentration on the task in hand.

We descend, the lift slowly rattling down the levels, until, with the slightest jerk, it stops.

Our friend moves past me, sliding the inner door back.

I watch him. See how small and neat his hands are, yet he's heavily muscled. Every movement is smooth and practised. Yet before he steps out of the lift, he turns and looks at each of us in turn, as if to check some final detail. Satisfied, he steps outside.

It's dark at this level. There are maintenance lights, but they are only every ten metres or so, and the walls are bare, stained by the damp.

'Remember,' he says. 'Not a word. And act subservient, if you can. These people can be very touchy. Keep your heads down and don't meet their eyes.'

I don't know what he means, but we soon find out. He walks us down a long corridor and out into a broad, well-lit hallway. There's a chain fence here, blocking our way, and cameras, lots of cameras. Beyond is luxury. Plush carpets and paintings on the walls. Statuary and fountains. One of the enclaves.

Two men – big men, private guards – step out to block our way.

We show them our passes. While one of them checks them, the other eyes us. Like Burckel I keep my head lowered, my eyes on the ground before me, but I can sense the guard's hostility, his *disgust*. He thinks we're shit. A thousand miles beneath him. And that gives me a better inkling of this world – of what makes it tick – than anything I've yet encountered. This is a world of hierarchies, of rigid social orders.

We are passed through, down the plush corridor and into a dimly lit yet delicately scented room. Beyond it is another, bigger room, smelling of oil and machinery. And there, on the far side of the room, is a flyer – a *Schweben-wagen*. As we go across, our friend calls for light, and in the sudden brightness, we see it in all its polished beauty. It's a bright metallic green, its curved lines giving it the look of a tapered rocket, like a massive crossbow bolt. Its glass cockpit is ridged and armoured, and its twin exhausts look powerful enough to take it into orbit.

'It's a *Steuermann* L-8,' our friend says. 'There aren't that many of them.' He smiles and puts his hand fondly on one of the smooth chrome tail fins. 'They've quite a range. You could reach Moscow in one of these without recharging.'

I'm not sure why he looks at me as he says that, but I sense it has something to do with my comment the other day – about the Russians. Maybe he thinks I'm a Russian spy. Or maybe he's just teasing.

'Okay,' he says, touching a panel on the side. 'Get in the back.'

As the door hisses open and lifts, I look to Burckel, but he seems as surprised as me. It's a beautiful machine, but I'm not sure I want to fly around in it. Yet it seems we've no choice. We climb in, sinking into the scented white leather of those luxurious seats.

I want to ask him what the deal is. This clearly can't be his. But cameras are watching, and he's told us not to speak.

He climbs into the front, and as the door locks shut he buckles himself in, then reaches out and starts the flyer up. There's the faintest vibration, and then the *Steuermann* lifts gently. As it does so the whole of the wall in front of us hisses open and we glide forward, out into the exit tunnel, the *Steuermann* moving smoothly, effortlessly on a cushion of air.

Our friend slows to a halt in front of a panel of lights, then, as the configuration changes and the outer door slides open, slips the flyer out into one of the air-lanes, banking to the left, then straightening out again, accelerating as he does so, joining the flowing stream of traffic in the massive concourse.

He handles the machine beautifully, climbing, banking, turning, finding his way without hesitation through the maze of giant tunnels. I relax, enjoying the sensation of flight, easing back in my seat, staring out at the massive struts and slabs that seem to flit by at a frightening pace.

There's never been a city like Neu Berlin, not before or since, and though much of it is architecturally quite brutal, its scale is something else.

Minutes pass, and then we slow again, finally coming to a halt at a major junction. There's a huge vertical shaft just ahead of us. I lean forward, looking up through the glass of the cockpit. It's like someone has dropped a massive rock through the city's levels. Up there, a long way up, I can glimpse the morning sky, though down here it's dark, the walls studded with faintly glowing lamps, embedded in the fine crash-mesh that covers every surface.

Our friend waits, watching the signal panel, then eases forward gently, beginning his descent. Down we go, down and down and down, until I wonder just how much further we can go. And then we stop.

Just across from us is a guard post. It's the only brightly lit point in the sea of darkness that stretches away on all sides. The ceiling here is fifty yards above us, yet despite the scale of things it feels intensely claustrophobic. The whole weight of the city seems to press down on us.

The lone guard yawns, sets his paper down, scratches himself, then steps out and comes across.

'Hi, Henny,' he says, as our friend raises the door. 'Nice flyer.'

They talk for a while. Inconsequential stuff. But I now know more about our friend than he would probably wish. A name, an occupation. So much for his anonymity.

Henny. It could be Heinrich. Unless that's his second name.

Eventually they exchange papers and, closing the door, we fly on, our headlights penetrating the darkness, until, in their glare, we see a big, low building of steel and glass. It looks old, abandoned. We steer to the right, and as we do, a queue of other flyers comes into sight, their engines idling, waiting to be admitted, but he ignores them, glides past and on round the back of the massive building, then slows as we approach a ramp.

There are more guards, armed this time and wearing body armour and visors.

'It's a secure area,' he says quietly. 'They'll need to see your passes.'

One of the guards steps up and, seeing us in the back, gestures with his gun for our friend to open up.

'Who are these?'

'I'm taking them to see the Supervisor. He's expecting them.'

The guard takes our passes, scans them, then straightens, listening to something in his head. He nods and hands them back. 'Okay. Go through.'

The gate opens and we glide inside, into some kind of airlock. As the doors slam shut behind us, three men approach, scanning the flyer with tiny, hand-held sensors. Looking about me I note the automated guns that are trained on us.

Satisfied, the three step back. One of them raises his hand. A moment later the inner doors hiss open and we go through.

The noise and activity hit us at once. It's a regular beehive. To both sides the *Werkstätte* are stacked up, floor to ceiling, each one a fully equipped service station, hundreds of them, piled one atop another, level after level, the single row in front of us stretching away out of sight, one of Urd knows how many rows.

I am astonished. It's a giant repair and maintenance shop. Big enough, by the look of it, to cope with half of Neu Berlin.

As we glide slowly down the row I look about me. Technicians are busy everywhere, working on flyers of every shape and size. The bright flash of welding arcs and the buzz of machinery form a stark contrast to the darkness and silence outside. The whole place must be sound-dampened. Our friend 'Henny' seems to have relaxed now that he's inside, and he half turns to us, even as he steers the big *Steuermann* towards the far side of the hangar.

'Its okay. You can talk now if you want. There are cameras here, but it's our people monitoring them.'

'*Your* people?'

He smiles, then slows the craft and eases it over to the right. 'That's right. The *Unbeachtet.*'

The unnoticed. The ignored.

I smile. 'I like the name. And the Supervisor?'

'He'll see us when he can. Maybe an hour from now. It depends.'

'But I thought—'

He kills the engine, and, as the flyer slowly sinks to the ground, he turns, looking directly at me, his grey eyes serious.

'Be patient, Otto. He's a very busy man. You're lucky that he's seeing you at all.'

101

We hang around, waiting, wondering if the delay's deliberate, to make some kind of point, yet when our friend returns, he seems apologetic.

'I'm sorry. There was a problem. But he can see you now.'

He leads us up a dozen flights of steps and then out along a kind of wire mesh walkway that leads across and between the stacks, high up, near the ceiling itself. At the far end of it is a kind of metallic cabin. It looks makeshift, hanging there by four great chains from the ceiling overhead, yet the underneath of it bristles with guns and cameras, and I wonder why.

The walkway ends at a gate. Our friend unlocks it and lets us through. It's not much of a barrier, but I can see its usefulness. It's not meant to stop anyone, it's meant to delay. The guns overhead would do the rest.

I step inside, following our guide, expecting what? A control room of some kind, maybe. But it's nothing of the sort. It's a simple living space. There's a bed in the corner and another to my right. There's a small kitchen, marked off to my left and, in the centre, two old-fashioned sofas and a coffee table. Shelves of books fill every other bit of wall space. But this much I take in only at a glance, for my attention is immediately taken by the Supervisor and his companion.

'Urd's breath,' Burckel whispers beside me. 'I never thought ...'

The Supervisor is a small man, unimpressive in all but one aspect. His head. As he stands and smiles a welcome, so ancient instincts awake in me, making my skin crawl; the hairs at the back of my neck stand up.

The skull is huge, like two skulls sewn together, side by side, the strange double bulge of the hairless dome tapering down to a boney ridge that seems to sit like a frill beneath both ears and around the top of his neck. Broad shoulders and massive neck muscles hold the doubled head in place, but otherwise his body's fairly normal. Nor is he alone. His companion, smaller than him and clearly female, has the same shaped head. Her smile is very like his, her mouth tiny in that broad face.

I've read about this. It was a Mechanist trick, to put two brains into one skull and somehow make it work, linking the two with bridges of ultra-fine fibre-optics. *Doppelgehirn*, they called them. But I'm surprised, even so, to meet one. I thought they'd all died out long ago.

'You look shocked,' the Supervisor says, more amused than offended. And why not? He has probably seen this response a thousand times and more. His voice is soft, pleasant, like the voice of a homely uncle.

'No, no I—' And then I laugh. 'Forgive me. I didn't mean to be rude.'

He gives me his hand. 'It's understandable.' Then, smiling, he turns, indicating the girl beside him. 'Otto, Albrecht, this is my daughter, Gudrun. And I am Michael Reichenau. A *Doppelgehirn*, as you see, and Supervisor of *Werkstätt* 9. Heinrich you've met.'

'Though not by name.'

Reichenau smiles, his mouth seeming exceedingly small in that huge face. 'You blame him for his caution?'

'Not at all.'

'Then be seated. Gudrun, bring us drinks. Something a bit stronger than coffee, eh?'

Heinrich leaves, and as we take our seats, I find I can't stop looking at Reichenau – or rather, at his head. Two brains, two distinct minds, sit in that skull. I'd read that many of them attained a kind of wisdom, what one might term a genuine supra-human enlightenment, but that was rare. Most simply went mad.

'It must be difficult.'

'*Difficult?* How do you mean?'

'Living with yourself.'

Reichenau laughs at that. 'No more than for any other man. There's always more than one voice in our heads, wouldn't you say?'

'Yes, but ...'

He lifts a hand to interrupt me, and so I pause.

'Even in our heads,' he says, 'it's argued that there must be a master and a servant. But why should it be so? Let me assure you, Otto, we who live closer to the matter know better. One *can* live in harmony, two minds conjoined and in agreement.'

I smile. It's a pleasant theory, but it's also a lie, because very early on in the process one of the brains *always* took control – the one with the strongest will. Yet Reichenau denies it.

Why? For some political reason? Or does he really believe it? Has he fooled himself into believing it?

Gudrun brings drinks in frosted tumblers. There's the sharp taste of aniseed from the clear liquid, but it's like drinking molten fire. I cough and put my glass down, noting Reichenau's amusement.

'Heinrich was telling me you were looking for a power source. Well, there you are!'

And he laughs again, not bothering to explain the joke. But I guess it probably has to do with the name of the drink. My throat is burning, like I've just swallowed pure alcohol. And maybe I have. All I know is that if we keep drinking this stuff I will get drunk. As drunk as a Russian.

'Seriously though,' Reichenau says, his tiny eyes narrowing. 'Why do you want to know where the source is located? You couldn't get to it, you know. Couldn't *harm* it.'

'It must be heavily guarded.'

His laughter this time surprises me, because I don't think I've said anything funny. Yet he seems to think so, and I begin to wonder if I'm wasting my time here, if Burckel has made another of his mistakes.

He smooths his left hand over the huge dome of his head, then shrugs. 'The Guild take good care of their captive star. It would be easier for you or I to kill the King, yes and to fuck his daughter too, than to even get close to the power source.'

Gudrun didn't even blink at the notion of fucking the King's daughter, yet anyone else in this society might have been shocked by the words. But then, these are *Undrehungar*, and I've no doubt Reichenau has raised his daughter to curse the King's very name.

'I'll find a way.'

This time he doesn't laugh, but simply stares at me curiously. 'You're an odd fish, Otto. Oh, you may look normal, but ...' He takes a sip of his drink, then, smiling, looks at me again. 'You're not from *here*, are you, Otto?'

'No.'

'Good. I'm glad to hear that you don't deny it. Because I had you checked out. There are all kind of entries in the record for you. Enough to satisfy any official who might come looking for you. You have a *Werknummer*, for instance, tattooed on your right arm. And yet ... well, according to *our* files, you don't exist.'

I smile, prepared for this. 'I'm American.'

'Ah. I see. An *American*. And why should an American be meddling in the affairs of Greater Germany? Are you a *spy*, Otto?'

I could say yes, see how he reacts, then jump right out of there and go back, enter the timestream earlier and do this all again, taking more care, but things are delicate and I'm not sure what I'd upset. My smile broadens.

'No, just an envoy.'

'An *envoy*?'

He leaves it. But his eyes tell me that he doesn't believe it for a moment. He thinks I'm a spy, and probably for the Russians. Yet here I am, speaking to him, so there's almost certainly something he wants from me. Something he doesn't think he can get by any other means.

Reichenau leans towards me, that huge head delicately balanced on those powerful muscles. Its closeness makes me feel uneasy. In a world of 'evolved' and variant humans, he is one degree too strange for my liking.

'Your interest in the power source ... why is that?'

'My masters – my *American* masters – wish to enter into negotiations with the fortress. But before they do, they need to have a proper sense of, well, of just how powerful you Germans are.'

Reichenau seems surprised. 'They do not *know*?'

'They know how it looks. You have limitless energy – energy provided by the black hole your scientists have tapped. And yet ...'

'And yet?'

Reichenau seems almost affronted. It seems he is perversely proud of the regime he wishes to bring to its knees. A revolutionary he may be, yet he is also, curiously, a patriot.

'And yet the Russians, who have no similar power source, appear your equals.'

'Our *equals*?' He roars with laughter. Beside him, his daughter is strangely silent, her face never changing from its sombre expression.

'But of course,' I say, sensing how restless Burckel is becoming beside me. 'Why else would the war have continued so long? If Germany is so much more powerful ...'

'Oh, my friend, do you understand nothing? The war is not prolonged because we are incapable of winning it, it is prolonged because it is *necessary*. If we wished, we could crush those vodka-swilling peasants in a single day, a single hour. *Eradicate* them. But that would not suit our masters' purposes. Oh no. For them the war is a means of control – each German who dies on the front, dies to keep that scum in power. So long as the war continues, then their rule is safe, the status quo maintained. But as for *equality* ...'

I am silent a moment, as if considering his words.

'It may be so. And yet ...'

'Oh damn your "And yets"! It *is* so. But things are changing. Even now ...' He hesitates, as if he's said too much, then sits back, glaring at me.

'What is it?' I ask, confused by his sudden change of mood. It feels almost like I'm facing a different person.

'Your interest in the source,' he says quietly. 'It proves ... convenient.'

'Convenient?'

He nods his huge head. 'We need to know.'

'Know?'

'Why the power is fading.'

It's the first thing he's said that genuinely surprises me. Burckel, beside me, tenses. The atmosphere in the room has changed. It has a sudden, dangerous edge.

'I don't understand,' I say. 'How can it be fading? The black hole ... the power from that won't run out for half a billion years.'

His eyes search mine. 'And yet it is,' he says, as quietly as before. 'Oh, they don't know it out there – the feed to the city is but the smallest fraction of its total power – but the Guild is worried. *Very* worried. These last three days …'

Ernst, I think. *The power-anchor to Ernst is draining the black hole's energy.* Yet how could that be? The total energy to be tapped from a neutron star was phenomenal. Almost incalculable. To drain it in the fashion they were talking of was impossible, surely? Or was I missing something? Some crucial piece of information? Maybe they could only channel so much. Maybe …

But Reichenau is talking again, and I jerk my attention back to him.

' …was the only reason I agreed to see you. Your interest seemed, how shall we put it, much more than *coincidental*.' He pauses, then. 'It would suit the Russians perfectly, after all.'

I smile coldly. 'We are not Russians. Nevertheless, what you say is true. Were the power to be … *diminishing* …'

The thought astonishes me. This has never happened before. Not, at least, in any of the time-lines we have explored. Yet if the time-anchor is new and untested …

It makes me wonder if the Russians actually know just how dangerous this is. If so, maybe the effects of their tampering is accidental, and not some deliberate plan to undermine the structure of what follows.

For this is where it all starts – where the loop begins and ends.

You see, certain things *must* happen here. If they don't then time travel will never come about, and without that …

My head spins. It *has* to happen. *Has to.*

Unless the whole damn thing gets blown to hell and back.

Reichenau has been silent, staring at me as if trying to make up his mind. Then, abruptly, he puts his hand out and snaps his fingers. At once the girl stands and, going over to one of the nearby shelves, takes something down and hands it to him. He stares at it a moment, then hands it across to me.

It's a map, a simple, hand-drawn map like something a child might have sketched. I take it in, memorising all of its aspects, then hand it back to him.

He's surprised, maybe even impressed. 'You don't want this?'

'I have it.' And I touch my forehead.

He smiles, then screws the piece of paper up and throws it away. 'How do I get in there?' I ask.

'You don't. No one does. Unless they're authorised.'

'So I get authorised.'

He laughs, a laughter that rolls on and on and on. 'You are so funny, Otto. So very, very amusing.'

102

Heinrich sees us home. I can sense he's not happy. He's still polite, but now he's monosyllabic in his responses to my questions, and when I ask when we'll see him again, he simply shrugs. I don't understand his sudden change of mood, but it doesn't matter. I have what I need. All I have to do now is find a way in.

Burckel wants to talk; wants to chew it all over and make plans. But I've already made my own plans, and I tell him so.

'But Otto …'

'No. You stay here. Until I get back. If I get in trouble I'll jump.'

He's unhappy, but he does as I say. Leaving him there, I return to the gaming club. It's mid-morning now, and most of the population are at work, but there are a scattering of people in Van Richtofen Strasse. All seems normal, until I step into the side alley and see, where the Club Rothaarige should be, a smouldering ruin. The place is cordoned off, visored SS officers – State Security – standing in the alley talking.

I stare for a time, pretending to be a curious bystander, and in a moment am moved on, but my heart is hammering in my chest.

What happened here? Was it gang related? Or was it an attempt on the Guildsman's life? If so, was it successful? And what about Dankevich?

I decide to jump back. To find out just what went on after I'd left the club. But first I decide to go back and tell Burckel what's going on.

Only Burckel's not there. He's gone AWOL again. I curse him, then, because time is of the essence, I jump back.

Hecht is waiting there, like he's expecting me. And maybe he is. We *are* time travellers, after all. Yet for once it seems strange.

'Trouble, Otto?'

'They burned down the club.'

'I know.'

You *know*?'

'It's in the histories. Only a footnote, admittedly, but ...'

'Ah.'

This is the part I don't like. The thought that Hecht knows more than I about the situation. It makes me feel *exposed*.

'I was going to ...'

He interrupts. 'Otto. I want to show you something.'

And so we jump. Back to the clearing. Only the clearing is no longer clear. There are makeshift tents among the surrounding trees – crude bivouacs – and there, about Ernst's glowing form, a dozen or more pilgrims kneel, praying to him.

I shake my head, astonished, then look to Hecht, speaking quietly, so as not to disturb the pilgrims.

'How much time has passed?'

'A week subjective.'

'Urd save him. And he's conscious?'

'We're not sure. But if he *is* ...'

It's a dreadful thought. One of the kneeling party notices us and, with a bow to Ernst, breaks away from his prayers and comes across.

'Sires,' he says, in that ancient, heavily slurred Russian that they speak in these parts. 'Have you come to make offerings to the angel?'

He's relatively young, but his hair is long and his beard thick, and he gives off the air of a priest. His clothes however are rough, undyed, and he smells like an unwashed peasant.

Hecht stares at the young man a moment, then brushes him aside with the disdain of an aristocrat. What's more, it works. The young man, noting our manner, backs off, bowed low, like he's in the presence of a great lord.

I turn, looking across at our trapped 'angel'.

Seen close, I note how much clearer Ernst now is. One cannot touch him, however. The air surrounding him crackles with static and I can see from the dark, burned patches on the ground nearby that those that have tried have been badly shocked for their pains.

'There,' Hecht says, indicating what appears to be a lump on Ernst's left hip.

I look closer, feeling the hair bristle on my head as it's drawn towards the field.

'What is it?'

'We think it's what's generating the field. We scanned him, a few days back, and that seems to be one end of the anchor.'

The lump is small and fleshy – no bigger than a largish coin – yet it seems to sit *beneath* the surface of his skin.

'It's made of his own DNA, of course. That's why it's taken hold so firmly. We can't cut it out. We tried and almost lost a man doing so. But if we could switch off the power ...'

'I have a map,' I say. 'I know where it is.'

'Good.' And Hecht looks to me and smiles. But it's quickly

gone, even as he turns back and looks at Ernst. In its place I see a great compassion fill Hecht's eyes.

'You mustn't fail, Otto,' he says. 'This time you *must* succeed.'

103

I shower and change, then return to the platform, wondering all the while what Hecht meant by *this time*. Have I been before? Are we trying again and again until we somehow get it right? Or have I already failed? Am I stuck in a loop, forever repeating this futile succession of actions, forgetting what I've done each time, as the field about Ernst grows stronger and stronger?

Only I don't ask, and Hecht doesn't offer. He isn't even there to see me off.

And so I go back again. Back to Burckel's room. Back to Neu Berlin, my head full of Ernst and the burned-down club – and Katerina.

Standing there, just before I make the jump, I wonder how I might persuade Zarah to send me there, to see Katerina briefly, to hold her and kiss her and tell her that I love her, only … how to ask? How to explain that, for me, seeing her is almost as urgent a need as freeing Ernst? As urgent as saving every last one of us, here at Four-Oh?

How to ask, indeed. And so I find myself back in Burckel's room, waiting on the man; wondering where he's gone this time, and who he's talking to. And while I sit there on the edge of his bed, I take a piece of paper and, from memory, begin to sketch her face, looking upward and to the right, her bright eyes shining with the morning light.

Katerina.

Finished, I fold the paper and place it in my inside tunic pocket, feeling now that I have at least some small part of her with me.

Two hours pass, and I'm about to go out and start looking for him, when Burckel reappears.

'Well?' I ask, keeping my temper.

'I had to deliver something. For Hecht ...That package you brought with you.'

I narrow my eyes. It seems he's telling the truth. Only now he's got me wondering why Hecht didn't ask *me* to deliver it.

'So where did you go?'

He turns away, as if he's looking about for something. 'Oh, in the north city. I found the man ...'

I'm tense now. Strangely angry. 'Man? What man?'

He glances at me, almost unable to meet my eyes. 'Otto, please. I can't tell you. Hecht was very insistent. So don't ask. You *mustn't* ask.'

It all seems very stupid, but I acquiesce. After all, Hecht must know what he's doing. Mustn't he?

I squash the doubt even as it rises in my mind. The only thing I've got to worry about is getting to the power source and turning it off somehow. Nothing else matters. If Hecht is playing other games, then that's not my concern, even if – this once – he chooses to exclude me from them.

'Have you heard about the club?' I ask, wondering if he, like Hecht, already knows.

'No ... what's happened?'

So I tell him, and see the genuine surprise in his eyes. 'Do you know why?'

'No. But I'd guess it has something to do with Dankevich and that Guildsman we saw. In fact, I'd bet a small fortune on it.'

Burckel nods then turns away, once again seeming to be looking for something.

'Have you mislaid something, Albrecht?'

'No, I ... Ah, here it is.'

I frown. 'What is that?'

He holds it up, the chain winking silver in the light, then slips it over his head.

'It's a charm,' he says. 'A lucky charm.'

104

We return to Van Richtofen Strasse. It's mid-morning now, and the sky threatens rain. Burckel and I tour the bars nearest the club *Das Rothaarige*, asking questions of waitresses and barmen, trying to piece together what's known. It's not much but we get a clearer picture. Rumour is that the first alarm was sounded just after four. And then – and this everyone agrees on – there was an explosion.

A bomb. It *had* to be a bomb.

No one seems to know anything about casualties, however, and so we keep going, hoping to find someone who knows something a bit more specific. Here Burckel's a help for once, for he seems to know most of the owners, and at a club some hundred metres or so from the ruins, we are brought drinks by a man named Meissner, whom Burckel seems to have known some years. With an air of secrecy, he tells us that he has a friend who's got the inside track on what happened, and would we like to meet him?

I hesitate, then nod, and, taking our drinks, we go through, into a back room. And there, sitting in a chair behind a desk, gun in hand, is our old friend Dankevich.

As the door closes behind us, I see the anger burning in his eyes and realise we've made yet another mistake.

'Sit down!'

His voice is cold, no-nonsense. The gun is aimed at me, as if Burckel is of no consequence.

'Andreas—' Burckel begins, but Dankevich barks at him.

'Shut up and sit!'

There are two chairs, like we've both been expected. We sit.

'Well?' I ask. 'Do you know what happened?'

'You were there,' he says coldly. 'You saw him. You *knew* he was there.'

'Who?' I say. But I know who he means. The Guildsman. And I know now that Dankevich *was* in the club when Burckel and I paid our visit, probably watching us on one of the club's security cameras.

'Don't fuck with me,' he says, and the gun in his hand trembles, like his anger's genuine. And maybe it is. Maybe he really doesn't know who Burckel and I are. But that's unlikely.

'So what's your angle?' I ask. 'Why are *you* so concerned?'

'It was my club, that's fucking why! My money. And now my fucking loss!'

It's a good act, only I know he's a Russian agent, and any money he may or may not have put into the club was *Russian* money, not his.

'How did you get out?'

'Me?' He looks puzzled. 'I wasn't there.'

'And the Guildsman?'

'Dead. And eighteen others with him. The fucker used a sticky bomb. Placed it right dead centre on the Guildsman's chest.'

I narrow my eyes. 'How do you know all this? I thought the cameras were destroyed.'

'They were. But there's an external feed. We saw it all.' He's staring at me still, but there's a slight question in his eyes now, as if he's not quite as sure of me as he first thought.

'And the assassin?'

'Dead. When the bomb went off he was only a metre or so away.'

'But you got a good look at him?'

'No. The fucker was masked.'

'Ah ...' And I wonder if our friend Reichenau was involved. One of his men, maybe. 'All right ...but why are you so pissed off with me?'

'Because you were there earlier. Your first visit. A bit of a coincidence, wouldn't you say?'

'That's because it was.'

'So you say. But I'm afraid you're under suspicion. The Guild are furious. They want answers, and fast. If you hadn't come here ...'

Too late, I realise what he's done. Nor can I jump, because then Burckel will have to jump, too, and our operation here will be completely blown. That is, if it isn't already. But Dankevich is acting as if he really doesn't know who we are. As I stand and turn to the door, so it flies open and two SS men, heavy snub-nosed automatics in their hands, block the way.

'I'm sorry, Albrecht,' Dankevich says. 'But if I hadn't handed you in, they would have come for you anyway.'

The apology is unexpected – and it makes me glance back at him. But then we're grabbed and cuffed and half pushed, half carried out to the cruiser which is waiting in the broad avenue outside, hovering a foot above the ground, all black metal plate and bristling guns.

Burckel looks sick, but I'm not about to let these bastards take us in and torture us, and as the cruiser lifts and banks, so I jump and jump back almost instantly, artillery in hand, and open fire, taking out both the guards and another four of their companions, including the pilot. One of them manages to fire a shot off, however, and suddenly Burckel's squealing like a stuck pig. As the cruiser dips towards the ground, Freisler appears from nowhere in the co-pilot's seat and, taking the controls, keeps the flyer steady until I can see to Burckel. It takes a moment to stop the bleeding; then I go forward to join Freisler in the cockpit.

'Thanks,' I say, hauling the dead pilot out of his seat and clambering in, getting the feel of the joystick.

Freisler nods ... then vanishes.

105

We dump the cruiser in wasteland to the south of the city. There I jump back to Four-Oh and return an instant later with a proper medical kit to patch Burckel up. It's his leg. The bone is smashed, but I can deal with that. I dose him up and put the limb in a walking cast, its neuro-transmitters by-passing the nerve-ends in the shattered leg, its artificial muscles allowing Burckel to walk while the bone heals.

We make our way by foot to the nearest terminus. Burckel's convinced there'll be a full-scale alert out for us, so we try to avoid all checkpoints and security cameras, only in this world you can't scratch your arse without a camera looking on.

I'm tempted to go back and change things, to jump in down the line and sort this mess out at the source, only Hecht was keen that I didn't meddle, and what Hecht says goes.

The priority now is to find a hidey-hole. Somewhere to stay for the next day or two. I suggest contacting Reichenau's man Heinrich, and Burckel makes the call, only our friendly terrorists don't want to know. They cut us dead, like they're afraid to know us.

I'm at a loss, but Burckel has the answer.

'Werner. We can stay with Werner. He'll look after us.'

I'm not so sure, but as I know no one else in this world, I go along with him. Burckel makes another call and, half an hour later, a bright red flyer descends nearby and Werner leans out, beckoning us across. It's not as plush, nor as powerful as the *Steuermann-L8*, but I'm surprised that Werner owns one at all . He's alone in the flyer, no sign of his two goons. Once we're strapped in the back he asks us what happened, and for once I let Burckel do the talking.

'You *shot* them?' he asks me, amazed. 'How the fuck did you manage that? I thought you were cuffed?'

'A trick I learned,' I say. 'But thanks. For this …'

'Shit. Don't thank me. Anyone who whacks one of those bastards …'

I'm about to say that I didn't, only Burckel lays his hand on my arm and I keep quiet.

Werner's 'place' is a big penthouse studio on the eastern side of the city. He sets the flyer down on a pad, then hurries us inside.

The apartment is the very height of luxury. I look about me, impressed. Werner is a far bigger man than I thought. 'Where are your friends?'

'I sent them away for a couple of days,' he answers, pouring us drinks. 'I thought it best.'

His smile is kindly, unthreatening, and I begin to wonder whether my earlier judgement of him was too hasty.

'I've some business to do,' he says, 'so I'll be gone for three or four hours, but you'll be safe here.'

I look up and find he's holding something out for me to take. It's a gun. A large calibre automatic, with laser sights.

'Just in case,' he says and smiles. 'I don't think anyone followed me, but you never know.'

I nod, and smile back at him gratefully. 'Thanks. You don't know how much this means.'

And that's true. Germany owes a debt to 'Werner'. That is, if we survive the next two nights.

When Werner's gone, I see to Burckel, checking his wound, then dose him up again. I want to give him something stronger – something to put him out, to let him rest so that his body will heal faster – but he won't let me. He wants to keep awake. He wants to talk. And so, finally, I let him, taking a seat by the window, looking out across the city, the gun across my lap, as, sprawled out on the couch nearby, Burckel tells me how it's been, here in 2747.

'This is a cold place, Otto. A frightening place, at times. No place to raise a family, if you know what I mean. Not that we two have much sense of family, eh? Not in the traditional sense.'

'We are a people ...'

'I know, but sometimes, well, I miss the more intimate stuff ... you know, being a father, having children ... that kind of thing.'

'Not the sex, then?'

'No. Strangely enough I don't miss the sex. I never liked being part of the programme. You know, servicing the *Frau* ...'

I look away, before he sees the agreement in my eyes.

'Anyway,' he goes on, 'even if I could, there'd be no point in this world. These people live in constant fear.'

I look to him, querying that.

'The fortress has the power of life or death over all,' he says, 'and it chooses its servants, well, let us say *arbitrarily*. Who knows on what criteria the choice is made. All that anyone knows is that at any time – day or night – the King's men might call and take a child, any child they wish, and take it back to the fortress to be changed, turned into one of the *do-hu*, the domesticated humans that serve the Masters. Nor is there any right of appeal. All here are the property of the fortress.'

I know, yet to hear Burckel say it so clearly – and with such bitterness – makes me see it anew.

'There are things we cannot change, Albrecht. How people live ...'

'You believe that bollocks?'

I stare at him, surprised.

'No, Otto. *Think*. We can change Time itself. Recast events and make things happen. So why not this? Why not make changes that affect the common people's lives? Why always the grand histori-cal gesture?'

I could answer, and at another time I might, only I want to hear what he has to say. Want to learn just how deeply this madness has taken hold of him.

'We act like policemen, Otto. Time cops, when we really ought to be acting like revolutionaries. *Undrehungar*. We could change things. *Really* change things. Not piss about meddling in historical events – what good does that do ultimately? The Russians only change it back! No. We need to get to grips with the underlying phenomena, with the *infrastructure* of history, not the surface froth.'

I have heard this argument before, but only from my younger students. To find it in an agent of Burckel's maturity stuns me, for he really ought to know what he's talking about.

'Have you been lonely here?'

He blinks, surprised by the question, then looks down and, after a moment, nods.

'You know,' he says. 'Some days I've been so lonely that I've thought I was going mad. I've thought ...'

He hesitates, and when he doesn't continue I prompt him. 'Thought what?'

He takes a long, shuddering breath, then nods to himself.

'Go on,' I say. 'I'm listening.'

'It's just ... sometimes it feels as if I've reached the edge.'

'The edge?'

'Of what's in my head. It's like ... you know how the ancients used to view the world as a great flattened circle, surrounded by a void, and that if you came to the edge you would fall off? Well, that's how I feel. That's what my memory seems like sometimes. There are limits to it. Like, well, like something has been taken from me.'

My mouth is dry now. This is what I saw, what I read, in Burckel's journals – the very thing that set alarm bells ringing, both for me and for Hecht.

'And to what do you attribute this ... *feeling*?'

There's the slightest frown now. 'I don't attribute it to anything, Otto. It's how we are. How human beings are made. Only ...'

Only *I* don't have that feeling. And as far as I know, no one normal has it either. Yet Burckel does. Why? Was he captured by the Russians and re-conditioned? Or is it something simpler – something physiological, brought on by a blow to the head or perhaps a mild stroke?

'Albrecht ... I have a confession to make.'

'A confession?'

'I read your journal.'

He laughs. 'Read it? But ...' And then he sees what I have done and his face changes, and he nods, as if it all now fits into place.

'I'm sorry,' I say. 'But we had to know. *Hecht* had to know.'

'Yeah ...' But he doesn't sound happy. He sighs and lets his head fall back, closing his eyes. 'So what did Hecht say?'

'He told me to watch you.'

'Ah ...' He's silent for a moment, then he smiles. 'At least you're honest, Otto. Some other bastard ...'

He doesn't finish the sentence, but I know what he means. Some other bastard would have kept quiet about it; pretended to be his best friend.

'Albrecht?'

'Yes, Otto?'

'Where did you meet Werner? In that bar we went to?'

'Urd no!' He laughs. 'It was at a party. I had these two friends – they're dead now, but – well, I went to this party with them, in the east lowers. In Friedrichshain, I think it was.'

'When was this?'

'Three, maybe four years ago.'

'And he's been a friend ever since?'

'No. At first I found him quite hostile. I remember we argued that first time. I found him … arrogant, I guess. Self-opinionated. But then I met him again a couple of times and things improved. First impressions … they're not always right, are they?'

I think of Kravchuk and I'm not so sure. But I don't argue. I want Burckel to talk. I want to find out where the edges of his memory lie.

'You've been *here* before, then?'

'Once or twice. Not often. He had a gathering here once, a year or so back. It wasn't so much a party as … well, Dankevich was a guest.'

'Go on …'

'Oh, I know what you're thinking, but there's no connection. Werner is as German as they come. He's like Reichenau in that, fiercely proud of his nationality. He'd never dream of getting involved with the Russians.'

'Okay … but how does he know Dankevich?'

Burckel shrugs. 'I don't know, but that's how I came to meet Dankevich – or Schmidt, as I knew him. That's how I got to hear about the club.'

'*Das Rothaarige?*'

'Yes. Mind, I didn't know that he owned it. If I had—'

He yawns deeply. The shots are clearly having an effect, but there's also a degree of shock setting in.

I look out across the rooftops. The city looks abandoned almost, *dead*, the only movement the dark shape of a flyer, two, three miles distant

'You say you had Werner checked out. What did you do?'

'There are ways,' he says. But he doesn't elaborate, and it gives me a moment's unease. Then I think about what Werner's done and

I relax. If he'd wanted to, he could have handed us over straight away – led the authorities directly to where we were. No. Werner's all right.

'Do you ever have doubts, Otto?'

I look across. Burckel is watching me now. 'Doubts?'

'About what we do? About *why* we do it?'

'No.'

And it's true. If we didn't do this, the Russians would eliminate us, down to the last man, woman and child.

'*Really?*'

I nod.

'Only, what if we *do* win, Otto? What if we finally destroy the Russians? What then? What kind of world would it be that our children inherited?'

I smile. 'A German world.'

There's the flicker of a smile, but he's in deadly earnest now. 'A *German* world, certainly. Not a *better* world. Not a more *humane* world.'

I look away. 'You've been here too long, Albrecht. All German societies are not like this.'

'No?' He laughs sourly. 'Only this is it. *The* world. *Asgard.* This is what was foreseen in the Myth, Otto. It's the singular pattern that underlies it all. We *derive* from this.'

'Maybe ...' I change the subject, steer away from the rocks. 'How's the leg now?'

'Comfortable.' And then he laughs. 'You don't want to, do you, Otto?'

'Don't want to what?'

'Question it.'

'What is there to question? The war is real, Albrecht. If it wasn't, you wouldn't be here.'

'No. Yet sometimes I wonder just what purpose I serve. I mean, all of this energy we've put into waging this war – three generations now – and what have we achieved? What have we really changed?'

That isn't quite the point, but again I don't want to go down that path. I know why *I'm* fighting this war – what I need to know is why Albrecht Burckel has given up on it. For he has, as sure as Dankevich is Dankevich and not Schmidt, a Russian, not a German.

'Was there never anyone, Albrecht? Here, I mean, in Neu Berlin.'

He knows what I mean. A *woman*. But he doesn't answer me. Instead he perseveres. 'You can keep on avoiding it, Otto, but one of these days you'll wake up and wonder what the fuck you've been doing all these years.'

I shrug. You see, I don't believe him. I don't believe it's possible.

'Oh, you're very smug about it now, Otto, but one of these days something will happen to you and, well, your eyes will be opened. You'll see ...'

I stand, angry with him now. 'Shut up, Albrecht! For fuck's sake ... can't you see it? There's nothing wrong with me. It's you.'

'*Me?*' He laughs. 'At least I have self-knowledge. At least I *know* who I am. You? Do you ever ask yourself anything, Otto? Or do you just accept it all blindly?'

I realise that I'm holding the gun much too tightly and relax my grip. Burckel is so wrong – so far gone down that road – that he can't see it, but that's no reason for me to lose it with him.

'You ought to sleep,' I say.

'What, like you, you mean?'

'I'm not sleeping, Albrecht. I'm wide awake.'

'Are you?'

But he doesn't pursue it. Sighing, he lays back and closes his eyes, and in an instant he appears to fall asleep, his mouth open, his breath sighing from him.

I wait a while until I'm sure he's sleeping, then, putting the gun down on the chair, go for a little tour of the apartment, checking it out.

The kitchen's luxurious, but not as luxurious as the bathroom, with its sunken golden bath – big enough to hold a small party. There's a large study, and several bedrooms, again decorated in a manner that suggests great wealth, but what interests me most is a room at the far end of the main hallway – for the door to it is locked.

Another time I wouldn't bother. Another time – with less at risk – I'd accept things at face value and leave it be. But this is no time to take chances, and so I jump to Four-Oh, then jump back again on the other side of the door.

Looking about me, I smile. Light glints from a hundred polished silvered surfaces. It's a work-room, a laboratory of sorts, with part of it used as an operating room. It's state-of-the-art, of course, which doesn't surprise me. What does is the fact that Werner works from home. That feels wrong, somehow. I don't know why, but it does. I was sure he'd work elsewhere.

I walk across. At the far end, beyond the work benches and the operating tables, is a whole wall of massive drawers. It has the look of a morgue, only when I pull open one of the cabinets it's no corpse I glimpse inside.

'Thor's breath!'

I swallow, shocked by the sheer oddness of the creature laying there. It's alive. Tubes snake from the cabinet into its brain, its mouth and chest – a chest which rises and falls with a calm yet, for me, disturbing regularity.

Werner's a gene surgeon, sure. This *is* his job. But who the fuck is ordering *these* monstrosities?

I check other drawers. They're not all as odd as the one I first saw, but they're none of them human – at least, not in any normal sense.

Or so it seems at first. And then it clicks. I open up one of the cabinets again and look more closely – this time with an anatomist's eye – and realise that they *are* human, all too human. Only I've been looking at them from the wrong viewpoint. The reason they don't look normal is because they aren't finished. They're being *grown*, but not as babies are grown, from a foetus, but piecemeal – each individual organ changed for some purpose, just as the limbs and torsos and heads have been changed. Each individual part tailor-made by our friend, like custom-made flyers.

It makes me reassess things. Makes me ask just who Werner *is* working for.

I jump back and reappear an instant later back outside, in the hallway. Burckel is still sleeping, so out of it that, when I shake him, he gives a little grunt, then begins to snore loudly, like nothing is going to wake him ever again.

I walk across and stand there at the window. Cloud drifts across the deserted rooftops. More than ever, Neu Berlin looks like a dead city.

Or a city of the dead …

Maybe it's what I know about the coming days that makes it seem so, yet I can't shake the impression now that it's taken hold, and when I see a cruiser approaching fast, I barely react until it's almost too late.

'Shit!'

I grab the gun then turn and try to shake Burckel awake. 'Come on!' I yell. 'We've got to get out of here!'

I don't know where or how, but it doesn't seem to matter. I can't wake him. And as the cruiser sets down on the roof just outside the window, I turn to find guards jumping down out of the craft, their guns trained on me through the glass. And then the room floods with light and a voice booms out.

'Throw the gun down, Otto! Throw it down or you're dead!'

106

'I had to,' Werner says, as if I shouldn't take his betrayal too hard. 'If I didn't hand you in, someone else would. So why not make a profit on the transaction? I'm a businessman, after all, and—'

'Shut up!' Dankevich says irritably from across the room. But I understand it now. Werner auctioned us to the highest bidder. And the highest bidders were the Russians. Not that they can keep what they've bought.

That said, I can't make Dankevich out. Surely he knows I'm a German agent. If not, then why buy us back? Yet he's acting as if he doesn't. In fact, he seems almost nervous. Edgy about something.

As I watch, he sits on the edge of the couch next to Burckel and feels his pulse, then turns and looks to me.

'Is he okay?'

'It's the medication.'

'Ah ...'

But that too seems odd. Why is he so worried about Burckel? And there's another thing – why did Dankevich hand me over to Security in the first place?

Werner leaves the room. He's not gone a second or two when the air beside Dankevich shimmers and three of his fellow agents appear from nowhere. Dankevich stands, smiling a greeting at the newcomers.

I know two of them. They're brothers, Ivan and Grigori Kalugin. The third is new to me, however, a small fellow with receding hair and pinched features, a real weasel of a man, not unlike our friend Dankevich.

Werner returns, holding two bulbs of drink. He's smiling, but, seeing Dankevich's friends, he starts and drops the bulbs, his eyes gone big and round.

'What the ...?'

'It's all right,' Dankevich says. 'They're just friends.'

But Werner's reaction, more than anything, convinces me that he doesn't know what's really going on. He looks about him, seeking some explanation for the sudden appearance of the men, but I can see he's having trouble. More than that, he's frightened.

'Sit down, Werner, before you fall down.'

Werner swallows hard, then sits. 'What's going on, Andreas? Where did these three come from?'

'They're Russians,' I say.

'Russians?' Werner stares at me as if I've gone mad.

'That one, the one you call Schmidt. His real name's Dankevich. Fedor Ivanovich Dankevich.'

'You *know* each other?'

I smile and nod. 'Know him? I've killed him.'

Dankevich's eyes widen. I look at him and laugh. 'Oh, you're much younger than you were then.'

And as I say it, I realise what that means. Dankevich will survive this episode, whatever happens to the rest of us. He'll go on to live another twenty years, skipping back and forth in Time. Which means ...

But Werner cuts into my thoughts. Standing, he shakes his head and laughs with disbelief. 'What the fuck are you two talking about?'

'Time,' Dankevich says, staring at me now as if he's seeing me for the first time. 'We're talking about Time. About *controlling* Time.' He pauses, then, threateningly, 'You, Otto. Cause us any trouble and I'll kill your friend here. Understand?'

'What do you want?'

'From you? Nothing.' He turns and looks to his companions. 'Grigori, wake him up.'

The elder Kalugin brother steps across and, taking a hypodermic from his pocket, gives Burckel a shot to jerk him awake.

Burckel sits up, like a dog on speed, twitching, looking about him anxiously. 'Otto? What?' Then he sees the Russians and goes quiet.

Dankevich crouches again, his face on a level with Burckel's. 'The package, Albrecht. What did you do with the package?'

'I ... delivered it.'

Dankevich looks round. 'Grigori – jump back and find out where he went. And bring it back.'

The small man nods and vanishes, and as he does so, Werner groans. I glance at him and see how he's rocking back and forth in his chair, as if he's only hanging on to sanity by a thread. Then I look back.

I expect our friend Grigori back in an instant, and clearly, so does Dankevich. But a full minute passes and there's no sign of him returning.

Dankevich straightens. 'What's keeping him?'

I look to Burckel; meet his eyes. 'Jump,' I say.

'What?'

They're all looking at me now. I look to Burckel again, willing him to obey me.

'*Jump*, Albrecht! For fuck's sake jump!'

But Burckel shakes his head. 'I can't. I've ... tried. I ... I just can't.'

Dankevich is smirking.

'What have you done?'

'Done?' But he's distracted. He gestures towards the younger Kalugin brother. 'Ivan ... go and find out where the fuck Grigori has got to.'

Ivan vanishes, then reappears. He looks distraught, and before he can say a word, Dankevich takes him aside. They talk, quietly yet with real animation, in Russian. And while they do, I turn again to Burckel.

This is strange. So strange it almost makes no sense. Dankevich knows now who we are, but he's not worried. We could jump out and come back armed, and he knows that. Only it feels completely wrong.

'Albrecht,' I say quietly. 'We have to get out of here, and we have to do it now.'

Burckel turns away.

'What is it? Why can't you …?'

But my words only make him hunch into himself, like he's ashamed.

And so, because there's nothing else to do, I step across and, wrapping my arms about him, I jump …

107

And come to in agony. My ears are ringing and there are pains in my arms and legs and chest. I can't see out of my right eye. I feel limp and damp, but also like someone has stuck a thousand tiny needles into me. My skin stings, like it's been burned, and my whole body tingles with the pain, so much that I black out again, and when I come to a second time, it's to find a small crowd gathered around me, someone fixing a drip into my arm even as Zarah strokes my forehead and tells me it's going to be all right.

I blink my right eye, trying to clear it, but that's a big mistake and the pain engulfs me, almost sending me back into the darkness for a third time. I groan aloud and clench my fists against the hurt, but the hurt is everywhere and it won't go away. Then, slowly, so slowly that I think I'm dreaming, it begins to wash from me as the drugs take hold.

My head swims and, for the first time, I realise that it's Hecht who's crouched over me; Hecht who's been talking to me this last minute or so without it registering.

I turn my head the slightest degree, trying to take in what's happening. The platform is a mess of blood and guts and jagged bone, and there's an overpowering stench in the air. Someone is sewing me up now, but I'm confused. What did they do? Bomb us?

And then I remember. We were in Neu Berlin. Burckel and I ...

'Albrecht ...' I croak, barely able to get the word out. 'Where's Albrecht?'

Hecht says something, but it gets carried away. I try to focus on him, but my left eye closes. It feels much lighter than the other, as if someone has replaced my right eye with a piece of lead. But the stabbing pain has gone now and I feel relaxed, like someone has doused me in a bath of cool, liquid silk.

Yet even as I slip back into unconsciousness, I see Dankevich's face as we jump, see the shock there as he throws himself belatedly towards Burckel and I, his lips forming a single word;

'No-ooooooooh!'

108

I don't understand at first. Hecht hands me the ragged gobbet of flesh and I frown at him. It looks like a locator, and I tell him such, but Hecht shakes his head.

'It's what's left.'

'Left?'

'Of Albrecht Burckel. Of the *real* Albrecht Burckel. That's why the signal never stopped. The focus was still working. But the rest of him ...'

I feel nauseous. So that's where our friend Werner came in. The Russians must have paid him to make a 'doppelganger' – a 'copy'

– of Burckel, then switched the live focus from the real Burckel to the copy, embedding this gobbet of flesh into the copy.

Only Werner didn't use Burckel's DNA to make his doppelganger, so that when Burckel jumped ...

I get a flash of the platform – that awful bloody mess, that hideous, gut-turning stench – and close my eyes again.

And immediately blink awake, because the eye is healed up, and my body ...

'Two months,' Hecht says, answering my unspoken question. 'But don't worry. I sent you back. Repaired you in the past.'

I nod, relieved. At least that means Ernst hasn't suffered too much from my absence, though Urd knows how it feels inside that stasis field. Each second might seem an eternity.

'You're good as new,' Hecht goes on, 'only I want you to hang on a day or two before you go back in. There's been a change of plan. You're going back, but this time I want you on the inside.'

'Inside?'

'In the fortress. It's all arranged. You have an audience with the King.'

But it doesn't properly sink in. Not yet. Because I keep thinking about what happened. About Burckel and the 'edges' of his memory. No wonder the poor bastard felt like that. No bloody wonder ...

Part Six

Rassenkampf

'A people is a detour of nature to get to six or seven great men. – Yes: and then to get round them.'

– Friedrich Nietzsche, *Beyond Good And Evil*

109

That night I dream of her.

Night has fallen and we're in the forest, running, naked in the moonlight, the paleness of her body flashing between the trees ahead of me. I can hear the breath hiss from me, while ahead, in that moonlit dark, her laughter peals out, like the laughter of enchantment. All night we run, hunter and prey. Slowly I gain on her, leaping fallen logs and rocks, running silently, tirelessly through the endless forest, until, in a glade at the bottom of a long, rock-strewn slope, she turns and faces me, a surging, silvered river at her back, a dark stand of pines beyond. She looks about her, like a wild and cornered animal, beautiful in her savagery, but I am upon her and, as I step from the trees, she smiles.

The dark and perfect buds of her breasts are aroused, and as she steps into my arms so her flesh is warm and moist against my own. Her soft mouth lifts to meet mine in a kiss.

And as she kisses me, I wake, aroused, wanting her.

'*Katerina* ...'

I turn, burying my face in my pillow, then turn back, groaning, unable to bear it.

You might think that I could go to her. But how? Every second of my waking day is taken up. Even so, perhaps I could slip back in Time and spend a day or two with her? After all, I could make it seem that I'd been gone only a moment.

True. Only to do so I would need to be *sent* back. To travel in Time I must use the platform. And why go back to that particular time right now? For what purpose? To help Ernst subvert Prince Nevsky? But Ernst is trapped, and until he's freed ...

Or, to put it more simply – *how would I explain it all to Hecht?*

You see my dilemma. And even if I *could* go back, to what point would I go? If I *have* married her, then that's done and in the Past and you might think that I could go back to some moment when she was mine – when, without a moment's hesitation, I might slip into her bed and, waking her, make tender love. But such a moment does not as yet exist. As things stand I have yet to make her mine. Nor is it certain that I shall, for all that's in the future – *my* future, not the world's.

'Otto?'

I look up, and find Leni standing there in the doorway. She smiles apologetically, an embarrassed smile, and it's only then that I realise my condition.

I throw a sheet over my nakedness, then sit up, taking the sealed envelope from her. As I open it, she crouches, meeting my eyes.

'Are you ... *in need*?'

I know what she means. Do I want to sleep with her? It would not be the first time. Far from it. But things are different now.

'No, I ...'

I fall silent, reading what Hecht has written.

'Otto?'

I look at her again. Leni is beautiful. Oh, all of our women are beautiful in their different ways, but Leni especially so, with her strong yet narrow face, her short blonde hair and her neat, full-figured body.

'I have to go,' I say. 'It's time.'

'Ah ...' And her eyes seem regretful. She smiles. 'Another time, perhaps?'

'Perhaps.'

When she's gone I shower and dress then gather together what I'll need for the journey. It isn't much: a gun, a knife and a picture I drew last night of Katerina, the old one having disintegrated in the jump that did for Burckel. Or what pretended to be Burckel. All else will be awaiting me at the platform.

Hecht too is waiting there. He smiles and briefly grips my shoulder. 'Good luck, Otto. You know what you must do.'

I nod, then step up on to the platform, my bundle in one hand. Urte meets my eyes from behind one of the work-stations and smiles. 'Good luck.'

And she brings her hand down on to the pad.

110

As the cruiser banks to make its final approach, I look down through cloud at the city below. The Jungfernsee is directly below, the lake's surface shining like a long, burnished mirror in the last hour of daylight. From this height you can see what a vast, sprawling metropolis Neu Berlin is, a strange, black, crystalline growth, filling the North Brandenburg plain. Even so, the fortress dominates the view, its central tower a vast, extended peak.

There's a faint murmur of exchanges from the cockpit – our pilot speaking to the control tower – then we begin our descent, swooping down out of the evening sky.

Glancing across, I smile at Heusinger. Klaus knows this age, this place – he's been here many times – but this once he's taking a minor role. This time he's secretary to me, the new ambassador of the Confederation of North American States. I've not worked with Klaus before, but he seems an amiable young man, polite, enthusiastic, and thoroughly – *thoroughly* – German.

This is Hecht's plan, evolved and carried out while I was being put back together – a thousand tiny slivers of bone removed from my flesh, my right eye rebuilt, my hair and skin re-grown.

Until now we've kept our agents on the hinterland of the action, in the suburbs of Neu Berlin and in several other cities of the Empire – in Cologne and New Magdeburg, Hamburg, Lodz, Munich, Oslo and Lisbon. But now we are to move inside, into the fortress for the first time. It's time to break bread with the deci-sion-makers. Time to meet them face-to-face.

I understand Hecht's reasoning. It has not been possible to play it otherwise before now. Much of the success of our game depends on subterfuge, on our agents being kept in the shadows, indistin-guishable from any native of the Age. But life inside the fortress is lived in the glare of the spotlight. Inside, we must be open and bold. Such a 'throw' as this cannot be attempted more than once. Not without alerting the Russians.

Moreover, there are historical factors that we must not disturb – things that *must* happen. Hans Gehlen, for instance. Right now, in June 2747, Gehlen is a young man of twenty-eight, a genius who, in the coming days – and I do mean days, not weeks – will unravel the mystery of Time and, in so doing, begin the great cycle within which we all exist. Nothing must happen to him. Nor, indeed, to several others who must fulfil their destinies, here in this Age. We have agents in place, of course, protecting them, overseeing them at every moment, yet we must be careful that some action – seemingly harmless but historically fatal – does not unweave our careful planning.

Oh yes. And for once Germany must fall. And everything – everything – be blown to pieces. For that is what happened. That is what awaits us, down the line in 2747. Ragnarok. The twilight of the gods … And afterwards? The *Nichtraum*. Four-Oh. And war. Eternal racial war – *Rassenkampf* – with Russia. All else can change, but not that.

We land on top of the garrison building, in the shadow of the massive back wall of the fortress. Stepping down, I look across and up at the huge bulk of the central tower which climbs a thousand metres into the sunlight. Everything's on a massive scale, yet as I turn to face the welcoming party I register a moment's shock.

They're huge, the smallest of them ten feet if they're an inch.

The five stroll toward us across the open space, then stop and, with a strangely disconcerting uniformity of movement, bow to us. As they straighten, I note how their heads and shoulders are in direct sunlight, their features golden in the sun's last rays, while their bodies – like us, *like every part of us* – lie in deep shadow.

The tallest of them stands at the centre of the group, a pace or two in front. He's head and shoulders bigger than his companions and wears a long black cloak. His face is old and lined, yet also strong and deeply tanned. His grey eyes meet mine with a smile.

'Ambassador. I am Tief, the King's chancellor. Welcome to Greater Germany.'

Tief. It means 'deep' in the old tongue.

I thank him, yet all the while I'm conscious of the difference in our physical statures. I feel like a child before him, yet he seems to make nothing of it. There's a kindness in his face that's wholly unexpected.

'Come,' he says simply. 'You must be hungry after your long journey.'

We walk among those giant figures across a narrow bridge – a giddying drop beneath us, like a chasm in a mountainside – and through a massive circular portal, the curved beams beautifully carved, into a huge yet shadowed banqueting hall.

I say hall, only it's really a massive slab of stone – or *Kunstlichestahl* – jutting out into the centre of what is, in essence, one vast single chamber. It's like being inside a giant lighthouse, to the walls of which have been affixed hundreds of these vast platforms. I can see others above and below us, and between them strange shapes move slowly, drifting between the levels.

I look about me. The black marble floor is empty but for one long table at the far end, set with silver and piled high with huge platters of food.

We take our places and, for a time, indulge in pleasantries. Nothing too profound, and nothing that touches on my business with the King. Tief and I do most of the talking, but eventually the meal comes to an end and, with a smile, Tief stands and, beckoning to me, turns from the table.

I follow, joining him at the edge of the floor. It's a remarkable sight. Above us and below, other platforms, similar to our own, jut out from the great curved inner wall of the fortress. No stairways link these giant slabs, and in a moment I understand why, as a portion of the floor we're standing on breaks off and, with a movement that seems almost motionless, glides down towards one of the lower platforms.

I feel a kind of excited fear at being suspended above the drop. A moment's loss of balance and I would fall a thousand metres. Yet the view beneath me is magnificent. There are kitchens and halls, workshops and classrooms, and – everywhere I look – hundreds of servants, tiny, dark, anonymous-looking figures, moving slowly, silently about their business. Not to speak of the guards.

I glance up, seeing how the platforms above me seem to defy gravity, everything here on a scale to make us lesser beings – we *Naturlich* – feel smaller, inferior. Or maybe I mistake the intent. Maybe it's just that the gods build like gods.

Another platform now approaches, a hall with pillars and a dozen great throne-like chairs along one side. As the segment of floor that's carried us melds with the edge of it, so two silent guards bow low, averting their eyes. Beyond them, the servants they have been supervising fall to their knees, their foreheads pressed to the floor. There is a profound silence to the place, such that our foot-falls echo on the stone.

We cross that great, empty floor, approaching a huge archway, each of the massive wooden doors carved with the giant figure of a bear, symbol of Berlin throughout the ages.

Tief turns to me. 'The King awaits you within. You may look at him, but you must not speak. Not without his permission.'

'And you, Chancellor?'

He smiles. 'I shall wait here for you. When you are done, I will take you to your quarters. Meanwhile your secretary will be attended to.'

I smile. 'You are most kind.'

He bows once more, his long body folding elegantly within its cloak.

The throne room is dark, the ceiling a long way overhead, lost in the shadows. We seem 'indoors' here, cut off from the openness of the rest of the fortress. Huge wooden beams cross the darkness above me, the dark forms of ancient banners dangling from their heights. There is a musty smell of age, as if this place has stood a thousand years. Lamps flicker in iron cressets to left and right, high up. I walk forward slowly, hesitantly, my eyes straining to make out the figure of the King. Just ahead of me is an imposing flight of steps – each broad stone step a good metre deep – at the top of which is an enormous marble throne. I make my way towards it and, kneeling at the foot, bow low, resting my forehead on my knee.

'Please stand, Herr Manninger.'

The voice comes from behind me, to my right.

I straighten and turn, even as he takes a step closer, looming over me.

If Tief was big, the King is massive. He's three times the height of me, so big a man he seems not made of flesh but of rock. His bare arms ripple with muscles, and though I know he is over two centuries old, he looks no more than fifty. He wears a great fur about his shoulders, like he's king of the primeval forest, but no ancient king ever looked so mighty, so magnificent.

Looking at him, I am awed. King Manfred is the end result of centuries of selective breeding – a creature at the very limits of what mankind might possibly be. But there's another reason to be awed by Manfred, because here is the longest serving king in Germany's long history. He has ruled this land for eighty-seven years, surviving six coups and nine assassination attempts. Yet as he gives me his hand – my own engulfed by it – he seems untroubled, almost free of cares. His blue eyes smile down gently at me.

'It's okay,' he says, in a deep rich voice. 'You may speak, Herr Manninger. Or should I call you Lucius?' His smile broadens momentarily. 'How was your flight?'

'It was long, Meister, and, I confess, rather tedious ...'

I know it's rude, but I can't stop staring at him. He is – and it might seem a strange thing to say about another man – quite beautiful. It's little wonder that his people consider him a god.

The Russians have their own genetic elite, of course – their *podytyelt* – but they are as nothing beside these *Adel*.

'I was, I have to say, surprised.'

'Surprised, Meister?'

'Yes.' And he sits, on the fifth step up, his long legs sprawled out before him like two fallen pines. 'Oh, I knew that things were happening out in America, that it was no longer such a barbarian wilderness as once it was, but ...'

I bow low, acknowledging that. 'Things have changed. Since the Confederation was formed we have striven hard to eradicate disease and hunger among our people.'

I pause, and am taken by surprise by the interest in his eyes. His is a powerful nation of a billion and a half, America a ragged conglomerate of states totalling no more than eighty million souls

– less than the southern quarter of Berlin itself – and he knows this, yet he listens as if we were equals, and I realise what a clever, well-balanced man he is. One might expect a degree of arrogance from such a being, yet he shows no sign.

'So I've heard. Indeed, I understand that you've made great strides.'

'Small steps, Meister, but in the right direction. These fifty years …' I pause and lower my head slightly. 'Our achievements might seem modest compared to your own, yet we are proud to have emerged from the darkness.'

There is history here – a lot of history – yet it can be simply stated. At the end of the twenty-first century, the United States came into conflict with its main trading rival, China, and fought what it hoped would be a decisive war. It was. America lost. Not that China won, exactly. Only Europe survived the conflict. Or rather Germany and European Russia.

'Six centuries of darkness,' he says, and looks away, as if he sees it clear. 'It is hard to imagine your people's suffering.'

'Meister …'

Only I *have* seen it. I've been there, along with Ernst. Long ago, admittedly, but not so long that I can forget the awfulness of it. After the bombs had fallen there was nothing. Nothing but ashes.

'Your king?'

I am loath to correct him, yet I must, if only for the sake of consistency – of getting our story right. 'Our *president*, Meister …'

He smiles, indulging me. 'Your president, then. Does he send me word?'

I take the sealed envelope from my pocket and, bowing low, offer it to him. He opens it and reads, then looks across at me.

'I see …'

It's not what I expected him to say. He doesn't seem surprised. But then, what could surprise a man as old and worldly wise as he?

It is a request to become his ally. Unsurprising, maybe, only the document, like all else about us, is a fake. Only the seal is genuine. The writing is Hecht's, the sentiments his alone. Even so, it seems to do the trick.

I kneel. 'Meister?'

'Yes, Lucius?'

'Should I kiss your ring?'

111

It might seem that my business here is done – that all it takes is for the King to say yes, but that's not so. Though Manfred is lord and master here and has the power of life and death over all, he still needs to consult those who matter in his realm: his many sons and brothers on the one hand; the Guild on the other.

The one body he doesn't need to consult is the army, and that's his one great strength, for the army is fiercely loyal to Manfred. And not merely his *Leibstandarte* – his fortress elite – but the greater mass of the *Wehrmacht* – the people's army.

There's to be a meeting of all parties later this evening, which we are to attend. A feast. Until then Heusinger and I are granted the freedom of the fortress.

Tief offers to be our guide, to show us whatever we wish to see. It's a generous offer, yet I wonder just how far I might push it.

'You have heard tell of the Hall of Kings?' Tief enquires.

I stare at him, surprised. 'That is a story, surely?'

'No, no. It exists. Would you like to see?'

'Why yes, I—'

Tief speaks to the air. 'Arrange it.'

And so we follow, in a kind of daze, because this is the stuff legends are made of, and true enough, as we step through the massive door, the Hall stretches out before us, a long, comparatively narrow space with a series of high, domed ceilings. The floor is marble, not fake, but a beautiful Italian stone, pure white, with the thinnest streaks of black.

The first of a dozen large glass cases faces us, not a dozen paces distant, like a giant bell jar, its massive, rounded dome reflecting the light of a circle of glow-globes that hover just above.

Tief strides across, then turns, awaiting us. We walk across, then stare.

'This was the first of them,' Tief says. 'The prototype. It's a lot bigger than a normal man, as you see – a good metre taller – but compared to what followed it's a crude attempt.'

I look up at Tief, surprised by his comments. Or perhaps they're sanctioned. Perhaps this is the official view – for this is one of Manfred's ancestors, the very first of the *Adel*. Not a king as such, but in the direct genetic line. I stare at the thin, sickly looking creature and can see how it must have suffered. Not so much a man as an experiment in gene-manipulation, this creature looks as alien as anything I glimpsed in Werner's makeshift morgue.

'You can see the problems at a glance,' Tief says. 'Though the genes had been stripped down and cleaned, and though they did their best to choose for strength, health and intelligence, what resulted ... well, you can see it with your own eyes. The first of the *Adel* were unsustainable.'

And preserved here for all time, I think, wondering what the living creature would have made of such a humiliating fate.

We walk on, to the second of the great glass cases. This one, though little taller than the first, is slightly more human. Not so thin or sickly looking. Yet he shares the pallor of the first, and the same look of unarticulated misery is in his swollen eyes.

Tief smiles at it fondly. 'With Hans here the geneticists thought they had solved most of the problems, or at least that they were moving in the right direction. The muscle-development, while not good, was much better than in the prototype, and – as you can see – Hans is much stronger, much more viable. Even so, he lasted only twenty-eight years.'

'And the first? The prototype?'

Tief makes a sad face. 'Seventeen.'

I nod and walk on, following Tief, listening as he tells me the history of each of these sad creatures. Some are an improvement, others – some markedly so – a regression. Yet every last one of them suffers from those problems that beset humans with greater height, greater body weight: problems of bone-weakness, of poor muscle-development and inadequate heart capacity. For the first nine generations of *Adel* these problems seemed insuperable. Sickly dinosaurs, they seemed. An evolutionary dead-end. Not only that, but they rarely bred true, nor naturally. Right up until the tenth generation they were, to all intents and purposes, an artificial race, needing the constant help of experts to sustain their line.

We stand beneath the ninth and last of the jars as Tief finishes his tour. Ahead of us the Hall stretches away, echoing empty, not a single glass case between us and the exit a hundred metres distant.

For with the tenth generation the geneticists finally got it right. With Manfred the quest was ended, the 'greater man' – the *Übermensch* – finally made flesh; a viable species, bigger and better than anyone had dreamed of: one that bore live children, and whose lifespan was twice that of mere old sapiens. It was an awesome victory over nature, a staggering vindication of scientific pride. And to the people? To the people it was as if the gods had returned to the earth.

'Are you tired yet?' Tief asks. 'Or would you like to see more?'

'Lead on,' I say, and smile. And there's much to see. The fortress is a wonder in itself, nine palaces in one. Here is luxury – self-indulgence, some might say – quite beyond imagining, yet I quickly tire of it. Besides, there's something else I want to see, and after a while I take Tief aside and whisper to him.

'Hmmm ...' he says. 'That may prove difficult. But who knows? Let me ask, anyway. The Grand Master may just be in a mood to show you his domain, and if he is ...'

Tief smiles.

If he is, I think, *then we are done here.*

I have the map in my head, you understand – the map our two-headed friend Reichenau gave me, identifying the position of the power source. All I need is to match one single point on it with some reality, and then ...

But that's to jump ahead.

We wait, among the furs and tapestries, the marble statuary and the endless gold, while Tief goes off to see what he can do.

I'm silent, thoughtful, but Heusinger's excitement makes him talk. He loves being here inside the fortress. For twenty years and more he's dreamed of this.

'Did you see that painting? That was a Petsch, surely?'

It was. But not one of them will survive. The greatest art works of a thousand years and all – *all* – will be consumed by the coming fires.

Petsch too will die, and his beloved Pauline. And the thought of it suddenly makes me think of Katerina, and of her mortality. Curiously, her natural lifespan is something I've not thought of before that instant and a pang goes through me to think that she will grow old and die.

I look down, distressed, for no good reason fearful for her. Where is she now? And what is she doing?

The answer is that she is everywhere back there; anchored in a million moments to her world, her life like the wake a ship makes in its travels. I can go back and dip into the stream of her being, but she ... she is tethered there, tied to her eternal Now.

I look up, meaning to say something to Heusinger, when I realise we are no longer alone. Across from me, seated in a chair by the doorway, is another giant – one of the *Adel*. And not just any giant. This is clearly the King's son, for that face, though different in its way, is similar enough to make its source quite clear.

I glance at Heusinger, then quickly bow.

He is dressed like a barbarian, in tight-fitting black leather trousers and a sheepskin jerkin that leaves his hugely muscled arms bare. In his thick, studded leather belt there is a short stabbing sword, like the Romans used to wear. I say short, but the whole thing is bigger than me. He could cleave me crown to groin with such a weapon.

I say he is like his father, but the likeness is that of caricature. Whereas Manfred seems confident and calm with a serenity that suggests great wisdom, this seed of his – if indeed this creature is a direct fruit of Manfred's loins and not concocted in some vat of chemicals somewhere – seems cruel and spiteful. He has said nothing, done nothing, and yet I see it in his face. There's a sneering arrogance to his features. His lips, his nose, his deeply blue eyes, all suggest a vicious, petulant nature, and when he speaks, the nasal tone of his voice confirms it for me. Here is a man not to be crossed, not even to be argued with.

'Who the fuck are you?'

'Meister,' I say, bowing low. 'I am the envoy of the Confederation of North American States. Your father ...'

'*Quiet!*'

I keep my head lowered, my eyes averted. Though I have the King's protection, I do not wish to anger this man in any way, though I sense my mere presence is provocation enough.

He stands and, towering above me, walks round me.

'*America* ...' And the sneer within that single word becomes a laugh. A laugh that is snuffed out suddenly like a candle. He leans closer, his voice lowered, as if offering me a confidence. 'We do not need you, whatever *he* thinks …'

I know by '*he*' he means his father, the King, but I say nothing. I wait for more, secretly praying that Tief will choose that moment to return, but when someone comes it isn't Tief, but a woman, another giant, a sister to this sneering demon. She wears a long, revealing cloak of purest white, against which her ash-blonde hair cascades like fine strands of precious metals.

'Who's this?' she asks, her tone dismissing me out of hand.

'*Americans*,' he answers, and they both laugh, a cruel laughter, as if they would enjoy watching us be slowly tortured. My eyes slide sideways, looking to Heusinger. He no doubt knows who these two are and how important they are in the pecking order inside the fortress, but there's no way I can ask him.

'He's a *puny* little specimen, don't you think?' she says, walking round me, then lifting my chin with one frighteningly enormous finger.

'Hideous,' her brother says. Yet as my eyes meet her sapphire blue eyes, I note a flicker of interest. Of curiosity. Her scathing disinterest is, it seems, a front, a mask put on to satisfy her brother. But she herself is wondering why I'm there, and why my own eyes show no fear, no awe of her.

I'd smile, only that would let her know that I'd seen through her, and then she might be angry with me.

She turns away, her finger drawing back from my chin, my flesh tingling where she has touched me.

And strangely – strangest of all, perhaps – I find I am attracted to her. As her long, elegant body turns from me, I am aroused. I look down, confused and dismayed, and force myself to think of Katerina, hoping that somehow her image in my head will displace this sudden, unwanted sign, yet my body continues to betray me. The feel of her finger on my flesh, that strange, hard pressure of her touch, has made me wonder what it would be like to sleep with such a goddess.

I shudder, frightened by the thought, appalled that I could even think it.

'*Lucius* ...'

For a moment I do not recognise my alias. Then, with a strange jerk of my head, I glance across at Heusinger. He gestures towards the empty space in front of us.

'They've gone.'

'Ah.' But I feel cold. The shock of the encounter has quite thrown me. 'Who were they?'

'The male was Manfred's sixth son, Hagen. His third wife Gunnhilde's son.'

'And the female?'

There's the slightest quaver in my voice, but not enough to betray the reason for my interest.

'I'm not sure. Gudrun, probably. They're twins, you see. Her and her sister, Fricka. Manfred's nieces.'

'Ah ...'

But then Tief returns, his open, smiling countenance refreshing after such sneers, such lofty arrogance.

'I'm sorry,' he says, 'but I'm afraid it isn't possible to see the Guild quarters just now. The Grand Master has called a special session of the Council and it would not do to intrude upon them. Tomorrow, perhaps?'

'Of course,' I say, far more interested by this development – expected as it is – than Tief knows. 'Tomorrow, then ...'

But I know now that it has begun. Just as in the history books. Only I shall be there this time.

112

Our quarters turn out to be a single monstrous bedroom, strewn with awnings that keep those above from spying on us. Alone there, sprawled out on a double bed large enough to house a dozen of my kind, I ask Heusinger to brief me on the internal politics of the court.

'What you have to ask yourself,' he says, 'is what each faction wants. They all want war, of course – unrelenting, perpetual war – but how that war is fought and who controls it, such details are at the heart of their disagreements.'

He pauses to pour me a cup of wine, then continues.

'The King, naturally, wants things kept as they are. Peace would be disastrous for him. The army is his chief support, and he needs to keep his generals happy. But equally an escalation of the war could prove just as dangerous, in that it would mean giving too much power to those fighting the war on his behalf – power that would, of necessity, be removed from *his* hands. No, what Manfred wants is stability – no one rocking any boats and the status quo maintained indefinitely.'

'And the Guild?'

Heusinger shrugs. 'It's hard to read. The Grand Master keeps his cards very close to his chest. There's no "official" Guild policy, but it would seem that the Guild wants precisely what the King wants. You'd think from that that they'd be his staunchest allies in council, only the days when the Grand Master had influence over the King are long past. Manfred acts without consulting them these days, and that infuriates them. More than anything, they'd like to see a new king, one they might *control*.'

It seems a harsh analysis, and if the Guild are listening – which they undoubtedly are – they'll not take kindly to it. But we are not here to make friends. We're not even here to forge the alliance we are supposedly seeking; we're here to disable the power source, and we must survive in this snake-pit until we can discover where it is and make our move.

'Do the Guild speak with one voice?'

Again Heusinger shrugs. 'Once more, it's hard to tell. If there are disagreements among them, they're kept well hidden. But it wouldn't surprise me. They're not as machine-like as they look. Bio-mechanisms they may be, robots they're not.'

'Which brings us to the King's close family.' Heusinger laughs, then sips his wine. 'I say close, but only in the genetic sense. There's more hatred among this parcel of relatives than in a roomful of cats on heat. The King's brothers and his sons might be envied for what they have – for a lifestyle matched only by the gods – yet they see themselves as prisoners here in the fortress. They feel impotent, *powerless*, much more so than the Guild. Like the Guild, they *want* power, but the only way they could gain it would be to kill the King.'

'They've tried, I take it?'

Heusinger nods. 'That difficulty aside, their main problem is in agreeing on a replacement. Killing Manfred would be only the start of their difficulties. With the present king dead there would be coups and counter-coups and – who knows? – maybe even civil war. There are at least four separate "pretenders" to the throne and their hatred of each other outshines their hatred of the King.'

'I see. So in essence there are three factions ...'

Heusinger laughs and shakes his head. 'If only it were that simple, Lucius. No, beyond the internal politics of the court, there's a much greater problem, that of the *Undrehungar*, the revolutionary parties, especially the *Unbeachtet*. They may not have a voice in the King's council, but their existence cannot be ignored. They're a real thorn in Manfred's side. The Security forces try their hardest to deal with them – to *eradicate* them – but like the famed hydra, cut off one head and another quickly grows. No, Lucius, the Empire is in turmoil; it festers with discontent. And that's where our friends the Russians come into the picture, for though they cannot hope to win the war, they can still dream of undermining things here. Their agents ...'

Heusinger stops and smiles, imagining what the listeners are making of this, then continues. 'Well, put it this way ... I am told that there are places in the city where half the population speak German with a Russian accent.'

We both laugh, but the thought of that troubles me. I think of Burckel and what they managed to do to him, and I wonder just how far, how *deeply*, the Russians have infiltrated our network here.

'So to whom should we be most friendly? The King?'

'He seems our greatest hope. But it wouldn't harm to court the favour of the Guild. The Teuton Knights are far from being a spent force in this land. They are – or so I'm told – building a spacecraft.'

I can almost hear the indrawn breath, the sudden panic among the various listeners. For this is a secret, and Heusinger has dropped it into the mix as if it were well known. The Guild will want to know how we found out and who the traitor is in their midst. The King, for his part, will want to know why the Guild is building rocket ships without his knowledge.

'I guess we should get ready,' I say, as if nothing has been said. 'You have the gifts for the King?'

There is a knock, not loud or hammering, but firm and sharp. Tief's knock, if I'm not mistaken. I look to Heusinger and smile.

'Come in.'

Tief pushes back the massive doors and enters. Was he listening? His face betrays nothing. 'Gentlemen,' he says, bowing low. 'Forgive me for intruding, but there's to be a ceremony – an offering to the gods – and the King ...' He smiles. 'The King asks if you would like to witness it.'

'It would be an honour,' I say. And it's true. Not only that, but it is some while since I gave thanks to Urd.

Tief waits while we prepare ourselves, then leads us out, across the platform and then down – floating on a piece of *Kunstlichestahl* no bigger than a desk top – on to a broad balcony that looks out over what seems a cross between an ancient chapel and a woodland glade, the one transposed inside the other. The walls are bare stone, with stained-glass windows in a medieval style, but there is also earth and rocks, pines and flowing streams, and at the centre of all a great ash tree, towering above the rest, its crown on a level with where we stand, above it all.

The World Tree, Ygdrasil.

Before it stands the King, and others so very like him that I assume they are his brothers and his sons. Those closest to him. Those that hate him most. Sensing me there, he turns, then gestures to me to come down. I glance at Tief, then descend by way of a small stone stairwell, walking out among those giants until I am at the King's side.

He towers above me, wearing a cloak of midnight blue so dark it seems made of the night itself.

I stand to his right. To his left stands a boy – taller than I, yet a child – holding a basket of apples. But not any just apples. These are huge, gilded apples that glow from within, silver and gold, like they were grown on some magical tree.

Manfred reaches into the basket and plucks out one silver apple and one gold and, holding them high before him, offers them to the World Tree. His voice booms deeply in that silent, enclosed space, deeper than any human voice I've ever heard.

'Urd, daughter of Mimer, who is mind and memory, Goddess of Fate, Queen of Life and Death, accept my offerings and, with your sisters Verdande and Skuld, guardians of the Past and Future, vouchsafe our destinies.'

The Tree shimmers, as if alive, and I see, high in its branches, a great bird, an eagle. Vedfolner, perhaps. It is a movement of the bird's great wings that has made the Tree shimmer, yet the illusion that the gods responded is strong.

Two handmaidens, half Manfred's size, dressed in virginal white, step out from the shadows to either side and, accepting his offerings, step across to the foot of the great trunk. They place them there, then step back, and as they do, so a fierce beam of light crackles in the air above, consuming the apples.

Manfred waits a moment, then, taking two more apples, holds them high and speaks again, his voice deep and resonant.

'All-Father Odin, one-eyed God of War, grant us your love and protection. Wisest of gods, you who were at time's first dawn, you of the nine and forty names who sees the fate of men and gods, watch over us and give us victory over our enemies.'

Again the handmaidens take the apples and place them by the World Tree, and again they are consumed by the blazing light.

For a third time, Manfred takes two apples and holds them high. His eyes shine now with belief, and his voice, when it sounds a third time, seems to resonate in my bones.

'Freyja, Goddess of Fertility, whose handmaidens sit beneath the boughs of the great World Tree, grant us long life and happiness and many children. May your beauty be our inspiration always.'

From all sides there comes a deep murmur of agreement. All about me and above me, heads bow towards the great Tree. Again it shimmers.

It is the simplest of ceremonies, over in a moment, yet I find myself moved beyond all expectation. I am used to the forms and phrases, for this is *our* religion, yet rarely have I heard them uttered with such conviction, such *belief*, never have I felt so certain of the gods' existence, and so, after a moment, I bow low, as if in Odin's eye, and Manfred, seeing this, places one of his great hands upon my shoulders.

'You have gods in your country, Lucius?'

'We do, Meister. But none as powerful as these.'

And I mean it. For though I have believed in the gods since I was a child, rarely have I felt their living presence as I did today.

We walk on, across the soft dark soil, and through, beneath the boughs of the great World Tree, into a long, lamp-lit corridor and thence into the Hall. And once again I am surprised, for what surrounds me is no less than an ancient chieftain's lodge, a huge, log-walled chamber with great shields and swords and axes on the walls, built in the ancient style. At the centre nine great trestle benches have been set up, eight in the main body of the Hall, in four rows of two, and one at the head, raised on a platform above the rest, as in olden days. There's straw on the cold stone floor, and, as in centuries past, a great fire roars in a massive grate to one side. The scent of burning pine fills the Hall.

I have sat in halls like this – smaller, danker halls, admittedly – when Germania was but a scattering of tribes hated by Rome and unified by lust and aggression. I have sat and eaten thus with many an ancient king, even with the great Hermann of the Cherusci, known to Rome as Arminius, whose armies defeated three legions in the Teutoburg forest, back in AD 16, but this is the strangest gathering I've ever attended; for while those ancient kings sought to impress me with the 'luxury', the *modernity* of their lodges, these *Übermensch* approach things from the opposite direction. They play at this retrograde simplicity, as if it suits them to be plain, unadorned brutes. Barbarism is in their blood, like a drug, yet their brutality is a matter of *style*.

It's a strange gathering in another respect, too, for rarely have I seen such a mixture of types of people – huge and tiny, gene-sculpted and bio-mechanical. The Guildsmen are conspicuously absent, and I note immediately that two of the benches at the centre sit empty. While the King goes among his people, shaking this man's hand or speaking to another, I look about me, surprised to see so many *Naturlich* among the ranks of the *Adel*. Heusinger, at my side, is pointing out various ministers, explaining their role in things, when I notice Gudrun, seated to my right.

It's barely an hour since I saw her last, yet she seems more beautiful than ever. Not only that, but when our eyes meet, she seems to start with surprise.

That moment's startlement confuses me. What does it mean? Surely she can't be interested in me? Yet to my surprise she stands and, coming across, smiles and gives me her hand. Her eyes are strange. If I didn't know better, I'd think they were filled with gratitude. But why should she be grateful?

She leans down and whispers. 'Thank you, Otto.'

This time I'm shocked. Shocked that she knows my proper name. But I also haven't a clue why she should be thanking me.

'I'm sorry?'

But there's no time to find out. Tief appears at my side and, hurrying me on, leads me across to the high table.

Everything here is manufactured to the scale of the *Adel*. Massive silver platters, bowl-sized cups, knives the size of swords, the forks like tridents. Even so, the King has made concessions to his guests, and though it makes us feel like infants at an adults' table, we have been given special chairs, special bowls and plates and cutlery.

The King, indeed, has honoured us, placing us to his left at the high table, above many who are patently brothers and sons – princes all of this mighty race.

Many an eye is on Heusinger and me. Many a scowling face scans us haughtily and looks away, as if we are – quite literally – *beneath* their interest. Among them I notice Hagen, seated with several of his brothers on one of the tables below and to my left. His sneering smile seems to welcome me, though I know he wishes me nothing but ill. I look to Gudrun again, seated among a group of maidens to the right, Valkyrie all, their blonde hair braided for the feast, plate armour beneath their silken, flowing robes, like illustrations from some ancient book of myth. And as I look, so she meets my eyes again, then looks away, as if flustered. As if something has happened between us when I know for a fact that it hasn't. And I wonder if this is some kind of game she's playing, to wind up Hagen, maybe. To make that bastard jealous. Only Hagen isn't conscious of it.

There's a strong buzz of talk, then a trumpet blows and all there stand, looking towards the two great doors at the far end of the Hall.

They march in like a cohort of ancient legionaries, four abreast behind the Grand Master, awkward, mechanical-looking creatures in pale blue full-length cloaks trimmed with purple, each of them identical to the Guildsman I saw at the club. Yet though they are huge by comparison to ordinary men, beside these *Adel* they seem diminutive. As they march to their places, I notice a kind of mocking superiority in the eyes of the *Adel*, as if the *Adel* know they don't have to march four abreast to intimidate their enemies.

We wait as the Grand Master bows before the King, then wait a moment longer, the silence strained, as the Guild Knights take their places. Then and only then, does the King sit again, relaxing, turning to me with a smile, even as the Hall fills with talk and laughter once more.

'Our friend Adelbert does love to make an entrance ...'

Adelbert is the Grand Master, and that sentence sets the tone, for from there on the King confides in me, letting me know just what he thinks of whom, and why.

'You see those five,' he says, raising his voice as he points out a group of *Adel* seated to our right, close by the maidens. They look to be of an age with him – brothers, not sons. 'They look full of themselves, don't they, Lucius? But they're lucky to be alive. I had them neutered. Made sure those sons-of-bitches wouldn't *breed*.'

I raise an eyebrow and he explains.

'They tried to kill me.' He smiles, then raises his goblet to them in a toast. 'I *could* have had them killed, only they are my *brothers*, after all.'

It's impossible not to see the bitterness in their eyes, the festering hatred, and I wonder how Manfred can live with this and still be sane. No wonder Burckel called this a hornets' nest.

He looks to me again, even as the first dish is served. A rich meat broth, with fresh-baked bread.

'Your king, Lucius, is he as *small* as you?'

'Our president ...'

'Forgive me, your *president*. Is he ...?' And he gestures to me with an amused smile, as if I ought to know what a pathetic specimen I seem. And maybe it's so, but I don't feel intimidated by him. I know that his kind are a genetic dead end. The Future, however it turns out, is not going to be ruled by these *Adel*.

I smile pleasantly. 'He's a small man, yes, and thin, too. But very clever. And *tough*. You don't know how tough such a *small* man can be.'

'Oh, I can guess, Lucius.' And, taking a spoon the size of a ladle, he begins to eat his broth, tearing at a loaf that's as large as a roasting pig.

I'm surprised at the way he launches into his food, for you would have thought there would be a taster, considering how much his own family want him dead, yet he seems to take no precautions against poisoning.

Or maybe I'm just missing something.

Between mouthfuls, he continues our conversation. 'You've met Hagen, I understand. A nasty little brute, isn't he? But typical of my children. Ingrates all. And none too bright, either, despite their genes. At least, not as bright as they *need* to be. As for their mothers, my wives ...'

He gestures to his right, where, at the end of our table, a group of women have been sitting all this while in total silence, not eating, their sour expressions an indication of just how little they want to be there.

'Grasping bitches, the lot of them! Not a pinch of kindness in any of them, even the youngest! They think only of their sons and who will rule when I am dead. But what do you expect when you have to fuck your own family?'

I don't know what to say. His candour throws me. I stare, then shake my head, as if I'm dreaming, but Manfred seems not to worry whether I answer him or not. He merely wants to talk, to berate those about him.

'They say it's our destiny. That the future belongs to the better race. Well, so it is, Lucius. We *are* the future. But getting there ...' He laughs bitterly. This is a different king from the one I met earlier in the day, and it makes me wonder what has happened to make him so.

'Take this war we're having with the Russians. This "race war", or *Rassenkampf,* as my ministers love to call it. What's that all about? How in Thor's name did we get ourselves embroiled in that? Is that too part of our genetic destiny? Must we obliterate all of our rivals to succeed? Because if that's so ...'

'Meister ...'

Tief interrupts, sensing, perhaps, that the King is about to over-step the mark.

'Yes, Tief,' he says, turning towards him, a weary sigh escaping him. 'What is it?'

'The Grand Master wishes to speak to our guest. He asks if he might take a place at the high table.'

'Ho ho!' Manfred says, and rubs his massive hands together, as if delighted. 'Tell him to approach. Oh, and set him a place ... *there* ... facing me. I'd like to see him struggle with the broth.'

My eyes clearly have a question in them, because he leans towards me and, in an exaggerated whisper says: 'They don't eat, Lucius, they *re-charge*.'

And he giggles. At least, as much as such a big man *can* giggle. It's a rich, deep chortle that goes on and on and only stops as the Grand Master steps up on to the platform.

The Hall falls silent.

The King stands and puts out a hand, as if offering a place to a friend, but I can see how little friendship there is between the two men. The Grand Master bows, then, at the King's gesture, sits, facing us. And as I look at him, I have my first surprise. Though he is mostly metal and wire, plastic and lubricant, there is someone in there. Two bright eyes sit back some way in that great mask-like piece of circuitry, like someone has been trapped inside.

Hydraulics hiss. Metal creaks. 'Ambassador.'

The voice is smooth and deep, without a trace of machine-enhancement.

'Grand Master,' I reply, with a little bow, conscious that, for all his title claims, there is only one real '*master*' in this Hall, and that's the King.

His head moves slightly, like a tank turret, taking bearings on my face. 'I understand that you wished to see the Guild apartments. I am most regretful that we could not grant you that today. But if you would be my guest? Tomorrow, at dawn?'

Though Tief has undoubtedly told the King of my request, the Grand Master's courtesy clearly surprises Manfred, and he glances at me.

'That would be most kind,' I say, 'unless, of course, the King has other plans for me.'

'No, Lucius,' he says. 'You must go. I'm told it's very Spartan there. But you'll like their theatres, I'm sure ... I'm told they have *plenty* of theatres ...'

I look down, trying not to smile. Manfred doesn't mean places of entertainment, he means *operating* theatres. For Guildsmen aren't *born* Guildsmen, they're *made*, transformed into the kind of complex bio-mechanism that sits before me only after hundreds of operations. Manfred might make a joke of it now, but it's why, as a breed, they're so well used to pain. So capable of transcending it.

The Grand Master waits a moment, as if expecting more, then speaks again, looking to me as he does.

'Forgive me, Ambassador, but I'm curious. Why did your masters send so small a mission? There are, I understand, just two of you.'

I smile. 'That's so.'

'Ah ... yes ... yet it would seem ...'

'*Inadequate?*'

Manfred, beside me, smiles. But I sense he too would like to know the reasoning, so I continue.

'It's a matter of simple expediency, Grand Master. A larger mission would have required a much bigger craft, and we do not have one. As you probably realise, we are rebuilding fast, yet our level of technology ...' And I shrug, as if my admission of our weakness is endearing, but the Grand Master looks far from amused.

'There is another matter,' he begins. 'You say you have come from America, yet our agents report that you flew in from Africa. From the Tunisian coast, to be precise.'

'That's true,' I say. 'We have a base, in Dakhla, on the coast of the Western Sahara. One of several small outposts that facilitate trade.'

'Ah. And you flew there first?'

'And refuelled. It would not have done to have flown in over

Germany with an empty tank. Who knows where we might have dropped out of the sky – and on to what …'

Manfred laughs, amused, but I am beginning to wonder what the point of these questions is. Don't the Guild believe us? Have they *other* information about our mission?

'You've heard why they've come?' Manfred asks, looking directly at the Grand Master.

Again that turret of a head revolves, like it's about to take aim. 'No, *Meister* … though I believe we shall be discussing it.'

Manfred, however, is not so polite. 'Oh, he *knows*, Lucius. Our friend Adelbert here has his spies everywhere. And so do we. *They* know what we are doing and *we* know everything about them … or *almost* everything.'

The Grand Master is staring at Manfred now, his head seemingly frozen in one position, as if some mechanism has locked.

'They love the *pretence*,' Manfred says, an edge now to his voice. 'They love to make people *think* they're on my side, even while they're spying and prying and building spaceships …'

'*Meister!*' the Grand Master protests. 'We are not!'

'Not? You mean, not spying on me? Not prying into my affairs?'

The Grand Master's head unlocks, makes a fluid sideways motion. He seems about to say more, then decides against.

Manfred, though, does not leave it. 'It will be destroyed, Grand Master. And you will give me proof that it has been destroyed. And as for its architects – you will hand them over to me, tomorrow, before midday.'

'*Meister*, I …'

'*Tomorrow!*'

The Grand Master bows, then stands, waiting to be dismissed, and for a moment I begin to think that Manfred will keep him there, only even the King can only take things so far, and after a second or two's delay, he waves his hand, dismissing him.

'I'm sorry, Lucius,' he says, as the Grand Master takes a seat below us. 'I meant to keep that business until later ... but he annoys me. He's so humourless ... so pompous and self-righteous. Yes, and such a hypocrite. They say he likes boys. *Young* boys ...'

I glance at the King, surprised. Then again, these are people who have lived in each other's pockets for a century and more. That's time enough and more for nerves to fray and tempers be shredded. The only wonder is that they haven't self-destructed before now.

These *Adel* have been bred with great wisdom, yet they're also, in some crucial way, like children. Spoiled, petulant children. Even Manfred, now that I see it. Yes, even Manfred.

I'm about to be indiscreet – to ask Manfred about Gudrun – when the trumpet sounds again. I look across, and as the end doors open, I get a glimpse of a woman – an *Adel*, fully Manfred's own size, cradling something in her arms. As she comes closer, so I make out what it is. A child – a baby, to be more precise – though no baby I have ever seen was quite so large, so obscenely over-weight. Though a newborn, he must be four feet, maybe even five head to toe. And I know, without attempting it, that I'd as easily lift a horse and run a furlong with it on my back as lift and cuddle this child of Manfred's.

Coming up on to the platform, the woman hands Manfred his child and he stands, the proud father, showing it to everyone, no trace of his earlier bitterness extended to this innocent. Yet as he hands it back, I note a flicker of sadness in his eyes, as if foreknowledge of the child's inevitable corruption has darkened even this for him.

It's at this point that I notice Gudrun stand and, with a word to those about her, leave hurriedly. I've noticed that she's been distracted for some while, staring down into her untouched bowl and tugging almost compulsively at her braided hair, yet the way she leaves – without a sign, without a backward glance – makes me wonder just what's been going through her mind.

She has been gone only seconds when there's a huge explosion from somewhere below us. The platform shudders, and in the silence that follows, I turn to Manfred and see a strange, almost withdrawn expression in his eyes.

'Tief,' he says quietly. 'Go find out what that is.'

As his chancellor hurries off, so Manfred sits there, picking absently at the half-eaten loaf, looking about him at his relatives, a kind of vacant yet predatory glare in his eyes.

Tief returns and, leaning in close, speaks softly to Manfred's ear. For a moment there's nothing, and then I notice how the King's hands have clenched into fists; see, at the same moment, a strange, almost excruciating pain in his face.

Manfred stands, looking about him blindly, pain and rage at war in his face, tears coursing down his cheeks. And then he bellows at the watching *Adel*.

'You cunts! You heartless fucking cunts!'

Eyes watch him warily from the body of the Hall. No one's laughing. No one wants to draw attention to themselves. The King looks deadly in this mood. They know he'd as soon slit their throats as talk to them.

He gasps with pain, then looks to me. 'Lucius. Come with me. You must see this.'

I don't know why he asks me, but I follow hastily, running to keep up with his gigantic strides. Members of his special elite – his *Leibstandarte* – hurry to join us, forming a bodyguard about us as we hasten down a long curve of steps and out on to a kind of balcony.

It breaks off and floats out into the central space. There's smoke below us, and a strong smell of burned plastic and roasted flesh. As we descend into it, I see that one of the lower platforms has been badly damaged, a large chunk of it blown away. It's a sleeping chamber, and the place is a wreck, pieces of debris scattered everywhere.

Manfred groans as he takes it in. 'Father Odin, weep for her,' he says quietly, tears running one after another down his massive face.

I look to Tief, but he shakes his head, as if he's loath to say a word. But Manfred notices my curiosity, and, with a shuddering breath, tells me what I'm seeing.

'Her name was Signy, Lucius, and she was my aunt. The best of them. The sweetest, kindest of women. My mother's sister. Her best friend, and, after my mother died, mine.'

And I see in that instant just what a blow this is to him. Whoever did this meant to cripple him. To strike right at the heart.

We step out on to the damaged platform, to a scene of carnage. There is a body in the bed but it would be hard to identify it. It looks like it's been flayed. In fact, there's so much blood about that I realise it can't have come from just one person, no matter how big she was.

Manfred staggers, then straightens. 'I'll find them, Tief. And when I do ...'

His face is filled with horror at the sight, but there's also a hardness there now, a determination, and I know that his vengeance will be horrible. Such a vengeance as might empty Asgard. Or would do, were there time. But Manfred's time is running out. This is the start of it. The beginning of the end.

'Do we know who was here?' he asks a captain of the guard, who presents himself before us.

'There were six in all, Meister. Your aunt, two of her serving women, a guard, and her grand-daughters ...'

Manfred blinks, shocked. 'The twins? Gudrun and Fricka?'

Impossible, I almost say. Gudrun could not have got down here in time. Only ...

Only what? Only she *should* have been here? Or was, and then wasn't ...?

It doesn't quite make sense. Not yet. But I'm beginning to have an inkling of what happened. Or part of it, anyway.

I need now to get away. To be somewhere where my absence won't be missed.

'Forgive me,' I say quietly. 'But I feel quite ...'

Manfred reaches out and holds my arm with one of those huge hands, as if to keep me standing.

'You understand now, though? You *understand*?'

'Your Meister, I—'

'I'll find out who did this, and be sure I'll make their lives a living hell. Only ...'

Only what? He never says. Just looks to Tief and nods. And, releasing me to Tief's care, he turns back to stare at the figure on the bed – that awful bloodied scarecrow of a corpse – his eyes so bleak I cannot bear to look in them again.

A king. Who could bear to be a king?

113

Tief sees me back to my quarters. Heusinger's waiting there, and when I tell him what I want to do, he shrugs, as if he's expected all along that I'd do something crazy.

'You're going to consult Hecht, though?' he asks, but though I nod, he doesn't believe me. Only I know now with a gut-driven certainty that my fate and Gudrun's are tied together somehow. She would have died there, at her great-aunt's bedside, but for my intervention. Which must mean she's important. Just why I don't know as yet, but I do know – or think I know – what I'm about to do.

'Wait for me,' I say to Heusinger, then jump. Back to Four-Oh.

Hecht is busy, but it doesn't take much to persuade the women. I have them send me back first to the moment after the explosion, armed with a camera. Then that done, they send me back again, to the moment after I first met her – after that meeting with her and her odious brother Hagen.

As she steps out of the chamber, so she finds me there, her eyes widening in surprise.

'But I thought …' And she looks back.

'Oh, I *am* in there,' I say quickly. 'But I'm here too.'

'But you can't be. I mean …'

'Listen,' I say, with such unexpected authority that she falls silent. 'I am not what I seem to be. My name is Otto Behr and I come from the future. If you want proof of it, just look.'

And I hand her the holo-prints.

'Urd's breath,' she says, horrified. 'Who is …?' And then she recognises the hangings behind the bed and gasps.

I feel sorry giving her such pain, but it's necessary, even if I'm not sure why just yet.

'I can't prevent this from happening. But I can prevent *you* from being there. You were going to see her, weren't you?'

She nods, shocked now, silent.

'Well, don't. Go to the banquet instead. You'll see me there. You must thank me and use my proper name. Okay?'

'Okay …' But then she looks at me, a moment's uncertainty in her eyes. I can almost read what she's thinking. What if this is a trick?

'You want me to prove it?'

'If you *can* travel in time …' She blinks, then nods to herself. 'I broke a cup, a favourite of mine, just this morning. If you could bring it to me whole.'

I nod. 'But first you must take me to your rooms. I must know where I am jumping to.'

'Of course.' And then she shakes her head as if she's gone mad. 'Otto, you say? A time traveller?'

'You want proof?'

She hesitates, then nods.

'Okay,' I say. 'Then let's go at once. There's no time to lose.'

114

I hand her the cup, a pretty lavender-glazed thing the size of a small punch bowl. In her hands it seems fine almost, delicate.

'What's happening, Otto? Why are you here?'

'There's a war going on,' I say, breaking all the rules in saying it. 'A war in time. And for some reason I need you to be alive. I don't know why just yet, but ...'

'My aunt, my sister Fricka?'

I shake my head. I can't save everyone. And the explosion has to happen. It's part of the chain of events that leads ... Well, you'll see, I hope. Only I can't disturb that part of it. It *has* to happen. Manfred *has* to be riled by the act. He *has* to seek his vengeance.

Even now he's giving orders, rounding up the suspects. Bringing them in to his torture chambers, happy to tilt his kingdom into anarchy for the sake of his dead aunt.

Gudrun puts the cup down, then looks at me, her eyes now filled with wonder. 'Otto ... what's *really* happening?'

'I can't say,' I say. 'Only that I need you.'

She almost smiles at that. And then I jump, leaving her there, the loosest of loose strands that somehow – I hope – will come to make sense.

I jump back, to those moments after the explosion. Back to the beginning of the madness that will rip everything apart. Tief has left, to do his master's bidding, leaving Heusinger and I alone. Much will happen this evening, but we cannot be a part of it. No, this evening we must trust to history. It is tomorrow at dawn that our part in events begins.

Or so I've been led to think. Only it doesn't happen that way. Already things are changing. The simple fact of our presence there has changed it, maybe, or the act of involving Gudrun. Whichever it is, I am summoned again just after midnight, and taken down to the very roots of Asgard – to the great dungeons – where I am brought once more into Manfred's regal presence. I ought not to be, perhaps, yet I am surprised by his appearance. His hair is matted and he is wearing a butcher's apron that is encrusted with blood.

The bitter anger – one might almost term it madness – that was in his eyes, has grown, intensified, one might say. To see such a huge man in his rage is fearful indeed, yet he smiles at me graciously and has me sit, before gesturing to Tief.

'I wanted you to see this, Lucius,' he says, one great, blood-stained hand resting lightly on my shoulder. 'I wanted you to bear witness to the depths of iniquity of my *kin*.'

He says 'kin' like it's the foulest blasphemy he could utter.

I swallow, wondering what's in store, but I don't have long to wait. One by one they are dragged out into our presence, the marks of torture clear on them. Sons and brothers, Guildsmen and ministers, wives, uncles, even his daughters. Not a single one of them has escaped investigation. His torturers have been busy tonight, and this is the result, this series of confessions and betrayals.

But lest you think me soft, I have seen worse than this. I was in Novgorod, in the winter of 1570, when the tsar, Ivan IV – known to history as 'the Terrible' – earned his name by putting whole families through holes in the ice. I was there when he boiled one of his own ministers – Nikita Funikov – alive, and when he forced his cousin's wife and children to drink great cups of poison.

Oh, I've seen worse than this, but not from such a man. History is filled with the acts of demons. Such is nature. It is only when such a great man – a man filled with the potential for good – is brought to such wickedness, that the gods weep.

And the last of them to be brought is Gudrun. I stand, shocked to see her in that condition, her head shaved, the torturer's scars livid on her pale flesh. Is *this* why I saved her? For *this*?

'Otto?'

Manfred has turned, staring at me. I am standing, I realise, staring open-mouthed at Gudrun.

'Why her?' I ask quietly.

'*What?*' Manfred asks, as if my question makes no sense. 'She was supposed to be there, and she wasn't. She ...'

I don't wait to hear any more. I jump, and find Hecht waiting for me this time.

'What is it, Otto? What's happening?'

I tell him and he frowns. 'I don't understand.'

'Nor do I,' I say, interrupting. 'But she's important.'

'You know that for a fact?'

I shake my head. *No, it's instinct. Pure gut instinct.* Only Hecht won't buy that. Or will he? If we've failed before, maybe he's willing to take a gamble on my instincts. Or maybe that's why we've failed. The truth is I don't know.

'Otto? What do *you* want to do?'

I hesitate, then say it. 'I want to go back again. To change it somehow, so that she'll be safe.'

'This isn't ...?'

'A love thing? No. It's instinct. Pure gut instinct.'

Hecht smiles. 'Then let's go with that.'

'What?'

'You heard me. We've tried everything else.'

'Sorry?'

Hecht's smile fades. 'We've done this thirteen times now, Otto, and every time we've had to unravel it all and start all over. But this time … this thing with Gudrun. It's a new twist. It didn't happen before. The thing with the cup …'

Hecht turns and clicks his fingers. At once Urte comes across. In her hands is the lavender-glazed cup I went back and 'saved' as proof to Gudrun that I could travel in time.

I stare at it, amazed.

'It was in Gehlen's trunk,' Hecht says, 'among his things. We asked him where it came from, but he never understood why it was there. But now, perhaps, we know. It's a time-loop, Otto. It can't be anything else.'

116

I jump back, to the moment after I left her, and watch her blink, almost in disbelief, as – having vanished into the air itself – I reappear an instant later.

'Change of plan,' I say. 'You must leave here. If Manfred finds you …'

It proves difficult to persuade her. There's no 'cup' I can return with to prove what I'm saying, yet she believes me. Only she doesn't like it. Running away, she feels, will only 'prove' her guilt. But she has no choice. Manfred – Manfred, that is, *after* his aunt's death – will be in no mood to listen to the truth. Guilty and innocent alike will feel his wrath, and I can't change that. If *that* doesn't happen, then the rest of it won't happen either, and neither we nor the Russians can allow that. But I can save Gudrun, and it seems I *must*.

'Where will you go?' I ask.

'To Erfurt.'

'Erfurt?'

'In Thuringia. We have a castle there. It's not often used, but my aunt ...'

She stops, then looks to me again. 'Is it true? Is it *really* going to happen?' I nod, then, taking the images from my pocket, hand them to her. 'Here. Keep them. But go. There's no time to lose. And let no one else know where you're going. Every second counts now.'

She hesitates, then stoops and, unexpectedly, kisses me, that huge mouth of hers leaving the softest, most delicate touch upon my lips. And then she's gone.

I stare after her, then put my hand up to my lips, amazed.

And jump. Back to the room. Back to the moment, just after midnight, when Manfred summons me again.

117

I watch the dawn come up from the battlements of Asgard, Heusinger beside me. After the night's events I fully expect Adelbert to overlook his invitation to me, yet even as the first light breaks over the eastern suburbs the Grand Master sends for me.

'What a night,' he says, as I am ushered into his presence.

The room's a high-tech cell. Bare stone walls surround a central nest of cutting-edge technology. But what did I expect? These are warrior-brothers, after all. The same thinking that drove their distant ancestors, the Teuton Knights, drives them.

'I didn't think ...' I begin, then stop, seeing how he's watching me from where he's seated before his screen.

Like Hecht, I think, surprised to be making that connection. Yet it's true.

'That I'd keep my word?'

But there's no edge to that. If anything – and this is the greatest surprise of all – Adelbert seems amused. But why? Because he survived the night?

'You seem … *unconcerned* by what's happened.'

'Unconcerned? No … everything that happens in the palace *concerns* me. Unsurprised might be better. It was only time before Manfred lost it.'

It's such a casual comment, that I actually wonder if I heard aright. '*Lost* it?'

'His patience. His temper. His *sang-froid*.'

Unexpectedly, Adelbert laughs. Distinctly human laughter from what looks like a machine.

'Were you …?'

'Behind the bomb? No. Not that I'd admit it if we were. Manfred will be watching us even now, sifting our words. Especially now. But this once, no. I rather liked his aunt. Or maybe "liked" is too strong a word. *Respected*.'

He pauses, then his head rotates again, his eyes meeting mine.

'You want to know who did?'

'You *know*?'

'I'm fairly sure.'

'Does Manfred know that?'

'Not yet.' And there's a mischievous tone to his voice. 'Not until I tell him.'

'But …'

'Our king is a great man. Passionate. Strong. Wise, even. Yet he could learn something from the Brotherhood. How to distance himself, for instance. How not to succumb to anger.'

I'm not sure I want to have this conversation. It feels like I'm betraying Manfred simply by talking to Adelbert this way.

'Anger can be a useful tool,' Adelbert continues, 'only it must be controlled, *channelled*. To let it shape one's actions ...'

He stands, then slowly comes across, speaking quietly to me, leaning in, as if confiding some great secret. 'I have the men who did it. Would you like to see them?'

This is all a game, I realise. Through me, Adelbert teases Manfred. Or torments him, maybe. Yet if Manfred really *is* watching ...

I nod, and he gestures to me to follow. And so I follow, down a long, steep flight of steps into the very depths of the earth. There, in a long, dimly lit cell, chained to the wall, their feet dangling, are three men. Two of them are strangers, the other ...

He meets my eyes briefly, then looks away, giving no hint that he knows me. And maybe he doesn't, not in this time-strand. But *I* know *him*. He's Reichenau's man, Heinrich.

Adelbert stands there, contemplating his prisoners, so still he seems switched off.

'How did you find them?'

His great head swivels round. His eyes, peering out from that mass of metal and plastic, meet mine.

'We were trailing them. There was an incident, two nights back. One of our Guildsmen was killed in the Tempelhof, and these three – known agents of a revolutionary clique – were observed in the immediate vicinity. It might have been coincidence, only last night they entered the *Konigsturm*, under the pretext of undertaking basic maintenance work. They were there, in Signy's chambers, less than an hour before the explosion.'

'I see ...'

Only I don't. Why, after all, should Reichenau want Signy dead? What did he hope to achieve, other than to bring Manfred's deadly fury down upon his over-sized head?

It makes no sense. And yet, historically, it's true. It's what happened, every time.

And what has happened yet again. Only this time *I'm* here, mixed up in it, and Gudrun's free, and ...?

I turn and look at Heinrich once again. Reichenau's the key. Only the key to what? To de-stabilising the whole situation? If so, then why? Does he – patriot that he is – *want* Germany to fail? Is that his aim? To bring the whole thing crashing down?

Or doesn't he know? What if it's just some vast miscalculation on his part?

Manfred's voice sounds suddenly in the air about us. 'Meister Adelbert ...'

'Yes, Majesty ...'

'You will deliver them at once.'

'Of course, your Majesty.'

I'm sure he'd smile; if he could. As it is, he turns and, gesturing to me, says simply, 'Come.'

118

'Well?' Heusinger asks, when I'm back with him. 'Did you ...?'

Find it? I shake my head.

'You saw ...?'

'Everything.'

Yes, and nothing I saw correlated in any way with the map Reichenau gave me. The power source, wherever it is, isn't here. Not in the *Konigsturm*, anyway.

Heusinger hesitates, knowing that every word we say is being listened to. Then he shrugs. 'So what do we do now?'

'Gehlen,' I say. 'We go and see Gehlen.'

'But that's—'

'Not permitted? Maybe not. But if anyone knows where it is, he does.'

Heusinger stares at me. 'Maybe, only we don't know enough about him. I don't know about you, but I haven't been briefed about Gehlen.'

I haven't either. And that *is* a weakness. But that isn't going to stop me. My instinct is so strong at this moment that I can almost touch it, and didn't Hecht himself say I should go with that?

I smile, and that only makes it worse for Heusinger. He wants to argue with me, only that would only make things worse, because if they *are* listening to every word and acting on them, then they'll be busy right now, asking themselves why we're so interested in one of their leading physicists and whether there's a connection.

Which there isn't. Not yet anyway. Only they're not to know that.

'Trust me, Klaus. I know what I'm doing.'

'Do you?'

'Yes.' And I make it sound convincing. Only the truth is I don't. What I'm doing now is operating on the basis that if all else fails, try Chance. Flip a coin, roll a dice, turn a card and see what turns up.

'Do you know where he lives?'

'No. But I can ask.'

'Lucius, can I ask you something?'

'Go on.'

'What if you're wrong? What if this is why you've failed each time?'

119

If it is, then we're fucked, because I've no other strategy right now. I'm trusting to a glazed lavender cup, a beautiful goddess and pure gut instinct. Reason has nothing to do with it.

Tief comes at our summons, looking tired, as if he hasn't slept, which is probably the truth. His secretary, a small, nondescript man – a *Naturlich* – stands just beyond him, very much in his shadow.

'Gehlen?' Tief says, looking surprised by my request. 'I don't see why not. Only ... may I ask why?'

I look to Heusinger. 'Our president...he much admires the man. His most recent work on positronic collision ...'

Tief stares at me, then shrugs and makes a gesture to his secretary, who hurries off at once. 'Okay. I'll arrange it. But forgive me now, I—'

'How is he?' I quickly ask. 'The King, I mean.'

Tief hesitates, then, softly, 'I fear for him, Lucius. This business ...'

He says no more, but I understand. This business has unhinged Manfred. Reason has fled. What lies ahead is darkness, and Manfred at the centre of it all, like a black hole, sucking everything – every single last thing – into himself.

'Good luck,' I say. 'And thanks.'

'Think nothing of it,' Tief says, then turns away and is gone.

I turn, looking back into the chamber. Heusinger is still staring at me.

'You should go back,' he says. 'Consult Hecht.'

'No,' I say, and as I say it I feel a strange certainty welling up in me. 'This time I'm doing it strictly my way.'

120

The coincidence does not, of course, evade me. We are in Erfurt, in Thuringia, just about to touch down, and as the craft descends towards the platform, I am conscious that she is nearby, and that Fate has shaped it so.

Fate or the gods.

Gehlen is here, too, for this is where he works three days of the week. Just south of here, to be precise, in Orhdruf. And it's there, if anywhere, that the *singularity* – their tame black hole – is kept.

'Rather you than me,' the pilot says, as he gently touches down.

I look to him. 'Sorry?'

'This place …' He shudders. 'When they turn the power on, all manner of strange things happen.'

'What?'

'The big accelerator … it jumbles up reality. I was here once when they switched it on. One moment I was clean-shaven, my hair neatly trimmed, the next … bushy as a bear, holes in my clothes.'

'You're kidding.'

He laughs. 'As I said: strange things happen near that place.'

I frown. It isn't possible, is it? I mean, the place is only a particle accelerator. A powerful one, maybe, but even so …

I stare at the pilot, wondering if he's joking with me. All Ages have their superstitions, after all – their urban legends, if you like – and why not this for the Age of Super-Science?

One of Tief's men greets me from the craft and ushers me quickly through customs and out to a waiting hover-car. It's only when we're in the air that I realise that we're not heading south but west.

'It's okay,' the man says, not looking up from the controls. 'She's expecting you.'

'She?'

'The Princess.'

And now I *am* confused, because Tief isn't supposed to know about that. Unless this isn't Tief's man at all.

'How did she …?'

'She's been waiting. She knew you'd come.'

I'm quiet after that, looking out over the landscape as the urban sprawl that surrounds Erfurt gives way to countryside, until there, in a fold of the land just ahead of us, lies a castle – an ancient-looking *Schloss* with turrets and a keep. We head for it and touch down on the battlements.

Gudrun stands there in the doorway, waiting for me. She looks more beautiful than ever, in a pale blue full-length gown, her golden hair, let loose from its braid, falling in twisting ringlets down to her waist. There is a necklace of fine gold about her lovely neck and as she sees me she smiles.

'Otto.'

What do I say? That I'm not here to see her? That I have to see Gehlen, and soon?

I smile and walk across, letting her take my hands in hers, overwhelmed once again by the sheer size of her, by her unearthly beauty.

She has been crying. Tears stain her cheeks. She smiles and gently laughs.

'Forgive me, Otto, it's just ...'

'Does Manfred know where you are?'

She looks away. 'I don't know. If he does ...'

If he did she would be dead. Or maybe not. Maybe he's content to wreak havoc only on those within his reach. Maybe he's too distracted thus to worry too much over one absent face.

'And Tief?'

'Tief is my uncle.'

'Ah ...'

So that's it. That's why I'm here, and not with Gehlen. Even so ...

'Gudrun – can I ask you a favour?'

'Anything.'

'I need to see someone. A man. He works not far from here, In Orhdruf.'

'Gehlen, you mean? But he's here already. I had him brought.'

'You had him ...?' I stare at her, surprised.

She smiles. 'My uncle said you wanted that. But I had to see you. And so ...'

What was it Hecht once said to me? That Fate is a boat without a rudder. Well, so it seems right now, as, my hand in hers, I walk beside her, like a young child beside his mother.

She takes me through to a nearby chamber where a massive table has been set for just the two of us. We take our seats at one end of it, then, at her command, the servants leave us.

We are alone.

Gudrun looks to me, her blue eyes smiling through some deeper sadness. 'You know what has been happening, Otto?'

'In the *Konigsturm*?'

She nods.

'Yes. I saw some of it,' I say quietly. 'Manfred summoned me down to the cells to witness what's been happening. It was awful.'

She sighs and reaches out to cover my hand with her own. 'Why does it have to be like this, Otto? What went wrong?'

That, perhaps, is the hardest question to answer. But I try.

'Because it has to go wrong. Because all of this is fated.'

'*All* of it?'

I smile. 'Almost all. There are things that *can't* be changed. Otherwise ...'

'Otherwise what?'

'Otherwise I'm not here at all. And if *I'm* not here ...'

'I don't see that,' she says with a passion that once again surprises me. 'I don't see *why* it has to be so.'

'Because this is where it begins. Time travel. Gehlen invents it. Here, within the next two days.'

Her eyes widen, her mouth falls softly open. 'Oh ...'

'So now you know.'

She removes her hand and sits back, lost for a moment in her own thoughts. Then she looks at me again. 'So I'm ... part of the circle?'

Her understanding pleases me. 'Yes. But don't ask me how. Don't for Urd's sake ask me how.'

121

Gehlen is furious. As I step through the door he almost runs at me and pokes me in the chest.

'What in fuck's sake is going on? I've work to do, and you bastards bring me here and make me kick my sodding heels ...'

He stops, seeing how strangely I am looking at him.

And what do I see? A youngish man of twenty-eight, slight of build and short – less than five feet six – who has already lost most of his hair. Yet his eyes are unlike any I have ever seen. If intelligence can be seen, then Gehlen has intelligence. It fair burns in those dark green eyes of his.

'I'm sorry,' I say, bowing to him slightly. 'It wasn't at my order. But I did need to see you as a matter of some urgency.'

He stands back a little, his whole manner arrogant, superior.

'And who the fuck are you?'

I almost smile. Here he is, our hero – creator of everything we depend on at Four-Oh – and he's acting like an odious little toad.

'My name is Lucius Manninger and I'm the American ambassador.'

'So *Lucius Manninger*, what do you want?'

How direct can I be? More to the point, how far can I trust Gehlen?

'Not here,' I say, conscious of the camera on the wall just above and beyond him.

'Then not anywhere. I have no secrets. My masters know what I am.'

Only that's not true. They've no idea what's in his head. Not a clue.

I smile. 'Okay. Then I'll ask you straight. Has there been a drain on the power source these last few days?'

It isn't 'straight' at all, but it does get a reaction.

'How did you know that?'

Reichenau, I could say, only I don't. 'A little bird told me.'

Gehlen gives the faintest nod. 'And this little bird ... why were they talking to you? More to the point, what's *your* interest?'

How do I answer that? Do I just press on and hope that Tief and his master, Manfred, are so distracted that they'll not notice what I'm up to? No. I can't count on that. So I keep to my cover story. At least, until I can get Gehlen alone, and out of range of a camera.

'It's like this,' I say. 'We – America, that is – are considering an alliance with Greater Germany. We thought that we would benefit from such an arrangement. Only ...'

Gehlen's eyes bore into me. 'Only what?'

'Only things are falling apart here. You've heard what's happening at the *Konigsturm*?'

Gehlen laughs humourlessly. 'Why would I know what's happening *there*? I'm a physicist, not a courtier.'

'Maybe. But even physicists can be affected by what's happening at court.'

'There's been another *cull* has there?'

'You could say that.'

'So what's different about this one? They happen. Nothing changes.'

'I think you're wrong. But the power drain ...'

'Is a fault somewhere. It has to be.'

'Why?'

'Because the maths doesn't work. The power has to go *somewhere*. Energy can't just vanish, that's a universal law – it *has to* be conserved.'

'Somewhere? Or *somewhen*?'

He looks at me strangely, then laughs. 'You really don't understand, do you?'

'Maybe not. Only there is drainage, correct?'

'Correct.'

'And you don't know why.'

'Not yet.'

'Where is it kept?'

'Pardon?'

'The singularity. Where is it? It isn't under Berlin.'

Gehlen smiles, then looks up at the camera. 'Can I go now? I've work to do.' He looks back at me. 'Oh, and I'd curb that curiosity of yours, if I were you. People have been killed for less. Even ambassadors.'

'It's under Erfurt, isn't it?'

Gehlen doesn't even so much as blink. 'Even if it were, I wouldn't tell you.' He pauses. 'I serve my masters well, and honestly.'

That may be so, only his masters are about to let him down. And I still need to find out where the power source is so I can shut it down and free Ernst.

Or maybe I *do* know. Maybe my guess was spot on. Erfurt. It would make sense. If Gehlen were using immense magnetic forces to bend the trajectory of basic particles, then he'd not do it under Berlin. He'd do it elsewhere. Somewhere much smaller. Like Erfurt. Which would explain the pilot's strange comments.

Time-jumps, caused by the manipulation – the distortion – of the basic laws of reality.

Gehlen waits, and after a moment a door opens at the far end of the chamber we are in and a servant bows his head as Gehlen walks across and, without a word, without a backward glance, leaves the room. Leaving me alone.

'Otto?'

The voice is hers. She has been watching our exchange. Listening in.

'Yes, Gudrun?'

'Why did you want to know those things?'

122

I explain it to her, when we're alone together, and she laughs.

'How silly you are. You only had to ask.'

'What?'

'You want to see the accelerator, right? Well, I can take you in with me, as my guest. I have clearance.'

I stare at her. 'But you're ...'

'A princess. Of the royal blood. And Tief's niece. And people do what I tell them to.'

'But Manfred ...'

'Is busy. And while he is – while he's looking elsewhere – I can get you inside.' She smiles. 'Maybe that's why.'

I stare at her, then laugh. She's quick. Quicker than I expected. And maybe it *is* why I 'saved' her. To be my key. My way in.

'Okay,' I say. 'But can we go there now?'

Her smile seems a foot wide. 'The flyer's waiting. We only have to get on board.'

123

Seeing me, Gehlen groans, then gives a great huff of exasperation.

'*You?* What are *you* doing here?'

'He's with me,' Gudrun says, squeezing in through the hatch.

The flyer isn't designed for someone her size, but she makes do, taking two seats and stretching her long legs out along the aisle. And I find that being inside such a small space with her has a strange, dream-like quality, like sharing a rabbit hole with Alice.

As the ship lifts and glides towards its cruising altitude, Gehlen tries to ignore us only Gudrun has other ideas. Looking to me, she gestures towards the overhead cams.

'They're off. You can speak freely if you want.'

I look to Gehlen.

'No,' he says. 'Not even with the cameras off. I've nothing to say to you.'

'You've been working on it,' I say. 'Trying to understand the fluctuations. The discontinuities.'

His head jerks round, alarmed.

'Oh, nothing visible, nothing out loud. Nothing the watchers could make out. But in your head ...'

He seems shocked. 'How do you know that?'

I don't say. I let him dangle a moment. Then – 'You want to talk?'

'No!' But he says it too quickly, and that's the give-away. He *does* want to talk. In fact, he positively aches to share his thoughts.

I shrug. 'Okay.'

He's still for a while, then he turns and looks at me. 'Who *are* you?'

'A friend.'

'I don't believe that. A friend wouldn't expose me like this.'

'*Expose* you?'

'To suspicion. I've children ...'

'I know.'

'Then you'll know I can't take risks. I can't talk. I can't ...' He looks down, then sighs heavily. 'I just *can't*, that's all.'

I like him better when he's not being so cock-sure and arrogant. And I take his point about his children. Only ... they'll be dead two days from now. Dead. And there is nothing any of us can do about it.

I soften a little. 'Look ... I'm sorry. But what's done is done. I've met you now. And if Manfred has any suspicions, he'll have them whether you speak to me or not.'

'Only I won't.'

'So you've said.' I leave a brief silence, then, as if to Gudrun, say: 'It's the equations. They keep running off to infinity. And that's bad. It indicates that the laws of physics are breaking down.'

I look back at Gehlen, who's now staring at me open-mouthed.

'Either that,' I add quietly, 'or the maths is wrong.'

'The maths is right,' he says, so softly that I have to strain to hear him. 'I've checked it endless times. In my head.'

'And now there's drainage, too.'

Gehlen meets my eyes and nods.

'Some*when*,' I say.

'Yes ... only it isn't possible.'

124

They're waiting for us at Erfurt – four of Manfred's ships. As we land, their guns are trained on us.

'Shit!' Gehlen says, his face pressed to the cabin window. 'Shit!'

He turns and glares at me. And who can blame him? Only I *can* change it; make it all right again.

I concentrate, thinking it through. I could jump, back to

Four-Oh, then jump directly to the moment before I first meet Gehlen. There, confronting myself, I could tell myself not to board the flyer with Gehlen, but let him return alone, unhindered, to Erfurt. The rest could be left to transpire as it did until that point.

Right. Only there's a problem. If I *don't* get on the flyer, then I won't be there to make the jump back to Four-Oh when things go wrong. If I take myself out of the loop, the loop will vanish.

In other words, we're fucked.

'I'm sorry.'

'Sorry?' He looks at me despairingly. 'You've ruined me! You and your stupid fucking questions!'

And he puts his head in his hands and groans.

Get a grip, I want to say. *No one is going to harm you.* Only I don't know that. Because this is a whole new train of events I've set in motion. And if I can't jump out ...

But before I can even begin to think of a solution, Gudrun takes matters into her massive hands.

I hear the sound of safeties being taken off, feel a new tension in the air and, turning round, realise that Gudrun is no longer in the craft.

She's outside, talking to one of the soldiers. I can't make out what's being said, but suddenly the man's voice rises to an angry shout.

I rush to the hatch and look out. Gudrun is standing there, towering over the man – a captain – while all about her his men point their weapons up at her. It's a tense moment and I try to defuse it.

'Gudrun ... move back from him. And for Urd's sake do as he says.'

She looks at me, surprised. I sense that it's against a habit of a lifetime for her to take orders from a common *Wehrmacht* officer. Even so, she does as I've asked.

Things relax a little.

The officer looks to me and nods. 'Ambassador. I have orders to take you back to Berlin. To the *Konigsturm*.'

'And my friend?' I ask, indicating Gehlen, who can be seen through the thick glass of the cabin window.

But the officer doesn't say. 'If you would come now, Herr Lucius ...'

125

What have I done? What in Urd's name have I done?

On the flight back to Berlin, I picture it. Gehlen in chains in a cell in the *Gefangnis*, the Guild prison, unable to complete his work. Unable to come up with the equations that will be the saving of us all.

In which case ...

I stop, mentally staring out over an abyss. Surely, if I *have* fucked things up, then it will simply end? If Gehlen doesn't complete his work, then we'll all just disappear, like so many ghosts – isn't that so?

Isn't it?

But here I am still, bound hand and foot, a prisoner, sitting between two visored soldiers in the back of a troop-carrier.

So maybe it isn't over yet. Maybe ...

No. No maybes. It *can't* be over. Something *has* to happen. Something which sets it right. Which allows Gehlen to complete his work and forge the circle.

After all, the snake has to swallow its tail.

Back at the *Konigsturm* I am taken straight to Manfred's private suite where, roused from his bed, he comes out to face me, draped in a dark blue silk gown the size of a sail, a deep anger in his clear blue eyes.

'Lucius, oh my dear Lucius, what *have* you been up to?'

'It's Otto,' I say. 'Otto Behr. And I'm German.'

But he seems not to hear me. Or ignores me. Whichever, he gestures towards the centre of the great chamber, and as he does, so a holo-image forms, life-size in the air.

'Do you know this man?'

I do, if only from the distinctive double head. It's Reichenau.

'No.'

'He says he knows you.'

'You have him prisoner?'

'We did. In the *Gefangnis*. But he blasted his way out. He and his accomplices.'

I am quiet for a time. When I look up again, I see that Manfred's watching me. He seems less angry now.

'Tell me,' he says. 'What were you doing down there? Why were you so interested in the power source?'

'I had heard rumours, my lord.'

'Rumours?'

'That there was leakage. That the impossible had happened and that the black hole was failing.'

Manfred studies me a moment, then turns away. 'Are you working for *them*, Lucius?'

'Them?'

'The Russians.'

I laugh. It's so preposterous, it's almost funny. 'No. For us.'

'*Us?* Who's us?' And he half turns towards me as he asks, like he's teasing a child.

'The *Volk*. The German people.'

'Ah.' He's quiet a moment, then. 'Your arrival. It was ... *timely*, shall we say. Just as things began to go wrong. The drainage. The bomb. Perhaps ...?'

He doesn't finish his perhaps, just leaves it as a general insinuation.

'I have done nothing, My Lord.'

'Nothing? Smuggling my niece out of the palace. Trying to get in to our highest security establishment. Mixing with the leader of the *Unbeachtet* – the most powerful *Undrehungar* sect. You call these nothings?'

'I've never met the man.'

'And yet he says he knows you. Made a great point of it, in fact.'

'Before he escaped.' I pause, then: 'I didn't think it possible, to escape from the *Gefangnis*.'

Manfred turns and faces me. 'I ought to have you killed. You, and Gehlen and that stupid meddling niece of mine. Only ...'

I wait and he finishes. 'Only I've seen too many die these past few hours.'

So I'm to livc. Good. It saves me disappointing him and jumping straight out of there.

He crouches, his face almost at the level of my own, yet not quite. Even on his haunches he is still a good few feet taller than me.

'So what were you talking about? In the flyer ...'

'My lord?'

'Just tell me, Lucius. Save yourself the pain. I really don't want to hurt you. I rather liked you. You seemed ... *fresh*. Untouched by it all.'

I'm silent, and so he sighs and straightens, his tall, well-proportioned body seeming to climb up and up until his head almost touches the ceiling of the room, high as that is.

'Oh, Lucius, why don't you simply tell me? It makes things so much easier. So much ... nicer.'

'I asked him about the leakages.'

'And he said?'

'He wouldn't answer. He's very loyal. Was fearful for his children.'

'A boy and girl, I understand ...'

I look up at Manfred. Is he teasing me now? Being sadistic? Has last night's work broken something in his mind?

But he only looks disappointed.

'What will happen to him?'

'Gehlen? Nothing. He's far too valuable. Besides, I believe him.'

'And Gudrun?'

Manfred doesn't answer, and after a moment there's a knock. It's Tief. He stands there in the huge doorway, his grey head bowed, awaiting his master's orders.

'Your niece,' Manfred says. 'She must tell us everything. Unless she does ...'

Tief seems to bow even lower. 'Master.' And then he turns and leaves, obedient to the last.

Manfred looks at me. 'You say your name is Otto?'

'Yes, My Lord.'

'Then tell me, Otto. What's happening? What's *really* happening?'

126

I want to help her, only I don't know how. I don't even know where she is.

Jump, I tell myself. *Go back. Unthread it all, stitch by stitch, then put it back together differently.*

Only how? And, more to the point, when?

My mind's a blank. For once I'm totally at a loss. Gudrun's important – she has to be – only I don't know in what way. I've not a clue what part she has to play, except that she clearly does.

Manfred didn't like it that I refused to talk, but for some reason he's loath to torture it out of me. Or maybe he's trusting to Gudrun telling him everything he wants to know.

Guards take me back to the guest quarters. There's no sign of Heusinger, and when I ask, they refuse to tell me where he is.

I sit on the bed and wait. I could jump, sure, but why jump until I need to? Why not see first where this time-strand leads?

An hour passes and then, at last, someone comes.

It's Tief. He looks at me, a grave sadness in his eyes, then shakes his head. 'You should never have intervened,' he says. 'You should have let things take their course.'

I frown. What does he mean by that? Does he know I'm a *Reisende*? Has Gudrun told him everything?

'How is she?' I ask.

'Alive.'

It's an ominous answer.

'Will she be punished?'

'That's not for me to say.'

'She had no part in it, you know.'

Tief says nothing. But it's noticeable how he won't even look at me now. As if, like Manfred, he's badly disappointed in me. After a moment he says, 'You must come now. The King wishes to speak with you again.'

I go with him. I have no choice, unless, of course, to jump, and as I said ... I want to know where this all leads.

Manfred is in his War Room, one great wall of which is dominated by a giant map. Germany is in black, to the left of the great screen; Russia, in red of course, is to the right. And that is all there is, almost as if nothing else exists.

Death and blood, I think, looking at the stark contrast of the colours.

'Herr Behr,' he says, greeting me. 'Come, take a seat. I want you to see this.'

That seems my role, as far as he's concerned. To be his witness. To sit there watching while *he* acts. And so I shall, for a time.

There's a nest of computer-stations just below where we are sitting, between Manfred and the giant map. In each small semi-circular station sits one of his commanders. As he speaks to each, so they swivel round in their great padded chairs and look up at him through dark glass visors on which quick strands of colourful lettering run.

Ge'not, I note with surprise.

'Marshal von Pasenow ...'

'Yes, Your Majesty?'

'You can begin the assault.'

Von Pasenow gives a beaming smile of pride within the darkness of the glass, then swivels back. On the map a bright line of gold begins to glow in the most northerly sector, broadening by the moment.

Manfred looks to me, then gestures towards the map.

'They'll hit back. Or try to. Only this time my commanders will be operating under zero restraint. This time it's total war.' He meets my eyes. '*Us* or *them*.'

The thought of it chills me, but only because I know. Billions dead, and the great Earth itself a wasteland.

We could stop it, only if we did, we too would disappear, and immediately it would happen yet again, for this alone is 'locked in', like there's some sick set of scales at work, creating this warped balance. We get time travel, yes, but at the greatest cost imaginable.

So it is. For this is how it happened. And how it's happening now, for all my attempts to meddle.

I might have known. Only ... Ernst is still trapped, and if I don't free him then I won't get back to Katerina. And that – though it seems so very little in the great scheme of things, so *selfish* – is, for me, unthinkable.

'What if they use their bombs?' I ask.

'We'll shoot them down.'

'And what if they've bombs in place, right here, in Neu Berlin?'

He looks at me pointedly. 'Have they?'

'If I were them, I would. Wouldn't you?'

He almost smiles. 'We have. In Moscow.'

'Then …?'

'Our agents are at work right now. Rounding them up. *Neutralising* them.'

'You're that confident?'

He nods. 'We infiltrated them long ago. Sleepers. Counter-agents. It began last night, after we freed Reichenau.'

'You let him go?' That *does* surprise me.

'And watched where he ran to.'

'So you have him under observation?'

Manfred looks away, for the first time uncomfortable. 'We did. But he vanished.'

'Vanished?'

'Into thin air. One moment he was standing there, the next …'

My mouth falls open. *Reichenau … Reichenau the patriot. Another fucking Russian.*

I stand. 'Forgive me, but I have to go.'

'Go?' Manfred looks both confused and annoyed. 'But I haven't said you could go anywhere.'

'Forgive me, Your Majesty,' I say and bow. And as I do, so I jump, leaving him staring at the air in shock.

127

Hecht, for once, is anxious to see me. He hurries me from the platform to his room, and there, an infinity of space between us and any listening ears, I tell him what I know.

'And that's it?' Hecht looks almost as disappointed as Manfred was in me.

I nod. 'Gehlen wouldn't speak. He just wouldn't cooperate. If I could get in closer to him, make friends with him somehow ...'

Hecht laughs. 'No one makes friends with Gehlen. Even his wife was a stranger to him.'

'But he has children.'

'Yes, but they die, along with everyone else. What use are they?'

It's harsh, but I know what he means. 'Maybe they're the key. Maybe if I can get close to *them*, then I can get close to Gehlen.'

Hecht sits back, staring at me sceptically. 'I thought *Gudrun* was the key.'

'She was, only ...'

'Look, Otto, you're playing blind man's bluff, and you know it. Your instincts ...' Hecht sighs. 'There's something you ought to see. To make you understand why I'm taking you off this case.'

'But ...'

Hecht raises a hand and I fall silent. 'Just come with me. Back to the platform. I think it's time you understood something.'

128

I stand there, staring about me in awe.

Bare rock climbs from the green, a half mile and more, into a vividly blue sky, the deepest blue I've ever seen, while down here, on the floor of the valley, a crystal-clear stream meanders its way through the lush grass that covers the lower slopes like moss in a bowl.

I reach down and pluck a blade at the base. It's thick and long and as broad as a man's hand, greener than green, so it seems, and fat with moisture; a sword of greenness, the very grass of

Eden. Among its rich, ripe verdancy, the great nodding heads of flowers – their massive petals garishly bright, red, yellow and purple – tower over me on every side, while great orange and blue butterflies the size of dinner plates flutter and dance in the air wherever I look.

The encampment is further down, nestled at the lower end of the valley, alongside the network of caves that pepper the lime-stone walls. It's hot, humidly so, the sun a large, flattened ball of orange at our backs. A tropical sun.

Hecht turns to me and smiles. He looks transformed out here; a new man. His grey eyes gleam as he looks about him, taking in deep lungfuls of the sweet-scented air.

'Urd save us, Otto. Just *look* at this place!'

But I don't need to be told. I am already struck by its beauty.

'Where are we?'

'Three hundred and ten thousand years BC. Give or take a century or two.'

I stare at him, astonished. As far as I know, this is the furthest back any of us have ventured. Here, we are on the very edge of things, the very limit of the platform's reach. Not that there isn't power enough to go back further, but beyond this we can't guaran-tee the accuracy. Beyond this, as Hecht's assured me many times, it's all hit and miss.

We walk on, and as we descend towards the far end of the valley and the huts come into view, so someone steps out of the largest of them and, raising his left hand to shade his eyes from the sun, waves to us with his right. It's Hecht – another, younger Hecht, but him, definitely him.

Beyond the huts are a few tended plots and pens for the animals, innovations Hecht has clearly brought with him, for the natives of this age were mainly hunters, and were for the best part of a million years.

'Are those what I think they are?' I ask, the slightest anxiety in my voice.

'They are,' he says. 'See if you can tell the men from the women.'

The creatures are gathered in a tiny group to the right, a dozen or so of them, the long auburn hair that totally covers their bodies making them seem more ape than human, but these are no apes, these are Neanderthal.

As we come closer, young Hecht calls out to us.

'Did you remember the gifts?'

Hecht lifts the sack he's carrying, and as he does, so there's an excited keening among the creatures.

Closer to, we see how they hold back, as if shy or frightened, keeping their distance. But as Hecht takes the sack and turns to them, they crowd about him, stroking his arms and back and shoulders as he hands out the gifts, a low, deeply burred murmur of sound coming from the creatures.

They're much shorter than us, but stouter and, I'd guess, much heavier. Though their arms and legs are shorter, they're built like bulls, their heads especially. And, of course, they have those famous pronounced brows, which give their eye sockets a deep, almost cavernous appearance.

Hecht's eyes are shining with an excitement I've never seen in them before. 'Look at their hands, Otto,' he half whispers. 'Look how delicate they are!'

I've noticed it. And though one cannot call these people gentle exactly, they seem quite sensitive. You only have to see their paintings in the caves to realise that.

The gifts given out, Hecht turns back to me, still smiling, a very different Hecht from the one I'm used to. He's relaxed and totally off guard here in the distant past.

'They call themselves the *huuruuhr*,' he says, making a deep rolling sound in the back of his throat. 'As you saw, they have their own language. But I've been teaching one or two of them our language, and you'll have a chance later on to talk to them. First let me show you around.'

I want to ask him what we're doing back here, wasting time, when Ernst is still trapped; only I know that no time's passing up the line. We can step back a second after we've left and carry on. But Hecht seems to need this break. Indeed, I can see now how he manages to carry on. *This* is how he recharges. By coming here.

The creatures have begun to wander away, yet as they do I note how one of them – a female? – looks back at us, an expression of pure curiosity in her deep-set eyes. She has a picture book, I see, holding it to her thickly haired chest as reverently as any priest ever held a bible.

'Who is that one?' I ask Hecht quietly.

'That's Ooris. You'll meet her later. I think you'll be surprised. But first come and meet my older brother, Albrecht.'

His *older* brother. That, naturally, surprises me. Even that Hecht *has* a brother is a revelation. Yet it makes sense now that I know. I always wondered who it was *he* confided in. Who shared *his* thoughts, the way he shares ours.

Albrecht leads us inside, into his hut. It's one big, open room, with a large bed in one corner and a desk in another. All very simple and unadorned. Albrecht smiles and offers me the chair, but I'm happy to stand.

'So you're Otto,' he says, his eyes taking me in. 'The *Einzelkind.*'

I look to Hecht, surprised. But Hecht seems unperturbed. 'Albrecht knows everything,' he says. 'And I mean *everything.*'

I wonder what that means, because there are surely things that even Hecht doesn't know, if I'm anything to go by.

'He's the Keeper,' Hecht says. 'But you'll see that later.'

I'm not sure what Hecht means by 'Keeper', but I let it pass. *All in good time*, I think, trying to take in what this all means.

413

Hecht has a brother, who knows everything.

I look about me, taking in small details. There's a picture of a woman in a silver frame on the table beside the bed. Their mother? If so, I've never seen her before.

Albrecht, meanwhile, is looking to his brother. 'It didn't work, I take it?'

'No.' Hecht hesitates, then: 'It was another blind alley.'

I guess he's talking about my last trip back to Asgard.

'That's why we're here,' Hecht says. 'I thought it was time Otto knew.'

Albrecht nods. 'I thought so. But why now?'

Hecht shrugs. 'Because ...'

I don't quite follow, but it would seem that our failures have brought Hecht to a decision.

'It's becoming impenetrable back there,' he says after a moment. 'There has to be a path through the maze, but what it is ...'

Albrecht nods. Then, looking to me, he smiles again. 'Forgive me, Otto. I'm being a dreadful host. You must be hungry after your travels. Would you like something? A sandwich, perhaps, or a drink of some kind?'

It's an odd thing to be asked when you're back in Neanderthal times, but I smile and nod. 'That would be nice,' I say, and watch as he goes to the door, and in fluent Neanderthal, bids one of the natives bring me something.

129

An hour later the three of us are climbing the grassy, tree-covered slope beyond the cabin, emerging on to a broad ridge, from which we look down across a landscape which – though I've seen many landscapes in many times – is the most spectacular I've ever seen.

In the distance, running the length of the horizon there's a mountain range, its seemingly endless peaks dominating the skyline from north to south.

'The Alps,' Hecht says, and I nod, realising where – geographically – we are.

Between us and the mountains is an Edenic country of rock and pool and tree; an undulating landscape of such magnificent wild beauty that it makes me think that there really *was* a Fall, and that this is what we yearn for when our imaginings turn to such things.

'They're out there now,' Hecht says, 'hunting.'

'*They?*'

'The rest of the *huuruuhr.*'

'Ah ...' And I relax. For a moment I thought Hecht was speaking of the Russians. But this is one place they surely don't know about. One place they'd never guess we came to.

'Come,' Hecht says. 'It's just there, down the path.'

We follow a dirt path down through the rocks, then turn left, through a screen of cypress trees, into a dark and narrow space. There, between two smooth, white stone walls, lies a steel door.

It looks like a vault.

'Otto, I have to ask you not to look for a moment.'

I avert my eyes as Hecht taps a code into the keypad by the door. A moment later it hisses open, a draft of cool air reaching out to envelop us.

We go inside, into a marvel of high-tech efficiency. It's a library, a massive storage room, with endless screens and shelves stretching floor to ceiling and, in one corner, a long *kunstlichestahl* work surface on which are all manner of tapes and files.

'Welcome,' Albrecht says, turning to me and grinning that by-now-familiar grin of his that separates him so distinctly from his brother. 'This is where it's all kept.'

The Keeper ... And I understand, instantly and without needing

to be told, that this is where Hecht stores it all. All of the information about all the different pasts we've visited. Details of all the
changes are here, of all our failed attempts to make it different.

Hecht sees the movement in my face and smiles, a pale smile
compared to that of his brother's, but similar.

'I see you understand. I knew you would. It's all here. Everything.
And Albrecht is the curator. He makes sense of it all. When I
lose direction, I come back here and he shows me what I need to
see.' Hecht looks to his brother fondly. 'It would be too much for
one man.'

I see that at a glance. There must be tens of thousands of files
stored here, in all manner of formats. And not just files, I note, but
things. Things from a hundred Ages and more.

'It's unaffected, you see,' Albrecht says, walking across and
picking up a file, then inserting it into a nearby touch-screen. 'If it
were further up the line, then any changes that you made would
make changes here. But being so far back ... nothing changes.'

'That's right,' Hecht says, 'so when I come back here after a major
paradigm shift, say, Albrecht *reminds* me. He shows me what was.
All of those realities that I'd forgotten, that had been *erased* from
my memory by Time.'

'So just how different is it?'

'Not much,' Albrecht answers, concentrating on what he's doing.
'At least, not as much as you'd think.'

He's quiet a moment, then gestures for me to come across and
join him.

'Look,' he says. 'Here's one of your earlier de-briefings.'

For the next half hour I stand there, half-crouched over the
touch-screen, watching myself answer Hecht's questions about
where I'd been, and what I'd seen and what was done. And not a
single word of it remembered.

As it finishes I look to Albrecht. 'Which of them was that?'

'That was your sixth trip back,' Hecht says, answering for him. 'That's when we knew that something odd was happening; that it wasn't going to be as easy as we'd anticipated. That's when we started going out on a limb – though nothing as left-field as your last trip back.'

'And nothing works?'

They don't need to answer that. Of course it doesn't. That's why we're here. But I'm thinking aloud now.

'But the cup ...'

Albrecht looks to his brother. 'The cup?'

'The lavender-glazed cup,' Hecht explains, then looks to me. 'What about it?'

'Just that it has to get into Gehlen's possession somehow. That *has* to happen.'

'Okay. But what's the *significance* of that?'

'I don't know. Only that ...' I close my eyes and try to concentrate.

There are certain things that *have* to happen. Gehlen *has to* discover the equations, and Germany and Russia *have to* be destroyed. We know that and the Russians know that. But what about the power source? Does that *have to* be found? Do we *have to* free Ernst from the time-trap? Or is that something we have no control over?

Hecht, it seems, doesn't know, and nor does Albrecht, because if they did, then we'd not be making these wild stabs in the dark.

Opening my eyes again, I look to Hecht. 'One more try.'

He shakes his head.

'Why not?'

'Because the Russians know you're there.'

'They must have known that for some while.'

'Maybe ... but it grows riskier each time. If they get *you*—'

Albrecht looks to him sharply, and he falls silent.

'*What?*' I ask. 'What don't I know?'

'Nothing,' Hecht says. But he's lying. And he doesn't do it well.

'What if we keep someone close this time,' Albrecht says. 'Someone who can jump in and pull him out of there immediately if there's any trouble.'

'No!'

'*Why?*'

I'm almost pleading with him now.

'Because it's too risky. Besides, someone new—'

'Won't know what's going on,' I interject. 'Look. Why don't you show me what happened – all of it; all thirteen attempts – then send me in again, armed with what I know. After all, if this *is* a maze, then maybe knowing what *doesn't* work – what paths *not* to follow – might just work.'

Hecht stares at me thoughtfully, then, quietly,. 'You really want to do that?'

I nod.

'*All* of it? I warn you, some of it's quite gruesome.'

I frown. 'What do you mean?'

'I mean you died. Several times. We had to jump in and get you out – change time and unweave events. It wasn't very pretty.'

'I *died*?'

Hecht nods.

I swallow, then, knowing there's no other course, look to Albrecht. 'Show me. Every last little thing you have.'

130

That evening, as the sun sinks below the rim of the valley, Hecht ceremonially lights a massive fire at the centre of the encampment. It's burning bright – throwing flickering shadows across the huts – when the hunters return, stepping out of the darkness in threes and fours, throwing down their captured prey on a great pile beside the main hut before joining the rest of the tribe about the fire.

And even as the men return, so the women get down to work, skinning and cutting up the dead animals, preparing the meat for the fire. Among them I notice Ooris. Indeed, it's hard not to notice her, for she seems to be at the heart of all the activity, organising the women, making sure each task is done well. And when the first of the food is ready, it is Ooris who brings a great wooden platter of it across to us, where we sit in front of Albrecht's hut and, bowing before us, makes an offering.

There is a kind of silence – a silence breached only by the roar and crackle of the fire – as she bows low, waiting for us to take the well-charred meat from the bowl.

Hecht looks to me and smiles. 'You first, Otto.'

I take a large chunk of meat – the leg of some beast – and almost drop it, not realising just how hot it is.

'Here,' Hecht says, handing me a carved wooden plate.

I drop the meat on to the plate, then look up, smiling. 'Thank you, Ooris.'

And as I say it, I almost feel she blushes. Only how would I tell in this half-light, and in that deep-set face? Yet there's a distinct movement of her body, which seems to indicate a certain pleasure at my thanks, as well as a feminine shyness.

Finally, Hecht takes the last piece and, raising it, offers a word or two of thanks to the hunters, his voice richly burred as he utters their strange and ancient speech. And then the feast begins.

After a while, Ooris comes across again and, with that same, gentle shyness, sits down in front of us.

'Hello,' she says, her voice strangely deep. 'Did you ...' She hesitates, then, more confidently. 'Did you *enjoy* the meal?'

Her *Volksprach* is excellent. Hecht, I note is looking on, wearing a more earnest expression than I've seen him wear all evening, like he himself is being tested here.

'I did,' I answer, nodding exaggeratedly. 'You speak our language very well.'

'Thank you,' she says, and this time – from this close, and in the fire's light – I see that she does blush. Indeed, though her form is somewhat heavy, somewhat frightening, there's something about her face that's almost attractive. There is a definite sweetness to her, and – I guess because she speaks our language – I find myself re-categorising her there and then, elevating her, I suppose you'd say, from ape to human. She is like us, despite her outer form.

She glances up, then looks down quickly, averting her eyes, that gesture so human, so like a love-shy teenage girl of some later Age, that again she comes suddenly alive to me, no longer just a creature. And it's that image that stays with me as, later, I drift into sleep: of a Neanderthal woman, smiling shyly, reminding me, despite all physical differences, of something that I'm missing so acutely that it brings me close to tears.

131

Heavy rain, falling on the roof of the hut, wakes me before dawn. I go to the doorway and look out at a valley transformed. Mist drifts like clouds of dense smoke, obscuring vision briefly, then clearing to reveal a landscape washed fresh and new.

It's only when I turn to speak to Hecht that I realise he's not there.

I walk across to Albrecht's cabin, expecting to find the two of them there, but that too is empty. Stepping outside, I look about me, but the encampment is silent, the *huuruuhr* sprawled in their huts, sleeping off last night's drunken feast.

The rain is still falling, a warm, pleasant rain. Peeling off my top, I walk out into it and stand there, looking out along the length of the valley, enjoying the simple beauty of the view. My hair is plastered to my head, my trousers soaked, but it doesn't matter. This is the best feeling – being alive on a morning like this.

'Otto?'

I turn, to find Hecht and his brother there. Hecht's carrying a pack. He smiles at me. 'You're an early riser. I thought you'd still be asleep.'

'I couldn't,' I say. 'The rain ...'

'Have you had breakfast?'

'No.'

'Are you hungry?'

'Famished.'

'Then come. I'll cook you a breakfast you'll never forget.'

I wonder where they've been and what they've been doing, but there's something else I want to raise.

'I had a dream,' I say as we walk back, 'just before I woke. It was about Reichenau. You know, our two-headed friend.'

Hecht turns and looks at me. 'Go on.'

'In my dream he was speaking Russian. Fluent Russian. With a Suzdal accent.'

Hecht laughs. 'Suzdal, eh? So he's a Moscow boy, perhaps?'

'It wasn't just that. In my dream he was fishing ...'

'Fishing?'

'Yes ... sitting there on the bank of a river, on a lazy summer's day, just fishing. I was on a boat, you see, drifting downstream, the faintest breeze in the sail, and there he was, on the bank, as casual as could be. He looked up and spoke to me, just as if he'd been expecting me.'

'In Russian?'

'Yes.'

'And what did he say?'

I smile. 'I can't remember. It's like the words themselves didn't matter. It's what lay behind them.'

'And what *was* behind them?'

'I'm not sure. Only it got me thinking. Why did he tell Manfred that he knew me? Was he trying to get me into trouble? Or what was he trying to do? It just seems strange that he even mentioned me.'

'Maybe Manfred asked him about you. Directly, I mean. Maybe he showed him a holo-image.'

'Maybe ...' Only I don't think that. In fact, I'm pretty sure that Manfred implied that Reichenau raised the subject.

Hecht's silent, then he turns and looks at me again. 'So you think Reichenau's a Russian agent?'

'I don't know. In my dreams ...'

He stops, and Albrecht and I stop too. 'Do you *trust* your dreams, Otto?'

'What do you mean?'

'I mean that maybe they tell us the truth sometimes. Truths that we'd otherwise never come upon?'

'I don't know. They're only dreams, after all.'

'And yet you trust to your instincts. How do they differ from your dreams? In what fashion?'

I stare at Hecht, surprised. Maybe it's being back here that makes him so, but he seems very different right now.

He smiles. 'Maybe *he's* the key. Not Gudrun, nor Gehlen, nor Manfred, but Reichenau. Maybe he's the one you need to go back and see.'

'You're kidding.'

'Why should I be? It's the one place we *haven't* been. Not in the last few days of it, anyway.'

'I don't know. The map he gave me ...'

'Wasn't of the *Konigsturm*, I know. That doesn't mean it doesn't locate where the source is. You just have to find out where that building is.'

'And how do I do that?'

Albrecht laughs. 'By asking Reichenau?'

'You think he'd answer me?'

'Not if he *is* a Russian agent,' Hecht says. 'But we don't know that yet. Besides, why give it to you unless it means something?'

'To waste my time?'

'There are other ways of doing that. No. I think the map is genuine.'

That puzzles me – why should Hecht think that? – but I let it pass.

We are still standing there, in the rain, the cabin fifty yards away, waiting, it seems, for Hecht to say something, or do something. But all he does is smile, then turn and walk on. As if, in that moment, he has seen it all clearly.

132

I never get that promised breakfast. The decision made, Hecht wants to act on it at once. He has Albrecht compile a dossier of all we know on Reichenau – not a lot, as it turns out – then has me study it.

I don't learn a lot that I didn't already know, only a few incidentals about his past, gleaned from the state records. His 'daughter', so-called, is no relation at all. Nor could she have been, now that I think of it. *Doppelgehirn* aren't born that way, after all – they're manufactured: their two brains sewn into a single skull. What surprises me is that he should make that claim. As if he needed family.

'Maybe it makes him feel less of a freak,' Albrecht says, speaking bluntly.

'Or maybe he's just a liar.'

Hecht looks to me and smiles. 'Well, there's only one way to find out ...'

Which is why, a mere half hour later, I am back in that tiny cabin, perched high above the vast metallic floor of *Werkstätt 9*, awaiting Reichenau's return.

It is the evening of the bombing in the *Konigsturm* – only an hour before Manfred turns everything upside down in his quest for vengeance. A poised moment. And Reichenau is out there some-where, *involved* somehow, while his 'daughter' serves me tea and makes small talk. Or so it is at first. But then it changes.

'Your friend, Burckel ...'

I look to her and smile. 'Yes?'

'Do you trust him?'

It's a strange question. 'Why?'

'It's nothing.'

Only it clearly is. She has a reason for mentioning it.

'Burckel's a dear friend,' I say, remembering what happened. 'I'd trust him with my life.'

'And yet he's not what he seems. You can see it at a glance.'

I don't answer, but it tends to confirm what I've been think-ing – that these are Russian agents. If so, they would know about Burckel. But then, why mention it now?

She looks at me, then shrugs. 'It's true what my father says. You're not from here. You have an aura.'

'An aura?' I almost laugh. It's the strangest thing anyone has ever said to me. 'You mean I glow or something?'

'Or something.'

That's much too cryptic for my liking. I pause, reassessing things. She's far from stupid, and she's not saying these things merely to break the silence. They have a purpose. But what?

'What *do* you see?'

She hesitates, then says, 'Burckel watches you, did you know that? Like he's waiting for the outer shell to crack open and some stranger to step out. But he's not wrong, is he? That's how you are. I can see it for myself.'

'Yes, but ...?'

'What do I *see*?' Her eyes in that strangely broad face stare back at me with a real intensity. 'I see a man walking in a maze, not knowing who he really is. A man cut off from the true meaning of his actions. A man ...'

She stops, then walks over to the shelves and pulls something down. It's an old leather-covered photo album.

'There,' she says, and hands it to me.

I open it and catch my breath. The first photo, the print almost the size of the page, is of me, standing at Nevsky's side beside a stream in northern Russia. And there, in the background, is Ernst.

I go to speak, but there are heavy footsteps on the metal walkway outside, and then the door creaks open.

It's Reichenau. He takes me in at a glance – sees what I'm holding – and gives a knowing smile. Then, as if nothing's happened, he takes off his jacket and throws it down, then pours himself a big tumbler of the clear liquor that we shared last time I was here. He takes a sip, then turns to face me, using his 'reasonable' voice – the 'pleasant uncle' voice of his controlling half.

'Herr Behr. I wondered when ...'

He knows my name, and has an album of photographs which – I turn the pages one by one – seem to be all of me.

'It's begun,' he says to her, and she nods. 'Where's Heinrich?'

'Gone,' she says. 'I sent him south with Karl and Gustav.'

'What is this?' I ask, holding the album out to him.

'I had you checked out,' he says. 'I had to be sure who you were.'

'Yes, but why?'

'To make sure you weren't a threat to me.'

'A threat?'

'You've got the map. What more do you want?'

'I want to know where it's for.'

He laughs. 'I thought you knew.'

'Are you Russian?'

It's not what I meant to ask, but this is all so strange.

'No,' he says. 'I'm German. Doubly so.' And he laughs.

'But you can't be.'

'No? Why not?'

'Because I know all our agents.'

'Like Hecht's brother, I suppose.'

That stops me dead. Just what *is* going on? Is this some strange reality shift? I mean, the album … it must have taken a great deal of effort to compile it, and for what purpose? And then there's his last comment.

I feel a small frisson of fear. I have never felt so cut adrift, so far from understanding what's going on.

'You're near the hub here,' he says, as if he reads my mind. 'Where things are at their most chaotic. Step back a little – a day or two – and it becomes much simpler, but the further in you go, the closer you get. Well, I think you understand, eh, Otto?'

Hecht called it a maze. A maze I've failed to navigate no less than thirteen times now – one that's left me dead on more than one occasion. And maybe this, strange as it is, is part of it. Only … how do I make sense of it?

Is Reichenau friend or foe?

I watch him change his shirt, and then he turns to me.

'You want a lift?'

It's so unexpected, I laugh. 'A lift?'

'To Gehlen's. I can drop you there if you want.'

'You'll take me?'

'If it's the only way.'

The only way to what?

'I don't understand ...'

It's an admission of weakness, of ... well, of *ignorance*, I guess. Only I need to know what's going on, before I go even further out on a limb.

'Come,' he says simply. 'We'll talk as we go.'

133

The flyer is a bright red *Angestellte* – an 'Executive' – which is ironic considering that Reichenau is supposed to be a revolutionary. It's a regular tank of a machine, stately yet brutal, the very type that 'executives' seem to like, and Reichenau handles it like it's a sports model.

Oh, and there's one other thing I note as I slide in beside him. There is a sticker on the passenger window, like one of those jokey things you often see, only this one reads '*standig Verandern*' – 'perpetual change'.

'Why doesn't Hecht know more about you?' I ask, without preamble.

'Because I've kept myself to myself. Until now.'

'Okay. So what's changed?'

He glances at me, then returns his gaze to the packed traffic channel, easing the flyer into a faster stream.

'It seemed to me that you needed help.'

'Help?'

'To complete the circle. To close the loop. We none of us exist without that.'

I stare at him, astonished. 'But—'

'I've been waiting for you to come to me a second time.' He pauses, then – 'It was fore-ordained.'

Nonsense, I think. Then again, this tiny sector of Time seems dense with loops; as if everyone's been trying to change it subtly without altering the major currents.

Which is probably the truth.

Only I've still no handle on Reichenau, and the fact is I still don't trust him.

'You *know* Gehlen?'

'For some years. I helped him once.'

This isn't in the histories. 'Helped him? In what way?'

'He killed a man, in a bar-room brawl when he was much younger. I went back and changed things.'

'And he knew about all this?'

'Of course not. He mustn't know. It doesn't work like that.'

'Then …?'

'I befriended him…before the brawl, that is. Bought him a drink and talked with him. Got him home in one piece. He was grateful. We became friends.'

'I don't believe you.'

He laughs. 'Fine. *Don't* believe me. But you'll see.'

134

He's right. I *do* see. Because Gehlen greets him at the barrier like a brother, hugging him close and patting his back, not put off by that awful, overlarge head of his. Maybe he feels that they're both freaks – one physical, one mental – but whatever it is, the connection seems genuine.

We are in the stacks of Hellersdorf, in sprawling East Berlin, at the gates of a 'secure' enclave, a drop of a mile and a half beneath the semi-circular platform on which we stand.

Gehlen steps back from Reichenau and looks at me coldly. 'Who's this?'

'This is Otto,' Reichenau says. 'Otto Behr. He wants to speak with you.'

Hearing my name, Gehlen starts. 'Behr? B. E. H. R. Behr?'

I nod. 'Yes, why?'

'That's strange. Very strange. There's a package, you see. It was delivered to my assistant two days back ...'

'There,' Reichenau says. 'Loops.'

Gehlen looks to the *Dopplegehirn*. 'Sorry?'

But Reichenau just smiles and shrugs. 'It's nothing. But I have to go now. I'm expected at the *Gefangnis* ...'

Again, the way he casually drops that in makes me feel he knows much more than he's telling me. Even so, I'm here, with Gehlen, and there's a package.

'Has he ...?' Gehlen begins.

'Here,' Reichenau says, and hands Gehlen a security pass, made out in my 'official' name and with my holo-image on it.

Gehlen frowns. *'Manninger?'*

'It's what the authorities know him as. But Otto's fine. You can trust him.'

The words send a little tingle down my spine. *You can trust him.* Why? What does *he* know that *I* don't?

I watch him climb back into the flyer, then turn to see Gehlen watching me. He says nothing, just turns and heads towards the gate, leaving me to follow.

135

I am here for one reason only – to locate the far end of the time-anchor so that we can free Ernst. Nothing else matters. But this business with Reichenau has thrown me. As I follow Gehlen down a long corridor and up a narrow flight of stairs, I ask myself a few questions.

If Reichenau *is* one of our agents, then why have we never seen him at the platform? Is it because – as he seems to imply – he's kept himself to himself, further up the line, or is it because he's Russian, and thus wouldn't pass through the screens without self-destructing?

But if he's Russian, why is he helping me? Why did he give me the map? Why also did he deliver me to Gehlen?

After all, the Russians have tried their best to kill me almost every time I've come here bar the last, and that was only because I jumped out early.

And then there's the photo album – where does *that* fit?

In fact, none of it quite fits. All of the pieces seem to come from different puzzles.

Or different realities?

I think about what Reichenau said – about things growing more chaotic the closer you get to the hub of things – and wonder if that might not be true. Maybe that's why I keep failing.

Gehlen stops and turns to me. He's standing before a plain black door. 'This is it.'

I look about me, surprised by just how nondescript the place is, considering. You'd think a man of Gehlen's stature would live in something more luxurious than this.

Not that this isn't expensive.

We go inside. A child is crying somewhere off to the left, and as I step through into the main living room, a small, blonde-haired woman – tired-looking, dressed in a pale blue one-piece – comes out of the state-of-the-art kitchen on the far side.

'Hans, I—'

She stops, surprised to see me there.

'This is Otto,' Gehlen says. 'He's a friend of Reichenau.'

The mention of Reichenau clearly doesn't please her. In fact, from her reaction, I'd judge she doesn't like the man. *And me from association* …

'Hi,' I say, but she doesn't answer. She looks to Gehlen again.

'Meister Lofthaus was on while you were up at the gate. He says we have to go to the safe haven. The King himself has ordered it.' She pauses, then: 'I've sent the servants home already.'

Gehlen sighs. 'Then we'd better pack.' He looks to me. 'Forgive me. It seems you've made a wasted journey.'

'I'll come with you,' I say. 'We can talk on the way.'

Gehlen looks at me oddly, then shrugs. He crosses the room, then takes down a small trunk – the very same that still exists, up the line at Four-Oh – and places it on the low coffee table in the centre of the room.

'What do you want to know?'

I wonder how direct I can be, and whether he'd answer me. Probably not. This too is probably being watched.

'I've heard rumours,' I say, remembering the last time I said this to him, in the flyer back from Gudrun's palace, 'that things have become … unstable.'

He glances at me, then continues packing. 'What did Reichenau mean by *loops*?'

'I don't know.'

But I can see he doesn't believe me.

'Things are fine,' he says, after a moment. 'The rumours are wrong.'

I take a pen and notepad from my pocket and write down the

equations – memorised earlier – then tear off the top sheet and hand it to him. He reads it almost carelessly, then double-takes. 'Thor's teeth!'

Straightening, he looks directly at me – for the first time the whole of him there in his gaze; an intense, powerful gaze that, for the first time, reveals his true intelligence.

'Where did you get this?'

'It's right, isn't it? The equations go off to infinity, which indicates that the laws of physics are breaking down.'

'It isn't right. It *can't* be right.'

'But it *is*.'

He nods.

'Drainage.'

'Impossible,' he answers, and again I get a strong feeling of déjà vu.

'The discontinuities,' I say. 'They have to mean something.'

Gehlen stares back at me and shakes his head slowly, but his eyes say yes.

His wife returns to the room, their little girl in tow, a bundle of clothes in her arms. Placing the clothes down beside the trunk, she begins to pack while the child stares sullenly at me.

Gehlen turns away. His chest rises and falls, as if he's been running. This whole business has agitated him greatly. He turns back, as if about to say something, when his three-year-old son, Manfred, runs into the room. Seeing him, Gehlen smiles; a very different Gehlen suddenly there before me. Crouching, he hugs the boy, then listens attentively as this son says something to his ear.

'Okay,' he says. 'But three things only. That's all you can take.'

And Manfred runs off, back into his room.

Gehlen straightens, then looks at me again. 'How do you know all this?'

'Things get out ...'

He nods. After all, this is a society of spies. Then, as if he's remembered something, he goes over to the shelves and takes something down. Stepping across, he hands it to me.

I stare at the label on the package. It's Hecht's handwriting but it's addressed to me, care of Gehlen, and I wonder why. This is what Burckel delivered two days ago, when he went AWOL. The same package that Dankevich sent his men back to get, when they, for some reason, failed to return.

As I begin to pick at the wrapping, so young Manfred runs in again, saying something about a missing toy. Gehlen, watching me, makes to turn and go with the boy, to search for it in his room, and it's then, as he takes the first step across the room, that I see what's in the package and call out to Gehlen, my voice urgent, telling him to stay exactly where he is.

Gehlen turns, surprised, then laughs, seeing what I'm holding. 'There he is,' he says to his son. 'There's George ...'

And he takes a step towards me, his son's tiny hand in his own, both of them smiling ...

The explosion in the bedroom is deafening. It knocks us all off of our feet. The room is filled suddenly with smoke and dust. But as I get up, I see that no one's badly hurt. The bomb has failed. Gehlen is still alive, and as I stand, brushing the dust off my clothes, I notice how he's staring at me like I've been transformed.

Neighbours come running, asking if we're okay. Both children are crying, and Gehlen's wife just sits there, badly shaken. An alarm is going off somewhere now, its repetitive drone shredding the nerves, *but no one's hurt.*

I let out a long, sighing breath, then look down at the object I'm holding and shake my head. It's a child's toy. A small, yellow giraffe, twelve inches long and made of soft rubber.

Gehlen comes across and takes it from me, staring at it in

wonder. 'George,' he says. Then, looking up into my face, he asks: 'How did you …?'

Loops, I want to say, but I just shrug.

Only he's too intelligent not to make connections. Too clever not to unpick this conundrum stitch by stitch and put it back together. Oh, and I know what you're thinking: that Hecht could simply have *sent* him the equations, only that isn't how it works. Not for something as essential as this. This once the 'fallacy of inaction theory' doesn't apply. We know, because we've tried.

But maybe *this* is enough. After all, Gehlen has been working on Q-balls for some time now – trying to fit them into the general picture – and though thus far he's failed, maybe this will give him the jolt that will allow him to think the unthinkable.

A toy giraffe named George …

I stare at it in his hands and laugh, and he looks up at me.

'Hetty,' he says, speaking to his wife, his eyes never leaving me. 'Leave that now. Just take the children and go to the safe haven. I'll join you later. There's something I have to do.'

136

It is happening, even as we're in the air. It is ten past two and the Russians, reeling under the first massive, five-pronged assault, have withdrawn their forces to a line that runs from Riga in the north to Odessa in the south. They are regrouping, ready to push the Germans back after this latest feint in the Great Game. Only they're mistaken, for the rules of the game have changed.

They have yet to realise that, this time, Manfred is in earnest.

Vast fists of heavy cloud dominate the sky outside, their sculpted shapes so dark and bruised they're almost purple, yet between them I can see great swathes of sunlit meadow. Indeed, the whole landscape has a brooding, unnatural look to it. The great world of field and wood and stream looks super-real in these, its final moments.

Soon – not long now – the first of the bombs will fall.

I look across at Gehlen. His face looks strange, mask-like, in the golden light from the portal just beyond him. I study him a moment, as one might study any natural phenomenon.

Gehlen is lightning. Gehlen is pure electricity, fallen to the Earth. He is a sun, throwing out energy and ideas – enough for a hundred thousand lesser men. And yet he is also a man, flawed and mortal.

Conscious of my attention, he turns to me.

'I don't know why you need to know any of this, but you get one shot, okay?'

'Okay.'

I have been mulling things over on the way down. Wondering why, for instance, there were no guards on Gehlen's apartment, and why, other than his importance to Manfred, they should want to bomb him, and whether it was Russian agents who did it. Time agents, that is.

Only time agents would have monitored the results and jumped back in again just as soon as they saw they'd failed. And then … but that gets complicated, so it can't have been that.

Reichenau?

More than anything, I want to know what Reichenau's part in this is, because if anyone's setting off these bombs – and from the news reports we've heard, there's been a whole spate of them – it's Reichenau's *Unbeachtat*, his revolutionaries.

But why should Reichenau put me in a position where I could save Gehlen, if it was he who planted the bomb in the first place? Or is there something glaringly simple that I've overlooked?

I look to Gehlen once again. 'Why are you doing this?'

'Because I owe you a life.'

I gesture towards the cameras. 'You aren't afraid of . . .?'

'Of being watched? I don't think *anyone's* being watched right now. It's chaos out there. But if you must know, I've permission to show you round.'

'Permission?' That surprises me more than anything he's said. 'From whom?'

'From Tief. He has instructed me to show you whatever you need to see.'

And he hands me a sealed document, from Tief's office, granting me access to the facility at Orhdruf.

Which makes no sense at all.

Or rather, it makes me want to jump back, right there and then, and present it all to Hecht; to let his cool reason play over everything I've seen and heard like a searchlight, making sense of it all.

'I see,' I say, although I don't. 'I see.'

137

Rain is falling, spotting the soft, pale stone of the battlements as we step down from the ship. Orhdruf, I note with some surprise, is another castle; a fact I completely overlooked last time, distracted possibly by Manfred's cruisers, waiting to arrest me.

Gehlen takes Tief's pass from me and, waving it overhead for the security cameras, walks across the pad and through the gate, leaving me to hurry after.

We make our way down several dark twists of steps and along dank, dimly lit corridors until, at the bottom of one last twist of steps, we come out into the most curious of laboratories.

It was a chapel once, I'm sure. Two long lines of slender stone pillars form walks to left and right. Between them are several huge work-benches, piled high with electrical equipment. Two assistants – one young, one surprisingly ancient – look up as Gehlen approaches, surprise registering on their faces as they see me there.

'This is Otto,' Gehlen says, looking about him for something. 'He's come to see how we do things here.'

It's a strange thing to say, and almost humorous, only the two assistants don't laugh. They simply stare at me suspiciously.

I look about me, surprised by how chaotic everything appears. It looks more like a dump than a *workplace*. Notebooks lie open everywhere you look, their pages filled with strange diagrams and scrawled figures, many of which are crossed through. It makes me think – not for the first time – that Hecht ought to have sent someone with a better scientific grasp. Then again ...

'Okay,' Gehlen says, pocketing a small, round object. 'You want to see? Then let's see. We'll take the lift down to the seventh level.'

138

We step into the room and there it is, spinning slowly in the darkness, so dark it almost seems bright. You can't actually see it, of course, but then again you can't fail *not* to see it. The brain registers it somehow as an absence.

We are wearing protective clothes, and dark visors, and I wonder how we can stand only a metre or so away from a black hole and not be sucked in ... only we can. It might seem like magic, but as Gehlen himself has said: 'It's not magic, it's physics. If the maths works, it works.'

I don't claim to even *begin* to understand this; the equations are so far beyond my comprehension that my mind simply rejects them. It was hard enough memorising them to do my party trick.

Only they work. And because they do, Gehlen has been able to create a 'field' in this room that *contains* the singularity.

'Where is it?' I ask, expecting some *visual* sign of the fluctuation, of the 'drainage' which, I know, is linked directly to Ernst back across the centuries.

'It's inside,' Gehlen says. 'Just within what we call the Cauchy Horizon.'

I haven't a clue what he's talking about, but I'm disappointed that I can't see anything I can 'switch off' to end Ernst's misery.

'*Pions*,' he says quietly, musing aloud. 'It has to be something to do with the *pion* emission rate.'

I know what pions are. That's something all of us at Four-Oh learned in our studies. They're particles that travel faster than the speed of light.

I turn and look at him, but I can't make out his features through the doubled thicknesses of glass.

'How is it actually used?'

Gehlen turns and points through the wall. 'There are catchment spheres – huge great things – in separate chambers surrounding us on all sides. Above, below, all around us. It's complex, but essentially we use the accelerator to fire particles into it, and they "jump" – that is, they disappear in one position and reappear in another – over there, within one of the spheres. And this is happening all the time. Every nano-second. Huge amounts of energy jumping from here to there through ... well, through nowhere really.'

'And the spheres ...?'

'Feed energy – huge amounts of energy – into the grid. There are dozens of them in all, so if one of them fails ...'

'And do they?'

'No. Not until now, that is.' He smiles. 'It's all switched off at present, otherwise we couldn't have come in here. We'd have been bathed in Cerenkov radiation ...'

I wait for an explanation and – of a kind – it comes.

'*Not* a good thing.'

'So what are you going to do?' I ask. 'Just how are you going to get inside that ... *thing?*'

Gehlen laughs. 'You know ... for once, I haven't a clue.'

'You haven't ...?'

I fall silent as the 'absence' at the centre of the room swells momentarily, and then seems to vanish to the tiniest point.

'What's happening?'

But Gehlen's not listening. He's staring at the singularity, unable to believe his eyes, for it has begun to burn an intense golden colour, like the darkness at its pinpoint centre has caught fire.

'Out!' Gehlen says, as if having a wall between us and that thing will make any difference. 'Out of here now!'

139

For the next hour, Gehlen sits in the gallery, watching the screen as the singularity goes through a terrifying series of metamorphoses. I sit there next to him, dry-mouthed, wondering just what's going on, and whether this is the end. But Gehlen is silent, pondering the significance of what he's seeing – as if he reads each change as a set of figures.

Which is perhaps the truth. After all, he does see things differently from the rest of us. But time's passing, and Ernst is still trapped, and if even Gehlen can't see a solution, then maybe there isn't one.

Maybe Ernst has to be trapped for it all to work.

It's a dreadful thought, but I'm forced now to consider it.

Yet even as I do, something else occurs to me. There's nothing in the histories about what happened to the singularity during the coming conflict. Nothing that survived, anyway. Within the next fifteen hours everything on the surface of the planet will be destroyed, but we're deep down here, just like the command bunkers in Moscow and Berlin, and there's the possibility that this too survived the general devastation. Only ... there's no record of it.

From the perspective of Four-Oh – anchored up the line in 2999 – this doesn't exist, and therefore *didn't* survive.

But is that so?

If the black hole *had* been destroyed, or even freed from its restraints, then surely it would have taken the Earth with it? I mean ... something this powerful ...

I look to Gehlen, meaning to ask him what *would* happen, but he raises a hand, as if to deflect my question, and I can see from the intensity of his manner that he's thinking something through.

And then he smiles.

'Of course,' he says. 'I should have thought of that before.'

140

And so it happens. As simply as that. Gehlen stands and nods, the smile remaining on his lips. Yet if he realises just *how* significant the moment is, he doesn't show it.

Time travel. Pions and Q-balls and energy that appears and disappears contrary to the laws of normal physics, that jumps from 'now' to 'then' and back again. Oh, he hasn't got it all. Far from it. But I can see he has enough. Enough to keep a smile on his lips that don't often deign to register amusement. And he'll work on that, these next few hours, until it's there, complete – ready for us to use ...

He looks across at me and shrugs. 'I guess I'd better write it down.'

I frown, as if I don't understand, and he laughs.

'I'm sorry. Just that it's come to me. What was wrong, that is. Or not wrong ...'

Yet even then he keeps it to himself. He doesn't want to say – not explicitly – what it is he's seen.

'Can you stop it?'

'The leakage?'

'Yes.'

'I guess so. If I wanted.'

'Then ...?'

I don't understand what he's waiting for. If he *can*, then why doesn't he?

You think, perhaps, that I should just tell him the truth – about Ernst, that is – and be done with it. But I can't. It's a paradox too many. Gehlen has to get there all by himself. There *is* no other way, and believe me we've tried a few. It's like there's some cosmic watcher, waiting to whip the magic carpet out from under our feet should we open our mouths to Gehlen, or slip him a note, or ...

And now it's *my* turn to smile, because I realise that I've done, in effect, what others have failed to do. I've already jogged Gehlen's mind on to the right track, and I've done it with a toy yellow giraffe named George.

Or Hecht has, to be more accurate. After all, I was only the link-man. The messenger boy.

'Otto ...' Gehlen says quietly, handing me Tief's pass, which has been in his custody all this while. 'Forgive me, but I have to work. Take the lift back to the first level. There's a sun room there. I'll join you in a while.'

I look to him, meaning to argue, but I can see at a glance that it'll do no good. He has already dismissed me from his mind.

I turn away, meaning to walk over to the lift, then stop dead, realising where I am.

Reichenau's map. This is it! This room, not the one in which the singularity is kept. It's here.

Again it makes no sense, for the map was supposed to indicate where the singularity was. Only I've seen that. I know now where that is and it doesn't help. But this ... this correlates perfectly to the map. And where the singularity should be ...

I turn and stare at the point in space where, on Reichenau's map, the black hole was marked. Only it's not a black hole, it's a simple, old-fashioned computer screen, the word '*Werktafel*' prominently displayed across the top surface, while on the screen itself ...

... is the singularity. Or a detailed graphic representation of it.

I wonder what that means. I take a step towards it and Gehlen looks up.

'Otto, *please*. Go now.'

I glance at him, then nod and leave. Nothing – and I mean nothing – is more important right now than letting Gehlen work through the equations.

141

The lift, as I observed earlier, has no camera in it. Thus, as the doors hiss shut, I jump, back to Four-Oh.

It's quiet about the platform, the lights dimmed. There's no sign of Hecht, but the women are there. The women are *always* there.

'Where's Hecht?'

'Sleeping,' Kathe says, coming across.

'I need to see him.'

'You can't.'

'What?'

'You don't need to,' Urte adds, stepping alongside.

'I ...'

She hands me something, and I stare at it and laugh. And then I jump. Back again. Back into the lift, a second later.

142

The lift doors hiss open. I step out, looking about me for a sign, but even as I do, a guard approaches, gun raised, and demands my ID.

I show him Tief's pass, and he takes a long while staring at it through the dark glass of his visor. There's a delay as he mumbles something into his lip-mike, and then his head jerks up and he steps back, snapping smartly to attention, his head bowed, the pass held out to me.

Even now, even as it's all falling apart, they go through the motions. Not that the guard knows. Not as *I* know.

The sun room is, in fact, a great, glass-walled balcony, looking west. The view is spectacular, the peaks of the Thuringer Wald dominating the skyline. There's a long bar against the back wall and plush white leather settees facing the view. A steward looks up from behind the bar, then hurries over, all politeness.

'What would the Meister like?'

'A beer. A Beck's if you have one.'

He nods and hurries away, leaving me to walk over to the great curving glass and look down, five hundred metres and more, to the courtyard far below. People are milling about down there, getting into transports, hurrying like ants, for what good it'll do them.

It is seventeen minutes to five. Far to the east, more than a thousand miles from where I'm standing now, the second phase of the invasion is under way. Manfred's southern army is sweeping north even as I wait for my beer, making directly for Kiev, at whatever cost. The Russians, shocked by the ferocity of the fighting, are reassessing their strategy. Three of their seven armies have been over-run and the situation is becoming serious. They have already recalled all reservists, and their eastern forces – under-strength and ill-equipped to fight a major campaign – have been brought west to beef up the defences surrounding their capital, Moscow.

They have begun to think the unthinkable.

The steward returns, hands me my beer, drops of ice-cold perspiration on the glass. I sip at it and smile my thanks, then turn back, studying, for a moment, the way the afternoon sunlight falls upon the distant mountains.

Between them and where I stand, the land rises and falls in great folds of green, the Gera river snaking its way like a thread of blue across the rugged terrain.

There's no sign, from where I stand, of the great north German megapolis that sprawls like some deadly crystal growth across the continent, from Amsterdam in the west, to Berlin in the east. From here one might almost believe that it never happened; that the Germany of rolling hills and dense, dark copses still existed. A Germany of castles and principalities, of Saxons and Westphalians, Thuringians, Prussians, and all the myriad other German tribes.

I have seen it all, and nothing – nothing – is as poignant as this. To see the last of it. Before the Earth glows molten red. Before the Nuclear Winter that's to follow.

I sit, relaxing, content to wait for once, to let it all wash over me. And it's then that she comes, ducking beneath the lintel, then straightening, her head, even then, barely scraping beneath the ceiling.

'Otto?'

I turn on the settee and look across at her, surprised.

'Gudrun … What are you doing here?'

She smiles, then slowly comes across. 'I came to see you.'

I stand, facing her. 'How did you …?'

'My uncle's secretary. He told me you were here.'

'Ah ...'

The settees are huge, big enough even for her, and so she settles beside me, reaching across to take my hand, mine, as ever, engulfed within her own.

The steward is hovering again, clearly overawed by Gudrun's presence.

'My lady ...' he says, in an reverent whisper, and bows so low I almost think he's going to touch his knees with his forehead.

'A glass of wine. A *Lohengrin* ...'

She turns her attention back to me, then grins, seeing what I've placed upon the low table to the side. She lifts the lavender-glazed cup and turns it carefully in her hands, understanding its significance.

'How did you get this?'

'I brought it back with me. Gehlen must have it, in his trunk. It's a loop.'

She nods, then sets it down again. Looking back at me, she smiles again, a pure radiance in her face. 'I'm glad you didn't go, Otto. I would have been sad not to see you one last time.'

Me too. How sad I hadn't realised until that moment. I squeeze her hand, and feel her respond.

'How much time have we?'

'Until the morning. Only ...'

Her eyes look a query at me. 'Only?'

'There are things I have to do.'

She nods, a trace of sadness returning to her eyes. 'What is it like, Otto, where you come from?'

I smile. 'It isn't really a place at all. More a series of connected rooms. And there's the platform ... '

'The platform?'

'When I jump back. That's where I go. Where the women are.'

But I notice that she's looking past me, and I turn and see at once what's caught her attention. Two craft, coming in low – maybe no more than fifty metres above the surface.

'Ours,' says the steward, as he hands Gudrun her drink. 'They'll be coming in from—'

But we don't hear what he says, because suddenly an alarm is sounding, and the two craft have peeled off – one to the left, one to the right.

There's a sudden grinding sound from above our heads – the sound, I realise, of a massive gun-turret rotating to face the incoming threat – and then it opens up, sending out a vivid trace of shells

The two fighters change trajectory, cutting back in, heading straight for us now, coming in fast, and I realise that if they keep on their current course, they'll hit the castle right slap bang where we are.

Other guns have also opened up now, and a continuous, deafening hail of shells and lasers are arcing through the air. But still the craft come on.

And then, suddenly, one explodes, a searing ball of flame leaving its after-image on the retina, yet even as it does, so two missiles snake out from the other craft, cutting the air like torpedoes, haring directly towards us at a frightening speed.

I close my eyes and place my free hand on my chest, preparing to jump right out of there, when there's an enormous explosion; one that makes the whole castle shudder. My eyes jerk open, to see a great ball of smoke rolling up into the sky, fragments of super-heated metal cascading into the courtyard far below.

'Close,' the steward mutters.

My ears are ringing. I swallow, then look to Gudrun. She sighs, then gives a little shudder.

'Guildsmen,' I say.

'What?' she says, shocked by what I've said.

'I said they were Guildsmen. It's civil war, Gudrun. Meister Adelbert has had enough.'

'Enough? But he's—'

'A powerful man,' Gehlen finishes, stepping alongside.

I look up at him. 'I thought you had work to do.'

He looks back at me clearly now, like a veil has lifted from his eyes. 'I did. But it didn't take me long. I've finished now. It was ...' He shrugs. 'I've left it on the board. If you're interested. Which I think you may be.'

Gehlen turns, looking to the Princess, then bows. 'My lady ...'

'Hans.' She leans forward and picks up the lavender-glazed cup. 'You must take this. Put it in your trunk. It's ... *necessary*.'

'A loop?' he asks, looking to me. 'Like the toy?'

I nod. 'A loop.'

Gehlen smiles. 'This is strange. I mean ... that you're here at all. It means that it works.'

I smile. 'Yes.'

'Then you can get me out of here.'

'I ...'

I am about to say no, but I stop dead, my heart racing suddenly. Why not? After all, all we have to do is get a team back here and fit a focus into Gehlen's chest. Even this late, there's time. Time for the graft to take, that is.

But it would mean leaving his wife and children to their fate, because there'd be no time to get *them* done. And besides it isn't always safe – not on children their age.

I'm quite certain that *I* wouldn't want to make such a decision. But Gehlen might think differently.

'Wait here,' I say, meaning to jump. Yet even as I say the words, I notice a movement in the air beyond Gehlen, then hear laughter. Familiar laughter.

Reichenau steps out and points the laser directly at my head. He's grinning, like this is the ultimate joke.

Gehlen whirls about. 'Michael …?'

'My name is Reichenau,' he says, introducing himself to Gudrun, 'Michael Reichenau.' And, stepping forward smartly, he rips Gehlen's shirt open and, with what's clearly a practised move, slaps a small, flesh-coloured circle against his chest.

'There,' he says, smiling across at me. *'Mine.'*

'Yours?' And then I realise. It's the same kind of 'plug' as was used on Ernst. Coded to Gehlen's genes, no doubt.

I'm about to say something, when Reichenau turns and gestures to the steward.

'You! More drinks! A *Lahmung* for me, and make it a large one!'

He gestures towards the settees with the gun.

'Come now. Sit down everybody … We've so much to talk about.'

143

Gehlen sits there, deeply uncomfortable. The plug on his chest is itching, only he can't get beneath it to scratch it and he can't remove it. Reichenau, sitting across from him, looks on, gun in one hand, drink in the other, amused.

Gudrun stares at him angrily. 'What manner of creature *are* you?'

'I am a *Doppelgehirn*,' Reichenau answers coldly. 'I was made thus, in the laboratories of the *Konigsturm* itself.' He smiles icily. 'You might say I am a *king's* man.'

'And that?' Gudrun asks, indicating the plug.

'It's as I said. It makes him mine. Ask Otto. He knows.'

Both Gehlen and Gudrun look to me, but I can't answer them.

Reichenau turns to me, waving the gun idly before him. 'Work it out. I'm sure you can. Only don't take too long. I know you won't.'

He's right. In fact, I've worked it out already. He needed me to save Gehlen, so that Gehlen might have the chance to 'discover' the time equations. But now that's done, he wants Gehlen for himself. Or – to be precise – for the equations that are in Gehlen's head.

'Why are you still here?' I ask. 'You have what you want.'

Reichenau raises his glass. 'I thought it would be pleasant to share a glass or two ... to toast *our* success.' Again he smiles, his over-large mouth stretched thin. 'That was some maze, huh?'

'Yes.' Only I sense that I haven't even got to the edges of this maze. Not yet.

I stand. If I can't do anything here, then I can at least jump back and change things earlier. But Reichenau is smiling again.

'No point,' he says. 'I only change it back ... And here we sit.'

I sit again, sip at my Beck's, and stare out at the sunlit mountains. Why is he waiting? Why *hasn't* he just jumped? And then it hits me.

The 'plug' is like a focus. It needs time to interact with the body. Maybe not as much time as an actual focus, but ... Reichenau finishes his drink, then throws the glass aside and stands. 'Wrong,' he says to me. 'It's immediate. But you'd have found that out.'

He reaches out, placing a hand on Gehlen's shoulder, then looks to me and smiles. 'Until the next time, eh?'

And they're gone. Like they were never there. I look to Gudrun, but she's looking down, into her lap, and I see – now that I've freed myself of my obsession with Reichenau – that she's been crying.

I walk over to her and take her hand once more. 'What?' I say gently. 'What is it?'

She looks up, her big blue eyes staring back at mine moistly. 'It's nothing. Really, it's nothing.' She sniffs deeply, then, forcing herself to smile, points past me.

'The cup,' she says. 'It has to be placed in Gehlen's trunk, doesn't it?'

I nod.

'Then let's do that. Let's at least get *that* right.'

'Okay ...' And as I think where Gehlen's trunk is, I remember what else is in that room, and what Gehlen said to me no more than fifteen minutes back.

I've finished now ... I've left it on the board. If you're interested. Which I think you may be ...

Interested? I laugh, and Gudrun stares at me, astonished.

'What?' she asked.

'Stay here,' I say, grabbing up the cup. 'I promise I'll be back.' And I hurry from the room, heading for the lift.

144

Diederich stares at the screen a moment longer, then looks up, giving me a beaming smile.

'It's all here. Everything we need. And more.'

'More?'

'Yes. He worked it out. Look.' And Diederich flicks through several pages until he comes to what might as well, to my eyes, be ancient Babylonian.

'What is that?'

'It's Ernst's position in Space-Time,' Hecht says, coming into the room. 'Gehlen pinpointed exactly where it is, and thus where the leakage was going to. That's the equation for it.'

'I thought we'd *lost* Gehlen.'

'We did. But now we've snatched him back. Or part of him ...'

'You've ...'

'No time,' Hecht says. 'We need to get a team back there to Orhdruf straight away. If we can plug the leak ...'

Ernst will go free.

'A team?' I ask.

'Three of us,' Hecht says, and looks to me meaningfully, as if to ask 'Do *you* want to come?'

'Why, yes ...'

'Then let's go. Horst ... make a copy of that. We'll need it when we're there.'

145

We jump back in – Hecht and Diederich and I – *directly* into the room where the singularity's kept.

We're suited up, of course, even though it's switched off right now.

'So what are we going to do?' I ask, staring at that dark absence that's at the centre of it all.

'We're going to flood it with energy, that's what,' Diederich says enthusiastically. 'In fact, we're going to push so much energy through it that it's going to overload.'

'And what good will that do?'

'No good at all,' Hecht answers, '*here*.'

'But if we're right,' Diederich adds. 'That is, if Gehlen's figures are correct ...'

I don't understand it at all. Least of all why we're inside here if we're going to flood the black hole with energy – presumably its own.

'But how do we ...?'

In answer, Diederich takes something from his pocket and holds it up. It looks like a pebble. A tiny, silver pebble. 'This here. We just toss it in like so ...'

And, like a child playing a game, he casually casts the tiny, silver pebble into the heart of the singularity where it vanishes.

I'm about to say something when I hear voices from the room next door. Gehlen's voice, and then my own.

'But ...'

'Now out,' Hecht says, placing his hand to his chest. And like ghosts, he, and then Diederich, and finally I, vanish.

146

'No wonder,' I say, back at Four-Oh, as I step out of my suit, thinking of the way the singularity changed colour so spectacularly while Gehlen and I were in the room with it. 'But what *was* that?'

'The gizmo?' Diederich combs back his thinning hair with his fingers and laughs. 'That's something Gehlen came up with. And not before time. He's been thinking on the problem for the best part of two centuries now.'

'Ah ... But has it worked?'

Hecht shrugs off the suit trousers and nods. 'If you mean, has it freed Ernst, then yes. Only ...'

'Tell him,' Diederich says. 'It won't harm.'

I frown. 'Tell me what?'

'He has his own platform,' Hecht says.

'He?'

'Reichenau. At least, that's what Gehlen now thinks. It's the only thing that makes any sense. And we think we know how. The black hole, at Orhdruf. He stole it.'

I laugh. 'He *stole* a black hole?'

Diederich nods. 'So Gehlen reckons.'

'And we think we know where,' Hecht says.

'Well, *where?*'

'You remember that huge gap in space and time we ran across, after Seydlitz's "Barbarossa" project in 1952?'

'Yes.'

'When we over-loaded the time-anchor, we made it unstable. In effect, it broke loose.'

'And?'

Diederich looks away. 'We didn't realise ...'

'Realise *what*?'

Hecht gives a long sigh, then answers me. 'Imagine you've got a really taut steel hawser, keeping a ship tight to the shore, and then you cut it. Imagine it flying back, all of the tension in the cable suddenly released, so that it whips back. Well ... it was like that. When we made the time-anchor unstable, it whipped back through time, burning a huge great hole through it.'

'A hole?'

'More like a gash,' Diederich says.

'It'll heal,' Hecht says, 'given time. Only ...'

'Only that's why,' Diederich finishes for him.

'Why what?'

'Why we can't see him. *Reichenau* ... Because that's where he's been. Inside that tear in Space-Time. Only now that we know where it is ...'

'Back in 1952?'

Hecht nods.

'Then why don't we ...?'

'Not yet,' Hecht says. 'Not until we know more. Anyway, there's something else we have to do first.'

'Ernst?'

Hecht nods.

'Come on,' he says. 'Let's go bring him home.'

147

The clearing is different this time. The bivouac-style tents are still there, and the stalls, yet there's no sign of Ernst. The place is still and dark, no shining presence in the air.

I look to Hecht, alarmed, but he seems unperturbed. He walks on, towards one of the larger bivouacs and, ducking beneath the awning, goes inside.

I follow, and there, on the floor, surrounded by a kneeling host of pilgrims – two or three dozen of the ragged fellows – is Ernst. He looks deathly pale and his breathing is faint. As I step closer, he mumbles something and then groans, such pain in so weak a sound.

Hecht claps his hands. 'Out!' he yells. 'Now!' And he kicks out at the nearest peasant.

I'm shocked. I have never seen Hecht this angry. He turns and looks at me, raw emotion in his face.

'If I *ever* get my hands on him ...'

Reichenau ...

I nod, then get to work, clearing that dark, malodorous tent, the toe of my boot pushing the last, reluctant pilgrim from the place.

I turn and look. Hecht is kneeling over Ernst now, listening to his chest. He looks up, deeply concerned, then reaches out and, cradling Ernst, lifts him.

'Burn the place,' he says. And then he jumps.

I stand there, looking at that awful, disease-ridden pallet on which they'd lain him; then, shuddering with disgust, I draw the laser from my belt and aim.

148

They send him back six months and repair him physically. But mentally?

Mentally, Ernst is in bad shape. Whatever he went through inside the time-trap, we can only ever glimpse the tiniest part of it. Imagine Time standing still. Imagine it freezing about you. Just imagine yourself embedded in ice. Eternally.

Then imagine being conscious all the while it happened.

Ernst smiles up at me from his bed, then lifts his head and shoulders from the nest of cushions in which he lays.

'Otto ...'

He's clearly pleased to see me, yet his smile is so pale, so wintry, that it chokes me up. This is the first time I've seen him since he came back, and I can see the difference.

Ernst will *never* be the same.

I sit down beside him on the bed, looking at him, studying his face, then reach out to embrace him.

He's so light; there seems so little of him. Like a cancer patient. Only the problem isn't physical. Physically there's nothing wrong with him.

As I move back from him, I notice the cards and flowers on the table on the far side of the bed.

'From the women,' he says, seeing where I'm looking. 'They came and saw me earlier.'

'They're glad you're home,' I say. 'And so am I.' I pause, then. 'It must have been hard.'

Ernst says nothing. He doesn't have to; the damage is in his face.

'Are you okay?' I ask, after a moment.

'Yes ... yes, fine.'

Both of his hands are in mine. I look down at them, noting

the translucency of the flesh, the strange, angular thinness of the fingers. They lay there in mine, impassive, *switched off*.

I meet his eyes again. 'What did they say? I mean … about getting you back into the programme?'

Ernst looks down. 'I've not asked him yet. But I guess they'll need to be careful.' He's quiet a moment, then: 'I understand that. If I were him …'

I wait, then, when he offers nothing more, I say cheerfully, 'I'll speak to him, maybe. See if we can't ease you back into things. Something simple. Familiar.'

He smiles wanly, like there's only so much energy to generate it. 'Thanks, Otto. It's so good to see you …'

'Time heals …'

Only, coming away from him, I wonder. Maybe there are experiences that leave so deep a scar they never properly heal.

I have to go back. To Orhdruf. To complete the circle. Only first there's someone else I have to see. Someone else who thinks he's seen the last of me.

149

Manfred is alone in the War Room. It's late – after three in the morning – and he has sent the others to their beds. This is the last night. When the sun comes up, it will all blow away in the wind.

I appear in the shadows by the door, stepping silently from the air.

Sensing something, Manfred looks up. He doesn't see me at first, but then he does.

'Lucius … or is it Otto now? How did *you* get in?'

If he fears assassination, he doesn't show it. But he *is* tired, I can see. I walk across, then sit, on a bench seat close to him.

'How goes the war?'

'It's ...' He stops, then, remembering what happened last time we met, stares at me directly. 'You *vanished*.'

'I know.'

'But how do you ...?'

'It doesn't matter.'

The great map behind me is mainly black now. Manfred's armies have routed the Russians. But it isn't over. Far from it. The final phase is about to begin.

'You know how they'll respond,' I say.

'I know.'

'Then why? Why destroy it all?'

But he has no answer. Only that he must. He stands up, towering above me, then turns as the great door on the far side of the room hisses open. It's Tief.

'Are you all right, My Lord?'

'Yes, Meister Tief. As you see, Otto has returned. Stepped out of the air.'

Tief nods. 'I saw, My Lord. One moment there was nothing, the next he was there.'

Manfred turns and looks down at me. 'I always knew.'

'Knew?'

'That there was something strange about you. All that talk of alliances ...' He pauses, then. 'But not a Russian?'

'Never a Russian, My Lord.'

Tief clears his throat, and Manfred looks back at him. 'Yes, Tief?'

'They have an answer.'

'They?'

'The Russians, My Lord. To our ultimatum.'

'Ah ...'

'And My Lord?'

'Yes?'

'The *Konigsturm* is burning. The Guild ...'

'I know, Tief. I know.'

It is civil war. Guild against King. Army against *Undrehungar*. As if one enemy wasn't enough.

I watch Manfred walk across and climb up on to the raised, semi-circular platform. Across from him the great screen changes. The map dissolves and in its place appear seven seated figures, as over-large as they are in life; greybeards in pale grey full-length cloaks. They look curiously ancient – medieval, almost. This is the Russian *veche* – or seven of the nine, at least – their supreme council of rulers. Like Manfred and his kin, they form a genetic elite among their kind – *podytyelt*, as they're known– yet they have nothing of Manfred's grandeur. They're poor specimens by comparison, and I find myself thinking that, like the Guildsmen, it needs full seven of them to match a single one of Manfred's ilk.

The two who are missing are already dead, their leader, Chkalov, one of them, assassinated at the very outset by Manfred's agents in the Kremlin.

'Gentlemen,' Manfred says, giving them a sweeping – ironic? – bow. 'You wish to surrender?'

The eldest of the Russians – seated at the very centre of the group – leans forward slightly and looks from side to side before he speaks.

'We have come to a decision.'

'A *decision*?' Manfred gives a short, humourless laugh, then shakes his head. 'I'll have no *terms*. You will surrender *unconditionally*.'

There's a moment's silence, and then the elder speaks again. His face is bitter now, his hatred for Manfred showing clear suddenly. 'You leave us no choice.'

Manfred lifts his head slightly. 'You capitulate then?'

The old man seems exhausted. Even so, he is defiant to the last. 'Never. Not until hell itself freezes over.'

Or the Earth boils . . .

Surprised, Manfred points towards their spokesman. 'You *will* surrender. You have no choice.'

'We shall destroy you first.'

And all of us, I think. But this is all written. Unchangeable. Manfred has backed the rats – as he's so often called them – into a corner from which they can't escape. And now the rats are biting back. If they must die, they will die – as they see it – honourably.

Such pride. Such stupid, self-destructive pride.

'So be it,' Manfred says wearily. And he cuts contact. On the screen the figures vanish, the great map reappears.

I stand there, shocked. Knowing about this was one thing, but seeing it . . .

And I do see it. I see it in Manfred's eyes, particularly; in the way he bends over the rail, like a runner whose energy is wholly spent. This isn't war, it's suicide. Only Manfred didn't want to go alone. He wanted to take everyone with him. Like that bastard Hitler. That's why he pushed them to the edge. Not to win. He could never *win*.

'You can't,' I say quietly, stepping towards him. 'You *can't*!'

He looks up, meeting my eyes, then turns and speaks to the air: 'Code Black Cloud,' he says. 'Target: Moscow . . .'

My mouth works soundlessly. There have been exchanges of missiles already. Cities have already been destroyed. But thus far it's been tactical. Brinkmanship. Now the *real* destruction begins. Hell itself will gape.

Already – even at that moment – the missiles are soaring upwards in great arcs towards their targets. German missiles, and Russian too.

Manfred looks to me again, and to my unspoken question

answers: 'Why not? Rather this than a world run by the Guild. It's over, Otto. *Finished.*'

And as he says the word, so there's a loud commotion outside and a sudden, violent hammering on the door, as if Thor himself is demanding entrance. A moment later it hisses open. Two Guildsmen step through and take up position, their weapons raised.

Adelbert enters a moment later, slowly, cautiously, his head swivelling from side to side. If he's smiling, then he's smiling deep within that nest of wires and plastic and metal that's his head.

'My Lord,' he says, and bows, as if the title means anything any longer. For Adelbert has won. Germany is *his* now.

'Guild Master,' Manfred answers, and again he gives that low, ironic bow. 'Or should I just call you … Master?'

Step by mechanical step he comes, until he's just below Manfred, at the foot of the metal steps that lead up to the platform. He looks up, his turret of a head tilting slowly back.

'You will be treated well …'

Manfred laughs tonelessly. 'I will be dead. And so will you. Unless, of course …'

Adelbert seems puzzled. '*Unless*, My Lord?'

'Unless you can stop the missiles in mid air.'

'My Lord …?'

Manfred moves back a little, allowing Adelbert to see the map. On it now are a series of tiny, colourful streaks, to the right and left of the central mass, like tears – or claw marks – in the surface of the screen.

'It's the final phase,' Manfred says, coming slowly down the steps until he's on a level with Adelbert, facing him, towering over him.

'But they …'

'Told me to go to hell.' Manfred laughs once more, then walks past Adelbert, towards where I'm seated.

'Otto. You know what happens. Tell him.'

'It's over,' I say, feeling sick to the stomach now that I've seen what really happened. 'Nothing will survive.'

It's not strictly true. Something *will* survive. The two deep bunkers for a start. And Reichenau, perhaps, if we're right about him. But it's as close to the truth as I can say.

'But why?' Adelbert says. And, strangely, there's real emotion in his voice.

'Because you bastards would fuck it all up. Make it a living hell.'

Adelbert doesn't answer. He stands there, still and silent, like he's been turned into a pillar of salt.

Manfred sits alongside me, his long legs sprawled out before him.

'How long before the first one falls?' he asks, his overlarge head turned towards me, his eyes – which I once thought wise – defying me to challenge what he's done.

'Eighteen minutes,' I say.

'And the last?'

'Approximately four and a half hours.'

'That long?' Manfred gives a long sigh. 'And you'll be gone, I take it?'

'Yes, My Lord.'

He nods, then turns away and, closing his eyes, yawns deeply. Getting to his feet, he walks back to where Adelbert still stands, silent and motionless.

'What is it, Grand Master? Seized up? Rain got to you?'

Adelbert's head swivels round. His voice is angry now. 'You're a fool, Manfred. A *wicked* fool.'

'As if you care for a single one of them!' Manfred huffs contemptuously. 'No! Let the bombs fall! Let the earth be wiped clean of our kind! Let there be no more wars, no more *Rassenkampf*! Thirty centuries is quite enough!'

He falls silent. The colored streaks on the map have lengthened, reaching out from west and east, the foremost missiles crossing trajectories. In a while they will all cross over. More are joining them by the moment, as matters escalate. Soon the whole map will be cross-hatched with the trails of missiles.

For me, it's time to depart. I have borne witness to the final act of this tragedy – this dark comedy of two nations, hell-bent on each other's extinction. There is no more.

Or rather, there's one last thing. One last person I must see.

I stand and bow, first to Adelbert, and then, finally, to Manfred. 'My Lord ...'

But as he shapes his mouth to answer I am gone. As he too will be gone before the dawn. Into the air. Ashes to ashes ...

150

She is not in the sun room. The great lounge is empty and burned out, the great glass window cracked and darkened by smoke. I go up and find her on the battlements, staring out towards the east, her long, golden hair falling to her waist. Beyond her the sun is rising for the last time on a living world.

'Gudrun?'

She turns to face me, her face in shadow. 'Otto? Is that you? Have you come?'

'I said I would.'

'Yes, but ...'

I go across to her and see, as I come closer, that her eyes are gone. Burned from her face. She is blind now. She will never see the dawn. Even so, she seems to stare down at me.

'What is it?'

I am wearing protective lenses. Fast-reactors, that form a thick film immediately there's a change in the light. And fortunately so ... for as she speaks, there's a blinding flash, like the whole world has been turned into a negative of itself. Gudrun's dark shape is outlined in liquid silver.

As it fades – the light bleeding back into the dark – I feel a tingling on my face. My eyes hurt, but at least they're not damaged.

'Leipzig,' I say.

'Leipzig?' And then she realises. 'Oh, sweet mother …'

I step closer, reaching out to take her hands. 'Your eyes …'

'It surprised me,' she says. 'No one told me …'

Looking up into her ruined face, I could cry for all that spoiled beauty. Even so, she smiles, and as she does, I remember how she looked.

'There can't be many left,' she says. 'I've heard them. Felt the heat from them on my cheeks and on my arms.'

Her arms are burned, I realise. The flesh is peeling from them.

I swallow and make to answer, but at that moment the sound hits us in a wave, the air throbbing and growling, making us both clamp our hands over our ears, for it's like the sound of a million souls howling forlornly on the wind.

Such an awful, bestial sound.

And then that too fades, and the stillness that follows is strange, for the silence is perfect. It is dawn, but not a single bird is singing. Not a single cock crows. There's no sound of trains, or planes or—

Gudrun kneels, facing me, her hands reaching blindly for my face until she finds it. Her fingers cup my cheeks.

'Otto?'

'Yes, sweet lady?'

'Do you have someone you love? Back where you come from?'

I am about to say no – not where I come from – but this is no time to be pedantic.

'Yes,' I say. 'Her name is Katerina. And she is as beautiful as you, my lady.'

'As I am now?'

'Oh, you are still beautiful.'

'But my eyes.'

'I remember your eyes. If I close mine, I can see them perfectly.'

Her fingers make a small movement on my face, then move back. She stands and looks about her, as if she's sensing the air, her head turning slowly this way and then that.

'When ...' Her voice breaks. She takes a moment, then begins again. 'When do they bomb Erfurt?'

'Soon, my lady.'

'And you ... you will be gone?'

'Yes ...'

And it feels like a betrayal. Like I could do something. Only I can't.

'Will you ... will you come back and see me?'

'See you?'

'In the Past. You could remind me. Show me the cup. Maybe ...' She falls silent.

'Maybe?'

She turns, smiling again, looking down at me, almost as if she can still see me. 'Oh, it would never have worked ... the size of me and the size of you ...'

I shiver. 'I—'

'Oh, I know, Otto. You love Katerina. And you're an honest man, not a rogue. But it would have been so sweet, to have had you, somewhere, *somewhen*. In some loose strand of time, maybe. You and I ...'

I close my eyes, tormented, for there is nothing I can do. I cannot return. I cannot grant her wish. And even if I could ...

'I must go,' I say, and find that I hate myself for uttering the words. 'I ...'

'I love you, Otto. Did you know that?'

I give a tiny, surprised laugh, then look to her. But *why* is it absurd? Why could I not be loved by such a one as her?

Because she is a goddess, Otto. Because such unions are not meant. And besides, there's Katerina.

There is. Only this once, I feel, perhaps, she'd understand. For Gudrun, at that moment, burned as she is, still has an unearthly beauty. And maybe that's why. Maybe such beauty had to perish, because …

But there is no 'because'. Here at the end, all I can register is the pointlessness of it all. As the last bombs fall, what can I say but that this never should have happened.

Rassenkampf. What madman conjured up the notion?

'My lady …'

And I jump, because if I stay a moment longer my heart will break.

My lady …

Dead, I think, as the platform shimmers into being all about me. *She is dead.*

And my heart feels heavy like a stone, and when Hecht asks me what it is, I turn from him and walk away, unable, for once, to trust myself to speak. Wanting only to find some dark and lonely spot and grieve. For that's what's needed now.

151

'Otto?'

I roll over on to my back and look up. Ernst is sitting there, in my chair, across the room from where I lie. 'What time is it?'

'It's now.' And he laughs at the old joke. For it's always 'now' in Four-Oh.

He hesitates, then asks. 'Are you all right?'

'Me? Yes, I'm fine. You?'

'It's just that …'

'Go on.'

'Just that you seemed hurt.'

I give the faintest nod, then sit up, knuckling my eyes and yawning. 'How long did I sleep?'

'Two days.'

'Two …?' I laugh. 'Urd help us, was I that tired?'

'It would seem so.'

Ernst stands. 'Hecht wants to see us.'

'Us?'

'Yes, *us*. And he wants to see us now.'

152

For once, Hecht comes to the point slowly. 'It was Ernst's idea … a good one as it happens.'

I glance at Ernst, who's sitting cross-legged beside me, then look back at Hecht.

'Go on …'

'It's a sector you both know. Somewhere familiar …'

'1239,' Ernst says.

I try not to look surprised. '1239?'

Hecht nods. 'Novgorod. You both know it well, so there shouldn't be any problems. The idea is to ease Ernst back into things.'

'Right. And the pretext?'

'To meet Nevsky,' Ernst answers. 'And to get in tight with him.'

'But Nevsky is in Moscow all that winter.'

'That's right,' Hecht says. 'So you go to him. You and Ernst. It'll allow you to acclimatise. To get to learn a bit more about conditions there.'

'But …'

I stop. I don't know why I'm objecting. It's what I want, after all. To go back there and see her. But I'm concerned for Ernst. Worried that this might be too soon, that such a trip might prove too demanding for him.

'When would we go?'

Hecht shrugs. 'When everything's prepared. Ernst will brief you. He's come up with a neat little scheme. And besides ...' He meets my eyes. '...it'll be good for you both to take things easy. These have been difficult times.'

That's true, but when I get Ernst alone again, I ask him exactly what he's got planned.

'It's a thank you,' he says.

'A what?'

'For doing what you did. For freeing me. You put yourself in grave danger ...'

'Of course I did. You'd have done the same.'

'I know, but—'

And he begins to spell it out, until finally I stare at him and laugh, surprised by just how devious he can be. Devious ... and yet as honest as they come. I reach and embrace him, holding him to me tightly.

'You're a good friend, Ernst. The very best of friends.'

'And you, Otto, are quite mad.'

I move a little away from him. 'Mad?'

'Yes, and me too ... for pandering to you.'

I grin. 'So just when did you come up with this little scheme?'

'Oh, I had time,' he says, and his eyes take on the slightest sadness as he says it. 'Or do you forget? Six months lying on my back. That's a long time. Time enough to come up with a dozen such schemes.'

I look at him thoughtfully. In the last few days he seems to have changed a lot. And all for the better. So just maybe ...

'Ernst?'

'Yes, Otto?'

'You mustn't hide anything from me, understand? You must tell me if it ever gets too much.'

'Of course,' he says, and reaches out to clasp my hand again. 'Of course.'

153

One dream, one final dream, before I let them 'purge' me of the memory.

It is of her, of course. Not Katerina, but Gudrun.

In the dream we are on the battlements again, at Orhdruf, standing side by side as the dawn breaks. Turning to me, she lifts me up on to her massive shoulders, my legs wrapped tight about her thick, exquisitely pale neck. And there I nestle, her long golden tresses like a blanket beneath me, the perfumed scent of her in my nostrils, as I look past her at the beauty of the surrounding countryside.

Slowly she turns, and as she turns, so she lifts, light as a feather, from the flagstones, and drifts out, as the birds freeze in the air and Time stands still.

Her head turns, until she's looking up at me, her beautiful blue eyes smiling back; and then she speaks, her voice slow and deep, like the tape's been slowed.

'You see, Otto? You see?'

And I wake, cold and shivering and alone, and call out. And Urte comes and lies with me, holding me until the morning, until they can locate the memory and remove it.

Because sometimes it hurts to dream. Sometimes you can see too much.

Acknowledgements

I'll keep it simple. Thanks this time must go to my agent Diana Tyler, for finding the very best of homes for this, and to my dear friends, Mike Cobley, Andy Muir, Ritchie Smith, Rob Carter, Brian Griffin and Brian Aldiss, for their intelligent and immensely helpful readings of the manuscript in progress. Thanks also must go to my editorial team at Ebury – Michael Rowley and Emily Yau – who gave the work its fine tune and asked all the right questions. May we make many more books together!

As ever, thanks must go out to my darling wife and life companion, Susan Oudot (long may she write for Coronation Street!) and to my four beautiful daughters (now grown), Jessica, Amy, Georgia and Francesca. Any resemblance to Otto and his *five* daughters is purely coincidental.

And, finally, huge thanks must go to Al Stewart, whose marvellous song, 'Roads To Moscow' set me off on this journey through Space and Time.

Otto's story continues...

Read on for an exclusive extract of

THE OCEAN OF TIME

Part Two of

THE ROADS TO MOSCOW

DEL REY

Part Seven

Up River

154

It is August 1239, in Novgorod. The weather is hot and dry, the sky the deepest, cerulean blue. Close by, the window – a western touch – is open wide, giving a view across the central garden.

This is *my* house, the land purchased with *my* silver, the house itself built only this spring to my own design. A Russian-style house, of course, but with Western touches, such as the sanitation.

Ernst stands beside me at the huge pine table, poring over the hand-drawn map. It looks crude – as crude as anything in this god-fearing, god-forsaken century – but the details are accurate. It only mimics crudity.

Ernst is frowning, as he always does when he's concentrating, then he looks up and, meeting my eyes, smiles.

'It looks fun. I only wish I was coming with you.'

'You can if you want,' I say, but he knows I don't mean it.

'No, no…I've plenty to do here. Besides, when winter comes…'

He doesn't say it, but I know what he means. When winter comes, it would be best to be inside a town, not out there in the wilds of Russia.

'You'll need to keep good time,' Ernst says, tracing the course of my prospective journey with his finger. 'If you delay…'

Again it doesn't need to be said. There are few roads in the Russia of this age and none at all between Novgorod and Moscow. Russia's rivers are its main means of transportation, and when winter comes…

The rivers freeze. Those roads are closed.

Besides, Ernst has been ahead of me already, checking out the route beforehand and making deals. Arranging things.

There are four points marked along the way in bright red ink. Those are my supply dumps, already set up and in place. Again, this is Ernst's doing. At each dump are duplicates of everything I need: food, equipment and weaponry.

And a focus. To jump to if in need. Or to send a message up the line to Four-Oh. We've worked it all out, you see. Each dump is marked by a tracking signal, which only I, in this non-technological age, will be able to locate. To make the hazardous journey safer, less subject to accident.

And there's a good reason for that this time. Because I'm not going alone.

Ernst looks past me, and, in his quaint Germanic manner, comes to attention and bows his head. I turn and smile.

'Katerina… you didn't have to get up.'

She grins. Her long, dark hair is tousled and she's still in her sleeping gown. But that doesn't worry her this once. It's Ernst. She squeals and hurries over to him, hugging him to her like a long-lost brother.

'Otto… why didn't you tell me Ernst was in town!'

For a moment, in her happiness at seeing Ernst, she doesn't notice the map spread out on the table. But then she does and she looks at me sternly.

'Otto…?'

'What?' I say nonchalantly. She turns and looks at the map, struggling to take in its details, but knowing what it means. Then, looking up at me again, she scowls, a hurt expression in her eyes.

'Otto… are you going away again? Is that why Ernst is here?'

'Yes,' I say, and see the disappointment – the almost child-like hurt – increase in her eyes. But I'm teasing now, and I really shouldn't. She goes to speak again and I raise a hand. 'And before you ask, no. Ernst *isn't* going with me. Ernst is staying here in Novgorod for the winter.'

'You're going *alone*?'

And now I smile. 'No, my pet, my darling little one. You're coming with me.'

155

The apprentices have wandered from their benches to come and stare over each others' shoulders at the drawings that their Master, the chief carpenter, has unrolled and fastened to his worktop.

The old man is frowning heavily and pulling at his beard, in a state of what, for him, is almost agitation.

'I've never seen the like,' he says. 'Never in all my life.'

It's true. The design comes from the future. It's one of Hans Luwer's, a beauty if you ask me, but the Master can't see that. All his life he's been used to making sleds a certain way – the way his father made them and his father before that – and this is too new, too revolutionary for him.

He sighs deeply, then straightens up and looks at me across the bench.

'No, Meister Behr. I am afraid I cannot make this. This... blueprint, as you call it... it makes no sense.'

It makes perfect sense, of course, but that's not what he means. He is frightened of it. Frightened of the departures in its design. It is, after all, radically different from any design he's seen or is ever likely to see. But next to him, his senior apprentice is staring and staring at the diagram, his eyes filled with pure wonder at what he's seeing. He wants to make this new thing. In fact, he absolutely burns to turn my drawing into something real, something he can *touch* with the palm of his hand.

'But Master...' he begins, daring to interrupt the old man in his excitement. 'This is—'

'Be quiet, Alexander Alexandrovich. I cannot make this thing. It would not be *safe*.'

'But Master—'

This time the old man turns and even raises a hand. Alexander Alexandrovich desists. But his eyes still burn.

I take the old man aside.

'Here,' I say, handing him a small bag filled with silver coins – dirhams, freshly-minted in Four-Oh not six hours past subjectively. 'Let your boy take this on. If it doesn't work...' I shrug, '...I'll pay you anyway, understand? Another twenty dirhams.'

The Master's eyes have lit at the sight of all that silver and the promise of yet more. I have paid him lavishly – ten times the worth of the sled; as much and more as a prince might pay – and so he bows low before me.

'Whatever you wish, Meister.'

'Good. Then I want the job done for St. Vladimir's day.'

His head jerks up. 'St. Vladimir's day? But that's—'

'Ten days away, I know. Is that a problem?'

Before he can answer, Alexander Alexandrovich steps in. 'It will be done, Meister. I guarantee it.'

'Good. And there'll be a bonus if you do a fine job.'

But now I've overstepped the mark. Both the Master and his senior apprentice straighten, almost bristling at this insult to their pride.

'Meister Behr,' the old man says sternly. 'Understand one thing. When Yakov Arkadevich takes on a job, it is done not just well, but perfectly. We are the best, you understand. The finest in all of Russia.'

156

Walking back to Katerina's father's house, I find myself smiling broadly. I know the sled will be built to my design. I knew it long before I knocked on Master Arkadevich's door. After all, with the slight improvements Alexander Alexandrovich makes to it, it forms the basis of those sleds we copied and which wait, even now, at the supply dumps along the way – the same basic design that will be used throughout Russia for the next seven hundred years.

Razumovsky greets me off-handedly. Something is bugging him and he's in a bad mood, even for him. I tell him of my plan to travel east and he asks me why I should want to do that. Isn't everything I need right here in Novgorod? I tell him no; that I'm taking a very special cargo of goods inland with me and that this single trip could make my fortune, and that with the proceeds I plan to buy an estate and a thousand serfs. That impresses him, but when I tell him that I'm taking his daughter with me, he objects strongly.

'That's no place to take a woman, Otto! There are thieves and bandits and ruffians of every kind out there!'

'I know,' I answer, 'but there are thieves of a different kind right here in Novgorod and I am as loathe to leave Katerina here as she is to let me go alone. Besides, I *am* her husband!'

That, irrefutable as it is, settles matters. But Razumovsky still doesn't like it. He comes up with a dozen reasons why his daughter should stay. And most of them have merit, only...

I can't bear to be parted from her. And this journey gives me a valid excuse to be with her every day for the next six months.

And every night...

Razumovsky is saved from coming up with further reasons by the arrival of Ernst.

Ernst, I know, has been back to Four-Oh to get the latest news, but he tells Razumovsky that he's just come over from the Peterhof, the German Quarter of the town, where he's struck a deal for fifty furs. Ernst wants to celebrate, and this surprises me somewhat, but I can't ask why. Not with Razumovsky there. It's not the 'deal', that I know, but there is a definite spring to Ernst's step as he calls out to Razumovsky's servants to bring us wine.

Razumovsky needs no encouraging. When the servants bring three flasks of wine, he sends them away for a dozen more. So it is that, as evening falls, the three of us sit drunkenly at the bench, laughing and slapping each others' backs.

Razumovsky's ability to consume endless amounts of liquor without needing to excuse himself is legendary. Even so, he eventually needs to use the midden, and when he does, I lean across and ask Ernst what's going on.

'They've killed Shafarevich!' he says, his eyes gleaming. 'Freisler shot him between the eyes. Then they snipped off time behind him, neat as a sewn wound!'

I laugh, astonished. Shafarevich is the Russians' equivalent of Freisler, and he's been a thorn in our side for as long as I've been an agent – yes, and for long before that. No wonder Ernst wants to celebrate.

When Razumovsky returns, I call for more wine, then climb on to the table and raise a toast to my father-in-law – a toast that has the sentimental Razumovsky in tears.

'You're a good son to me, Otto,' he says, hugging my legs, not letting me get down from the table. 'A man could not ask for a better son.'

Only I'm glad I'm not Razumovsky's son, for if I was, how then could I have married Katerina?